"Nice-looking man," Mavis [...] of thought.

"Who is?"

"You know." Mavis's eyebrows wiggled as though Jenna did know and was just pretending to be dense. "The Grisham fan."

Oh. Him. The guy who'd bought the snazzy hat yesterday, and looked darned good wearing it today. Jadeite-green eyes. Styled not barbered hair. Took his coffee black and had a crosshatched scar on the back of his right hand.

Jenna shrugged. "I didn't notice."

"Not Pierce Brosnan handsome, mind you." Mavis's feather duster twirled over the cast-iron cookware displayed on a possum-bottom Hoosier cabinet. "More of a Don Johnson without the dimples."

Jenna's face assumed the huh? position it was wont to do when Mavis Purvis held the conversational floor. She was like a second mother, even though Aggie Franks hardly needed a backup to drive Jenna nuts on a regular basis.

Both of them meant well, wanted the best for her, insisted she put on a sweater when they caught a chill and viewed every single male not currently on life support as the answer to her commitment phobia.

"The Grisham guy didn't look anything like Don Johnson," Jenna said. More like Sam Elliott's taller, huskier brother. Ageless pretty boys don't have shaman eyes and jawlines as blunt as cast bronze.

Mavis moved to a hutch laden with Roseville, Rockwood pottery and art glass. "Thought you said you didn't notice."

Also by SUZANN LEDBETTER

WEST OF BLISS
NORTH OF CLEVER
SOUTH OF SANITY
EAST OF PECULIAR

And watch for SUZANN LEDBETTER'S newest novel
Coming September 2004

SUZANN LEDBETTER

In Hot Pursuit

MIRA

ISBN 1-55166-687-1

IN HOT PURSUIT

Copyright © 2003 by Suzann Ledbetter.

Visit us at www.mirabooks.com

Printed in U.S.A.

For Dave, the love of my life

ACKNOWLEDGMENTS

From page one to the end, this book was a doozy to write. The crack team of law enforcement professionals usually drafted into assisting mostly sat this one out, but dear friend Ellen Wade, R.N., was as always instrumental in helping me get the medical references right, meaning any glitches in that vein—so to speak— are mine.

Enormous gratitude also goes to Paul W. Johns, Judy Chilton, the Godfather's Pizza gang and innumerable others I whimpered to and was steadfastly supported by. However, the largest laurels must be heaped on my editor, Martha Keenan. Her patience, understanding, editorial smarts and savvy, and her beyond-the-call dedication and devotion to this story spurred it and me across the finish line.

Heaven knows my agent, Robin Rue, and Emily Kim rate major thank-yous, too, for readily supplying an "Atta girl" or a butt kick, whichever I needed at any given moment.

1

Paul Haggerty had been playing visual chicken with Jenna MacArthur for over an hour. He'd caught her looking nearly as often as she'd caught him.

One of her getaway glances wasn't fast enough to hide a grin—the sheepish kind usually associated with little kids and cookie jars. Since then, the table where Paul sat nursing a cup of MacArthur Perk's excellent coffee had received no attention—subtle or otherwise.

He cut his gaze to the older woman restocking a wood-and-wire-mesh case with fresh muffins, then to the novel splayed in front of him. Sufficing as a bookmark was a cash-register receipt stamped with the previous day's date and the shop's name in lavender ink.

Yesterday's scouting mission at the combination flea market-bookstore-coffee shop was to have been a ten-minute, lay-of-the-land proposition. Except that dawdling through MacArthur Perk's array of art deco, art nouveau, Danish modern, oak and pine primitives, advertiques and fifties memorabilia was like revisiting his childhood.

The pink and gilt ceramic fish blowing ceramic bubbles up one wall were once as common to bathrooms as girdles air-drying on towel bars. Granddad

Haggerty used to hoard bent nails, odd screws, bolt-less nuts and nutless bolts in Maxwell House coffee, ZuZu cookies and Uneeda biscuit tins like those displayed in a rubber-tired grocery cart. The old pack rat would swear the world had gone mad if he knew the prices those colorful cans fetched now.

Nearer the front door, a retired post office's sorting cabinet held hardcover bestsellers, lesser-known personal recommendations and paperbacks, along with antique toys, lava lamps, kitchenware and knick-knacks. A wire rack beside a magazine gondola offered *USA TODAY,* the *Wall Street Journal* and Sunday editions of the *St. Louis Post-Dispatch, Kansas City Star,* and *The New York Times.*

The sales counter was a rib-high mahogany bar salvaged from a turn-of-the-century tavern. When Jenna teased Paul about the vintage homburg he'd inexplicably liked the look of, her smile had lit up her face, just as it had the last time he'd seen it, twenty-three years ago.

She'd approved of the newest Grisham thriller he'd selected. Beside it, he laid a forty-five rpm record by an obscure artist singing ''I Can't Get You Out of My Mind.''

''As is,'' Jenna warned, squinting to read the title. ''That's flea market-speak for 'You pays your money, you takes your chances.'''

Paul's response had been something incredibly suave like ''I know,'' or the ever-popular ''Okay.''

His belly gyrated throughout the transaction, but at no time did recognition glint in her eyes. Not that he'd expected it. After a team of plastic surgeons had worked their specialized magic, his own mother had passed him on the street without so much as a good-morning nod.

Returning to MacArthur Perk this afternoon assured him that nothing in his voice or mannerisms had since thumbed Jenna's "Don't I know that guy from somewhere?" doorbell. He was just a tall, sandy-haired stranger with a gunslinger's mustache who enjoyed good coffee and a quiet place to read— or faked it admirably.

Their peekaboo interlude had been fun while it lasted, but Jenna's stalwart refusal to look his way again had its advantages. A chance to meld the remembered with the real, for one thing. Or try to.

More than just her name had changed in the span of a couple of decades. He wondered how she'd chosen it; Jenna not Jenny, or Jennifer. It couldn't be in honor of a grandmother or favorite aunt. The Witness Protection Program forbade such tips of the hat.

MacArthur, he supposed, was for the World War II general who vowed, "I shall return" to troops marooned on an island about to be overrun by the enemy. Whether ironic or an inside joke, there was nothing for her to return to. Her former life was a footnote, vanished or banished from collective memory.

Save hers. And his.

She once wore her hair cropped as short as a boy's to tame the curls and minimize the fuss. Gray now threaded the black, unruly mane that skimmed below her shoulder blades, swinging and swaying with her every move. A man could sink his hands wrist deep in those lush, thick waves without fear she'd scold him for it.

Laugh lines fanned from deep-set, brown eyes that

had seen too much and forgotten nothing. The ten or twelve pounds she'd gained had softened her angular features and body contours. Though never drop-jaw gorgeous, she'd always been attractive in a way men noticed at a second glance and gravitated toward after a third.

Paul rubbed the thin scar behind his ear, raising his head enough to bring her into peripheral view. Her back was turned and she was talking to a customer—Tammy something-or-other, a clerk at the Feed & Seed next door.

He decided that *change* wasn't the right word for what time and circumstance had wrought on Jenna MacArthur. Reach that certain age when life is a perpetual hand of liar's poker and "You haven't changed a bit" can play either as an ace or a trump.

The visible differences were closer to osmosis. Like married couples who adopt each other's gestures and expressions until they resemble fraternal twins, the woman he'd known as NYPD Patrol Officer Liz Rivas fit the mental picture conjured by her alias. And it was disconcerting as all hell.

Then and now jumbled in Paul's mind as loud as rocks agitating in the kitschy, plastic polishing machine on MacArthur Perk's toy shelf. Past regrets and anticipation tangled with reproach for ever darkening Pfister, Missouri's city limits—much less Jenna's door.

The older man and young blonde seated behind him at the corner table offered a much-needed distraction. They were shouting in whispers about a pending divorce—his, not hers. Ultimatums were issued, then promises and threats as empty as their eavesdropper's coffee mug.

Tuning them out again wasn't difficult. Paul already knew how their story would end. His was only half-written, and half a lifetime ago at that.

"Are you reading that book or memorizing it?" The question coincided with fresh coffee purling into Paul's cup. He jerked his head up, irritated at himself for being caught woolgathering.

"Sorry if I startled you, Mr...." A nameplate rode the woman's bosom like a buoy on an ocean swell. Mavis the Manager was pushing sixty, but had Cleopatra's flair for eyeliner. Her spit-curled, magenta beehive could qualify as a ninth wonder of the world. Winged, rhinestone-encrusted eyeglasses hung from a pearl-and-gold neck chain.

"No need to apologize." Paul tilted his head toward the window. "It's too nice an afternoon to sit here with my nose stuck in a book, anyway."

Sunlight sparked off a gold crown when she smiled. "Fall's my favorite season of the year." Leveling a disgusted glance at the couple in the corner, her voice was shrill when she added, "No, it's surely not as hot as it was, nor nearly as cold as it's bound to get, by and by."

Silence fell, but for the sounds of two bodies shifting uncomfortably on their chrome and vinyl-upholstered chairs. Satisfied her dart had scored a double bull's-eye, Mavis said, "Hereabouts, we call this kind of weather Indian summer."

At the unasked *What's it called where you're from?* Paul bit his lip to stanch a grin. Small-town natives were too gracious for outright interrogations and too nosy to let a stranger remain one.

Mavis rested the coffee carafe on the Formica-topped table that would have looked at home in the

Cleaver family's kitchen. "I hear people travel clear to New England just to see the leaves turn." She chuffed. "What their trees have over Missouri's, I'd thank you to tell me."

He shrugged. "A better publicist?"

Her laugh evoked the rumble of bowling balls on hardwood alleys, beer frames and lucky socks. "Hey, that's a good one. I like a man with a sense of humor." She tossed a casual wave toward the counter. "Jenna MacArthur—she's the owner, like you hadn't guessed that already—sure doesn't lack for a funny bone. No-sir-ee, she's plumb had me in stitches more'n once."

"Has a great smile, too" slipped out so easily, Paul didn't realize he'd said it aloud until Mavis slanted him a cagey look.

Loose lips and all that crap, he thought. A clammy sheen spread across his forehead. Get a grip, man. The old girl knows you aren't blind. Complimenting her employer does not the cat into the mouse make.

He flipped a page of the book, as though it were impossible to put down. At twenty-six bucks, minus a ten percent discount, it was an expensive prop, but pretending engrossment in the daily newspaper was as clichéd as it was awkward. Especially the *Pfister Free Lancer,* whose content ran to banner headlines announcing the local poultry plant's expansion, homecoming-queen contestants, bow hunters poised beside their antlered prey and a quarter page devoted to the weekly soap-opera update.

Not one to take a hint, Mavis said, "Word to the wise. I wouldn't set much store in what Betty Bigelow says about Tommy Ballew's garage. Fair enough for Betty to send bidness to her son-in-law, seeing as how her daughter spends a quarter for every dime Tommy makes, but it's Don Junior Ulmer over yonder across the street that can fix anything with a motor—lawn mowers to them foreign cars, like yours.''

It took a moment to sort the whats and wheretofores. Betty Bigelow owned the all-frills bed-and-breakfast Paul had checked into late Sunday afternoon. The pear-shaped proprietress was sure to be a more effusive information source than a clerk at a franchise motel, or at the funky Route 66 vintage SeaShell Motor Court.

As for his vehicle, unless General Motors had merged with a German or Japanese automaker since he picked up the rental at Kansas City International, the Chevy Lumina he was driving was as American as the Smith & Wesson .38 Special strapped to his ankle.

He chuckled to himself. MacArthur Perk's second-in-command was no slouch at fishing expeditions. Mavis would just have to troll somewhere else for her catch of the day.

"I appreciate the advice," he said, "but my car is running fine."

A penciled eyebrow crimped at its center. Clearly, Mavis wasn't accustomed to being stonewalled and not about to surrender gracefully. Or soon.

Her free hand delved into a pocket of the carpenter's apron tied around her waist. An embossed business card with the shop's logo, address, phone, fax number and Web site skimmed across the table. "If you're gonna be in town a while, get this punched at the register when you stop by. Buy five cups of joe and the sixth one's on the house."

"Thanks." He tucked the card in his book beside the register receipt. "I may stick around long enough to use it."

"On vacation, are ya?"

Damn it. A simple thank-you would have sufficed. "Um, not exactly."

"Here on business, then, is it?"

The woman was a purple-haired bloodhound in black Converse All-Stars. Laying on the charm was his best defense.

He winked up at her as he arched his back to remove the wallet from his jeans pocket. "No harm in mixing the two, is there? As long as the boss doesn't find out."

"None at all. You know what they say about all work and no play." Mavis picked up the carafe, muttering, "Time off for some fun would do a boss I know a world of good."

He laughed. "Mine just shows up at the office now and then so nobody will forget what he looks like." Before she could ask the obvious, he said, "Which reminds me, I do have a meeting in a few minutes."

It was the whole truth and nothing but, even though his appointment was with the county library's microfilm machine. Paul pointed at his coffee mug. "How much do I owe you for the refill?"

Mavis looked over her shoulder at Jenna, then back at him. Her lower lip curled over her teeth, as if a gallery of mug shots broadcast on *America's Most Wanted* were scrolling behind her eyes.

"No charge," she said absently, then blurted, "Do you like Mexican food?"

He didn't particularly, but answered in the affirmative.

They both jumped when chair legs shrieked on the linoleum. The young blonde marched past as erect and stiff-jointed as a drunk taking a field sobriety test. The brass bells above MacArthur Perk's door clanged a parting epithet.

The man hastened after her, the skin above his shirt collar a mottled crimson. The shop's phone rang just as the door suffered a second glass-rattling slam.

Apparently inured to customers' melodramatic exits, Mavis said, "We close up at five-thirty on Tuesdays so Jenna can have supper with her son—"

"Telephone, Mavis," Jenna called, waving a cordless handset.

The manager cursed, turned away, then halted. "Sam—that's her son—is out of town. No guarantee she'll be there tonight, but Casa Juarez is as decent a place to eat as any in this burg."

Grins didn't come any more genuine than the one Paul felt stretch from ear to ear. Better to be lucky than good, any day. Aloud, he said, "The minute I sat down here this afternoon I started thinking how a couple of tacos and a cold beer would really hit the spot."

As Mavis backpedaled for the phone, renewed faith in snap character judgments radiated from her every pore. She whispered, "Well, now, that's a coincidence just waiting to happen. Right?"

He closed his book, edged two singles under the coffee mug and took the homburg from the chair beside him. Grateful as he was for the information, someone really ought to tell Mavis why small towns were such popular hunting grounds for human predators.

2

"Have a great day," Jenna told the thirtysomething couple squeezing themselves and four shopping bags through the door.

Honeymooners, she guessed. Everything the woman touched had fostered his adoring "We'll take it." By their fifth anniversary, his tune would change to "And just *where* do you think you're gonna put it?" and her expression would convey the first location that sprang to mind.

Their purchases wouldn't meet the store's mortgage payment, but it was the largest single sale that month. If Tammy Zeman would quit using her coffee breaks from the Feed & Seed to visit the Jacobean davenport and club chairs she ached to own and actually *bought* them, October would be one of MacArthur Perk's most profitable months ever.

November and December should pay for themselves. January through March were always dogs, but there'd be inventory to complete, deep cleaning and refurbishing to do and stock to rotate.

By April, Jenna would own the building and the adjoining corner lot free and clear—just in time for the new section of interstate bypassing Pfister to open. Ribbon cuttings would also be held for the obligatory knot of fast-food restaurants, a chain motel and a convenience store purveying gasoline, diesel, clean rest rooms and ample parking for drowsy truck drivers.

It wasn't as if its nearest town lacked for amenities. Pfister had a junior college, a regional hospital, an enviable public-school system, a Wal-Mart SuperCenter, cable TV and a retro charm its young didn't appreciate until they had children and the big city's siren song sounded more like a call to arms.

What Pfister didn't have was a wax museum, a cave the James Gang was rumored to have used as a hideout, a theme park, a roadside Snakes Alive! attraction, a winery or a restored speakeasy once frequented by a vacationing Al Capone, Dillinger or Ma Barker and her boys. In other words, no kitschy or compelling reason for tourists to crank a left at the top of the new highway's off-ramp and detour to Pfister.

Aging baby boomers and nostalgia buffs would continue their sentimental journeys on Route 66's tar-veined two lanes. If the number of dying, dead and disappeared towns along the Mother Road's twenty-four-hundred-mile length were any indication, everyone else would cleave to the interstate's faster, straighter, shorter distance between where they'd been and where they were going—an equation of which Pfister was not a part.

The ace up Jenna's fiscal sleeve was selling merchandise on eBay and other electronic flea-market sites. The tide had turned on the popularity of surfing the Internet for collectibles, and top dollar was half or a third of what it once was, but a tidy profit was still makable.

In theory, that is. In practice, she'd rather be

chained to a chair to watch a *Dumb and Dumber* videothon than hunker in front of a computer monitor. Or scrub the bathroom grout with an ex-lover's toothbrush. Even sandwich herself between two cheval mirrors with all her clothes off and all the lights on.

Okay, the last one might be a tad over the top, but becoming accustomed to living middling well, eating regularly and blowing ten or twenty bucks on herself in blue-moon months left Jenna with two choices. She could dedicate herself to building the virtual end of her business to offset the inevitable decrease in foot traffic, or she could slowly go bankrupt, then move in with her mother.

Her stomach lurched, then loop-de-looped. She loved her mother. Very much. The sacrifices Aggie Franks had made would have crushed a woman of lesser substance and strength. It was just that sometimes their adopted hometown wasn't big enough for both of them. Far less frequently, but certainly worth noting, were those times when the entire freakin' *planet* wasn't big enough for both of them.

Rod Stewart's "Tonight's the Night" drifted through Jenna's mind, as if she needed a musical incentive to go straight home, boot up the computer and rattle the keyboard's plastic ivories until her fingers bled.

"Nice-looking man," Mavis said, derailing Jenna's ambitious train of thought.

"Who is?"

"You know." Mavis's eyebrows wiggled as though Jenna did and was just pretending to be dense. "The Grisham fan."

Oh. Him. The guy who'd bought the snazzy hat

yesterday, and looked darned good wearing it today. Jadeite green eyes. Styled not barbered hair. Takes his coffee black and has a crosshatched scar on the back of his right hand.

Jenna shrugged. "I didn't notice."

"Not Pierce Brosnan handsome, mind you." Mavis's feather duster twirled over the cast-iron cookware displayed on a possum-bottom Hoosier cabinet. "More of a Don Johnson without the dimples. Or the cleft chin. Or the Cupid's-bow mouth."

Yup, Jenna thought. On a nose, earlobe and hair line basis, the two were damn near dead ringers.

"Don's a Missouri boy," Mavis said, as though the state motto was Better Genetics Through Geography. "Same as Brad Pitt."

"So was Vincent Price."

"Well, there you go."

Jenna's face assumed the *huh?* position as it was wont to do when Mavis Purvis held the conversational floor. She was like a second mother, even though Aggie Franks hardly needed a backup to drive Jenna nuts on a regular basis.

Both of them meant well, wanted the best for her, insisted she put on a sweater when they caught a chill and viewed every single male not currently on life support as the answer to her commitment phobia.

"The Grisham guy didn't look anything like Don Johnson," Jenna said. More like Sam Elliott's taller, huskier brother. Ageless pretty-boys don't have shaman eyes and jawlines as blunt as cast bronze.

Mavis moved to a hutch laden with Roseville, Rookwood pottery and art glass. "Thought you said you didn't notice."

Well, hell. Jenna reached under the counter for the

giant economy-sized jar of calcium-fortified antacids. Cloning her mother and Mavis could make osteo-porosis a thing of the past. "And I thought *you* promised to drop the Auntie Mame routine."

"I'm doing no such a thing. Being a matchmaker, I mean."

A dust-mote cyclone glittered in the sunlight angling through the store's windows. "Which isn't to say a hot 'n heavy romp in the sack wouldn't bring out the roses in your cheeks."

A half-dozen semi-pulverized Tums whooshed down Jenna's windpipe. Arms flailing like a shipwreck victim, she wrenched open the beverage cooler's sliding door and grabbed a bottle of springwater.

"How long's it been, anyway?" Mavis went on, dusting and dithering. "A year? Two?" She licked her thumb and applied it to a smudge on a brandy warmer. "Heavenly days, it's a wonder your face hasn't pimpled up like a goose plucked for Sunday dinner."

Struggling to swallow the chalk-and-water mortar stuck to her soft palate, Jenna thanked God the shop was empty. Or might as well be. The teenage philosophers who slouched in every afternoon after school to stroke their peach-fuzz goatees and debate Nietzsche, Marx and *Buffy the Vampire Slayer* episodes were moochers, not customers. From the caffeinated, multivoiced buzz and their drum-major motions, the Platos weren't listening to each other, much less the wannabe Dr. Ruth wielding a feather duster like Zorro on speed.

"Now that I think about it," she said, "it's been

at least that long…unless you saddled up that sweet young cowboy sniffing around you last spring.''

''Mavis, for God's sake, will you shut—''

''Whether you did or didn't, the drought's been on you for months, and believe you me, that's just not healthy. Why, if I went without for weeks on end, I'd be chewing nails and spittin' out carpet tacks.''

She sat down in a rattan chair and daintily crossed her legs at the knee. ''Go ahead. Make all the sputtery noises you want, hon. I'm here to tell you, you're as grouchy as a caged bear. Everybody's worried about you and that's a fact.''

Jenna had heard of apoplexy. She just wasn't sure if bugged eyes, shortness of breath and the sound of ocean waves crashing off her cardrums was symptomatic of it or of spontaneous combustion.

''Everybody?'' she managed to ask, each syllable a stand-alone. ''And that would be…?''

Oblivious to the human teakettle simmering a few yards away, Mavis brushed wisps of down from her polyester slacks. Her voice was softer and its cadence slower, as though she were talking to herself, when she said, ''You like to think of yourself as a loner. You are, but having known you as many years as I have, your brand of it is spelled l-o-a-n-e-r.

''I guess I see it in you because I'm one, too. Hard as I've tried and much as I've wanted to, I can loan my heart to a man, but I can't ever quite give it away.''

A flatbed lumber truck hacking out blue fumes roared by on Commercial Street. One of the Platos seated at the corner table burst out laughing. Hot tears stung Jenna's eyes.

Mavis was wrong. She'd given her heart away

once. A little over three years later, it was ripped from her chest and ground into a thousand tiny pieces.

Funny thing about pain, be it physical or emotional. You remember having it—remember crying, blaspheming God and begging the devil for a deal—but you can't bring it back. Gone but not forgotten. Just like NYPD Detective Rick Rivas and his patrol officer wife, Liz.

They'd married in haste, three weeks after their eyes met over a derelict's frozen corpse. Rick was a big, beefy, third-generation cop, eight years older than her and seemingly invincible. He'd been married once before, swore he wouldn't make that mistake again, then fell as hard, fast and completely for Liz as she did for him.

A year later, they had a fat, happy, beautiful baby boy named Robby that frog-kicked and cooed whenever his daddy lifted him from his crib. Life was good. Couldn't be any better.

Okay, Rick wasn't home as much as he'd like to have been. Robbery-homicide units don't operate nine-to-five with weekends and holidays off. And at any given moment, being a wife, mother and wearing a badge were at least two jobs too many. Or so she'd whined to the refrigerator, the bathroom mirror, her sleeping toddler and the man in the moon.

Yes, if it were a perfect world, a few things could have been improved upon. But their life together *was* good, mostly better than good…until the night of their third wedding anniversary.

She and Rick were walking to the hotel where he'd reserved the honeymoon suite. They were giddy on champagne, each other and the hope of making a little brother, or sister, for Robby.

Then Rick stopped short, knocking her off balance. "Hold it—police!" His hand fumbled inside his topcoat for his service weapon. Gunshots. Four, maybe five. She'd never be sure. The world and everything in it shifted into slow motion.

Distant screams. Rick staggered backward. A sensation like superheated knives skewered the side of her head, her rib cage, her shoulder. An acrid slurry spilled into her mouth an instant before a sightless, soundless, pure black void swallowed her whole.

Maybe, as the adage went, they'd have eventually repented in leisure their whirlwind marriage. Statistics gave even odds without factoring in a two-cop household and law enforcement's higher-than-average divorce rate.

Blame fate, bad timing, worse luck, God's will— what have you. In less than thirty seconds, a mob hit gone wrong cheated them out of any chance of ever finding out. Cheated Robby out of a father. Cheated—

Stop it. Jenna's fingernails scraped the alligatored countertop. *Snap out of it.* Put on the game face— *now*—before you make a fool of yourself.

You're a divorcée, not a widow. Jenna MacArthur, small-town businesswoman, not Liz Rivas, big-city cop. Your son is a grown man named Sam MacArthur, not a chubby little boy named Robby Rivas.

Deep breaths, she told herself. Her shoulders pulled back to slough off the aftereffects of the flashback. She hadn't had one in...so long ago, she couldn't remember.

Why now? What had triggered it? Not Mavis's

loving but erroneous lecture. Truth be known, for the past couple of days Jenna had felt as if her skin had shrunk. Edgy, for no reason she could guess let alone diagnose.

Gradually, the room that had tilted like a carnival fun house leveled again. She inhaled the aroma of imported coffee beans, linseed oil, hand-dipped candles and the must peculiar to old, plank-floored buildings chock-full of treasures rescued from attics, root cellars and barn lofts.

"Call me a matchmaker or worse," Mavis was saying, "but mercy sakes alive, hon. Why do you think I spoke up?"

Drained and trembling on the inside, Jenna forced her lips into a smile. "Because you're a nosy old broad who couldn't keep her mouth shut if her jaws were wired together?"

"Well, there's that," Mavis allowed.

Her joints and the chair's creaked as she stood. Both were, after all, about the same age. "Don't take this like a woe-is-me 'cause it isn't, but I don't want you to wake up one morning wishing you'd set your heart free to fend for itself, instead of keeping it wrapped in tissue paper and muslin for fear it'd get broken."

Jenna's gaze averted to an ivy-patterned bone china service for eight that a World War II veteran had brought home from England for his bride.

"Forgot all about them," he'd told Jenna, "till I found them packed away in a trunk after my Millie passed on." A sugar bowl materialized from its yellowed paper-and-fabric cocoon. "I reckon she was saving them for good, like all those dresses in her closet with the tags still on."

He sighed, his thumbs caressing the piece's delicate handles. "They're as pretty as the day I bought them. Not a scratch or a chip anywhere. Ends up, Millie saved them for good, all right. Only something tells me, if she had it to do over, she'd have laid the table with 'em every Sunday and twice on Easter, and worn those dresses till they done wore out."

Jenna said, "And if I had it to do over, I'd have begged Rick to hail a cab that night."

"Rick?" Mavis repeated. "Rick who?"

Before Jenna could cover the gaffe with a second-nature lie, one of the Platos pointed to his chest. "You talking to me?"

Mavis whirled and knuckled a hip. "No, and why ever would you think I was?"

The boy's Adam's apple bounced. "You said something about Rick and that's my name, so—"

"You took it for an invitation to interrupt a private conversation between me and Ms. MacArthur."

"N-no, ma'am," he stammered. "I just—"

"Don't you argue with me, young man. Not if you and the rest of you eggheads want to help yourselves to the leftover muffins in the pie safe."

Necks craning, the boys exchanged glances and smirks. The one seated beside Rick nudged him, signaling him to play along.

"Go on now, before I change my mind." Mavis shooed them with the feather duster. "Get to chompin' and smackin' like usual and y'all wouldn't hear thunder if it clapped you on the back."

A blur of knobby elbows, stovepipe legs and untied high-tops sprinted for the pine and punched-tin cabinet on the opposite side of the room.

Jenna grinned and raked a hand through her hair.

Different day, same scenario. Why Mavis had to bait the boys in a faux-Gestapo fashion before giving them the day's leftovers was a mystery, but they adored her for it. The faces changed, but year after year unseen elves shoveled Mavis's walk in winter and mowed her trailer's scrap of lawn in summer.

Equally as reliable was the "Rick who?" question arising again. Jenna sleeved the dampness from her forehead. It's tricky, frightening, damnably hard work to be a liar most of your life. Any idiot can stick to the truth. Given time and compounded by circumstances, the proverbial web of lies morphs into a chain-link maze strung with razor wire.

If everyone she'd slipped and said her dead husband's name to compared notes, they'd think the neighborhood where she'd grown up, kindergarten-to-college classmates and previous places of employment swarmed with guys named Rick.

In truth, she'd known only one. He'd been her best friend, her lover, her husband, playmate and peer. Losing him, and all those things he was to her, was like losing the five people you loved most in the world in an irrevocable instant.

Better to have loved and lost than never to have loved at all? Even two-plus decades after the fact, the maxim had a pompous ring to it. Probably coined by someone who hadn't experienced either.

She jumped when Mavis blew past her so fast her sneakers cheeped on the wood floor. "Lady Lurch and the Loon at twelve o'clock," she said. "I'm not setting foot out of the back room till they're gone, either."

A showroom-shiny '59 Chrysler Imperial inch-mealed into one of MacArthur Perk's handicapped-parking spaces. Behind the wheel was Gerta Kleinschmidt, a dour, skillet-faced Amazon of indeterminate origin and age.

For forty-some years, lags in discussing the weather, or those jackleg Republicans in Washington, had been plugged with speculations on where Gerta had hailed from, exactly when she'd moved to Pfister and why. Privately, Jenna wondered if Gerta was one of WITSEC's earliest participants.

In the beginning, the U.S. Marshals Service had clustered witnesses for safety and case management purposes. The unintended consequences inspired the movie *My Blue Heaven*, where Steve Martin played a mob snitch who panics when he realizes his new neighborhood is swarming with relocated mafiosi.

The Chrysler's passenger seat appeared to be unoccupied. On closer inspection, the tip of a peacock feather peeked above the cot-size dashboard. Without a doubt, it was affixed to the band of a velvet chapeau wobbling large on the head of Miss Flogent Lee Pfister.

The spinster matriarch of the town's founding family took no guff from anyone—in particular her surviving great-grandnieces and nephews, Foster, Philoneous, Phoebe, Fayetta and Florentine.

Flogent Lee was the eleventh child born to Fagan and Lily Marquart Pfister, of the Saint Louis Marquarts. The couple's joy was tempered by the well having run dry of Christian names beginning with *F* or *Ph*, as ordained by generations of Pfisters.

Lily searched the Bible, a world atlas, church hymnals, and asked the advice of travelers who frequented the Pfisterses' mercantile and hotel. She found nothing that appealed, wasn't already availed or was unattached to a deceased Pfister, which Lily believed reusing would tempt the wrong kind of fate.

She was about to christen her daughter Elizabeth and be done with it, when a snake-oil salesman gave Lily a book of Robert Burns's poems. She'd never heard of him, or Scotland's Afton River, but was enchanted by his ode to it and ''my Mary'' slumbering on its bank ''where wild in the woodlands the primroses blow.''

Except, Flow Gently Sweet Afton Pfister didn't exactly glide off the tongue. Nor did Flow Afton Pfister. Lily and Fagan finally agreed on Flogent Lee Pfister and never regretted the choice. The same could not be said of their last-born child.

Jenna watched as Gerta Kleinschmidt assisted her ninety-two-year-old employer from the car, hoisted her by the armpits over the tall curbstone, then set her down on the sidewalk.

Flogent Lee's back might be bowed and her neck recurved to compensate, but once on level ground she rebuffed Gerta's or anyone else's assistance.

A collapsible cane emerged from Flogent Lee's huge tapestry purse that probably weighed as much as she did. She then inserted a nickel in the parking meter's slot. The city of Pfister had retired their last surviving meter maid in 1982, but Flogent Lee wasn't one to take chances.

Jenna swung open the shop's door. The courtesy would induce either a toothy smile or a scowl that could strip varicose veins. ''Beautiful afternoon, isn't it, Miss Pfister?''

''It is that, my dear.'' The rasp and quaver in her voice was like a rusty garden gate batted by the breeze. "If you overlook Wynema Owens passing away this morning."

"I'm so sorry. I didn't know." Jenna didn't know Wynema Owens, either, but that was beside the point.

"Her daughter said the doctor was going to dismiss Wynema from the hospital tomorrow, then sometime during the night—*poof*—she was gone."

With age came pragmatism about death. Jenna's mother always said, "The young believe they'll live forever. The old know better, and wouldn't care to, even if they could."

"The doctor wanted to do an autopsy to find out what killed her," Flogent Lee continued, "but the family said no." She sniffed. "I guess you can't blame them. Dead is dead, but there's been quite a lot of it going around lately."

Jenna supposed the elderly woman had outlived most, if not all of her friends, along with an entire generation of family members. It was quite a milestone to be born in the early part of one century and live on into the next, but sad to be the proverbial last man standing.

Flogent Lee's milky hazel eyes, magnified by thick-lensed spectacles, fireballed Mavis via the back room's pass-through, then slanted at Jenna. "That purple sweater becomes you. You should wear it more often."

"Why, thank you—"

"With a skirt. A black one or a soft heather gray, I think, and with a proper hemline." Her lips pursed. "Dungarees are for carpenters and farmers and their ilk. Not for a lady, and certainly not in public."

Jenna squelched a grin. A skirt might make a good

parachute whenever giant spiders, mice and, in one instance, a monster black snake hitchhiked inside incoming merchandise and had her climbing thin air like a ladder. "I'll keep that in mind."

"See that you do." Flogent Lee scuttled forward, her cane tattooing the floor. "I wouldn't want your reputation to suffer for want of decent attire."

I wish, Jenna thought, wedging her hands into the back pockets of her jeans. She hadn't anticipated the interlude between the onset of menopause and a horizontal ride to the mortuary to itch like a chigger bite she couldn't reach.

Contentment still reigned supreme, yet there were moments—when she locked the shop at night, opened up in the morning or stared out a window as if it were a porthole to another dimension—that the urge to jump into her Explorer and roar off into the responsibility-free sunset was strong enough to taste.

A doctor would prescribe hormone replacement therapy.

A shrink would say her inner child was sniveling for one last whirl on the merry-go-round.

Her mother would *tut-tut* in sympathy, then take her shopping.

Mavis had told her to get laid.

Joyce Ramsour, Jenna's best friend, would second that motion, then place ads in the Saturday *Free Lancer*'s "Love Connection" section and sneak into men's rest rooms all over town and scrawl Jenna's phone number on the stalls' walls. If that didn't work, Joyce would book a nonrefundable passage on a singles' cruise and call it an early Christmas present.

Ho, ho…hmm. Let us not be too hasty. Tropical

sun, salty sea breezes, exotic ports of call. No shop, schedule or house to keep. Not a soul aboard who knew her, thus couldn't possibly rat her out to anyone in Pfister, such as her mother.

No strings, no oh-promise-me's, no dumping. Just five days and nights of fabulous food, fun and—

"Ms. MacArthur." Flogent Lee's formality and tone implied the summons was not the first.

Jenna apologized, saying her mind was elsewhere. Which it had certainly been, but there was no need to identify the precise location or the happy tune it was still humming.

"Calling this piece gaudy would be a kindness." Flogent Lee pointed a shaky finger at a hand-painted *Gone with the Wind*–style lamp. "It is a reproduction, of course."

Jenna shook her head. "Not this one. I guarantee it. The Fostoria burner is the original and the globes are signed by the artist."

"Hmph." Flogent Lee's mouth disappeared, her chin bobbing as though she were chewing bubble gum.

The Platos took their leave, waving goodbye to Jenna and in the general direction of Mavis, who was most likely bent over a vatlike sink, elbows-deep in suds. With her rump twitching to a Travis Tritt CD on her Walkman, she'd scrub the kitchen's every cookie sheet and muffin tin ninety-two times before she'd share the same room with Flogent Lee Pfister.

The bone of contention between the dancing pearl diver and the town's queen bee depended on who was asked. None of the explanations Jenna had heard seemed worthy of their mutual animosity. Then again, the Pugh twins hadn't spoken to each other since 1987, when Hugh traded cards with Stu at an Elks Club bingo night, then refused to split the fifty-dollar jackpot with his brother.

Flogent Lee said, "The price on this lamp is highway robbery, Ms. MacArthur. You should be ashamed of yourself."

Two and a half times its book value, Jenna agreed silently.

"What would you take for it, cash on the barrel-head?"

"A ten percent discount is the best I can do."

"Twenty percent. I *am* a regular customer, not a tourist."

"Fifteen."

"Done."

Jenna removed the lamp from the wrought-iron fern stand it rested on. The upper globe shuddered in its filigreed brass collar. Her pulse hiccuped. God help her if she dropped it.

"Put it on my bill," Flogent Lee said. "And you will deliver it this evening, won't you? Say, five o'clock?"

"The shop doesn't close until five-thirty."

"Then Gerta will expect you at the back door at 5:35." She patted Jenna's arm. "It's always a pleasure doing business with you, my dear."

The lamp was disassembled and swathed in tissue paper before Mavis ventured out from the back room. She looked from the wrapped bundles boxed on the counter to the sales receipt Jenna was writing.

"Why you go to such trouble to humor that pickle-pussed bag of bones, I'll never know."

"Because I like Flogent Lee, and because she's a lonely old woman rattling around in that huge old house with no one to talk to except Gerta. Assuming Gerta *can* talk.''

Jenna slipped a preprinted, fill-in-the-blank note into an envelope addressed to Flogent Lee's great-nephew, Philoneous, owner and president of the First National Bank of Pfister.

Today's visit was the buy-back phase of the agreement Jenna had made with Philoneous shortly after she opened MacArthur Perk. To wit, on her next visit, Flogent Lee would carry in another family heirloom to sell. Jenna would pay her the item's book value in cash, bill Philoneous for the amount, plus the ten percent surcharge he insisted she add, then price the item so high nobody in his or her right mind would buy it. In a month or so, Flogent Lee would return to hem, haw and dicker as though she'd never seen the piece, then charge it to an account for which she never received a bill.

Mailing a receipt to Philoneous kept the transactions kosher and assured him the heirloom had migrated back into its rightful owner's possession.

Mavis advanced on the Platos' table, dragging a broom and a long-handled crumb catcher. ''Ever ask yourself what'll happen if one of those gimcracks gets broken? Or stolen? Or the shop catches fire?''

''No.'' Jenna shivered as though she'd been transfused with Freon. All three of those disasters had starring roles in recurring nightmares.

The building and contents were insured. Philoneous had signed a waiver absolving Jenna of any liability for damages from acts of God, arson, theft, vandalism or clumsiness. But from the wrath of Miss Flogent Lee Pfister, there would be no salvation.

Just another unexpected funeral, Jenna thought. *Mine.*

With that, she grabbed the cordless phone's receiver and punched three on the speed dial. What the hell. To be specific, what was an hour, one way or the other, before she applied butt to chair in front of the computer?

"Joyce? Me. Girls' night out. Margaritas. Dinner. Dessert. Five forty-five." She rolled her eyes. "Yeah, yeah, it's my treat."

3

The woman bearing down on the circulation desk was slender and leggy, with copper hair and bright blue eyes.

Paul Haggerty thought, if librarians looked like that when I was a kid I'd have been a Rhodes scholar.

"I'm Mrs. Haroldson," she said. "My assistant told me you're interested in local history."

He nodded. "Do I need a library card to do a little research?"

"It depends on what you're looking for." She turned and pointed at a closed, curtained door in the back corner of a reading alcove. "Some of our books on the area are in circulation, but none of the materials in the history room can be checked out."

The prohibition guaranteed the good stuff was under lock and key. Paul reached for his wallet. "Even with a contribution to the library's general fund?" Realizing the offer might sound like the bribe it was, he added, "I'm staying at Bigelow's Bed-and-Breakfast and I'm sure Betty would vouch for me."

"Rules are rules." A tapping, unpolished fingernail emphasized the statement. "However, if you mark pages with slips of paper from the basket on the table, I can photocopy them for you for fifteen cents each.''

Paul hid his irritation behind a smile. "I'm an old hand at copy machines. I'd hate to waste your time when I can do it myself, and pay the charges before I leave.''

Inside that attractive package beat the soul of a pinch-lipped, professional bibliophile with her hair in a bun, four house cats and pots of African violets in a neat row on her kitchen windowsill.

"Patrons are not allowed to use the copiers, sir. No exceptions.''

"All rightie then. How about archived issues of the newspaper? I'm told you have them preserved on microfilm.''

"We do.'' An ornery glint sparkled in her eyes. "In the history room.''

"Now *there's* a surprise.'' His chuckle was devoid of humor. Like Custer, he knew when he was whipped. "Are microfilm printers available, or will I have to flag you down whenever I want a frame reproduced?''

"They are, and no, you may print them yourself for—''

"Don't tell me, let me guess. Fifteen cents apiece.''

"Correct.''

And she'd count every sheet rather than take Paul's word for the total.

The librarian motioned to another staff member, then pushed off from the massive horseshoe-shape walnut desk. "If you'll follow me, I'll show you where everything is.''

The wonderful, fusty smell common to block-stone libraries of the Carnegie era filled Paul's nostrils. It fostered back to a young boy's memories of awe and intimidation at the thousands of books no lifetime was long enough to read, and teenage recollections of rainy Saturdays when he'd studied Diane Wallis, the cheerleader of his dreams, instead of Thackeray, Browning or the fall of the Roman Empire.

Row upon row of steel shelving units were buttressed by wheeled ladders. Their height blocked the sunlight from the building's sash windows and sliced to ribbons the ceiling fixture's wan illumination.

Two-person alcoves were equipped with computers, printers and swivel chairs. Small wooden tables and straight-backed chairs were provided for old-fashioned research. Devotees of newspapers and periodicals took comfort in frumpy upholstered club chairs and love seats.

Framed oil paintings competed for wall space with portraits of dead presidents, the current governor, library benefactors all surnamed Pfister and corkboards shingled with business cards, public notices, sale bills and church bulletins.

The history room was airless, windowless and jammed with file cabinets and shelves. The microfilm machine sat on a prewar utility cart. At the center of the room was a scarred table and a plastic bucket chair likely donated by the local chiropractor.

"Please leave all materials removed from their locations on the table," Mrs. Haroldson instructed. "Some holdings are quite old and fragile, so the less they're handled the better."

Paul scanned the jumbled collection categorized by gummed labels stuck to shelf edges and box fronts. He'd spent the morning leafing through records stored in the courthouse's basement. If dust and mold spores were fattening, he'd weigh a good two-twenty by nightfall.

"Any questions, Mr...?" the librarian asked.

He said no and thanked her for her help.

Switching on the microfilm reader to let it warm up, he started his search with a pictorial history printed for Pfister's sesquicentennial celebration.

Before U.S. Route 66 was designated such in 1926, the section bisecting the town was known as the Old Wire Road for the telegraph poles spiking its length. Route 66 now became Commercial Street at Pfister's eastern limit, then reverted to its highway enumeration a hundred yards west of the city's fourth and final traffic signal.

Black-and-white photographs showed that field rock, Missouri's most abundant noncash crop, was the building material of choice when the Mother Road put Pfister on the map. Other than modern plate-glass doors, thermal windows and burglar bars, the Feed & Seed's bow-roofed, cobbled facade hadn't changed in almost seventy years.

Its contiguous neighbor, MacArthur Perk, had started life as a Texaco filling station with a single-bay garage. The bay door was now the coffee café's bay window and the pump island had been removed. Still intact was its original rock-pillared canopy, left as a permanent awning between the sidewalk and the shop's transomed front door.

Paul committed a few lines to his pocket-size notebook, then laid it aside. The shelved books and loose files yielded little of interest—to him, anyway. Most chronicled the nineteenth and early twentieth century.

The *Pfister Free Lancer*'s archives had a wealth of photos of Jenna MacArthur's son, Sam. Unfortunately all were grainy and an f-stop or two from focused. There were action shots of Sam's prowess on the athletic field. His reign as prom king was published a few weeks before a thumbnail shot of his graduating class. Four years later, a larger photo marked Sam's police academy graduation, but his face was shadowed by a wide-brimmed campaign hat.

Paul thought back to the breakfast he'd eaten at the Ritts Café. Every small town had a throwback diner where the old-timers gathered every morning to drink coffee and chew the fat. A stranger with open ears and a closed mouth could learn an amazing amount of scuttlebutt during those bull sessions.

"You coulda knocked Jenna over with a feather when Sam told her he'd enrolled in the police academy," a hawk-nosed farmer had said. The ring and middle fingers were missing on his right hand. A hay baler has no conscience.

The man beside him, a walking billboard for Carhartt outerwear, agreed. "Mamas of only children are tetchy that way. 'Spect if Jenna'd married one of them fellas she took up with and had a couple more babies before she passed her prime, she wouldn't have pitched such a fit about Sam being a cop."

Oh, yes, she would have, Paul thought. Did Sam know about his father? That Jenna had been a cop, too? A third man snorted derisively. "How long's it been since you had your eyes checked, D.W.? The gal still looks plenty prime to me."

"Get your minds out'n the gutter," Hawk-nose warned. "Neither of them jakes was near good enough for Jenna. She was smart enough to show 'em the door before the 'I do's' were done."

D.W. nodded. "Once burnt, twice shy. Sam's daddy must have gored her deep when he left her high and dry. Bastard never visited his boy once, neither, far as I know."

"Stands to reason, him being dead and all," the third man said. "I hear they were fixing to marry up again when he went and crashed his motorcycle into a semi."

Hawk-nose said, "Drunker'n a skunk, too, except he was afoot when that train ran him over down south somewheres. Atlanta, I think it was. Coulda been Mobile, though."

Frank Ritts banged his spatula on the grill he was scraping. "Drunk or sober, I can't say, but I know for a fact that Jenna's ex and some others went fishing for muskie up Minnesota-way. I disremember exactly how, but the boat flipped over and every one of 'em drowned."

The ensuing moment of silence ended when Hawk-nose said, "For a smart gal, Jenna's sure had more than her share of man trouble."

No argument there.

"That first 'un she was sweet on," he went on. "What was his name? Navarra? Guevarra?" He hunched a shoulder. "Now, I don't have nothing against Mexicans, but what she saw in that swaggerin' son of a gun, I couldn't divine."

The Hispanic surname and description were all the explanation Paul needed to understand the attraction. It was almost predestination that she'd fall for the first man she could fool herself into believing might fill Rick Rivas's shoes. How much too big had they been? Five sizes? Ten?

D.W. shook his head. "I'd give him my blessing over that coach Joyce Ramsour fixed Jenna up with. He looked like a tromped-on bullfrog and didn't know beans from apple butter about football."

The third man said, "The wife says Jenna wasn't as much in love with those guys as she was in love with the idea of being in love."

"Huh?" D.W. snaffled a bite of biscuit he'd sopped in a pool of egg yolk. Around a cheek pooched like a foraging squirrel, he said, "What the hell kinda sense izzat supposed to make?"

Camel smoke streamed from a fourth, and thus far silent, man's mouth. He wheezed, then pressed an electrolarynx to his throat. "If anything women said...made sense...they'd...be men."

Belly laughs and Frank's remark about a future president wearing skirts instead of chasing them swung the conversation away from Jenna to speculation on a former first lady becoming commander in chief.

Paul hung around the café for another quarter hour or so, but the Liars' Club had their teeth sunk into politics and weren't about to let go. How they could argue when they were obviously in agreement was beyond him. Maybe like crying babies exercised their lungs, old men bellowed and bellyached to keep theirs in working order.

Chuckling at the probability of becoming a café congressman himself someday, Paul squinted into the history room's microfilm reader and printer as though his eyes were out of focus, not the newspaper photo of Sam MacArthur. With some expert tweaking, a color photocopier might sharpen the image. Reproducing the picture with the library's Stone Age equipment was a waste of paper.

Edition after edition of the *Free Lancer* appeared on the viewer's screen. The cursed start-stop-reverse-advance process unsettled his stomach like riding backward on a commuter train.

Eleven years earlier, Jenna MacArthur had received a Chamber of Commerce Businessperson of the Year award. The photo accompanying the article showed Mavis accepting the plaque in Jenna's stead. In a later issue, the owner was conspicuously absent from a Sunday "LifeStyle" layout on MacArthur Perk. In a shot of Jenna and Sam taken at an all-sports awards banquet, a slight blur indicated she'd turned her head to look up at him just as the lens snapped.

Both she and her mother, Aggie Franks, were members of various civic, charitable and social clubs. At one time or another, both had held offices in various groups, yet captions consistently noted their absence when incoming boards of directors' photos were taken.

Hadn't their camera shyness ever aroused curiosity? The canon that engagements, weddings or obituaries were the only proper events for photos to appear in the newspaper was as obsolete as the gravity-feed gas pumps that once stood outside Chenoweth's Texaco.

Paul switched off the machine, assuming their AWOL attitude toward Kodak moments wouldn't raise any flags to the casual observer. It was a pattern of behavior you had to look for to find.

Before he left the room, he reshelved books he'd thumbed through, and stacked others selected at random on the table. He reboxed microfilm reels and returned them to their cubbyholes, leaving two decoy spools beside the viewer.

Photocopies and microfilm hard copies would have been nice additions to his files, but he wasn't about to alert Mrs. Haroldson to his interest in the MacArthurs and Agatha Franks. Like mothers, librarians had eyes in the backs of their heads and sonar systems the navy could only dream of.

As he paused at the stairway landing that led to the basement-level exit, Mrs. Haroldson rounded the front of the circulation desk and strode in the direction of the history room.

Hands thrust in his pockets, Paul whistled softly between his teeth as he descended the stairs to the parking lot.

Twilight had sharpened the breeze curling around the building from the alley behind it. Crimson, orange and yellow leaves scraped the asphalt parking lot like fingernails on a window screen.

The faint scent of wood smoke laced the air. It wasn't chilly enough to stoke fireplaces or woodstoves, but there were always a few folks eager to throw logs on the grate, kick back in a recliner and feel at one with their pioneer ancestors.

Jenna took the carton with the *Gone With the Wind* lamp's upper globe from Mavis and nudged it beside the other box on the Explorer's floorboard. "Are you sure you don't mind my leaving early?"

"If I did, I'd say so."

The comeback wasn't snippy, but not exactly

bursting with glee. Jenna shut the truck's passenger door, then surveyed the otherwise empty parking lot and vacant spaces on MacArthur Perk's street side. "Customers probably aren't going to stampede through here in the next half hour. Let's go ahead and lock up, then we can both play hooky."

Mavis's eyes skittered in their sockets, then narrowed to hyphens. "You don't trust me to take care of the store, do ya?"

"What? Of course I—"

"I knew it." Mavis's hands shot up as if an armed robbery was in progress. "You're still mad about the bank deposit I screwed up last month."

Jenna's head tilted to one side. "Excuse me?"

She was convinced that math had been invented just to piss her off. She and the drive-in teller at First National had a running joke about Jenna intentionally transposing numbers on deposit slips to keep the bank honest.

Before Mavis semiretired and came to work part-time at MacArthur Perk, she'd tended bar at the Bottoms-Up Lounge—some said, since Prohibition was repealed. Jokes aside, her internal cash register could tabulate the cost of a cartful of groceries, minus coupons, plus sales tax. To the penny. Every time.

"You couldn't screw up a bank deposit if you tried, Mavis."

"Think so, huh? Well, I guess *that* shows how much attention *you* pay to what *I* say. For your information, I most assuredly did and I apologized for it till I was blue in the face, too."

Arms crossed tight to her chest, she added, "You've got about two seconds to get on your pony and ride, or it'll be a cold day in August before I believe you trust me worth spit.''

Jenna's teeth worried her lower lip. Flogent Lee's visits always irked Mavis, but her fuse had been shorter than usual all afternoon. "Why?" would be an excellent question. Mavis's drill-sergeant stance indicated that now was a lousy time to ask.

Jenna keyed the Explorer's ignition, mouthed *See you tomorrow* through the side window and wheeled toward the sloped apron accessing Commercial Street.

Years after the town council's decision to give the main drag a bona fide name, a highway department employee heard that Springfield, the state's third largest city, was replacing its old street signs and hauling the discards to the landfill.

An ad hoc committee outfitted in chest-high waders was dispatched to root around the dump site for recyclable signage. They returned with a truckload, including a slew from Springfield's Commercial Street.

An army of volunteers helped with the installation. Merchants donated food, coffee, soda pop and commemorative T-shirts. Naturally, when the project was completed, some residents grumped about every address in town being altered to conform with new street names or hundred-block designations. Out-of-towners were and would forever be flummoxed by South and North Streets running east to west, which was intentional, because South South Street or South North Street sounded like something out of the *X-Files*. However, virtually everyone agreed that the mayor and town council were fiscal wizards on a grand scale.

Jenna yielded to the stream of oncoming five o'clock traffic, hoping for a break or a disciple of the Golden Rule. A glance into the rearview mirror reflected no ticked-off store managers aiming the evil eye at the Explorer's tailgate. Mavis Purvis wasn't built for speed, but she'd vanished in a blink.

"Mine is not to reason why," Jenna muttered, waving a thank-you to the minivan driver who braked to let her pull out. "Mine is to deliver Flogent Lee's lamp, go home, clean up my act, then haul ass to Casa Juarez for a double margarita. And a straw."

Paul slowed the Lumina for the turn off Fairway onto Lyon. Tree branches clad in fiery autumn coats formed an arbor over the street, plunging it into a premature dusk.

It was a stable blue-collar neighborhood of neat lawns and half-brick ranchers whose floor plans could be guessed by their window placements, size and treatments. Skimpy front porches were decorated with corn shucks, bedsheet ghosts, jack-o'-lanterns and portly, well-dressed scarecrows sitting on bales of straw.

At 210 Lyon, a raised bed planted with brilliant chrysanthemums encircled the yard light. The house's blue-over-white color scheme and chateau-style trim was feminine without being prissy.

Aggie Franks was visible through the glass storm door, laying her dining-room table with dessert plates, coffee cups, saucers and drink glasses. Paperback books were stacked on one corner. The tablecloth was black, the drape bordered with white outlines of bodies in various postmortem positions.

When her name was Ellen Bukowski, she'd been

a rabid mystery-novel fan. The derivation of her surname, Paul didn't know, but felt certain Aggie was
short for Agatha, as in Christie. Of greater interest at
the moment was the fact that she wasn't planning to
have dinner with her daughter tonight.

An article in the newspaper's back issues told of
the book club she'd founded. The members met to
review new, old and obscure whodunits and to col-
laborate on the novel they were writing. Paul had
also heard that Aggie attended the funerals of widows and widowers with few relatives or friends,
whether she was acquainted with the deceased or not.

Why, no one seemed to know. Paul Haggerty
could have hazarded a pretty good guess.

Book clubs, charity work and volunteering at the
local hospital weren't Aggie's only activities. He
doubted if anyone, including Jenna, knew she'd established an Internet chat room for adoptees searching for their birth parents, birth parents searching for
adopted children, and the lost, the missing and the
presumed, but not proven, dead.

It had also led Paul Haggerty straight to her daughter's doorstep.

Three years ago, after a near-fatal car accident left
him trying to reconcile himself to life with a shattered face and confinement to a wheelchair, the Internet had been Paul's window to a world where he
was hale, hearty and whole again.

Plugging words at random into Google's search
engine began as a game and became a preoccupation.
Among thousands of hits, *orphan* introduced him to
a chat room whose moderator's screen name was the
title of a Dashiell Hammett short story.

He rarely revisited the sites he'd discovered. The

chat room was the exception. Before long, he was contributing techniques and sources used by police, estate attorneys, private investigators and, ironically, identity thieves.

A first-time chatter requested information regarding a sixty-eight-year-old man named Francis De-Smet. The moderator, aka House Dick, asked if Francis could be related to a Trudy DeSmet, last known address Astoria, New York.

The newbie had no knowledge of Trudy DeSmet, but for days the name nettled Paul's memory like a blister. His physical therapist was inflicting her special brand of torture when the answer shimmied to the surface.

Trudy DeSmet—nicknamed Trudy DeSlut—had been Earl Bukowski's mistress. Clichéd though it was, the skirt-chasing, boilermaker-swilling, ham-fisted husband of Ellen Bukowski and father of Elizabeth Bukowski Rivas, had suffered a fatal coronary in Trudy's arms and bed. Earl had to be extricated from both by a squad of paramedics.

Slowly, carefully, Paul gathered crumbs of information dropped by and about the chat room's moderator. Building a dossier flexed mental muscles he feared were as damaged as the nerves controlling his legs. Without realizing it, the cozy, listless depression he'd shrouded himself in loosened, then fell away.

Aggie Franks, aka House Dick, aka Ellen Bukowski, lived in Pfister, Missouri, with her daughter, Jenna, and grandson, Sam. The chat room was created in the hope of finding Aggie's long-estranged son, Jimmy. She had no reason to believe he was still alive, other than a mother's heart. If Jimmy was dead, she would know. Until then, she would keep looking.

"Hard to believe," Paul said as a weigela hedge obscured his hindsighted view of the house at 210 Lyon. "What WITSEC, the U.S. Marshals Service and a grab bag of cooperating agencies and entities joined together, one guy with a laptop and a new-found reason to live doth put asunder."

At the corner, he yielded the right-of-way to an urban cowboy's tricked-out pickup, then turned left and drove the short distance to 1423 South Dollison.

The Explorer parked in the driveway of the two-story stucco bungalow gave him pause. With Sam out of town, had Jenna decided to skip having dinner out? Or had Mavis confessed to divulging Jenna's plans to a nameless stranger?

His prior drive-bys had only hinted at a routine, but to date, she'd secured her vehicle inside the de-tached, gambrel-roofed garage at night. That she hadn't tonight suggested she wasn't home to stay.

Another possibility kicked up Paul's pulse rate a notch. The Ritts Café regulars hadn't mentioned a current boyfriend. Would Mavis have stage-set the evening if Jenna was seeing someone?

His eyes flicked to the dashboard clock. He ex-haled the breath he hadn't realized he was holding. In less than an hour, he'd know the answer.

4

Joyce Ramsour, the human chronograph, was never late.

As if being a size three petite, terminally cute and a natural strawberry blonde wasn't despicable enough, Joyce was always five minutes early, except on those rare occasions when Jenna was five minutes early. Then, thanks to some sort of psychic-alert mechanism, Joyce would have arrived *eight* minutes early to allow plenty of time to practice looking smug.

Jenna rested her chin on the heel of her hand and doodled swizzle-stick figure eights in her soupy margarita. Casa Juarez was medium-busy for a Tuesday night. A few booths and tables were available, but Ciencia de la Torres, the restaurant's owner, was ringing up take-out orders as fast as she could sack them.

A Hispanic population boom began shortly after Ciencia and her husband, Andres, settled in Pfister. The Jones Farms Fresh Fryers plant paid above-average wages, but the de la Torres family gambled on their countrymen yearning for a taste of home. When the restaurant became as popular with Anglos as Latinos, the couple opened an ethnic grocery, invested in a low-wattage Spanish-language radio station and converted a storeroom into a classroom where tutors unraveled the linguistic Gordian knot known as American English.

Jenna admired the de la Torreses' entrepreneurship, but wished they'd turn down the restaurant's blasted sound system. Until tonight, she hadn't realized the canned mariachi Muzak was as annoying as the neighbor kid practicing "Lady of Spain" on his trumpet.

The kitchen exhaled steamy, mouthwatering aromas that had half of Jenna's stomach pleading for mercy. Queasiness assailed the other half. She couldn't decide whether to be worried, pissed at being kept waiting or to celebrate the law of averages victory over her best friend's compulsive promptness.

Joyce did have a husband and two tweenage daughters, lived in a wedding cake of a house nicknamed the Money Pit and owned Pfister Ford-Lincoln-Mercury. To be fair, it was a miracle her knuckles weren't scarred from dragging the ground.

"Fair, hell." Jenna dunked a tortilla chip in a bowl of congealed chili con queso. "If life was fair, I'd have one, too."

The chip was taxiing for her tongue, when a man said, "Mind if I join you?"

Jenna's head whipped sideward. Three things registered simultaneously: the gist of the question, that the questioner liked homburgs and John Grisham novels and that the gooey, cheese-laden chip had landed four inches east-southeast of her mouth.

Her stuttered assortment of pronouns and sentence fragments ended in a perfectly enunciated "Aw, shit."

Currying his mustache didn't hide the grin spreading behind the man's hand. "Is that 'Aw, shit, yes, have a seat'? Or 'Aw, shit, no, I'd sooner cram dip in my ear than share my booth with you'?"

"Go for it," Jenna said, laughing, then tacked on a rueful "If you think my stupid appetizer tricks are special, wait'll you see what I can do with an entrée."

"I'd like to, Ms. MacArthur." His knees brushed hers as he slid into the booth, a barely-there tap that shouldn't have crackled like a static-electric charge.

He laid the hat he carried crown side down beside him, then reached between his bottle of Dos Equis and her margarita glass. His handshake was firm, businesslike. "Paul Haggerty," he said, as though refreshing her memory of a previous introduction.

There hadn't been one. Even Mavis, the Presbyterian yenta, hadn't pried a first name out of him, let alone a last one, or anything else worth grinding through the gossip mill.

He released her hand a beat later than convention called for, yet the reluctance didn't telegraph the smarmy *How do you do* perfected by horn-dog graduates of sexual-harassment seminars.

Or was it her hand that had lingered? Her reluctance to break the connection? It was impossible to ignore the nonsensical sense of familiarity Jenna felt whenever he was near, but there must be a simple, rational explanation for it. There had to be. Across-a-crowded-room simpatico was as true to real life as Elvis sightings.

Joyce would call it kismet. Joyce didn't know kismet from Kibbles 'n Bits. If she ever showed up, Joyce had some explaining of her own to do.

"Paul Haggerty," Jenna repeated slowly. Her mouth tucked at a corner. "So are you a nephew or a cousin to the Haggertys that own the Charolais ranch west of town?"

For an instant his sea-green eyes dulled and darkened, like a cloud shadow skimming over a meadow. "Neither, as far as I know." He leaned back in the booth. "Especially if their house is the one with the big white bull on the roof."

"It is." She peeled a napkin from the holder to dab at the goo in her hair. "If you think Ferdinand is an attention-getter in the daytime, drive by at night when the floodlights are on."

"You're kidding."

"No bull, I swear."

His groan matched his grimace. "Walked right into that one, didn't I?"

"As have legions before you. Second to the Mother Road, Ferdie the Four-legged Fiberglass Roof Ornament is the town's most famous tourist attraction."

"I can see why. That thing's almost as long as the house is wide. How did they get it up there?"

"Money, influence and being former world-champion bull rider Dolph 'Stick-tight' Haggerty doesn't hurt. Then all you have to do is borrow a crane, a fire department hook-and-ladder truck and an electric company cherry picker, then ice down a kegger or two for added incentive."

Paul munched the chip he'd swiped from the basket. "It kind of makes you wonder which came first—beer or the barter system," he said. "If I had a dollar for every eight-thousand-pound sofa bed I've hiked up and down eight-thousand flights of stairs, I could replace all the furniture my skunk-drunk buddies trashed every time they returned the favor.''

It was probably rude to picture Paul bare-chested, buffed and loading housegoods into a U-Haul. Imagine sweat glistening on his skin. Biceps bulging under the strain. His excellent mane of sandy hair damp and wind-mussed, the ends dark and curling at his nape—

Urrrrrt. Hit the brakes. Hold the phone. And furthermore, lay off the freakin' tequila. The soy extract, too, if it's replacing fallow hormones with atomic lust particles.

Exchanging primal for prim, which likely came off as constipated, Jenna continued the local-history lesson. ''The guys that hoisted Ferdie into position did get seriously hammered, but they must have known what they were doing. He's survived a tornado, a low-flying doofus in an ultralight and numerous kidnapping attempts by teenagers with more brawn than brains.''

''I guessed as much the minute I saw it,'' Paul said. ''A bull on the roof, like moths, are ever caught by glare.''

Interesting. A man who looks dashing and a bit dangerous in a vintage hat, who not only *can* read but does, and can paraphrase Lord Byron, doesn't happen along every day.

Determined to stay on topic, she said, ''Sam— that's my son—and the other seniors on his football team are the only ones who've successfully committed grand theft bovine. Their record stands at seven years and counting.''

A blush inched up her neck. What kind of mother brags about her child's youthful induction into the

Vandalism Hall of Fame? Well, contrary to three others she could name, the kind that made sure Sam participated in Ferdie's reinstallation, then helped Dolph Haggerty dig a new pond and mend miles of barbed-wire fence as penance.

"After the heist," she continued, "the boys hauled Ferdie to the high school, dressed him up in a tie, black dress socks, sandals, a PHS helmet and sunglasses, and braced him behind the principal's desk.

"Mr. Atherton was a good sport about it. He was still laughing when he gave the boys in-school detention until graduation night. Dolph and his wife got such a kick out of it, they hung a commemorative plaque beside their front door."

If Paul was listening, her jaunt down memory lane hadn't tickled his funny bone. As his thumbnail pared a strip of label from the beer bottle, he asked, "How many children do you have?"

"Just Sam. He isn't a kid anymore, but there were days when he was little that I'd have traded him for triplets so I could get some rest."

Paul snorted, apparently intent on crawling the label in one ruched piece. "From juvenile cattle rustler to cop, of all things."

Gooseflesh sprinted up Jenna's arms. "How did you know that Sam is a cop? And what do you mean by 'of all things.'"

He started as though unaware he'd spoken aloud. Gaze focused a fraction above her eyes, he licked his lips, then said, "I, uh, had breakfast at the Ritts Café yesterday and today. You probably know the Liars' Club holds court at the counter every morning. I presumed the Sam MacArthur they mentioned was your son."

The Nosy Old Farts Club was more like it. Between the Ritts and A Little Deb'll Do Ya, the most popular beauty shop in town, Jenna couldn't imagine why anyone in Pfister paid for telephone service, much less subscribed to the *Free Lancer*.

"But why did you say 'of all things'?"

Paul balled the torn, soggy paper between his thumb and forefinger. "I'm hell on jumping to conclusions. Wrong ones are a specialty. I suppose I thought it'd be tough on a single mom if her only child chose a career as dangerous as law enforcement."

Mamas, don't let your babies grow up to be lawmen. Jenna repressed a laugh certain to sound a bit manic. If only he knew. If only anyone knew, besides Aggie.

Sam's enrollment in the police academy had triggered a swirling, sickening panic that hurled Jenna backward in time. It was agonizing for her mother, too, but Aggie's marriage to Earl Bukowski had earned her a Ph.D. from the School of Let Sleeping Dogs Lie.

On occasion, when Sam entered the store or the house in uniform, his tall, backlighted build slammed past into present and the collision sent Jenna reeling. She'd have shouted out her dead husband's name if not for the heart lodged in her tight-closed throat.

Sam remembered nothing of Rick Rivas. He was too young when his daddy died for good-night kisses, Latino lullabies and wild hallway horsey rides to carve lasting impressions. A blessing, Jenna told herself so often she almost believed it. A child can't mourn what he never had.

According to the cover story hashed out with the

Feds, Jenna and the mythical Adam MacArthur had divorced as impulsively as they'd wed. They'd reconciled and were about to remarry when Adam and his parents were killed in a boating accident off the Gulf coast. Their bodies were never recovered, hence no graves to decorate on Memorial Day or absentee paternal grandparents to explain.

The script was as sappy as a daytime drama, but Jenna had refused to portray Sam's fictional father as a deadbeat dad who, along with his parents, had abandoned the boy like an unwanted puppy.

She flinched at the familiar stab of remorse for depriving Rick's parents of their grandson and Sam of them, along with a busload of aunts, uncles and cousins. Telephone contact between Jenna and her in-laws, arranged by the Marshals Service, had ceased when the Rivases petitioned the court to have her declared an unfit mother to gain custody of their absentee grandson.

Jenna shook her head, a metaphorical leap from a painful train of thought to another track. To Paul she said, "Of course, I worry about Sam—in or out of uniform. He's my kid and it was love at first sight before he was even born. Do you think I'd worry any less if he had nineteen brothers and sisters?"

The lines fanned at the corners of Paul's eyes, as though he was recalling the punch line to a private joke. "No, but there are those who'd argue that the larger the litter, the less a mama bear frets about each cub."

"*Frets?*" She laughed. "Geez, two meals at the Ritts and you're talking like a native. With a Brooklyn accent."

"Not Brooklyn." His grin widened. "New Orleans.'' It came out *New Orr-lins,* rather than the nonresident and national media's erroneous *N'awlins* or *New Orr-leans.*

Her breath caught. If the Liars' Club had made the same geographic error, then told Paul that she, too, hailed from New Orleans, she'd damn them for…well, liars.

New Orleanians—Ninth Warders in particular— did sound like transplanted New Yorkers, which is why that city was selected for hers and Aggie's re-birthplace. When eastern met midwestern, their accents gradually slowed and slurred into a God-knows-from-where melange.

Four, then five seconds ticked past without Paul connecting any communal dots. As if a reminder were necessary, this agony was why she'd prolonged a bevy of deadend relationships and clung to two Mr. Wrongs almost until the last prenuptial minute. For impostors the basic boy-meets-girl preliminaries were pungi-stick pits with flimsy grass trapdoors.

Jenna crammed the paper napkin she'd used to wipe the cheesy goo from her hair into a side pocket of her shoulder bag. ''By chance, did the café's fossilized parenting experts also say I might *fret* less about Sam if he didn't volunteer for every multijurisdictional drug task force that came along?''

''Is that where he is tonight?'' Paul asked. ''Out beating the bushes for dopers?''

Again her skin prickled. ''How'd you know…'' trailed off to a sigh. The counter stoolies had probably told him every dumb, embarrassing, sinful thing she'd ever done. Or would, if given enough opportunities.

''The Pfister P.D. sent Sam to Quantico for an antiterrorism seminar. Foreign and domestic. Everyone else on the force, including the chief, thought it sounded like a yawner.''

''Everyone except your son.''

''Yup. Mr. Gung-ho's duffel bag was packed a week before the flight to Virginia.''

Jenna recrossed her legs, taking care not to knee-cap Paul's shin with a stiletto-heeled boot. She supposed she should be grateful to Joyce Ramsour for intimidating her out of her work clothes and into a snazzier outfit, makeup and sexy footwear. Which was akin to sending Mattel, Inc., a thank-you note for inventing Barbie.

''What about you?'' she asked. ''Any children?''

''Not any—'' He chuffed. ''Not that I know of.'' A palm raised. ''Sorry. Dumb joke. Wish I did, but no, no children.''

A voice in the back of her mind whispered, *How about a wife or a significant other?* A snottier one chimed in, *Care to explain why it matters? He must be closer to Sam's age than yours and let us not forget certain promises made to yourself when Roger Ernst broke your engagement.*

It had been three years since that dreadful day, but her ego hadn't completely recovered from Roger telling her he was leaving her for someone else on his way out of town. Bonus points for candor aside, when a man dumps a woman for another man, she can't stand in front of the mirror and wail, ''If only my boobs were bigger....''

Paul said, ''You're divorced, too.'' A statement, not a question.

''Married once, twice shied from the altar.''

His eyebrows arched. "Do you mind if I ask why?"

"No."

After a pause of pregnant duration, Paul grinned and swigged his beer. Jenna grinned back and sipped zero-proof ice water. He surveyed the dining room, perhaps reckoning the distance to the closest emergency exit. She traced a Rorschach-like stain on the vinyl tablecloth.

His "Look, I didn't mean to pry" stepped on her "How about we start over at the introduction?"

They laughed, the tension leaving his face at the same rate it drained from her neck and shoulders. He reached across the table. "Paul Haggerty, expert lady-killer."

She clasped his hand. "Jenna MacArthur, sparkling conversationalist."

"My fault. I wouldn't appreciate a know-it-all stranger barging in on my evening and my private life." His tone implied a bygones opportunity for a *Nice talking to you, Paul. Do drop by the shop whenever you're in town.*

The waiter descending on the booth had twice inquired after her readiness to order. Seating was still available, but servers frowned on customers who thought a drink and a bowl of cheese dip bought indefinite squatters' rights.

Jenna checked the restaurant's foyer. No Joyce. Tomorrow heads would roll. Right now was freakin' awkward.

Twenty-first century or not, if she invited Paul to join her for dinner, he might feel obliged to pick up the check. A "my treat" offer could force an excuse such as a need to hie back to the bed-and-breakfast to rinse out some socks.

Then there was the prospect of eating alone, which sucked. She could have nuked a Maria Callendar at home and earned a virtual fortune on eBay by now.

"Okay, listen up," she said, resting her elbows on the table. "My ex–best friend was supposed to meet me here forty-five minutes ago. My stomach is rumbling like a cement mixer. I'd enjoy your company for dinner, but if you can't stay, fine. If you can, we'll go dutch."

The waiter's chin buckled as though the proposition sounded reasonable to him. His attention shifted to Paul.

"There's nothing I'd enjoy more than having dinner with you..."

Please. Spare me the lame intro and cut straight to the lame excuse.

"...but where I come from, a man opens doors for ladies, walks on the street side, never spits on the sidewalk and pays for dinner."

An old-fashioned guy. Not many of those on the loose, by golly. "I thought chivalry went out with *The Ed Sullivan Show* and leaded gasoline."

Paul accepted a laminated menu from the waiter. He slanted his eyes at her, and the tip of his tongue curled over his teeth.

"Yeah, I know," she said. "Not where you come from, it hasn't," and added ornery to dashing, a bit dangerous and too young—

His face, but not his hands.

The observation broke the surface of her mind like a movie or song title that's floated on the periphery for hours. Her slow-on-the-uptake brain finally supplied the *something* that had bothered her yesterday while they'd discussed the merits of commercial fiction versus literary fiction.

Present on the backs of Paul's hands were the ropy veins, coarsened skin and pleated knuckles of a man in his middle to late forties. Absent in his face were any corresponding marionette lines or the parenthetical age dimples that should bracket the corners of his mouth.

Great genes? Had he bobbed for apples in the fountain of youth? One thing for sure, manual labor hadn't caused the discrepancy. When they'd shaken hands, her palms were more callused than his.

To ask why the sum of his visible parts didn't jibe would be tactless. Except she couldn't stanch the hum in her bones. It had been half a lifetime since she'd worn a badge, but cop instinct was as ingrained as her ability to visualize the mahogany dresser cowering under layers of milk paint, dirt and grime.

Paul caught her staring. He angled his head, his expression pensive. "Why don't you order for both of us. Something light on the green chilis and jalapeños for me, though. I like them, but the feeling isn't mutual."

No problema. Jenna simply doubled her every Tuesday-night repast, minus another round of drinks. When the waiter was out of earshot, she said, "You may be tuned in to the good ol' boy network, but you aren't exactly an enigma yourself, Mr. Haggerty."

With an apology to everyone south of the Mason-Dixon Line, she drawled, "I know more about you than you think. A lot more."

The Dos Equis bottle toppled. Its last swallow

dribbled out on the tablecloth. Paul set it upright and mopped the foamy puddle with a napkin. "Clumsy of me," he muttered. "You were saying…?"

The dregs of her margarita were flat, room temperature and bitter. She made a face, an unladylike noise, then pushed away the glass. "Well, for starters, you checked into Betty Bigelow's house of frilly horrors on Sunday afternoon with a garment bag, a laptop computer, a metal briefcase with combination locks and no departure date."

His adenoidal "Uh-huh" languished. The Muzak's Spanish guitar mimicked hyperactive mosquitoes. "That's it? I'm supposed to be shocked by your supernatural knowledge of my luggage?"

Jenna waved a dismissal. "Of course not. I was just warming up."

"In that case, give me a minute to brace myself."

Lucky for him, she had a soft spot for smartasses. "You wear contact lenses, exercise when you waken and before you go to bed. You're left-handed, an insomniac, a social drinker, earn a six-figure income—minimum—and you didn't come into the shop yesterday to buy a book. You came in to scope me out."

Paul's jaw fell, his features as slack as a dental patient's after a root canal. He crossed his arms, a classic self-defense posture, and appeared neither impressed nor amused by the smirk she couldn't conceal.

"Not bad, Miss Marple. About twenty clicks short of blockbusting, but not bad at all."

Hmm. A wise guy and a bluffer. Would it be too much to ask for him to have an older brother? "Okay, then, do correct me where I'm wrong."

"Not wrong but not psychic. This afternoon at your shop during Mavis's fishing expedition, she already knew or guessed I was staying at the bed-and-breakfast. When I left, I'll bet she was on the horn to Betty before I got my car door unlocked."

Actually, Mavis had waited to call Betty until Jenna was busy with Flogent Lee Pfister. "And your point would be?"

"Your manager has a straight pipeline to my landlady, who's a snoop and a keyhole peeker. I don't figure you for an apprentice blabbermouth, but you are a good listener."

"So what if Betty isn't blindfolded when she changes the linens, collects the dirty towels and lays out fresh ones," Jenna countered. "As for eavesdropping, I guarantee she doesn't haunt the hallways. Not that she wouldn't, but two-inch-thick oak doors and a woman too vain to wear a hearing aid sort of puts the screws to effective spying."

By his beetled brow, logic was making inroads. An eagerness to battle wits was as evident as the razor-thin tracheotomy scar visible through the unbuttoned collar of his shirt.

A cruder, stitch-tracked line welting Jenna's neck had diminished, but scarves and chokers were as much her trademark as calligraphing the capital J, M and A in her name.

"That barn of a house's floorboards squeak," Paul said. "Hearing-impaired or not, anyone can tell the difference between somebody torturing himself with a hundred push-ups and wandering around owl-eyed at 3:00 a.m."

She bestowed a silent touché. "There are advantages to living in old, two-story houses. When Sam was a teenager, he couldn't figure out how the stairway risers creaked here, there and somewhere else one weekend, then broke out in new places the next.''

Paul chuckled. ''Mothers are the mothers of invention.''

''That's how mine caught me sneaking in and out after curfew, until I outfoxed her by mastering the art of sliding down the banister and shinnying up it without making a sound.''

''Sam never caught on?''

''Sure he did, except our stairway has a railing, not a banister, and he couldn't know in advance which risers I'd loosened. What really drove him nuts was when I didn't sabotage any of them. God, it was hilarious hearing his size fourteen clodhoppers tiptoe up the stairs, then him cussing a blue streak when he got to the landing.''

''You are a wicked, wicked woman.'' Paul clucked his tongue, clearly revisiting the days when sneaking into and out of the house was on par with taking the gold in an Olympic biathlon. ''Terrifying to think what havoc you'd wreak if you *were* psychic.''

The waiter arrived with a steaming ironstone platter in each mitted hand. He fetched schooners of iced tea, fresh chips and salsa from a tray resting on a folding stand, then left them to commit the third deadly sin.

''Pretty good,'' Paul said, shoveling in his third mouthful of south-of-the-border heaven smothered in enchilada sauce.

''Oh?'' Jenna scowled as though she'd slaved over a hot stove since dawn, only to be damned with faint praise. "What would you call the Hanging Gardens of Babylon? Nice landscaping?"

"Diversion will get you nowhere."

"Diversion? From what?"

"Telling when-Sam-was-a-boy stories—entertaining as they are—instead of explaining your other guesses about me."

"Oh. That." Tedium leavened her sigh, then her voice. "You wear your watch on your right wrist and carry your wallet in your right back pocket. North-paws might do one or the other, but seldom both. Hence, you're a lefty."

Switching his fork to the customary hand sufficed as confirmation.

She indicated the Dos Equis bottle corked with the damp paper napkin. "You nursed that a half hour before you ventured over, and it was a long pull from empty when you did. Bar dogs don't drink warm beer. Hence, social drinker."

"Aw, c'mon, Jenna." He laughed as men do when their ability to handle power tools is questioned. "There's no way you could know that. I was here before you were, and you can't see the bar from that side of the booth."

Squeezing lemon into her tea seemed fraught with symbolism. "Can so."

Paul craned his neck and looked over his shoulder. "Well, I'll be... Mirror, mirror, on the wall, huh?" He turned back, grinning. "Should I be flattered that you had me in your sights?"

She shrugged. "I was bored and thought Joyce might come in the rear entrance instead of the front."

"Ouch."

She glanced up. "Nothing personal."

"Gee, thanks. I feel better about myself already."

If Joyce were there, she'd kick the crap out of Jenna's ankle as a reminder that flirting was not the verbal equivalent of full-contact karate. Paul didn't seem aghast at her intermittent alpha-chick behavior, but Jenna was. Not that it was a departure from the norm. It was just unusual for her to step out from behind her shop face around someone she barely knew.

It wasn't as if she felt especially comfortable or relaxed. Oh, she liked him well enough. Liked his banter, his faux cockiness, the wisdom and humor in his mood-ring green eyes. That grin, more pronounced at one side of his mouth than the other, was borderline irresistible.

Yup, all systems would be go—at least getting there—if she could stifle the murmur, as capricious and indistinct as a whisper on the wind, that Paul Haggerty was no more a stranger to her than she was to him.

Horse hockey. She'd spent too many nights alone reading Dean Koontz and Stephen King novels, was all.

"While my ego's trying to recover from your painful honesty," Paul said, "you can admit you took a wild guess at my income."

"An educated guess," she corrected before her mouth closed around a bite of the sancho enchilada-style she no longer craved. Once the food was dispensed with, she teased, "And you're just dying to know where it came from."

"If it's from someone other than where I think it did."

Ignoring the barb, she cited as evidence his hand-stitched loafers and calf-skin sport coat, accessorized by a sliver-thin platinum watch. "Clothes don't make the man, but a man with your taste makes a chunk more than union scale."

"Trust fund?"

She shook her head. "Not unless you wear a neck chain you never take off except during surgery. Link-style. Twenty-four carat gold, minimum. Cross hanging from it, optional."

"Oops. Guess that disqualifies me."

"Thank God."

"But maybe I owe my soul to American Express."

Jenna waved a dismissal. "Doesn't everyone?"

She'd charged VISA to MasterCard and MasterCard to VISA a few times when Sam was outgrowing his clothes and the fridge's cubic footage faster than her income allowed, but Paul paid cash for his purchases yesterday at MacArthur Perk—a memorable transaction, for several reasons.

Ninety percent of her cash sales were for coffee, baked goods, magazines and newspapers. Items in the twenty-dollar-and-above range brought out the plastic. That general rule was particularly true of travelers, with the advent of credit card issuers' breakage-and-theft warranties. Rare were customers like Paul Haggerty who whipped out a hundred-dollar bill as casually as Jenna would a single. She'd almost emptied the register making change. The clincher was the fact that as unintentionally as English teachers notice misspelled words on signs, shopkeepers noticed the contents of customers' billfolds. The glimpse Jenna got at Paul's would give a pickpocket an orgasm.

Conclusion? He who has a personal ATM hugged to his not-bad ass isn't a credit card junkie.

She graciously bit back an "Aha!" when Paul said, "I *am* indebted to AmEx. Just not the way most people are. They were one of my first clients when I went into the security business."

"You're a stockbroker?" Novels and Hollywood had molded her conception of a Wall Street wonk, but Paul didn't fit the image or personality.

"Not that kind of security. Armored vehicles and discretionary surveillance systems, among other things." He smiled. "Bulletproof mobile bunkers and electronic sentries were once the domain of foreign diplomats and top-rung government officials. Now they're as much a status symbol as protection for celebrities and Fortune 500 CEOs."

Jenna surrendered all pretense of eating. "It sounds like an interesting line of work, but what brought you to Pfister? We're not exactly up to our earbobs in your type of clientele."

Paul groomed his mustache with a napkin, then replaced it in his lap. "My apologies for the James Bond impersonation, but I can't go into specifics. Strict confidentiality is a lot of what separates me from a burglar alarm salesman."

How can a lie be true? With the right amount of spin. The trick was figuring out which components were which.

How did she know he was lying—or, to be fair, not being a hundred percent truthful? The same way women had since Eve. Have a kid and you get a state-of-the-art bullshit detector at no extra charge.

The best thing she could do was plead weariness and go home, which was about ninety-three percent gospel. Dessert and coffee were declined, then an after-dinner drink, and finally, a drive to the Haggerty ranch to see Ferdie lit up like the Liberty Baptist Church's flagpole.

In keeping with his old-fashioned-guy lecture, Paul paid for their meal and refused to let her get the tip.

He helped her into the wool frock coat Aggie had sewn from a reproduction pattern, then lifted Jenna's hair free of the collar. The intimacy of the gesture startled her. No man had done that since her father died.

Paul's hand rode the small of her back as they exited the restaurant. Judging by the looks they attracted, if he took breakfast at the Ritts tomorrow, the grilling would not be exclusive to the kitchen.

The contrast between the sultry restaurant and the night air was at once invigorating and shivery. Paul donned the homburg and snapped the brim Bogart-style. Jenna hugged her foil-lined go-bag to her chest. The crunch of her boots on the pea-gravel parking lot sounded like gnashing teeth.

"Your powers of observation are pretty amazing," Paul said, picking up the conversational thread. Again.

"It comes with the territory, if you want to survive in the flea-market biz. Fluency in body language helps, too. It's as bright as Broadway when a little old lady whips out an heirloom, certain I'll faint dead away when I realize it's George Washington's denture cup. Breaking the bad news without implying Great-Grandma lied like a rug is an acquired skill."

She was babbling and couldn't care less. "Then there's the hucksters out to flimflam me with overnight antiques and garage sellers thrilled to get a quarter for a knickknack. Later, when they see it in my shop with a twenty-five-dollar price tag, they go ballistic and accuse me of cheating them.''

A few yards separated her from the Explorer. She mined the side pocket of her shoulder bag for her keys.

"I may be pushing my luck," Paul said, "but you haven't explained why you think I came to the shop yesterday to meet you, not just to buy something to read.''

The same way I'm certain you aren't asking why I think it, but how I damn well know you didn't just happen by the store.

"I was on a roll," she lied, brushing away the hair tickling her cheek. "Shooting for a bidda-boom, bidda-bah finale.''

Eyes averted, she thumbed the Explorer's remote entry button. The battery must be low. Two more tries were necessary before the taillights winked. The lock mechanism chirped "All aboard.''

Paul's hands clamped Jenna's shoulders. He hustled her bodily into the dark canyon between her SUV and the minivan beside it. His knee prodded the pressure point behind hers, forcing her downward.

In her ear, he whispered, "Quiet, Jenna. Don't make a sound.''

5

Jenna stumbled forward. Gravel pinged off metal, slewed beneath her boots. Her temple grazed the Explorer's chrome mirror. Caroming off the van's side panel, she wheeled around, flattening her back against her truck's cold, wondrously solid door.

Her heartbeat pounded in her ears. She whipped her head left, then right. The scream boiling up her throat withered to a gurgle. Paul Haggerty had disappeared.

A family of five ambled from the restaurant. The father yelled, "Hey, you—what'cha doin' over there," just as Paul's disembodied voice shouted, "Hands on your heads. Both of you. Out of the vehicle. *Now.*"

The Samaritan started forward, then paused. His wife yanked on his sleeve, herding him and their children in the opposite direction.

Adrenaline percolated through Jenna's veins. Long-dormant muscle memory snapped her hand to her hip. A forefinger groped for a holster's safety strap. She stretched up on the balls of her feet, but the minivan's tinted windows obscured Paul from view. By his voice, several cars separated them.

Backup. I've got to call for... Where she was, *who* she was, jolted her as hard as an uppercut to the jaw.

Sweat poured down her back, her ribs, the intensity of the flashback like a mental and physical tidal wave.

She brought a shaky hand to her temple, then hesitated, afraid to touch the elongated, pearl-slick scar where the bullet had pierced her skull. What was *wrong* with her? Why, after so many years, was the past leaping into the present and ambushing her?

She moved nearer the front of the van. Thirty yards away, Paul stood glaring at two black-clad figures. Their arms were winged, their fingers laced atop their sock hats. Behind them was a bright yellow Miata. The doors were wide open. Its interior light sparked off the car's ivory upholstery.

Jenna's hand closed into a fist. Anger rinsed away the metallic taste of fear. She stomped toward them, vapor gusting from her nostrils. "What the *hell* are you doing here?"

Turning her wrath on Paul, she yelled, "And who do you think you are, shoving me upside my truck and scaring the *shit* out of me?"

Jenna snatched off the hat from the taller of the pair's head. Mavis yelped, then cringed, speechless for perhaps the first time in her life.

The second beheading tumbled Joyce Ramsour's blond-red curls to her shoulders. She grinned at Jenna and said, "Is it okay if we put our hands down now?"

An hour later, Jenna was still fuming. She paced her kitchen under the watchful gaze of two exquisitely ugly dogs sprawled on the floor, a three-legged tabby draped across the top of the refrigerator and the blissful, unrepentant Joyce Ramsour seated at the round oak table.

"I don't know why you're so upset," Joyce said for the umpteenth time. "It's not my and Mavis's fault that your new boyfriend is paranoid."

"Paul Haggerty is not my boyfriend."

"He'd like to be. I haven't seen such a moony-swoony look on a guy's face since Barry and I went all the way in the back seat of his dad's Oldsmobile at the drive-in."

Her lips parted with her sigh. "The honeymoon's not over and I've taught Barry some mighty fine moves in twenty years, but those were the days, my friend."

"You're changing the subject again."

Joyce sipped from her wineglass. "I am not. It's obvious you're attracted to Paul, too. You sure didn't stand there in the parking lot reading him the riot act like you did us, even though he was just protecting you, the same as we were."

Jenna counted to ten along with the Kit Cat wall clock's shifty eyes and tail. Mavis's "You don't trust me" malarkey that afternoon was a ruse to get rid of Jenna so Mavis could call Joyce back, tell her about the half-blind date arranged with Paul, then conspire to stake out the restaurant.

"Cut the po'-widdle-me crap, Joyce. You and Mavis set me up, then went to a helluva lot of trouble to spy on me."

She flapped a hand. "It was no trouble at all. Really. I knew you'd recognize my duallie, but Tiffany Inwood traded in her Miata for a new Mustang this afternoon. Sweet car, but it needed the cobs blown out of it."

Joyce was just the Hot-rod Annie to do it, too. Speed limits were mere suggestions, and not very good ones at that. A vehicle in the hands of a less skillful driver would be lethal, but Joyce had a NASCAR-level feel for the road.

"I took Mavis home to change clothes," she said, "grabbed us a cheeseburger, then we sat with the heater on, toasty as bedbugs, waiting for you to come out."

Joyce examined her flawless, blood-red manicure. "Besides, you'd have done the same thing if I was meeting a total stranger for dinner. That's what friends are for, right? And if you want to get real about it, you didn't even know the guy's *name*."

Homer, the basset hound–cocker spaniel mix, wagged his abbreviated, pointy tail as if in agreement. Beside him sat Herschel, his muzzle at rest on the top rung of a ladderback chair—hardly a stretch for the son of a registered Great Pyrenees who'd gotten down and dirty with a mostly Great Dane.

Jenna wouldn't trade them for any other two dogs in the universe, much less a pair of attack-trained rottweilers, but at the moment would consider a short-term loan.

"I did not know I was meeting Paul for dinner," she said. "I thought I was meeting *you* for dinner."

"My point exactly." Joyce held a lighter under the tip of a Salem she'd quit smoking two years ago. She took a deep drag, then exhaled with a moan common to porn flicks. "Mavis and I weren't about to leave you alone, twisting in the wind. For all we knew, Paul was a homicidal maniac or something."

Jenna slumped into the opposite chair. She scratched a cigarette from the pack, lit it and choked.

After Joyce and Mavis slunk away from Casa Juarez, Paul apologized repeatedly for manhandling Jenna and for assuming the two figures he'd seen duck down in the idling Miata were car thieves, purse snatchers or worse.

He'd tried to make a joke of it. Assured her he didn't make a habit of rousting people from their vehicles. "I don't know what came over me. Maybe too many years of watching my backside. My antennae quiver when a parked yellow car with the engine running doesn't have a taxi meter on the dash."

Jenna accepted his apology and a kiss on the cheek, but declined his invitation to lunch. He had nothing to "make up" for, she told him. She had tons of work to do, having taken off on a buying trip the week before.

As she drove home, she didn't believe Paul would take no for an answer that easily and couldn't decide whether she wanted him to. The hinkiness she felt in his company defied explanation. Other than by association, the sudden resurrection of Liz Rivas wasn't Paul's fault. Leopards can't completely change their spots. If Jenna hadn't been preoccupied, she'd have noticed the car and occupants before he did.

Mavis said Jenna had declared herself the wall-flower at the dating dance so long ago, she'd forgotten the steps. Maybe she was right.

Yeah, and what if you did, Jenna's inner bitch taunted. Paul Haggerty is just passing through town and one-night stands aren't your style, even if they last a week, or two.

"Gimme that," Joyce said, startling Jenna and eliciting a harrumph from Herschel. The cigarette

Jenna wasn't smoking was snatched from her forked fingers.

"If you want to watch something burn, light a candle." Joyce tapped the ash worm into a Barney Rubble ashtray. "I have to drive clear to Saint Robert to buy a pack of smokes, or somebody'll rat me out to Barry."

"Why don't you just quit for good?"

"I did, for cripes' sake. Ages ago." Joyce's smile looked as though it had been drawn on by a palsied hand. "Smoking after you quit is a helluva lot more fun than everyday smoking. A couple of puffs and *whoa*—I'm higher than a kite in a thunderstorm."

Jenna stared at the pack lying beside Joyce's wineglass and mulled over the possibility of getting hooked, then quitting cold turkey, so she could fly high on down-low nights like this.

Paul Haggerty lay atop the lace-edged cabbage-rose comforter, fully dressed, but for the loafers he'd kicked off beside the bed. Fingers twined behind his head, his eyes roamed the titty-pink plaster ceiling. How, he wondered, had everything gone to shit in a matter of seconds?

The matchmaker and the ditz, otherwise known as Mavis Purvis and Joyce Ramsour, had put Jenna on guard—deflector shields raised and impregnable. Her face had been as white as bleached bone when she'd stepped out from behind that van. The look she'd leveled at him could have stopped a locomotive, much less a heart.

The hot-water pipe juddered in the adjacent bathroom. Betty Bigelow was taking her soak in her bathtub downstairs a half hour later than usual. Across the hall, a sitcom's laugh track shinnied out the cracks of the retired pharmacist's door.

Paul rolled onto his side to muffle the noise and the vanilla fumes from the potpourri basket on the night table. What stars were visible through the windows' chiffon swags winked as though mocking him for being improvident, impetuous, imbecilic.

What had he been thinking? Easy question. He hadn't thought—just acted. Now he had to start over at square one. Hell, try square one minus ten. Having frightened Jenna, any good impression he might have made at dinner was down the tubes.

Thank God he hadn't pulled the Smith & Wesson. He'd knelt and hitched his pant leg, then recognized Mavis an instant before the gun cleared its ankle holster.

The bedsprings twanged as Paul swung around and sat up on the edge of the mattress. He raked his fingers through his hair, then shook his head. No sleep for the wicked. Not tonight.

His eyes slid to the amber prescription bottle on the piecrust lamp table. Every nerve, every muscle pleaded for solace—for a few hours of pain-free oblivion.

Forget it. Sedatives chased with uppers to bat away the morning fog was a merry-go-round he'd sworn he'd never ride again. He locked the meds in his briefcase, then walked to the window, avoiding the treasonous floorboards under the broadloom carpet.

He'd been certain he'd prepared for any eventuality. Acknowledged well in advance that the odds of Jenna remembering his name were slim. What he hadn't realized, or had blocked from his mind, was how much he'd hoped she would, and the whiplash effect when she didn't.

A fickle memory resulting from her head injury had allowed Rick Rivas's killer to walk. The neurologists had said that time and the body's natural healing process would restore a percentage of it. How much and how quickly they couldn't—or wouldn't—guess.

The shooter, a cretin named Lenny Vildachi, had been obsessed with making his bones and earning the family's respect by avenging the murder of his father, John Vildachi.

For a son, particularly an only son, exacting an eye for an eye was Sicilian justice, except John Vildachi's death wasn't an assassination. After being diagnosed with Lou Gehrig's disease and told the prognosis, Vildachi set the scene to spare his wife and son the shame and stigma of suicide, praying God would choose that moment to blink.

Whether He did or didn't, the family, their priest and Vildachi's circle of friends and enemies allowed his death to play out as he'd planned. The truth was an open secret his son Lenny refused to believe. For reasons unknown, Lenny blamed mob boss Constantine Manetto.

His target's current mistress was stashed in a midtown penthouse. Lenny and the soldiers his uncle assigned to baby-sit him laid in wait for days, on the assumption boredom would overcome Lenny's misplaced hatred before Manetto had a hankering for female companionship.

In crude but precise terms, Lenny Vildachi's retribution was a cluster fuck from the outset. He leaped from the car, tripped on the curb and practically fell into Manetto's arms. The prodigal son scrambled up and managed to splatter Manetto to kingdom come, then panicked when he spotted Liz and Rick Rivas, who'd just exited a neighboring restaurant.

Lenny didn't know the Rivases were cops, but ignorance was no excuse. Murdering innocent bystanders violated La Cosa Nostra's peculiar code of honor. Gunning down an officer of the law and critically wounding another literally compounded the felony. The entire New York City Police Department came down on the Five Families' collective necks.

Liz's recovery was one of those medical miracles everyone prays for but are seldom granted. She wanted justice—the death penalty for Vildachi, or at least life imprisonment with no possibility of parole.

Unknown to her, so did Gerald Shur, the chief and creator of WITSEC. Vildachi's uncle had disowned his pathologically stupid nephew. If convicted, a bitter, betrayed Lenny could be an excellent candidate for trading information on the organization's top-feeders in exchange for a reduced or commuted prison sentence and government protection.

Liz's testimony was clear, concise and compelling. Vildachi's defense team chiseled away at her credibility when her recollection of events prior to the shooting and afterward were fuzzy, contradictory or irretrievable.

A week's deliberation found the jury split seven to five for conviction. When the judge declared a mistrial, Vildachi and his shysters celebrated as though it were a victory.

The district attorney and Gerald Shur blamed Mario Puzo's pop-fiction portrayal of Don Vito Corleone's quasibenevolence. Without additional substantiating evidence, the risk of a retrial ending in another hung jury or, God forbid, an acquittal, was too great. For the time being, the charges against Vildachi were dropped.

Except, murder has no statute of limitations. Word on the street was that Liz Rivas wouldn't live to testify again. Robby or Liz's mother might be used as bait to draw Liz out. To pea-brained Lenny Vildachi, such a bold move would restore his rightful place in the organization. Entering the WITSEC program was his targets' only recourse.

Paul absently watched a car cruise past the inn, then turn into a driveway two doors down. For Liz Rivas, her son and her mother, federal protective custody had turned into a twenty-five-to-life sentence.

Balding, morbidly obese Lenny Vildachi remained an embarrassment to his family and civilization in general, but he waddled the streets of New York a free man. There'd been no takers on the rumored contract on him. A hit would have been tantamount to a favor paid to Lenny's uncle, but even enforcers for whom torture was sport drew the line at old folks, children and retards.

The woman known now as Jenna MacArthur had sacrificed everything, including her name and her career, in the hopes of someday bringing Vildachi to justice. Underestimating her had been Paul Haggerty's second error in judgment.

Shades of Rick Rivas on that score. Rick's ego had always sold short his wife's perceptiveness and analytical mind. He loved her, yet had no sense of the woman he'd married. Of course, plenty of guys were guilty of that.

The haggard chimera reflected in the windowpane

glowered at Paul. *Wha'dya do, Romeo,* they all jeered. *Leave your smarts in your other jacket tonight? She almost nailed your ass with that crack about her son being a cop, "of all things."*

He'd also seen Jenna's hand poised near her hip, as though hovering over a phantom service revolver. Her tactical standing-cover position was textbook when she'd stepped around the van.

"Want proof of 'once a cop, always a cop?' Well, you got it in 3–D Technicolor this evening, sport. You'll do well to remember it in future."

The houses across the street, grand old dames all, dissolved before Paul's eyes. In their stead was a stucco bungalow with dormers and a sleeping porch on the second floor. He imagined Jenna MacArthur aglow from a hot shower, her hair wet and sleek and smelling of fresh peaches.

"Hello?" Jenna said into the phone. She glanced at Joyce, threw a leg over a padded chrome bar stool, then leaned an elbow on the counter. "Oh, hi, Mom."

"Mavis just called and told me what happened. Are you all right?"

"Sure. Why wouldn't I be?"

"Well, Mavis is afraid you'll never speak to her again."

Jenna blinked, though she should be accustomed to the tangents Aggie's conversations often took. "So instead of calling me, Mavis tattled to you."

"She did no such thing. Mavis knew you wouldn't say word one to me. Being a mother herself, she didn't want me to find out secondhand about that thug you're dating."

Take me now, Lord. "Paul Haggerty isn't a thug, Mother, and I'm not dating him."

At the table, Joyce crammed a fist in her mouth to keep from laughing.

"Whether you are or aren't is no business of mine," Aggie said. "You're a grown woman. Your choice of boyfriends has never been my cup of tea, but who am I to criticize?"

Fingers tented at her forehead, Jenna braced herself for the migraine due to detonate at any second.

"The point is, Mavis worships the ground you walk on. You should be ashamed of yourself for treating her the way you did."

Jenna pulled the receiver from her ear and squinted at it. "Are we talking about the same Mavis Purvis? Doesn't look a day over a hundred and twelve? RuPaul makeup? Kick-ass attitude?"

"Watch your language, missy. All she wants is what's best for you and you'd damn well better apologize for yelling at her at the top of your lungs right in the middle of town."

Casa Juarez wasn't anywhere near the middle of town, but the devil is in the details. Jenna accepted the glass of wine Joyce poured for her and knocked back a gulp. It was boxed wine, not bottled, but any port in a storm, so to speak.

"Okay, okay, I'll call Mavis and apologize." For yelling. Not for the content.

"At this hour?" It was nine-fifteen. "Tomorrow is soon enough, sweetheart. And it'll mean more to her face-to-face."

No argument there. Double-crossing the boss was a faster picker upper than a Geritol smoothie.

"By the way, tonight's book club meeting was a

dandy. Too bad you missed it to go out gallivanting with that thug.''

Jenna drained the glass and held it out to Joyce for a refill. She hadn't attended a meeting since Aggie begged her to critique the first chapter of the group-written whodunit. Actually, it was the four-hundred-and-forty-third draft of the first chapter. It read as erratically as sentences razored from pulp detective novels and glued in place, like a fifty-page, single-spaced ransom note.

Too late Jenna had realized that the geriatric wanna-bes weren't after constructive criticism. They wanted affirmation that their work beat the bejesus out of Chandler, Gardner, Hammett and Spillane combined—which it sort of did, considering how heavily all four had contributed to it.

"Everyone *loved* my lemon bars," Aggie went on, "and Racine Yount said my new drapes are simply gorgeous."

Jenna winced. That zinger was a payback for saying a fabric swatch brought projectile vomiting to mind, unaware that her mother's new curtains were a few seams away from finished.

"Then Blanche Filbert and Casper nearly came to blows when he told her that stabbing a victim with an icicle had been done to death. She huffed up—you know how Blanche is when she doesn't get her way—and said Casper was dumber than dirt on a stick if he thought anybody would fall for his lunatic plots."

Ah, yes, Jenna thought. 'Twas another dark and stormy night in the neighborhood.

When Casper Wetherby, a retired railroad engineer and Aggie's gentleman friend of ten years, wasn't proposing or plotting murders most foul, he dreamed up get-rich-quick inventions. The majority were totally off the wall, such as a rotary-dial cell phone for people whose fingers were too big to punch a keypad.

His few gems, like reducing collapsible fire hoses to garden-size scale, had the unfortunate habit of having been patented several years earlier by someone else. Rather than discourage him, Casper took those minor setbacks as proof that the only thing off was his timing.

Jenna didn't recall *right* and *Casper* ever coinciding in the same sentence, but she agreed, the frozen-dagger M.O. had grown much moss since the forties when John Dickson Carr employed it in a trademark locked-room mystery.

Aggie sniffed. "I wish you'd been here to tell Blanche that. When Casper tried, she acted like he'd mashed all ten toes at once."

"To be fair, Mom, Casper can be a little crotchety at times."

Joyce said, "Casper is a lot crotchety all the time," as though she were participating in a conference call. "Along with cheap, stubborn, a hypochondriac and the worst driver since Beryl Van Meter crashed the OATS bus through the senior center's back door, out the front, fishtailed across the street and demolished the embalming room at Tuft's Funeral Home."

Jenna scowled and tapped a finger to her lips.

Joyce simpered and tapped a different finger to hers.

Aggie said, "Is Joyce over there?"

"She most assuredly is." Jenna cocked her head

and made a you're-gonna-get-it face. "She's chain-smoking Salems and getting drunk on cheap wine."

"Oh, good."

"Excuse me?"

"I have something to ask you and two heads are better than one."

"Not necessarily," Jenna said. "Not when one of them is impaired and the other can't get that way fast enough."

A lengthy pause ended in a tragic sigh. "Never mind, then. It isn't as if I ask for help twenty times a day, like some mothers do. I wouldn't ask at all if I didn't respect your opinion, but if you're too busy to spare me a few minutes of your time, I wish you'd just say so."

Jenna smiled a salute. She really should take notes. When Aggie pulled out the stops, she could out-guilt anyone on earth. It was a gift.

"I'm never too busy for you, Mom. You know that."

Joyce toasted the comeback. Her own mother wasn't too shabby at troweling it on, either.

"I should hope not," Aggie said. "It isn't as if—"

"You did that part already."

"Oh." A throat-clearing and a cough were indicative of Aggie backtracking to pick up the original trail. "The homecoming game," she said. "Yes, that's it. Do you remember the night somebody spiked Sam's Gatorade with syrup of ipecac?"

"Like I could forget? The poor kid puked so long and hard, he passed out."

"The nurse at the hospital's Poison Control Unit that took care of him. What was her name? Wasn't it Mallory something-or-other?"

Jenna pondered a moment, then repeated the question to Joyce, who'd comforted Sam as best she could during the ride to the hospital. They stared at each other like Vulcans trying to whomp up a mind-meld, then gestured "Ya got me" in tandem.

"Sorry, Mom. That was too many years ago. In fact, I'm not sure I ever knew the nurse's name."

"Well, if you didn't, you should have. After all, she saved Sam's life."

A large exaggeration, even for a besotted grandmother. The nurse had mostly forced fluids and taken turns with Jenna holding an emesis basin under Sam's chin. "Why do you need to know her name now?" slipped out before Jenna could muzzle herself.

"Because Casper's new plot idea for the book is a scene with the butler canning raspberry jam. Later, the victim eats some on his toast and dies, but it looks like he choked to death. Nobody suspects murder except the detective. Brilliant as he is, it'll probably take him ten or twelve chapters to deduce who did it and how."

"That's, uh—that's very intriguing," Jenna allowed, "except 'The butler did it' is as clichéd as the icicle thing."

"It would be if the butler was our murderer," Aggie replied in a how-can-a-child-of-mine-be-so-dumb tone of voice. "The *real* killer poisoned the jam with pokeberries when the butler left the kitchen for a few minutes to answer the door."

"Ah, so. The twist in the tale."

"One of many. Tell Joyce and see what she thinks."

The designated second opinion wrinkled her nose,

then pinched it. Jenna nodded and hiked a shoulder, which was best friend–speak for, "You tell her. She isn't your mother."

It was possible the surrounding neighbors heard Joyce's "Good job, Aggie. This time, you've really outdone yourself," as it was rendered with the gusto and sincerity exclusive to politicians and professional car salespersons.

"Ooh, I just knew she'd like it," Aggie crowed, and turned away from the receiver to repeat the verdict to Casper.

"I liked it first," Jenna muttered.

"I appreciate that, sweetheart, but it means so much more coming from Joyce."

Jenna shut her mouth before something snide fell out. It had been a long night. God, she was exhausted. And wired. And desperate to be alone with her dogs, Festus the cat, and her thoughts.

"I see why you want to contact the Poison Control Unit nurse who treated Sam, but anyone in the department should be able to tell you about pokeberry poisoning. The plants shoot up all over the place every spring."

"Should be able to," Aggie countered, "but nobody will tell us a thing. Twice Casper called to ask how many berries he'd need to kill somebody and if cooking them into jam would boil away the poison. Both times, whoever answered the phone hung up on him."

In the background, Casper hollered, "It's those damn HMOs, I tell you. Nobody'll give you the time o' day, unless you wave a checkbook under their nose."

Jenna grinned. She adored the skinny old coot,

who was such a pessimist, he wore trousers with suspenders *and* a belt. "I'll see what I can find out," she said, then added, "tomorrow."

"After you apologize to Mavis."

"Yes, Mother."

"And tell Joyce to sober up and get herself home where she belongs. A woman out alone this time of night is just asking for trouble."

Paul switched off his headlights as he turned the corner. The Chevy's wheels hadn't straightened, when a cat streaked across the pavement in front of him. Reflex slammed on the brakes. Tires yipped loud in the quietude.

Letting the car glide along at its own speed, he glanced out the side windows, checked the rearview mirror. From one backyard to the next, dogs barked as though a watch commander were calling roll. Perspiration filmed his forehead. He swiped it away with the back of his hand.

Hey, it's a free country, isn't it? Relax, for Christ's sake. There's no law against driving around town on a full-moon night. The taut, stubbled face framed in the oblong mirror had no reason to look as guilty as sin.

A television's blue haze flickered in a few front windows, but most were dark. Pfister was a working-class town. Breaking the early-to-bed, early-to-rise rule made a five-day week feel like ten and Friday afternoons a hundred hours long.

Compared to its neighbors, the bungalow's ground floor was as bright as Grand Central Station. Joyce Ramsour's Miata was parked in the driveway. Jenna's truck must be in the garage.

Paul eased the gearshift into neutral. He feathered the hand brake to slow the sedan without activating the taillights. It rolled to a curbside stop two doors down and across the street from Jenna's.

As he cut the ignition, he chuckled, thinking of Joyce's amateur surveillance. When she left Jenna's house and walked to her vehicle, there'd be no telltale exhaust chugging from his Chevy's tailpipe; no idling engine to drown out the katydids and southbound snow geese; no cigarette ember glowing in the dark like a miniature harvest moon.

Neither she nor Jenna would guess he was within miles of 1423 South Dollison.

6

"Give me five good reasons why you won't go out with me," Paul said.

Jenna chuffed the way Sam once did to unreasonable demands, such as dropping his underwear in the hamper not beside it. "Good by whose standards? Yours? Or mine."

Paul propped his butt against the coffee bar. The heels of his hands he anchored on the stainless-steel countertop she'd just finished polishing. "I'm a fair kind of guy. How about three by yours, two by mine."

She peered over a shoulder at the kaffeklatschers at the tables. At the opposite end of the shop, Mavis was measuring a wardrobe a couple wanted to convert into an entertainment center. In a soft but scathing voice, Jenna said, "You, Mr. Haggerty, are a pain in the ass."

"See? That wasn't so hard, now, was it?" His grin begged to be wiped off his face. "One down, four to go."

Aerosol mist spat from the can of polish. Jenna buffed the counter with a rag-bag T-shirt until her bicep burned. "You don't live here."

"I have a condo in Baltimore, but I don't live anywhere to speak of."

"A Gypsy is worse than a tourist."

"I'm not a Gypsy. I telecommute."

"Semantics."

"No, it isn't." He leaned closer. "Do I strike you as the type who's happy chained to a desk?"

He didn't, but Jenna was of the opinion that desk jockeys were made not born. What little boys or girls ever dreamed of spending most of their adult lives with half their anatomy stuck in a three-sided box?

"Okay," she said, "it's like this. You're a nice guy, but complications I don't need. Or want. I like my life just fine the way it is. Peaceful, organized—"

"Boring."

Twitching her nose to stave off a sneeze, she couldn't nuke him with a look or a suitably obscene comeback.

He hadn't phoned or made an appearance since the Casa Juarez fiasco Tuesday night.

Wednesday morning she'd taken her laptop to work with her and had been almost too preoccupied to notice. That evening, Joyce ponied up the ten bucks she'd bet that Paul would send forgive-me flowers.

All day Thursday, Jenna's ears had perked like Pavlov's dog's whenever the bells jingled above the shop's door.

This morning she'd blamed a bad night's sleep for dragging to the shop in baggy leggings and the oversize sweater she couldn't resist buying at seventy-five percent off, but should have. A dab of moisturizer and mascara was consistent with the Sure As I Slouch to Wal-Mart Looking Like a Bag Lady, I'll Run Into an Ex-Lover in Aisle Six rule.

The location was immaterial. The concept was

graven in stone. It was a corollary to being involved in an accident on the one and only day in your entire life that you weren't wearing clean underwear.

"Aw, c'mon," Paul said. "If the idea was that revolting, you'd have told me thanks, but no thanks, instead of dredging up dumb reasons why two adults can't go out for a drink or a meal or something."

"The reasons game was *your* idea."

"You went along with it."

Their eyes met; his were as self-assured as a cat's, hers narrowed and obstinate. "If I'd given you a straight, flat-out no, would you have respected it?"

A eyebrow arched. "Yes. I would have."

Yes, he would have, she thought. Which is why I didn't give him a straight, flat-out no, which makes no freaking sense whatsoever. I've turned down thousands of dates before. Hundreds. Dozens.

She shook her hair back from her face. "So now you think I'm playing hard to get."

"You don't play anything, but I am kind of curious about who you're arguing with. Near as I can tell, it isn't me. In fact, it can't be me, because I'm not arguing."

The cleaning cloth hit the counter with a pathetically dull *fwup*. "All right. You win. Pride goeth before the fall and all that crap.

"Scratch your nonresident status and my happiness with life as I know it and that leaves me being too old for you. I have a reasonably high estimation of myself, but I need boy-toy jokes like Michelle Kwan needs ice-skating lessons."

Paul's laugh trailed off like polite applause at a PTA meeting. "Good God. You're serious, aren't you?"

It wasn't the reaction she'd expected. Most men would have automatically asked her age. He didn't, nor did he give her the up-and-down, estimating the miles left on her odometer before her chassis rusted. He just stood there, staring through her, his mouth gaped a fraction.

Pulling the plugs on the coffee urns could be construed as symbolic. For Jenna, it signified that a semi-abysmal day was limping to an end and that her yearning for a tub of Blue Bell Dutch-chocolate ice cream and a shovel would soon be realized.

A matronly foursome seated at one of the tables rose in unison. Their bridge club met every Friday for cards, lunch and Bloody Marys, then they tottered into MacArthur Perk to dish about everyone else in the club and sober up before carpooling home to scorch supper for their husbands.

As Unella Fogerty struggled with the intricacies of matching her arms to their corresponding coat sleeves, she said, "You'll be at the concert in the park Sunday afternoon, won't you, Jenna?"

Attrition had winnowed out Pfister's amateur philharmonic to four clarinetists, the triangle player and a conductor. Area bluegrass garage bands, barbershop quartets and gospel groups now laid claim to Frisco Park's gazebo. Whether the music was toe-tapping or shade tree karaoke, admission was free and church auxiliaries took turns selling refreshments.

"I wouldn't miss it," Jenna said. "Especially since it's the last concert of the year." She licked her lips, anticipating the hot, spiced cider and pumpkin cookies for which the Lutheran ladies were renowned.

A glowering Clara Jeanne Journegan rooted through her coin purse. A dime was plucked out, which she examined as though she'd minted it herself, then placed beside her coffee mug. She must be fresh out of nickels. Mavis would be thrilled.

"They say we're in for a gully washer," Clara Jeanne warned with obvious delight. "All day Sunday and into Monday."

Inez Petrie sniped, "Who does besides you, Miz Merry Sunshine?"

"Now, girls," said Tilda Donahue, their designated driver. "Let's not bicker and spoil a lovely afternoon." Moving to the door, she held it open for her unseaworthy passengers.

Unella paused at the threshold. Low-button shoes were the rage when she was a debutante, but a woman who'd survived three husbands left no man unflirted. "I hope we see you on Sunday, too, young man."

Jenna delivered a sidelong "I told you, so" look at Paul.

"Don't forget the lawn chairs." Inez winked. "Or better yet, a blanket for two."

Clara Jeanne snapped, "And an umbrella."

Refusing to acknowledge the young man's continued presence, Jenna drained each urn into its respective pump carafe. "Last chance for refills, everyone." For the benefit of the skinflint Schumacher cousins, she added, "Mugs only. No go-cups."

Paul nudged her aside with his hip to load the urns onto a wheeled trolley. The crusty stains left on the counter he dispatched with a spritz of polish and masterful swipes with the cleaning rag. The former he stowed in the cabinet below and he hung the latter on the trolley's handle.

Not to be outmuscled, Jenna hefted a rubberized bin full of dirty coffee mugs. Paul removed it from her hands and deposited it on the cart's lower shelf.

"Thank you," she begrudged.

"You're welcome." He steered the trolley toward the kitchen. "I'm forty-eight."

"I'll take the—" Her subtle attempt to wrest control of the cart from him halted as abruptly as she did. "You're what?"

"I'll be forty-nine in July."

She looked at him askance. Puffed out a raspberry. Said, "In dog years?"

From the flea-market area, a shrill "You want me to knock off a hundred bucks *and* throw in free delivery?" vibrated the plate-glass windows. The couple interested in the wardrobe recoiled, their expressions apologetic and a trifle horrified.

Reducing her volume, but not the venom, Mavis went on, "That's the trouble with you young folks. No respect for history. I'll have you know, this wardrobe was saved from the wrecking ball when they tore down the Hotel Pfister. None other than Harry S Truman himself stayed there back in '44 when he was campaigning for president, and it's said FDR did, too, when his touring car broke down on the way to Hot Springs, Arkansas."

The man blanched. "We had no idea...."

"Well, you do now." Mavis caressed a door panel as one would a lover's cheek. "I'll carry this beauty home on my back and bust it up for kindling before I'll give it away."

The woman clutched her husband's arm. "Oh,

Bradley, it's perfect for the media room. You said so yourself.''

He groaned, but reached into his topcoat's inner pocket. "Will you take a check?"

Paul wheeled the trolley around the sales counter, chuckling under his breath. "If I was smart, I'd hire your manager away from you. Mavis could put the fear of God in God, then sell him an armored SUV."

"She's a born huckster," Jenna agreed. "And amazingly good at judging when a piece will sell itself and when a little encouragement is needed."

"Is that what you call it?" Paul parked the cart alongside the kitchen sinks. His hand glided the length of her arm, then covered hers. "That's the trouble with you young folks. No respect for your elders. I'll carry that wardrobe home on my back and bust it up for kindling before I'll let you get away."

The warmth of his touch suffused her skin, and it was wonderful, so natural, she couldn't imagine why she pulled away. Because of a reluctance to be alone with him, she supposed, even though she'd missed him when he'd disappeared for a couple of days, despite the "whistling through a graveyard" feeling she had when he was near.

"I was in a car wreck several years ago," he said, his voice as detached as his gaze. "We were t-boned at an intersection. The car flipped, landed on its roof. The posts snapped and it smashed down on top of us. A gas leak caught fire before Rescue could get us out. The driver died. There was a time, a damn *long* time, when I envied him."

"Oh, Paul."

He motioned for silence. "Don't worry. I'm not going to give you an organ recital. Let's just say it took all the king's horses and all the king's men to put me back together again—from the face down.''

Walking wounded, she thought. Both of us. I should have guessed when I saw the trach scar on his neck at the restaurant. That and a shared survivors' guilt might explain the connectiveness, the eerie whisper of déjà vu.

"Uh-huh. Mavis told me I'd find you back here." The speaker's tone was brusque, accusatory and eminently recognizable.

Jenna and Paul whirled around. Aggie Franks advanced on them from the doorway like a guided missile in taupe wedge-heeled Soft Spots. The shoes matched her purse and the contrast piping on her black pantsuit, whose slacks had to be shortened the usual four and a half inches before they could be worn.

She peered up at Paul, her head cocked back at a severe angle to center him in the narrow field of her lineless trifocals. "You're that Paul Haggerty fellow, aren't you?"

He paused a moment before owning up to it. Jenna didn't blame him. Her mother was sixty-eight years old, shaped like an upside-down bowling pin, had a red belt in tae kwon do and ink-black, poodle-permed hair that appeared to have resulted from accidental electrocution. In other words, a force to be reckoned with.

"Still sniffing around my little girl, eh?"

"Mo-ther."

Paul nodded solemnly. "Guilty as charged, Mrs. Franks. From what I've been told, you're already taken."

Jenna's eyes rolled so far back in their sockets,

she should have seen light shafting in through her ears. How he knew her mother's name was a no-brainer. The Ritts Café regulars really should get lives. Of their own.

Ed McMann and the prize patrol couldn't have solicited a bigger smile from Aggie. Hand all aflutter near her bosom, the senior citizen who struck terror in social security clerks everywhere cooed like a lovesick pigeon. Turning on Jenna, she said, "Surely this isn't the same Paul you told me about on the phone, sweetheart. Why, if he's a thug, I'm Patricia Cornwell."

"*I* didn't call him a thug. You—"

"If you don't already have plans for this evening, Mr. Haggerty, we'd love it if you'd join us for a sandwich and a movie."

"We who?" Jenna said.

Paul's eyes flicked to Jenna. "Consider it a date, Mrs. Franks."

"Please, call me Aggie. All my friends do."

"And I'm Paul."

"All right then, Paul. You're staying at Betty Bigelow's, aren't you? We'll pick you up there at..." She consulted the watch held at arm's length. "Goodness, in about an hour, if that isn't too soon."

"We who?"

Aggie squinted at Jenna as though she knew her from somewhere but couldn't quite place her. "Oh. Well, the three of us, then. You, me and Casper." She squeezed Paul's wrist. "Casper Wetherby is my gentleman friend."

"Lucky man."

"In case you've forgotten, Mother, the shop doesn't close till six."

"Phooey. You own the place. You can lock the doors whenever you feel like it."

"Not if I want to stay in business I can't."

"Mavis is here. Let her—"

"Mavis should have been off the clock fifteen minutes ago. I can't afford overtime and I won't let her work for free."

Paul sucked his teeth, then heaved a sigh. "I understand," he said understandingly. "But tonight won't be nearly as much fun without you. Will it, Aggie?"

Head tilted, she spread her hands in *comme ci, comme ça* fashion.

Jenna's life passed before her eyes. Before the evening ended, Paul would know every intimate detail of it, beginning with the morning she'd finger-painted the bedroom wall with poop from her diaper.

7

The Lumina's front tire skinned the curb in front of Jenna's house. Paul yanked the steering wheel left before the rear tire followed suit.

He killed the ignition and took a deep breath, as if ready to scuba dive without a tank. *Whew*. Should've taken it a little easier on the cologne. Except the way I'm sweating, a double slap of Escada beats smelling like a dockworker.

On the dashboard was the map Aggie had drawn on a MacArthur Perk napkin. She'd decided it would be quicker for him to pick up Jenna, then meet Casper and her at Aggie's house.

"If Casper gobbles down his food, he gets gas like you would not believe," she'd said, a hand batting the air. "We could go to a later movie, but then he'd snore through most of it."

Paul's luck was on the upswing. He knew it when he'd kept Jenna under surveillance the last two days without being spotted by any of the increasing number of townsfolk with whom he'd become acquainted. The kicker came when he'd walked into the shop an hour ago and Mavis looked as if she'd been granted a stay of execution.

The bungalow's doorbell was the twist type that usually played "Edelweiss" or "The Lonely Goatherd.'' A single, crystalline *ting* chimed before basso profundo barking and a Hound of the Baskervilles howl exploded inside.

Paul stepped back, expecting the door to burst off its hinges at any second. What the hell kind of dogs did Jenna have?

The question remained unanswered even after she introduced Herschel, a hairy, sludge-gray haystack with feet as big as manhole covers, then Homer, a flop-eared, liver-colored Slinky on stilts. Somehow Paul wasn't surprised when he noticed that the cat weaving figure eights around his ankles was missing a hind leg.

''That's Festus,'' Jenna said. ''When he was a kitten, a utility lineman decided the most expeditious way to get him down from a tree was to chainsaw the branch from under him.''

Paul grimaced at the image. ''With Good Samaritans like that, who needs enemies?''

''The vet stopped the bleeding, but was about to euthanize him when Festus pulled himself up on three legs, hobbled a few steps and bit the crap out of the vet's hand.''

Paul knelt to scratch the valiant tabby's ear. Its purr riffed as loud as a snare drum. Herschel and Homer craned their muzzles as far as their necks allowed, whining, ''Me, too. Me, too.'' Festus yowled a warning. The dogs sat back on their haunches, then oozed belly down to the floor, a pair of unworthy subjects genuflecting to the king.

''Festus has 'em snowed,'' Jenna said, laughing. ''He scalped their noses a few times when they were puppies. They have maybe half a brain between them, but there's nothing wrong with their memories.''

Nothing wrong with mine, either, Paul thought, suddenly glad she'd retained none of him. He had nothing to live up to, and nothing to live down.

In under a half hour, she'd changed into slightly faded, five-pocket jeans and a white silk poet's shirt with a matching silk turtleneck underneath. Her hair was brushed to full volume—a wild, free-falling tumble women half her age must envy.

"You look terrific," he said.

"Flattery will get you nowhere, chum."

"Still mad, huh?"

"Who, me? Just because you blackmailed me into being a fourth wheel tonight? Jeepers, Wally, why would that make me mad?"

Her tone was haughty, but Paul saw a grin as she turned to open the entry closet's door. She let him take the leather Eisenhower jacket from her and hold it for her to slip into, but denied him the privilege of liberating her hair from the collar. But the scent of her, pure and unmasked by perfume, was his to savor, if only for a moment.

He had a vague impression of the living room's cream-colored walls, Mission oak furniture and a fabulous antique billiards table, before Jenna ushered him out the door again. "Sorry, but the place is a mess and there's no time for the nickel tour, anyway. If Casper eats too fast—"

"We'll regret it," Paul finished.

She glared at him, then batted her lashes. "My, my, it's jes' sweeter than combed honey how you and my mama done took to each other. Why, if I hadn't seen it with my own l'il ol' eyes, I wouldn't have believed it."

He closed her car door and laughed all the way around to his. "That's the worst Scarlett O'Hara impersonation I've ever heard."

"Oh, yeah? It's probably because I was doing Ellie Mae Clampett."

The Chevy pulled away from the curb, sidewalls intact. "In that case, if I were Uncle Jed, I'd sue."

"Oh, shut up and hang a left at the corner."

For someone arm-twisted into an evening out and carrying a serious grudge because of it, her doe-dark eyes surely had a sparkle in them.

"Did Mom also tell you how to play musical cars?" Jenna smiled. "By that blank look, I guess not." She supplied more directions he didn't need, then said, "When we get there, park on the street, not in the driveway next to Casper's car."

"Okay."

"Because he'll insist on driving tonight and you, the young whippersnapper, have to act like that's a splendid idea."

"Act?" Paul whistled. "I haven't been in the back seat of a car with a girl for thirty years." He leered sideward and winked. "Betcha it's like riding a bicycle, though. Don't you?"

She socked him in the shoulder. "Will you *listen?* Casper can't see his own hood ornament after dark. Mom's night vision isn't much better, but at least she drives a Volkswagen Beetle, not a Sherman tank with hubcaps."

"And she isn't male."

Jenna's perfect crescent eyebrows arched.

"And as the whippersnapper, it's my job to lavish

praise on Casper's car so he can offer to let me drive his pride and joy without losing face."

Jenna's expression was a picture of astonishment. "How'd you know that?"

"Every family has a Casper and this is America. Land of the free and home of Detroit. Take a man's car away and you might as well..." Her nod indicated the drift was gotten. He went on, "My uncle Ernie's Buick hunkered in the driveway for years, its body deteriorating at about the same rate as Ernie's.

"Aunt Belle kept nagging him to sell it while it was still worth something. To hush her up, Ernie agreed, then priced the heap triple what it was worth. Belle was a sweet lady, but I don't think she ever understood it wasn't a car to him. He was so frail, but as long as the Buick was there, he could tell himself he'd have the strength tomorrow, next week, next month at the outside, to hop in and cruise to the Elks Club for a scotch-rocks with his buddies."

Jenna stared at him for a full fifteen seconds. "You really are one of the good guys, aren't you?"

His chest constricted as though his ribs were suddenly too small. At the last instant he realized he was steering into the curb in front of a house he wasn't supposed to know was Aggie Franks's. He straightened the wheels, thankful Jenna's eyes were still on him.

"Could be I'm like Festus." His smile felt as rigid as the jack-o'-lanterns on the porch across the street. "Maybe I've got you snowed like he does Herschel and Homer."

"Possible." Jenna's thumb aimed out the side window. "But I know for a fact we just drove right on past Mom's house."

Aggie and Casper must have been ready to spring when the doorbell rang. Aggie's coat was on and her purse over her arm when she bustled out. She apologized for skimping on the hospitality and promised cake and coffee after the movie.

Following as close as a dinghy was an elderly gent with rust colored hair who could be mistaken for Walter Matthau's shorter, skinnier brother. Aggie simultaneously introduced the men and shooed them toward the driveway.

"Beautiful car you have there," Paul said as he shook Casper Wetherby's hand. By Jenna's description he'd expected a cousin to a two-tone Buick Electra—Uncle Ernie's six-passenger time machine. A four-door, white Bentley sedan hadn't entered Paul's radar frequency.

Behind him, Aggie said, "I just love that blouse, sweetheart. Very feminine."

A hesitation implied Jenna looked downward to see what the fuss was about. "Thanks, Mom."

"You should wear it more often." Lowering her voice, Aggie added, "But don't you think those jeans are a smidgen tight in the derriere?"

Paul swallowed hard to stanch a preemptive grin.

"Yep," Jenna said, a beat later. "They most certainly are."

Casper's "She's a one-owner, too" threw Paul for a second. "A '90 model," he went on, "but she's only got twenty-three thousand miles on 'er."

"You don't say." Paul scratched his jaw, his gaze traveling bumper to bumper and back again. Of two completely disparate minds at the moment, his "I'll bet the rings haven't ceded yet" sounded obscene.

"Shoot-fire, son." Casper's dentures were as worn

and yellow as old accordion keys. "She isn't due for a tune-up for another seven."

Aggie flounced past and opened the sedan's rear door. "I don't know about the rest of you, but I'm starving." As she tucked herself into the back seat, Jenna said, "So am I" and rounded the bumper.

Casper hurried after her. "Hold your dingblasted horses, Jenna-girl, so's I can get the door."

Jenna vanished into the Bentley's parchment-leather maw in accordance with the Unwritten Law of Vehicular Pecking Order. It was as responsible for siblings' mobile turf battles as women's reputations for being back-seat drivers. Worst of all, for two men to automatically take the helm and two women to settle aft without a peep of protest was incontrovertible proof that people do eventually turn into their parents, no matter how many times they swear they won't.

Paul's shoulders slumped in resignation as he gently closed Aggie's door. He was reaching for the requisite shotgun side's handle, when Casper jangled the keys above the roof. "I don't guess you'd want to take 'er for a spin, now, would you?"

The Bentleys Paul had driven in the past were fully armored vehicles. Casper's civilian model seemed lightweight and flimsy compared to an FAV equipped with run-flat tires, roof and gas-tank reinforcements, dual batteries, computer-activated armor and underbody protection from grenades, pipe bombs and land mines.

All the way to the Cow Palace, famous for its greasy deluxe cheeseburgers, skin-on curlicue fries and concrete-thick shakes, Casper iterated and reiterated the car's pound-sterling qualities.

"Geez, Cappy," Jenna said. "Why don't you quit bragging about the stereo system and turn it on."

"Anything for you, sugar." Casper clicked a knob and fiddled with others. Glen Miller's "String of Pearls" wended from the speakers—those mounted in the back seat only.

Paul delivered a visual "Nice try" to Jenna in the rearview mirror. Casper talked leg room. Paul nodded and grunted at appropriate intervals. The way Casper nattered, one would think he wanted to sell the damn thing.

Paul came to find out, he did.

"No bones about it," he admitted after they'd finished eating, and Aggie and Jenna had excused themselves to visit the ladies' room. "I need the money, and Joyce told Aggie that Jenna said you're sitting prettier than a goose on an ostrich egg."

Paul doubted the information string began with Jenna, which ruled out Joyce as a conduit. Like her daughter, the chat-room moderator known as House Dick was no piker in the shrewd department.

"I can't sell cheap." Casper leaned sideward and peered in the direction of the rest rooms. "My daughter, Vinita, threw a hissy fit when I bought it as an investment. She finds out I lost twenty cents on the deal, and I'll never hear the end of it. But for cash, I can be real reasonable."

Anxiety hastened his speech and aged his already timeworn face. "I'll understand if you're not interested, but I figure you might be able to put me on to somebody else."

A couple of bites of sandwich and half the curlicues remained in the red plastic basket in front of Paul. Jenna and Aggie had split an order. Casper had only nibbled at his sandwich and hadn't touched the fries, but drank most of the shake.

A man in his mid-seventies living on a pension and social security could have other needs for a chunk of fast cash. Paul thought of some, but kept circling back to remarks about Casper's chronic indigestion.

Folding his arms on the table, Paul said, "It's a great car. I'd hate like hell for somebody else to grab it, but I'm just not in the market for a Bentley at the moment."

"Hmph." Pop-bottle lenses magnified Casper's disappointment tenfold. "I was afraid you'd say that."

"Tell you what, though, instead of buying it outright, how about if I loan you the money with the car as collateral?"

Ignoring Casper's head slowly shaking from side to side, Paul continued, "It's insured, right? You'll have the car to drive—low as the mileage is, a few hundred more won't hurt its value. Anything happens to it, we're both covered, and I don't have to worry about losing out if you decide to go ahead and sell it to me—say, a year from now."

The head-shaking stopped before Paul finished speaking. On the jukebox—if that's what plastic, imitation Wurlitzer CD-players were still called—Terri Hendrix sang of places in between. A lethal smog of airborne cholesterol smelled like heaven should.

Casper checked to see if the coast was still clear, then sat back. "Well, shit. S'cuse the French, son, but much as I'm tempted, I can't." He snorted. "Can't borrow from Paul to pay Peter."

"Hey, if Paul's willing to—"

"No. I appreciate the offer, especially coming from a near stranger, but I'm already in debt up to my eyebrows. It won't be for long—I swear it won't—except I've been saying that for going on three years."

Relief that Casper's troubles probably weren't medical was chased by curiosity. Asking how he'd gotten so deeply in debt was more personal than asking his income. Paul said, "Look, I know what a bad case of the shorts feels like. I had a lot of help getting back on my feet—literally. The only way I can repay it is by helping somebody else."

"It isn't pride stopping me," Casper said. "Okay, there's a dab mixed in, I'd reckon, but this fray I'm in, I'm not keen on bringing anyone else into."

He scooted his chair nearer the table. "Short and sweet, before a soul around here realized the new highway was coming through, the Budget Zzz's motel chain bought a forty-acre parcel at a corner of the interchange.

"When they started laying natural-gas lines and such to the property, they plundered into some old mine shafts. Reading about it in the paper reminded me of the patent claims Grampa had on parcels all over the county. He was convinced a huge lead belt was his for the finding. For better'n twenty years, he sunk shafts here to yonder, looking for it."

Casper laughed. "Grampa died with nothing but a bunch of holes in the ground to his name. The patent claims passed down to Dad, then me and they're as valid as the day they were issued. Budget Zzz's owns the ground up, but what's underneath it is mine."

Paul knew that once rare, if not unheard of, patent-claim disputes were popping on court dockets from

Aspen, Colorado, to Phoenix, Arizona. Statutes dating back to the nineteenth century varied from state to state, but in general they allowed an individual or company that found land containing mineral deposits and performed a minimal amount of mining to apply for a patent. When granted, the applicant owned the parcel outright, even if mining was discontinued.

A hundred-plus years of record keeping and attendant errors meant that clear titles to patent-claimed land were virtually impossible. A cloud formed every time the land was sold without respect to the patent claim, which itself could be sold separately from the parcel or willed to the original grantee's heirs, as Casper's grandfather had done.

"Those corporate muck-a-mucks can't build their motel-restaurant-truck stop complex without a clear title," Casper said, "and I'll be damned if I'll deed over the patent for a measly ten thousand dollars."

Ten grand for a third-generation, worthless hole in the ground? Paul resisted an urge to grab Casper by his sparrow-narrow shoulders and shake some sense into him. From what he'd said, though, it was three years too late.

"By gum, that claim's worth a quarter million, at least. With winter coming and the new road scheduled to open next spring, my lawyer thinks they'll settle any day, but his fees have to be paid up front."

"Oh, I'll just bet they do," Paul said. If the attorney had taken the case on a contingency basis, he'd have shared in the risk and reward. Getting his fees and expenses up front could mean the lawyer wasn't very confident of a sizable settlement. "Which is why you're so eager to sell your car."

"I already took a reverse equity on my house,"

Casper said. "I've got a couple of inventions on the drawing board—a mop with a reservoir on the handle so gals can scrub and wax the floor in one swipe, and a Teflon-coated necktie. Trouble is, it'll be a while before the kinks are ironed out and I can interest a manufacturer in buying the designs."

He studied Paul's expression a moment, then flapped a hand. "Aw, don't worry, son. The settlement's practically in the bag and you've given me one dandy-fine idea."

"I did?" The only idea Paul could remember was the loan offer Casper had rejected.

"Like you said, forget selling the Bentley outright. Let 'er be collateral against that shylock's two hundred smackers an hour."

Paul recoiled. "I wouldn't do that if I were you."

"Wouldn't do what?" Jenna asked, startling them both.

Aggie looked from Casper to Paul. Whatever clues she'd expected to find on their faces weren't there. It was evident on hers that a plan B solution for Casper's financial problems was formulating in her mind.

"Well, if we're going to make the seven-fifteen movie," she said, taking her coat from the back of her chair, "we'd better shake a leg."

8

In color and size, the harvest moon looked like Mars had abandoned its orbit for Earth's. Cloud wisps suggested a pair of off-kilter eyebrows, a Vandyke beard and a ragged comb over. Optical illusion had it cruising across the night sky in a celestial drag race with Paul's Chevy sedan.

Jenna couldn't recall when she'd last felt as content as Festus napping on a sunny windowsill. The dreaded double date with Cappy and her mother had been the most fun she'd had in years.

The movie was so atrocious, they laughed until tears spilled from their eyes. Aggie flirted nonstop with Paul and vice versa. Cappy's eyes sparkled despite his deadpan, grumpy-old-man persona. And Paul…

Without moving her head, peripheral vision wouldn't extend to the profile illuminated by the dashlight's greenish glow. No matter. Having sat beside him for almost two hours in a darkened movie theater, she'd committed every angle and curvature to memory.

She wondered how much his features differed from the way he'd looked before the car accident. Had he been drop-dead handsome? Or had recon-

struction minimized a bulbous nose, a lantern jaw or
a recessive chin?

Lifting her head from the seat back's rest, she
glanced at him and tried to imagine seeing one face
reflected in mirrors and window glass over nearly
five decades of life, then suddenly seeing a stranger
there. The eye color was unchanged and some features would be familiar, but gone forever was the
man recognized by one and all as Paul Haggerty.

"Almost home," he said, turning onto South Dollison Street. "Unless I can accidentally get lost."

"Do you think I didn't notice you took the long
way here?" Jenna smiled. "A pretty good trick, considering Mom's house is eight blocks from mine."

"I thought you were asleep. As pretty as you are
in the moonlight, it would have been a sin to waken
you."

From anyone else, the sentiment would have been
high camp. Not from him. Not spoken in a low, slow
baritone that resonated in her belly and beyond.

Her laugh was jittery and too shrill. "Yeah, well,
when a woman hits a certain age, moonlight is about
the only kind that becomes her."

"Don't."

The gruff edge to his voice startled her. "Don't
what?"

"Answer a compliment with a put-down." He
steered to a smooth stop at the curb. "I don't think
you're fishing for more, like some women do, but
it's still a bad habit to fall into." He chuckled. "Actually, what it does is dig a trench for a guy to fall
into."

Heat suffused Jenna's face; her defense mechanism advised a yellow alert. "Trust me. Men do most

of the spadework themselves.'' She sniffed. ''Like now, for instance.''

''Not true.'' The engine dieseled then died. He left the key in the ignition and unlatched his seat belt. ''Let's say, for instance, I compliment you about something every day for, oh, six months. Each one's answered with a put-down. Seldom, if ever, do you say thank you, or even offer a simple smile.''

Jenna squirmed and looked away. Who came up with the effing stupid idea that men should learn to emote? Life was so much sweeter when guilt was a one-way street.

''Pretty soon,'' Paul said, ''it dawns on me that the best way to keep you from running yourself down is to lay off the compliments. You don't seem to appreciate them anyway.''

She motioned a time-out. ''All right already. I know where this is going. Later, or probably sooner, I'd nail you big-time for taking me for granted, not appreciating me—yada, yada—because jerk that you are and hard as I try to please you, you never act like you notice anything I do.''

''Cause and effect.''

''Whatever.''

He leaned closer, his arm sliding across the seat back. His grin was so wide, his mustache's handlebars went almost horizontal. ''You're even prettier in the moonlight when you're mad.''

''The hell I—'' An excellent imitation of Herschel in guard-dog mode rumbled up her throat. Fingers pressed to the corners of her mouth, she pushed up a smile. ''Thank you, Paul.''

''You're welcome, Jenna.''

''Five bucks says I can stay mad long enough to be freakin' *stunning* by porch light.''

By her expression, she was teasing, but he took the hint.

Accustomed as she was to Casper's door-opening, door-shutting perfect gentlemanly manners, it still seemed somewhat like Prom Night the Sequel waiting for Paul to liberate her from the car. Rick was the only other man she'd known who'd extended that courtesy. He was a cop, though. The post-arrest swing-and-shut was as hardwired as the cuff-and-stuff.

She took the hand Paul extended. It closed around hers and didn't let go for the short stroll up the patchwork stone sidewalk—an appropriate venue for a game of mental hopscotch.

She wished he'd never come to town. Telling him goodbye someday would hurt. She felt as though she already had and it did.

Wish number two was that he'd leave tonight, or first thing tomorrow, before she was in over her heart. The young were accused of falling too hard, too fast. Maybe they did, but age brings more losses than gains. With those losses comes a sense of urgency to have and hold just in case it's real. Just for now, if need be. Just because here *is* now and time is finite.

She wished he'd stay. Screw absence making the heart grow fonder. Give familiarity the space to breed contempt.

Their shoes scuffed the wide concrete step, then the porch's crackled floor. Insects swirled and tinked off the fixtures' yellow bug-repellent bulbs. Jenna slipped her hand from Paul's to rifle through her shoulder bag for her keys.

"I had a wonderful time tonight." She looked up. "Clichéd but true."

"So did I. I can't tell you how glad I am that Aggie asked me out, then let you tag along."

"Yep. Mom's a firm believer in spreading the joy."

Paul laughed. "You're more alike than I think either of you would admit."

The key ring jangled free of the screwdriver's handle it garroted. "I'll admit it. In fact, by your rules, I owe another thank-you for the compliment."

"Women." He shook his head. "I thought it was treason punishable by firing squad to compare a daughter with her mother."

"Depends on the principals, I guess. Mom has her faults and some quirks I hope aren't genetic, but for the most part she is what I aspire to be when I'm her age."

Smart man that he was, Paul didn't even try to fill that blank.

"A great old broad," Jenna supplied. "It's the Mount Everest of mature womanhood, according to His Eminence Casper G. Wetherby. Mother says she'll haunt me if I don't have it inscribed on her headstone."

The real one, not the decoy erected on the plot parallel to Earl Bukowski's. She'd gagged at the Beloved Wife and Mother scripted above the name Ellen Cransk Bukowski, yet entering the WITSEC program gave her the opportunity to attend her own funeral. In disguise, of course.

No doubt she'd spend the rest of her life bitching

to Jenna about the cruddy flower arrangements, meager attendance, the screech-owl soloist and the tin-can coffin chosen to minimize expenses. The U.S. marshal in charge laughed till he cried when she gave him a list of items she wanted to be buried in the casket in lieu of a corpse.

"The loves of Earl's life," she called his bowling bag and box of trophies, custom-made cue stick, a six-pack of long-neck Miller's Genuine Draft, a carton of Pall Malls and the TV's remote control. "If I could afford a bulldozer, I'd chuck that damn old recliner of his in the hole, too."

Jenna understood the hurt behind the humor, but it bothered her all the same. Earl Bukowski had been a lousy husband and no father-of-the-year to his son, Jimmy, but he was and always would be her daddy.

Paul said, "For whatever it's worth, I don't think you'll have any trouble fitting Aggie's shoes someday." He stroked Jenna's arm. "I'd say there's a better-than-even chance they'll be a little tight on you."

His touch caused a ripple effect that converged on her solar plexus. Purse jammed against her ribs and keys clenched in her fist, Jenna focused on the vee where his coat lapels overlapped. Standing with him on the porch, she felt all of fourteen again, and for the zillionth time knew why Joyce Ramsour married her high-school sweetheart a month after graduation.

Besides the head-over-heels-in-love factor, Joyce's march down the aisle had pretty much ruled out dating, at least until death did she and Barry part. Even then, with luck, the survivor would be too shriveled and senile to give a rat's rear end about pairing off again.

Thinking, no guts, no glory, Jenna tipped back her head and looked into Paul's eyes. The rippling sensation surged to whitecaps. If she hadn't felt the chill wicking from the concrete through her shoes, didn't smell his cologne, then register the penetrating warmth of his hand kneading her arm, she'd think she was drowning in a bottomless sea of green.

The intensity, the raw emotion startled her. Reflex took her back a step. "L-long day tomorrow," she stammered. "Saturdays. They're not always busy. Well, more often than not, they are. People off work, out shopping..."

The masklike tension in his face had dissolved, along with the disquieting hunger in his eyes. Had she imagined them? Of course she had. She was almost certain of it. They were optical illusions, like the moon's hot pursuit, contrived from shadows and glaring bug lights.

"I'm not good at this." She frowned. "Never have been, never will be."

"At what?"

"*This.*" She skimmed back her hair, wadding it in frustration. "The damn dumb dating protocol. Have a crappy time? The finale is like saying goodbye to the plumber. No muss, no fuss. But have a terrific evening and everything gets awkward and fidgety and pretentious at the end."

Paul's eyebrow crimped, as though unsure whether he fit the plumber category and should beat a hasty stage-left exit, or should stick around in the event a cup of coffee, a hug, a kiss or getting naked was in his immediate future.

"That's why women love Meg Ryan movies," Jenna said. "Who cares who her costar is? Her character is always a quart low on cool, which on Meg looks adorable and endearing and sexy in a rumpled, quasivirginal sort of way and gives the rest of us hope that sleek and sophisticated is *so* last year.''

Paul ventured, ''I, uh, like Meg Ryan movies.''

''See?''

He didn't appear to, but Jenna couldn't squelch the head of steam building since he began to star in her lascivious dreams and refused to take maybe for an answer.

She said, ''Life's too short for anxiety attacks over the possibly deeper, overt psychological meaning in a guy's tone and inflection when he says, 'I'll call you.'''

Paul pulled her into a snug embrace. ''I'll call you.''

Breathing didn't come easy, and not because of the lumpy purse threatening to puncture a lung. ''Yeah. Okay. That would be good.''

''Right now, though, I'm going to kiss you good-night.'' He slipped a finger beneath her chin and raised her face to his. ''Unless you have any objections.''

Eyes hooded, she licked her lips and murmured, ''No—no objections. None at all.''

His palm caressed her cheek, gently, tenderly. He brushed his lips across hers, his mustache as soft as down, heightening the tease. He kissed her slowly, as though every second must be savored, then his tongue found hers and he moaned, his pleasure sky-rocketing her own.

Her purse thudded on the floor. The key ring clattered nearby. Jenna's hands slid up his chest, encircled his neck, and she lost herself in the taste, the touch, the feel of him.

When they parted, she sagged against him, breathless and dizzy and replete. Paul looked down at her, his hand still cupping her face. A strange shadowlight glistened in his eyes as if tears rimmed them. Voice husky and quiet as a whisper, he said, "I've wanted to do that for a long, long time."

She cocked her head, then smiled, thinking he couldn't be as serious as he sounded. "Is that your way of saying time flies? I mean, we met on Monday and this *is* only Friday."

His gaze lowered, locked on a point an inch east and a thousand miles south of her shoulder. Deliberation furrowed his brow. The creases remained as he clasped her forearms, easing them from around his neck. "Which makes tomorrow Saturday. The more-often-than-not busy day you mentioned a minute ago."

The mood swing rattled her, but she could take a hint, too. When Paul "Leave 'Em Wanting" Haggerty says "a kiss good-night," it isn't a rough estimate.

He picked up her shoulder bag and keys. A semblance of the grin returned. "I can dial you direct, can't I?"

"From Betty Bigelow's house?" She keyed the dead bolt. Homer and Herschel snuffled at the door crack, whining to go out, or for her to come in. "Go up to the widow's walk and yell and I could probably hear you."

"I meant, without an assist from Aggie."

She made a face, said, "Guess there's only one way to find out, huh?" and ducked inside.

Homer and Herschel greeted her with open mouths. Tongues lolling and panting from the exertion of sitting upright, they whimpered doggie love-gone-wrong songs about the heartbreak of empty paws, empty rooms, empty food dishes.

Jenna tossed her jacket, purse and keys on the throne chair strategically located for that purpose. Festus she lifted off the white enamel dentist's cabinet where he perched, vulture fashion, when she went out at night.

"Haven't forgotten how to climb up there, huh?" she said, scratching his neck. He slanted her a look, reminiscent of her mother's when she'd been primed to shoot down yet another bullshit excuse for a curfew violation.

Herschel and Homer went into their dervish dance, butts wiggling and toenails ticking like castanets on the hardwood floor. They would have, even if she'd just come in from fetching the newspaper from the yard. Cats kept humans humble. Dogs made every homecoming a celebration.

Herschel prodded the small of her back with his nose, signaling it was treat time at the MacArthurs'. "Not so fast, big fella. No cookies till I'm sure you guys didn't eat any of the furniture while I was out."

The house was a Craftsman home designed by Gustav Stickley, rather a poor man's Frank Lloyd Wright. Jenna bought it at a court-ordered estate auction, then invested years of blood, sweat equity and tears ripping and stripping away improvements akin to modernizing Monticello with vinyl siding, flocked wallpaper, painted woodwork and two-dollar-a-yard shag carpeting.

Visions of the refinished product had alternated

with fantasies of committing felony arson. She didn't realize it then, and now wasn't sure how she'd survived, but raising Sam, running a business and making a hovel into a home had been her salvation. Precious little time was left to throw pity parties.

"Heck of a nice place for one, though," she told Festus, gazing upon hers and, eventually, Sam's handiwork.

Yanking down a tacky suspended ceiling had revealed red oak beams spanning the length and width of the large, rectangular living room. At one end, built-in china cabinets flanked a tapestry brick fireplace with an alcove instead of a mantel. At the other were small-paned sash windows with combination storage bins and seats beneath and open shelving above.

A heart-of-the-house staircase divided the library–sitting room from the dining room, also furnished with a fireplace and built-in china cabinets. Adjoining the library was a huge bathroom, and beyond it, Jenna's bedroom. Opposite them, the dining room and kitchen shared a common wall. The latter's wealth of deep-set, solid and glass-doored cabinetry, open cubbies, shelves and wide countertops epitomized the adage "They sure don't build them like they used to."

Festus poured himself from Jenna's arms to orbit the jack-in-the-box cookie jar. The tabby detested sugar wafers, but Herschel and Homer always went berzerknoid, convinced Festus was about to swipe their favorite snack.

Duly rewarding them for not destroying the house, Jenna let the dogs out to water and fertilize the fenced backyard. She was lobbing cheese-flavored goldfish crackers to Festus, who snatched them from the air like a trained seal, when the phone rang.

Late-night calls meant one of two things. Bad news, or Joyce Ramsour foaming at the mouth for a second-by-second recap of the evening. Come to think of it, the latter was the same as the former.

"Hello?"

"See? I told you I'd call."

"Paul?" She threw back her head and laughed. "Are you nuts?"

"I don't think so, but you're not the first to ask."

"Where are you?"

"In the car. On the cell phone."

"Uh-oh. I hate to tell you, but Pfister has a city ordinance that prohibits the use of cell phones while driving."

"Good thing I'm not then."

Jenna frowned. He couldn't have made it farther than a block or two. Why pull over to— "Don't tell me you're still parked outside."

"Okay."

She rolled her eyes. Laying the receiver on a dish towel, she strode down the narrow hall to the living room. After snapping off the lamp in the window, she pulled back the curtains, then spun around and returned to the kitchen. "Other than definitely being nuts, *why* are you still parked outside?"

"So I could tell you, first chance, how much I enjoyed tonight and how tough it was to leave."

Smiling, she leaned against the counter and crossed her ankles. "That's nice to hear."

"And to explain why I did, the way I did."

"There's no need for that." She tossed the last cracker to Festus. "After my wacko speech about dating and Meg Ryan movies and God knows whatever else I babbled about, I wouldn't have blamed you if you'd done the handshake-and-skedaddle number.''

Static crackled for several seconds. ''Darlin', the only thing that would have stopped me from kissing you was if you'd told me no.''

Jenna blew out a breath. The way she'd felt afterward, she couldn't be sure she'd have said no to anything he'd asked. Not because she wanted sex. Doing the horizontal boogie just to scratch what itched was like craving Cristal and settling for tap water.

When she was in Paul's arms, her body pressed to his, she had wanted to make love with him and knew he'd wanted no less. That aching, passionate, primal response to a man she'd met only five days ago was almost frightening.

''Jenna?''

''I'm here—sorry. I was, er, my cat was getting into something he shouldn't have.''

Festus looked up from licking crumbs off his paws, as if he knew he'd been defamed and didn't appreciate it.

Paul said, ''There's something I need to tell you that I don't have the guts to do face-to-face. I tried a couple of times when we were on the porch, but I couldn't. Too afraid of how you'd react. What you might say.''

Bad news it was then, eh? Jenna hiked her butt onto the counter and let her head fall back to rest against a cabinet door. ''You're leaving town tomorrow.'' Even in sit-down-and-brace-yourself position, she couldn't force out *and you're not coming back.*

''No. Not unless you want me gone after I say what I have to say.''

She closed her eyes. He'd lied. He's married. Has five kids and a house in the burbs. His wife doesn't understand him. They haven't slept together since Clinton was governor of Arkansas. As soon as the youngest graduates from college, he's filing for divorce.

''Tell me,'' she said, her jaws clenched.

A pause. Four beats...five. A heavy sigh, then, ''I've been looking for you for nearly half my life. Didn't know your name, had no idea where to start, but I knew you were out there somewhere. All I had to do was find you.''

A lump began to form, thick and hard, in Jenna's throat.

''After the accident, I gave up on everything. The doctors said if I'd done that while I was in ICU, I wouldn't have made it.'' Paul chuffed. ''Hang in too long to throw in the towel, and be convinced there's nothing to live for, and—well, hating the world and hopelessness are a shitty combination.''

''Yes, they are.'' Jenna winced and squeezed the curl out of the telephone cord. *Jesus.* What if he asked how she knew? A car accident was her cover story to explain away her scars to Sam, her physician, Joyce, two fiancés and a few lovers. To lie to Paul would be a mockery of the mental and physical torture he'd endured.

He must have assumed it was a sympathetic remark, for he went on, ''The opposite of dying isn't surviving, Jenna. It's living.''

She nodded, rocking now, holding her head in her hand. Stop, she thought. I know, I know, and I'm sorry you do, but please, don't make it all come back for me. Already the dreams, the flashbacks—they're scaring me sick.

"With life comes hope," Paul said, "and a gut-deep understanding that life really does turn on a dime and whatever there was left of mine, I was going to spend finding you."

Patchy static, a low electronic hum on the line counteracted the silence. Jenna looked up at the ceiling, emotions welling, the muscles in her neck as tight-corded as guy wires.

Then inch by inch, an elegant, weightless sensation crept over her and she knew...had never been more sure of anything in her life.

"Paul?"

"Oh, God, I was afraid you—"

"Be careful not to shut your car door too hard. The couple across the street has a new baby."

9

The front door's knob turned in Paul's hand. Reality jolted him. Every step from the car to the porch, he'd told himself he'd misunderstood what Jenna had said. That they'd have a good laugh and blame garbled cell-phone transmission for the miscue, then he'd kick his own ass all the way to Betty Bigelow's.

Now what? Ring the doorbell? Knock? Or just walk in as if he belonged there. As if he had a right to be there.

The door swung on oiled hinges. He blinked to speed the adjustment from porch lights to the darkened living room. No dogs barked. No cat nuzzled his ankle where a gun had been holstered until a few moments ago. Two clocks ticked off cadence to each other. The discord shortened full minutes to thirty-second increments.

He breathed in Jenna's scent; the subtle notes permeated her home, her sanctuary. Then he saw her, silhouetted in a narrow hallway, smiling, holding out her hand to him.

He visualized himself walking toward her, but his legs hadn't obeyed, his feet refused to move. Fleeting thoughts that the paralysis had returned, locking his knees and rooting him to the floor, shot white-hot terror through him.

No, it was anything, everything, but that. The sight of her standing there, haloed in the golden glow of the oil lamp behind her and beckoning to him was too much for his mind to absorb at once. Not after waiting over twenty years and, now he could admit, never completely believing this moment, this dream entwined with a fantasy, would ever arrive.

Arms rising to embrace her, his shoes tolled loud on the bare plank floor. *Make love to her and there's no going back.* He hesitated, then shook off the voice warning him from within. There was no choice. He'd made it the first time he crossed MacArthur Perk's threshold.

Jenna took his hand and lifted it to her lips. Without a word, she led him to the bedroom. Just enough light to outline the furnishings filtered through the sheer curtains. Eyes averted from his, she unbuttoned his jacket, slipped it off his shoulders. It fell on the bed, then tumbled to the carpeted floor.

Nimble, hasty fingers plied the buttons of his shirt. Paul caught her in his arms and kissed her neck, the plane of her jaw, her lips, willing himself not to lose control, not to hurry, not to let her rush, arousing as it was that she wanted to.

Tongue flicking, exploring, dancing with his, her hands cupped his bottom, pulling him against her. Hips slowly undulating, she pressed harder, mimicking the act of love, driving him to the brink of climax.

Groaning, he stepped away, holding her at arm's length. Desperately he tried to remember the multiplication tables, the Giants' starting line-up, the Mets'—hell, his *own* name, for Christ's sake.

He tugged her billowy shirt from the waistband of

her jeans. He fumbled with her belt buckle, then his, blanking his mind to the image of her dressed in moonlight and nothing else, before his body betrayed him.

A glimpse of the lush, womanly curves of an alabaster goddess crowned by a glorious tangle of dark hair was all he saw, then she was in his arms again. Her skin was velvet warm, her hands like satin caressing his bare back as he reached for the pull chain to the bedside lamp.

"Don't." She caught his wrist. Bowing her head, she sighed, then lofted her chin in defiance. "I have scars, too, Paul. I've been told they're a real turn-off."

Rage hit him like a knee to the gut. Now he knew the why behind the hurry. Some guy, some fucking fool, had left her believing her body would be repulsive to any lover who wasn't too stone-blind hot to notice.

Paul brought her hand to his chest, guiding it down the wide, bald ridge where the emergency-room doctors had cracked open his ribs to massage his heart. "I've been told that, too, darlin'."

Her eyes bored into his. Taking his hand, she made his fingers follow the puckered track low on her neck and a shorter one beneath her arm. He felt a wide, spear-shaped wedge at her left breast, the tapestry of stretch marks on her belly—shallower and thinner than his ex-wife's after their daughter was born.

"I want you, Jenna." He picked her up in his arms and laid her on the bed. "If you'll let me, I want to feel and kiss and taste every beautiful, imperfect inch of you."

He began with the salty tears rolling from the corners of her eyes. Her cheeks. That full, sensuous mouth, and down her lovely long neck. Her breasts were small, firm and high. The nipples swelled and hardened between his lips.

Moaning his name, her arms outstretched on the pillows, she surrendered to his touch, her body restless, conveying a demand to hurry, but for an entirely different reason.

"Not yet," he teased, kissing the hollow beneath her ribs, moving ever downward. "Soon. Very soon."

His tongue sought, claimed, reveled in the luscious core of her, perceiving her needs, her desires, and meeting them, then exceeding them. The intensity of her first orgasm rocked them both, aroused him nearly to the point of pain. Another shuddering wave crested and subsided, then another, until he could stand it no longer.

He entered her, filled her, felt her rise again with him. He slipped his arms under her back, curled his hands over her shoulders. Deeper, faster. She tightened around him, cried out, "Now, *now.*"

The control he'd fought to maintain shattered in a roaring burst of heat, of light, of oblivion.

Saturday was a cold, drizzly gray morning everywhere except in a room painted bawdy-house red, with butter-cream woodwork, crown moldings and a palmetto-blade ceiling fan.

Tangled sheets, blankets and pillows heaped a massive Jacobean bed with a modified frame to accommodate a king-size mattress. The aroma of amazing, incredible marathon lovemaking mingled with that of barbecue potato chips, beer and chocolate-fudge brownies raided from the kitchen.

Jenna lay on her side, gazing at the flowers budded and blooming and the twining foliage in the area rug's design. If Paul wasn't snuggled against her, spoon-fashion, she'd wonder whether last night had been only a dream.

She snickered under her breath. Like she'd ever dreamed a lover as remotely passionate and skillful and generous as he. Nice guys didn't just finish last. They gave a girl one helluva head start.

At some point between the junk-food picnic and unconsciousness, they'd showered together and rated each other's scars, by length, width and degrees of thickness. She was surprised but relieved that Paul didn't ask how she was injured, or when.

Their intimate, bizarre, hilarious game of Mine's Bigger'n Yours was no contest. Paul's body, as lean and well muscled as an artist's model, was also a living testament to heroic medical procedures, annexation to life-support machinery, serial operations and the whisker-thin signatures of gifted plastic surgeons.

In Jenna's eyes and heart, he was beautiful. Because it was fact, not selective vision, she could believe she was beautiful to him, as well. When she'd told him that naked was an excellent look for him, he'd laughed and said in the future he'd concentrate on seducing female flea-market owners who loved cast-off, dilapidated furniture. She'd then knelt on the shower floor to demonstrate a restorative technique she hadn't learned from watching Minwax how-to videos.

He stirred beside her, mumbling gibberish. An arm

encircled her waist, drawing her nearer. She smiled. They did fit together like spoons, all right, but also in many other wondrous ways, and quite possibly a few they hadn't discovered yet.

"In case you're wondering," he said, "I'm still sound asleep."

"Oh, yeah?"

"Mmm-hmm. If I was awake, I'd eventually have to get up." Kisses trailed down her bare shoulder. "The hell with that."

Jenna squinted at the coach clock on the nightstand. An hour and thirteen minutes to shower, dress, beg Homer, Herschel and Festus's forgiveness for locking them on the sunporch all night, feed and water them, then haul ass to the shop to open it for business, just as she had every freakin' Saturday since dinosaurs mutated into birds.

Rain pecked at the windows. A damp chill seeped in under the covers. The clouds must have thickened and clotted, for a gloom had fallen, cloaking the room in shadow. *Snick...snick...snick*—the clock's sweeping second hand was relentless. Shit...shit... shit.

Jenna felt Mr. Working Vacation's chest expand and contract with the rhythm of sleep, just asking for an elbow to the ribs. Maybe she wouldn't be so pissy if she started referring to days in the great outdoors— otherwise known as her driveway—stripping and sanding beau-nasty gunk off a trailerload of incoming merchandise as a *working vacation.*

She hadn't had a genuine, honest-to-God, get-outta-Dodge vacation since Sam was ten and they'd spent a weekend at Walt Disney World. He'd been old enough to travel well and young enough to think that sleeping in a rusty cargo van, surviving on a steady diet of bologna sandwiches packed in an ice chest and showering at truck stops was *awe*some.

Fifty-nine minutes sneered the clock that would be advertised on eBay before sundown. Gotta get up. Gotta get crackin'. Gotta go to work…work…work.

"Paul?"

Grunts. Snuffling noises. "At the sound of the tone, please leave a message."

Laughing, she grasped his wrist to lift the arm lassoing her waist. It didn't budge an inch, but something else was definitely beginning to defy gravity.

"C'mon, Paul. Let me go and I'll make it up to you later. I promise."

"How?"

"You'll see."

"When?"

She reached back and gave him a hug. "Not yet," she whispered. "Soon. Very soon."

Grumbling, he rolled over, pulling the sheet with him, making no effort to cover himself. *Jee-zuss.* Beautiful wasn't all he was.

Jenna reached for the Princess phone beside the clock, thinking, sexual myth number one: size doesn't matter. Performance-wise, no, but psychologically, the bigger a guy got, the more a woman felt responsible for creating the monster.

Sexual myth number two: men are aroused by sight, women by touch. (Refer to sexual myth number one and add that seeing isn't just believing.)

"Hey, Mavis," she said into the phone. "Sorry for the short notice, but I'm calling in well today."

"You're…what?"

"I'm calling in well. I can't call in sick, because I'm not, but I am taking the day off."

Pause. "Are you sure you're okay, hon? You sound kind of funny."

Jenna flapped a hand as though Mavis were in the room. "I'm fine." She glanced over her shoulder at Paul, who was wearing a corner of the bedspread like a loincloth and grinning ear to ear. "I'm totally fine."

Another pause, then an "Oh" ranged up one octave and down another. "You did like I said, didn't you? You've been doing the wild thing with that Paul Haggerty fella."

A full-body blush commenced at Jenna's toes.

"Lord-a-mercy," Mavis went on. "I can't remember the last time you took the whole day off. The man must've worn you plumb out."

To stave off further speculation, Jenna said she'd see her Monday, then amended it to Tuesday. "It's only fair to trade you today for Monday."

"Oh, for the love of Mike." In a trailer park not far away, an innocent telephone receiver was being throttled by an irate flea-market manager. "Take the week off. Take a blessed month off, if Paul's going to be in town that long."

Jenna's breath caught. She'd forgotten. Yeah, well, she'd stopped believing in happily-ever-afters a long time ago. "I'll be there Monday, as usual."

She hung up the phone and swiveled around on the bed. Cowlicks barbed Paul's razor-cut hair. One cheek was pillow-creased and both were stubbled whiskey-brown—shades darker than his hair and mustache. An arm was winged under his head.

"Is something wrong?" he said.

Emotion surged, the pressure distending her throat, temples, the back of her eyes. Something's wrong, she thought, if it means being lonely or stupid or middle-aged crazy enough to have fallen in love with you without knowing who you are, where you came from or how soon you'll leave.

Only that you will.

A tight-lipped smile was the best she could contrive. She bolstered it with a you-know-Mavis shrug. "I need a shower, coffee and food. In that order."

It was obvious he recognized evasion when he heard it, but didn't press. "Good plan." He swung his legs off the bed and wrapped the towel he'd used last night around his waist. "When we get to phase three, point me to a skillet and I'll make us some mean junkyard omelettes."

Jenna knuckled her hips. "I have to wash my hair this time, Paul." Her tone was sharp; the inner bitch personified. "There is another bathroom upstairs."

He looked at her, puzzled, then hurt. "I was about to ask if there was." Snatching his clothes off the floor, he wadded them into a ball. "I don't make a habit of barging in where I'm not invited, including shower stalls." He glanced at the bed, then at Jenna, then at the bedroom door. "And the breakfast table."

"What the— Good grief, Paul. Why are you so angry all of a sudden?"

Joyce Ramsour was the diva of the verbal bait and switch—a talent Jenna had failed to absorb by osmosis, as Paul's snide expression affirmed. Of course he was angry. She hadn't just gone on the offensive and put him in his place, she'd shoved him there.

Reverting to standard fall-back position, she waved her hands, signaling for a take two, a concession—however he chose to perceive it. "I'm not a morning person, okay? The less sleep I've had, the crabbier I am, until I can get a hot shower and a couple of cups of coffee down the hatch."

That ever-dubious eyebrow cocked, and his head along with it. He walked over and kissed her cheek. "Bullshit."

Watching his glutes rhumba behind the taut-stretched towel, she thought, now there's an exit line you don't hear every day. Very Rhett Butleresque.

She stared into the hall well after the stairway's treads drummed his ascent to the second floor.

A little under an hour later, Jenna took another tiny sip of her first cup of coffee. To ingest it straight from the carafe by intravenous drip would be splendid, except she'd specified two cups as the minimum daily requirement for jocularity.

No sense rushing things.

She sat at the breakfast table, facing into the kitchen, with the sunporch's door behind her. Her perspective was also a first. Police academy indoctrination against leaving her back unguarded—which was why she hadn't sat there before—almost guaranteed she wouldn't again.

Fatalistic, perhaps, but experience teaches. However long it lasted, there'd be enough memories of this love affair without someday being ambushed by the image of Paul Haggerty bent over the stove, the tip of his tongue clamped between his lips, cooking her breakfast.

When she'd entered the kitchen, Festus was on Paul's lap and the dogs were delirious from unrelieved petting, haunch slaps and guy talk. "I hope it was okay to let them in," he said, a chill in his tone.

It was, she assured, and proceeded to brew a pot of coffee. He would have taken the initiative, he told her, but heaven forbid she think him presumptuous for pawing through her cabinets and drawers for the accoutrements. Ditto rooting around for her cooking utensils and invading her refrigerator for omelette ingredients.

Yeah, well, after the way she'd acted earlier, her own petard deserved a hoist. Didn't mean she liked it. Didn't mean her defenses weren't at full mast, either.

They'd gone about their respective chores exchanging thank-yous, excuse-mes and you're-welcomes with the excruciating politeness of divorced spouses attending their beloved only daughter's wedding.

Jenna sipped another atom of coffee and focused on her cup being half-full, not the alternative. Ignore the awkwardness and taut silence, and the scene before her was domestic du jour. In the nine American households where Hubby cooked breakfast on Saturdays, anyhow.

Paul must have foraged the medicine cabinet in what had been Sam's bathroom. He was clean shaven, his damp hair combed straight back from the crown. His shirt and slacks were a tad rumpled, but presentable.

The countertop beside the stove was piled with produce bags, peelings, cartons and jars. Whatever Paul was doing with them smelled wonderful.

Festus, who wasn't allowed near the cooktop, roosted in an open cabinet drawer. His amber eyes followed Paul's every move, occasionally narrowing as if to ask, "You aren't really going to eat that, are you?"

Herschel paced the floor between the chef and the table, like a picketer issued a restricted parade permit. Homer plodded the same course, but slalomed between Herschel's fore- and back legs, just because he could.

"Breakfast is served." Paul deposited a plate with a perfect, puffy, golden-brown omelette in front of her. It figured that he actually could cook. Part and parcel with leaping tall buildings in a single bound.

Still, her eyes widened at first bite. "Gawd, this is delicious."

"Thank you." He hitched a shoulder. "Anybody can make an omelette."

"I can't. Well, I *can,* but mine usually wind up looking like mutant scrambled eggs." She speared another forkful. "What's in it, anyway?"

"Depends on what's in the fridge. Cheese, veggies, deli coleslaw. SpaghettiOs aren't bad. Leftover roast beef and potatoes are great. Hence, a junkyard omelette."

SpaghettiOs? Jenna decided the mysterious green and red and brownish-yellow things in hers were better left unidentified.

The phone rang when she was crossing the kitchen for coffee refills. She started to let the machine answer, as if she ever had when she was home. The few times she'd tried, her mother's, Joyce's or Mavis's voice had yelled in escalating decibels, "I *know* you're there, Jenna, so pick up...I mean it, Jenna...Jenna—so help me, *you'd better pick up the phone right now.*"

"Hello?"

"Oh, thank goodness you're home. Of course, if you weren't, I'd have tried calling the shop next, but I've been beside myself with worry for hours as it is, and like they say on TV, every minute may count."

It took half of one for Jenna's brain to process the gaspy monologue, which prompted the woman's panicky "Hello—hello—are you there?"

"Yes, I'm here, but…who *is* this?"

"You mean you don't recognize— Well, silly me, why would you? We haven't spoken on the telephone that often."

Jenna was about to hang up, when the speaker said, "Dear me, I'm glad I called you first instead of the police. Why, they'd have thought I was a raving lunatic." A tongue cluck, then, "This is Betty Bigelow."

"Oh?" Jenna's eyes slanted to Paul's back. "And the reason you're calling?"

"I hear that you're acquainted with one of my boarders—a gentleman by the name of Paul Haggerty?"

"We've met." Jenna's molars ground together.

"I certainly don't mean to alarm you, but I'm terribly concerned about him. When he didn't come down for coffee with the others this morning, I went up to check on him. You know, to see if he wasn't feeling well or something."

"Uh-huh."

"When he didn't answer the door, I peeked in and—" another tongue cluck "—well, being the mother of a boy as rambunctious as Sam was, I'm sure you can imagine how frightened I was to see that Mr. Haggerty's bed hadn't been slept in.''

Jenna didn't know whether to slam down the receiver or burst out laughing.

''I may have overreacted,'' Betty allowed, ''but he is a stranger to town and I'm sure you'll agree, Pfister just isn't the sleepy, safe little village it once was.''

''I wouldn't say it's changed *that* much, Betty.'' Jenna laid on a drawl as honey thick as the innkeeper's. ''People still keep a *real* close eye on each other. Like you, for example, concerned as you are about where Mr. Haggerty spent the night.''

Paul whipped around in the chair, his expression dumbstruck.

''I do take pride in treating my guests like family,'' Betty said.

''Listen, my breakfast is getting cold, but I'll tell you what. Next time you want to know who I'm sleeping with, why don't you just come right out and ask me?''

''Ms. MacArthur! Why, I never—''

''Have a nice day, Betty. I'm sure I will.''

Jenna dropped the receiver in the cradle. Beyond angry, with herself as much as anyone, she tipped back her head and bellowed, ''Shit on a freakin' damn stick. A girl can't even have a one-night stand without everyone in town knowing about it.''

She grabbed a dish towel and snapped it. Knocked a plastic tumbler into the sink. Slapped the faucet. Hugging herself, eyes squeezed shut against tears she didn't want to shed, didn't want Paul to see, she wedged herself in the corner of the counter like a misbehaving child.

He walked up behind her and wrapped her in his arms. "Is that what you want? A one-night stand?"

She stiffened. Tell him yes. Tell him last night was great, but—

"Because I don't. If I thought that was all it was for you, I wouldn't have stayed. If it was, tell me now. Better to leave it at one night."

"One, three, ten— What difference does it make? Sooner or later you *will* leave."

He spun her around to face him. "I'll ask you again, Jenna. Is that what you want?"

Head bowed, she nodded, then looked up at him, straight in the eye. "No. It *isn't* what I want. I realized it this morning when Mavis offered me a week, then a month off. Gave us plenty of time to screw each other's brains out before you left town."

Anger contorted his features. "Don't ever say that again. Don't ever call it that again." He looked away for a long moment, a nerve stitching in his jaw, then turned back and cupped her face in his hands. "You're going to say I'm crazy. That I've only known you for a few days and that this kind of thing only happens in Meg Ryan movies, not in real life. But…I love you, Jenna. As long as you want me here, that's where I'll be."

10

"Here you go," Casper said, handing Paul a beer from Aggie's refrigerator.

Paul thanked him and took a swig. Smacking his lips forced them apart again. The brew, an off brand he'd never heard of, was wet and cold. That's all he could say for it.

With difficulty, Casper hoisted himself onto the bar stool beside him. The built-in counter wasn't that high, but age lowered a person's center of gravity.

Aggie had tried to shoo the men into the living room, but Casper would have none of that. He said doilies, flowery stuff and truckloads of gewgaws begging to get broken made his neck itch. The kitchen was where the action was. And the beer.

Casper said, "I took your advice, son. Called that shylock of mine first thing yesterday. His girl went through this rigmarole about him having to be in court all day Monday. Today was already booked up. Wednesday he'd be out of the office—playing golf, I'd reckon. Said she could maybe squeeze me in Thursday afternoon." He grunted. "Four days to get an appointment with an attorney. Can you believe that?"

Paul nodded. "They're getting worse than doctors."

"Ain't it the truth."

They were drinking on it when Aggie and Jenna stalked into the kitchen. Both were flushed and flustered from running relays to the dining room, preparing a welcome-home dinner for Sam.

"This is my house and my table, young lady. I can seat company wherever I want to."

"Bull. You're just being stubborn." Jenna glared at Paul as she took a stack of plates from a cupboard. "And pushy."

He returned a "What did I do?" look.

Jenna said, "Isn't she, Paul?"

"Uh-oh," Casper murmured. "If you know what's good for you, you'll keep your lip zipped."

"I am not being stubborn," Aggie said, gathering up tableware from a drawer. "Even if I was, I have a right to act however I want to *in my own house. Don't* I, Paul?"

The drawer banged shut. She turned toward the bar. Knives and spoons gleamed in one fist and forks in the other. "Well?" she said to Paul. "*Don't* I?"

Sweet Jesus, hear my prayer.

Somebody must have, for Jenna said, "Criminitly, Mother. Will you leave the poor man alone and help me finish setting the table before Sam gets here?"

They stormed out, still pecking at each other.

Casper clapped Paul on the back. "Welcome to the family, son."

"Beg pardon?"

"When those two start arguing over you and *at* you, it's a sure sign you're in like Flynn. I knew you were close when Aggie let you into her kitchen. Take it from me, if she thought of you as company, she wouldn't have let you past the front room till the food was on the table.''

That made a trifecta of sorts. Joyce and Barry Ramsour had welcomed Paul to the fold over pizza Saturday night. Half the town saw him and Jenna holding hands and stealing smooches at the concert in the park Sunday afternoon.

He'd had to move to the SeaShell Motor Court when Betty Bigelow said she didn't harbor scoundrels, miscreants or fornicators, but thus far, his and Jenna's relationship had met with most everyone's approval.

Tonight was the acid test. He didn't expect Sam MacArthur to sing for Paul's a jolly good fellow. Not hating him on sight would be good enough.

Casper said, ''I don't recollect Aggie taking to any of Jenna's boyfriends as fast as she has to you. She's a wonderful woman, but slower than a fat hog in a deep wallow at making friends.''

Paul tipped the beer bottle and drained it in a secret toast to himself.

''Then again, I s'pose you and Jenna boinkin' like bunnies since we all had supper together the other night could've speeded things up a mite.''

Beer spewed up Paul's nose and down his windpipe. Coughing, choking, he pounded his chest like a self-inflicted Heimlich maneuver.

''Paul?'' Jenna asked from the direction of the kitchen door. ''Are you all right?''

Head down, clearing his throat, he nodded, grabbing for the wad of paper towels Casper ripped from the roll. He wiped his bleary eyes, his forehead, his mustache, hoping Jenna had returned to the dining room to escalate hostilities with her mother.

"Need a glass of water?" Casper asked.

"Thanks, but I'll be..." Paul felt the blood drain from his face. He gripped the counter, vaguely aware of its sharp edge slicing into his palms.

Rick Rivas stood in the doorway, his shoulders nearly as wide as the jamb. He was taller than Paul remembered and his glossy black hair was cut military style, but the dark eyes fixing him in their crosshairs still telegraphed equal parts good humor and menace.

"Paul Haggerty..." Jenna shimmied into view, her radiant face tilted upward, in profile, exactly as it was in the old newspaper photograph. "Allow me to introduce Sam MacArthur, the kid you've heard a lot more about than anyone should have to listen to."

Sam extended a hand. "Nice to meet you, sir." His grip was firm, not a bone-crushing insult disguised as courtesy. The accent was southern Missouri–bred—not to be confused with Southern, as two-fifths of his vowels escaped behavior modification.

"For the record, I'm half as ornery as Mom makes me out to be, twice as smart and, no, she can't still kick my butt. I just let her think she can."

Paul laughed, the shock subsiding, his equilibrium returning. Sam's resemblance to his father was uncanny, but he had Jenna's smile and some of her facial contours. He wondered, though, how much of Rick Rivas she saw in her son, and its effect on her.

Was Sam a living memorial to her slain husband? A constant reminder of all she'd lost, all that had been stolen from her? Paul guessed some of both, but the joy in Jenna's face said she believed herself the luckiest woman in the world.

"Paul's in the security business," Casper said to Sam. "The high tech end of it. Armored cars, mostly—not the bank kind, ones that's got grenade-proof glass, oil sprayers and such."

"Oh, yeah? Is the mayor getting paranoid or something?"

Paul didn't respond. He smelled a trap being laid. That, or he was the one getting paranoid.

Sam introduced Kathy Baker, a pretty, athletically built redhead with cornflower-blue eyes. "Pleasure to make your acquaintance, sir."

Paul winced. A young man calling him sir nicked his ego, but a young woman? Yeouch.

Jenna slanted a look at Kathy. It gave nothing away, aside from Sam's girlfriend registering a blip on Jenna's radar screen. But the glance she exchanged with Aggie spoke volumes. Being male, Paul was tone deaf.

Sam shook Casper's hand and pulled him into a bear hug. "Hey, old man, I brought back a batch of crime-scene photos from Quantico. All homicides. The db's were shot, strangled, stabbed, garroted—got you a floater, even."

"Hot damn." Casper peered around him. "Hear that, Aggie? Research from sources none other than the FB by-God I." He looked up at Sam. "I had my fingers crossed for a poisoning, but we can save that plot for the sequel."

Kathy said, "You mean you've finished your book? Gosh, it must be longer since I've seen y'all than I thought."

"Um, not quite," Casper allowed. "A few tweaks here and there, and we'll be off to the races on chapter two."

Sam moved to the stove and lifted the lid on a Dutch oven. Steam billowed up like a miniature mushroom cloud. "When's dinner gonna be ready, Grandma? I haven't had anything to eat all day, except a bag of pretzels on the plane."

Aggie said, "About ten minutes after everybody scrams out of my kitchen so I can dish it up."

The men didn't need to be told twice. Jenna and Kathy stayed to help Aggie, although she insisted she'd rather take care of things herself.

Casper dispensed fresh bottles of beer he'd cadged from the fridge when Aggie wasn't looking. Paul didn't want another—his stomach was empty, and since the accident, alcohol seemed to go straight to his brain—but there was no graceful way to decline.

Casper said, "So, Sam, you and Kathy are back together, eh?"

"Nope." Sam chugged half his bottle in what appeared to be one gulp. "You have to break up to get back together."

He looked at Paul and chuckled. "I was only out of town a week. How long have you been going out with my mother?"

Paul started. Somewhere between the kitchen and living room, Officer Friendly had changed into Officer Surly. "Oh, about a week," he said, then swigged beer as though he'd morphed into Cool Hand Luke.

"Is that a fact?" Eyes locked on Paul, Sam placed his empty on a coaster from the stack on the coffee table. "Must be, since I don't believe in coincidence."

Casper said, "Well, if you and Kathy were seeing

each other all this time, where the heck has she been the last four or five months?''

''Upstate, taking some special classes.''

''Law-school stuff? All week and on weekends, too?''

Sam shrugged. ''A crash course, in a manner of speaking.''

''I hope to shout.'' Casper grunted. ''Maybe that's why my attorney doesn't bust his chops. He's still worn out from getting his J.D.''

Sam hooked his thumbs in the woven-leather belt—cop stance whether dressed in jeans and a rugby shirt or in uniform. ''Are you passing through town, Paul, or thinking about moving here?'' His smile might be his mother's, but that sly grin was pure Rick Rivas. ''Pardon my curiosity, but I can't help having some, with you driving a rental car leased at KC-I a week ago Sunday and all.''

Paul had assumed Sam had driven directly from Lambert Field in St. Louis to his grandmother's. Maybe he had, but at some point someone must have told him about Paul. That, or the kid made a habit of asking Dispatch to run the license plate and registration on every strange car parked in Aggie's driveway.

A sweat broke at thoughts of Sam rifling through the glove box for the paperwork on the lease—the hell with locked doors and the Fourth Amendment. Rental companies demand ID out the wazoo. It doesn't take much to initiate a background check. Then it's a matter of connecting dots.

Paul had no good answer to Sam's question, including the truth. He polished off his beer and set the bottle on a coaster beside the other. ''My plans?

To enjoy the evening and eat all of Aggie's home cooking I can hold.''

''So, you're one of those live-for-the-moment types.''

''Hey, what's going on here?'' Casper looked from one to the other, finally wise to the jousting match. ''You boys in some kind of pissing contest?''

''No, sir. I'm just trying to get better acquainted with Mr. Haggerty.''

''You can start by calling him Paul.'' Jenna rounded the dining room's archway. Her brown eyes delivered a fair amount of menace when riled, too. She sidled between Casper and Paul and halted toe-to-toe with her son. He might doubt that she could literally kick his ass, but Sam cringed at the hundred-and-thirty-some pounds of figurative glaring up at him.

''Number two,'' she said, ''you will be as courteous to any friend of mine as I've always been to yours—including the jocks and jerks and bimbos you dragged home when you were younger. To act otherwise is disrespectful to me.''

''Sorry, Mom.'' Sam glanced at Paul. ''Sorry for the rousting, sir.''

Paul nodded.

''You can apologize to Cappy, too, for being rude. Grandma's bossed him around all day, putting this dinner together for you.''

''Aw, for Christ's sweet sake, Jenna-girl. So he went a little overboard looking out for his mama. Quit rubbing his nose in it. Paul knows he didn't mean anything by it, don'tcha, Paul?''

''Sure.'' An adjunctive *he did* Paul kept to himself.

Sam was protective of his mother, but a cop's intuition dictated his questions. His father had a sixth, even seventh, sense for evaluating crime scenes and suspect interviews by what was there, what was there that shouldn't be and what wasn't there that ought to be. A fraction of Rick's bloodhound genes in Sam's DNA made him a threat.

Paul needed time. How much? Weeks, months— enough to gain Jenna's unconditional trust. Sam would accede to her wishes in public, while privately sniffing out Paul's back trail. It would go cold in places and for extended periods of time. Except detours, delays and bureaucratic snarls were damn thin pegs for a man to hang his life on.

"Hey, Paul." A huge hand clamped his shoulder. Sam grinned down at him. "Let's see how wide a furrow we can plow down Grandma's table."

Laughing, Jenna threaded her arm through Casper's. To Paul, she said, "Beware that firsts on the mashed potatoes and gravy may be onlys. Sam is served last, for obvious reasons, but that doesn't mean you'll have a second chance."

Sam patted his flatiron stomach. "Truth to tell, amigo, I can guar-an-tee there won't be any second chances."

Paul got the message.

Jenna clasped Paul's hand, then Casper's, and bowed her head. Moored to two of the three men she loved most in the world didn't dispel feeling like the new kid at summer camp ignorant of her bunkies' sign language and codespeak.

Aggie and Casper were their usual, lovable, aggravating selves. Everyone else at the table was just trying to act normal, which seldom fools anyone, aside from the actor. Verily, normal is a steady-as-she-goes state of mind, not an emotional cloaking device.

Similar to a drunk faking sobriety, talking and laughing a beat too fast or too loudly, or neither talking nor laughing, and self-conscious gestures and eyes skittering like a rabbit suspecting a hunter behind every bush are all dead giveaways.

Being surrounded by bad actors harboring unknown agendas was as nerve-racking as it was infuriating. While Casper thanked the Lord for his bounty and asked for his blessing, Jenna asked a few favors. For Sam to start acting like Sam, not Marshal Dillon with a burr up his butt. For Paul to relax, make eye contact—if that wasn't too *much* to ask—and to stop jiggling his damn knee under the damn table. For Kathy Baker to lose the snotty attitude, or go back to wherever she'd been and stay there.

She'd zigged to Jenna's every zag while they were dishing up and laying out the food. The evasions were intentional; the smirk Kathy couldn't quite hide was hurtful.

She and Sam had dated on and off since high school and Jenna loved her like a daughter. When Kathy vanished midsummer, Sam tendered no explanation. He hadn't dated anyone, but didn't appear heartbroken. Tonight, the prodigal girlfriend had returned, and she was treating Jenna as if she was contagious and wasn't being particularly attentive to Sam.

"...Lord, bless us and keep us," Casper said, to which Jenna added, *from each other's throats.* Her amen joined the chorus a tick late and a little too loudly.

Sam raised his wineglass. "Before we dig in, I have an announcement to make." He bumped shoulders with Kathy and grinned. "*We* have an announcement to make."

Jenna stopped breathing and stared across the table at him.

Aggie shrieked, "You're getting married," and clapped her hands to her cheeks.

"We're getting married," Sam said, ignoring his dumbstruck mother and hyperventilating grandmother. "In the spring sometime." His grin widened. "Not soon enough for me, but Kathy says we've waited this long, what's another six months to do it up right?"

Jenna knew she should say something, do something besides sit there with her mouth hanging open. Married. Sam. Sam married. Then comes Sam with a baby carriage.

Kathy splayed her left hand, wriggling her fingers. Rainbow-colored sparks shot from a marquise-cut solitaire in a channel setting. Classy. Gorgeous. The sucker must have cost Sam three months' salary.

The excited bride-to-be's voice was as high as Minnie Mouse on helium. "Oh, Jenna—God, I'm so sorry for barely speaking to you before, but Sam wanted to surprise you. The ring was burning a big fat hole in my pocket as it was. If we'd been in the same room for more than a minute, I couldn't have kept my mouth shut."

"I understand," Jenna lied—not to Kathy, but to Sam, who was oblivious to the subliminal resentment. Yes, it was childish and petty to take offense for Sam not breaking the news privately, before dinner. Tough shit. The hurt was compounded by the fact that she couldn't tell him it had or why, because she'd sound childish and petty.

Perhaps he'd intended to, but forgot. What with the two-plus-hour drive from the airport, proposing to Kathy, giving her the ring, getting to Grandma's for his homecoming dinner and harassing Paul, no wonder a trifle such as telling his mother about his impending marriage had slipped Sam's mind.

Could happen to anyone.

"What's with the long face, Mom?" Sam's gaze shifted to Paul, as if he were the culprit, then back again. "I thought you'd be tickled to death."

"Of course, I am. Why wouldn't I be?" Jenna pushed out a laugh. "Hey, you wanted it to be a surprise—I'm surprised, already."

"To Sam and Kathy." Aggie held up her wineglass like the Statue of Liberty's torch.

"You okay?" Paul whispered.

"Yeah." Jenna nodded. "Just peachy."

"May they live long and prosper and be happy ever after." Aggie grimaced. "That's the worst toast I ever heard. There's a reason men do these things. Casper, you try."

"Hurry, Cappy." Sam chuckled. "My arm's going numb."

"All rightie. To Sam and Kathy, who don't need an old fart like me to tell them how lucky they are to have each other to celebrate the good times, help endure the bad ones and keep the in-betweens from gettin' boring."

Jenna's vision blurred. Forever. Please, let them have a forever together.

Paul's hand covered hers under the table. He didn't know that the emotions batting at her heart were miles beyond a mother accepting that somehow, when she wasn't looking, her boy had become a man and soon would have a family of his own. Paul simply perceived that she needed an anchor. Her fingers laced with his. Comfort for comfort's sake was all the sweeter for being unexpected.

Over the hear-hears and clinking glasses, Casper said, "Hey, Aggie. How's about we make it a double wedding?"

Sam's glass halted midway to his mouth. "Say *what?*"

Aggie squeezed his forearm. "Oh, don't go all white around the mouth, sweetie. I've always thought double weddings were tacky, and we wouldn't dream of stealing your thunder. Would we, Casper?"

"Hmph. It ain't looking much like it."

"Christmastime would be better, anyway. I do so love the holiday colors and the Holly and the Ivy Committee always does such a beautiful job decorating the church's sanctuary."

All heads swiveled from Aggie to Casper, except Casper's. His craned forward so far, he resembled a mongoose with spectacles and googly blue eyes. "Wha—wha—wha—"

"Put your tongue back in your mouth and stop making that hideous noise." Heads swung to Aggie's end of the table. "This isn't any huge shock, you know. You *asked* me this afternoon and I *told* you I'd think about it and give you my answer later."

"You did not. You said you were too busy to be bothered and to get the hell out of your kitchen."

"It's the same difference."

"My hind end it is." Casper patted himself down as though his clothes were smoldering. "If this don't beat all and back again. I've carried that dadblasted ring in my pocket for going on ten years, and the one time I need it, I leave it in my other pants."

Aggie puffed out her bosom. "Well, just never mind then. The food's getting cold, anyway. Jenna, pass the pickles, please."

"No—wait—here it is!" Casper leaped from his chair and scurried to the end of the table. He sank into a half crouch, grimaced then straightened up again. "Hang on, Aggie. I'll get there."

He switched feet, began a slow descent. Groaned. Staggered upright. Muttered, "Damn floor gets lower every day."

"Good heavens, you've asked me to marry you about five hundred times." Aggie held out her hand. "Skip to the next part before you throw your back out or something."

He shrugged. "You all heard her, if I need a witness later."

She gasped as he removed from a jeweler's box a star-sapphire ring encircled by diamonds and mounted on a filigree band. "Oh, Casper. You *remembered.*"

As he eased it on her finger, he explained, "As many times as I've proposed, I've never shown her the ring. I was holding out for a yes, don'tcha know.

"'Twasn't long after I fell for her hook, line and sinker that we were dawdling around window-shopping and she stopped cold, pointed at this ring and said she'd wanted a star sapphire for as long as she could remember."

Aggie looked up at him, her face aglow. In a quavering voice, she said, "I told him that when I was a little girl, the neighbor lady wore a sapphire as big as a lima bean. She said it was a genuine morning star the fairies brought to her from heaven—that accounted for the stone's deep blue color. Then she promised, if I was a *really* good girl the fairies would someday leave a star sapphire under my pillow, too."

She laughed. "I swan, I was a married woman with a baby on the way before I stopped looking for it."

Sam said, "From peeking under your pillow for jewelry to peeking under cabbage leaves for Mom."

"No, for Jim—" Aggie froze, her eyes wide, panicky.

As far as the others knew, Jenna was an only child. Aggie had chosen to keep her son Jimmy's existence a secret, for fear that declaring him dead might broker a self-fulfilling prophesy.

Paul's fingers tightened in Jenna's the same instant she blurted, "It was the stork. The stork brought me, right, Mom?"

"Yes—the stork. The stork brought *Jenna.* Brought your mother." Bright crimson lashed Aggie's cheeks. "She, uh…when she did something silly, her daddy used to say the stork must have dropped her on her head."

Paul teased, "That explains a lot, doesn't it, Sam?"

"Think so?" He turned to Kathy. "Pretty insightful for a guy that only met Mom a week ago."

She recoiled. "Why are you… Just cool it, okay?"

"What, he can make a joke and I can't?"

Paul said, "It's no—"

"Aw, fühgeddaboutit, man. Sheez."

Aggie said, "I love you, Casper, and I love my ring. Now go sit down so we can eat. Everyone's so hungry they're getting out of sorts."

Out of sorts? Jenna was about to launch from her chair. Maximum sensory overload. Good stress, bad stress—stress was stress. A time-out in the bathroom to breathe, splash cold water on her face and pull herself together would help.

Sam said, "Anybody object to me bragging on my fiancée, while Cappy floats down from cloud nine?"

Jenna wanted to shout, I do. Can't everybody shut up for a minute? If we have to talk, how about sports, gardening, the Eurodollar—anything dull and impersonal and as far removed from this suddenly dysfunctional family as possible.

"I suppose y'all have wondered where Kathy's been the last sixteen weeks," Sam said.

The number gonged in Jenna's mind. Oh, no...*no.*

"Has it been that long?" Aggie clucked her tongue. "My, my."

"After she quit law school in July—"

"Quit?" Casper hip-hopped his chair closer to the table. "You told me she was upstate, taking special classes for her degree."

Jenna's lower lip curled over her teeth. In her peripheral vision, she saw Paul watching her with concern. She wished he'd stop.

Sam went on, "I said, in a manner of speaking she was." He laid his arm across the back of Kathy's chair and squeezed her shoulder. "I'd have given anything if I could've been there Sunday to see Patrol Officer Katherine Ella Baker graduate from the police academy."

Paul murmured, "Oh, my God."

A montage scrolled behind Jenna's eyes. Her own academy graduation. Rick in his dress uniform. Her in her wedding gown. Standing profile, as big as an upended Volkswagen in a blue polyester maternity dress. The gold shield and tri-cornered flag presented to her at the hospital. The bagpiper's heel-toe march on video. The pallbearers in lockstep, their backs rigid, their faces grim.

Pallbearers...*pallbearers*. The room lurched, slowly began to revolve. A nightmare-go-round. She tried to tear her hand from Paul's. He wouldn't let go.

"We got us a two-cop family," Casper said. "Not many of those, I bet."

"No more secrets, Jenna, I promise," Kathy was saying, the syllables elongated, grotesque. "You were so upset when Sam enrolled at the academy, I thought it was better not to tell you. I mean, you know, I could've washed out."

"Yeah, right." Sam laughed. "Try third in the class overall and the top-ranked markswoman. If you've gotta worry about somebody getting shot, Mom, worry about *me*."

Head shaking, Jenna whispered, "Don't—please, don't say that."

"Hey, it's fact not brag." Sam sighted down his thumb and forefinger, elled like a pretend pistol. "Kathy hits what she aims at—"

Paul slapped the table. "Shut up, Rick. Just shut the hell up."

11

"**Y**ou lying son of a bitch."

"I never lied to you, Jenna. I just didn't tell the entire truth."

The front door rattled open. "Back off. I told you in the car, you're not coming in."

"We have to talk."

"*We* don't have to do a damn thing."

"Please. Hear me out. Give me a chance to explain."

"Explain what? Why you decided to stalk me twenty-three years after you were a pallbearer at my husband's funeral?" Her nails bowed to the door's unmalleable brass knob. "How you justified slithering into *my* life, *my* family, my *bed?* Or maybe you want to tell me what you hoped to gain from it?"

The tears streaming down her cheeks enraged her. No wonder women are called the weaker sex. We cry when we're happy, sad, at sappy movies, at love songs and when we're so angry and hurt and betrayed it feels as if our guts are being ripped out with tweezers.

Jenna swiped her face with the cuff of her jacket. "Screw the boss's wife? It happens. Comfort his widow? Not unheard of. But wait twenty-some years to screw the boss's widow?" Her laugh was caustic, malevolent. "That's gotta be a first, Detective-Sergeant Haggerty."

Rick Rivas had been more than Paul's unit commander. He'd been a mentor and a close friend. When Rick had a few drinks, he'd tease Paul about having a crush on his wife, then he'd exact a promise that if anything ever happened, Paul would step in and take care of her and his son.

"It wasn't—isn't—like that." Paul spread his hands. "Some things are impossible to fake. You know that better than most."

Like dispassion, Jenna thought. The opposite of love wasn't hate, nor was the opposite of hatred love. In both instances it was feeling nothing at all, to have no emotional investment in another person beyond basic human compassion.

Feign indifference? Sure. No sweat. How hard could it be to fool a man who knew her secrets?

She heard Sam's tricked-out Jeep Wrangler roar around the corner. Headlights and amber fog lamps played on the asphalt. Oversize tires crunched on the driveway, rolling to a stop adjacent to the porch.

The Jeep's interior was open to the elements. Kathy Baker, belted into the passenger seat, would be half-frozen if not for the hooded parka she was bundled into. Sam's antidote for hypothermia was an FBI-issue ball cap and nylon windbreaker.

"I hope you picked up my uniforms from the cleaners," he said. "The watch commander's short-handed. He needs me to work the third shift."

Steeled for another confrontation, the gist didn't register for a moment. "Tonight? But you just got back into town a few hours ago."

"Duty calls, Mom." He commenced the contortions necessary for a too-tall man to exit a too-small vehicle. "It would have tomorrow afternoon, anyhow."

Herschel's and Homer's noses poked through and pried at the crack in the door. Paul stood with his head bowed, his hands thrust in his coat pockets, as though awaiting a jury's verdict.

Jenna's gorge rose. She had no choice but to continue the performance begun at dinner when Paul called Sam by his father's name; when Paul's identity clicked in her brain; when she realized she couldn't expose the Judas seated beside her without exposing herself.

The ain't-life-grand grind would have to continue until she and Paul were alone again.

"Heel, you idiots," she commanded. Her dogs didn't know from heel, but they did know pissed from pleasant. They scuttled backward as she stepped inside and flipped on a light switch.

Sam bounded onto the porch. "After you, Paul," he said, his tone almost friendly. Why not? His priorities had changed with the watch commander's call.

The corollary to the difference between "my husband is a cop" and "a cop is my husband" was "my son is a cop" versus "a cop is my son." Spouses—including those also in law enforcement—and family members who don't accept those truisms come to despise the profession, then later the loved one who's never completely off duty and happiest when on the job.

Homer and Herschel break-danced in place at the sound of their second-favorite person's voice. Sam scrubbed their heads and thumped their flanks.

"Howya doin', Dumb and Dumber? Yeah, yeah, I missed you, too."

Jenna glanced toward the open door. "Isn't Kathy coming in?"

Sam shook his head. "I'm pushing it as it is to get to our place, change clothes and get back to the station so Sarge can bring me up to speed."

Our place? Gee, it seems like only last week when it was *your* apartment. Jenna shrugged off the thought. Where else would Kathy stay? Her mother's job had transferred the family to Nashville before Kathy's last semester of high school. She'd moved in with a girlfriend's family until graduation, then into an apartment near the University of Missouri–Columbia campus, then—surprise, surprise—to wherever she lived during her academy training.

"She's okay," Sam said. "I left the Jeep running and the heater on."

With no roof or sidewalls. Yes, Jenna, your boy has definitely become a man.

"Your uniforms are hanging in the upstairs closet," she said. "I'll put the cleaning bill on your tab."

"Thanks, Mom." Sam gave Festus an ear scratch, waded through legs and tails to reach the stairway, then halted. "I don't suppose you guys were going to put on a pot of coffee or anything, were you?"

Jenna tensed. Would this conviviality ever freakin' end? "I guess I could."

"That'd be great." Two steps up he paused to ask, "Do you have an extra thermos I can borrow?"

"Yes, dear."

Midway to the landing he snapped his fingers. "And some bread, too? Just a couple of slices. I tossed out the perishable stuff before I left for Quantico.''

''A couple of slices, huh?'' Jenna folded her arms. ''And what might you want between them?''

''Hey, anything's fine. Lunch meat, cheese, pickles—maybe slap on some lettuce and tomato if you have 'em.''

Another ''Thanks, Mom'' floated down as she strode to the kitchen. At no time since they walked through the door had she acknowledged Paul's presence, nor had he made it known.

She heard him take a seat at the table. The groans and squeaks of Sam, Homer and Herschel clomping around upstairs filtered through the ceiling. Cabinets and drawers *screeched* open. Water splashed into the coffeemaker's carafe and, in turn, its reservoir. Bottles and jars clanked in the refrigerator door's shelves. Cellophane rustled like wet leaves. The Kit Cat clock ticked at half Jenna's pulse rate.

Any second now she'd start screaming and she might never stop.

The lusty smell of hot water sluicing through morning-ground coffee beans filled her nostrils. It was her kind of aromatherapy, whether nerves needed a calming influence or a kick in the dendrites.

Constructing a Sam-size sandwich was rote, but she did so with a mother's just-so flair that fashioned valentines from the perfect amount of mustard and pickles arranged with jigsaw precision. The process also lent a few minutes' thinking time.

Jenna pushed aside the emotional damage Paul had done. What remained was the threat he posed. If given the chance, Lenny Vildachi would have taken her life. If he chose, Paul Haggerty could destroy it.

Hers was one of WITSEC's success stories. She'd obeyed the program's rules, severed all ties to the past and forged a new life for herself and her family. Yet, for those whose identities are made, not born, the fear of someone or something exposing them as frauds and phonies and liars gradually eclipses the fear of retribution from their enemies.

It's true, Jenna thought. The road to hell is paved with good intentions. Waiting for that idyllic *right time* to act on them has given Paul Haggerty the power to hurt me more than bullets ever could.

She and Aggie weren't just mother and daughter. Their relationship exceeded the usual bonds of love, blood, loyalty and trust. They were confidantes, exclusive to each other. The secret keepers. The two-woman guardians of a single Pandora's box. Someday, they'd agreed, Sam must be told what it contained.

When he was six, they decided twelve would be old enough to understand the agonizing choices they'd made to keep their family secret. When he was eleven, sixteen seemed a more mature benchmark. Then eighteen. Then twenty-one. Then a day or so after Sam's graduation from the police academy, when Jenna promised herself she'd tell him he was a third-generation cop and how proud he'd made her, his father and his grandfather.

Now, how *could* she tell him and provide any rational, believable reason for waiting, aside from the fear he'd hate her for deceiving him. For letting him talk to, brag to, cry on photographs of the blond, blue-eyed stranger he believed was his father. For cheating him out of any knowledge of the man who was.

At the *whump-whump* of Sam's big feet pounding the stair treads in descending order, Jenna slid the sandwich into a small, plastic bag. She felt Paul watching her, begging a glance, a word, a nod in his direction. Ceding none of them, she moved to the coffeemaker to fill the thermos.

If ever there was a right time for a confession, it was years—decades—past. Joyce Ramsour was her best friend, had been since almost the day Jenna, her mother and Sam moved to Pfister. Joyce would be horrified to hear why they'd come here. She'd understand that secrecy had been a life-or-death matter. She'd agree that no, they couldn't have risked telling anyone the truth.

Then, in a quiet, cold voice, she would say, "But you could have told *me,* Jenna. You could have trusted *me.*"

Casper Wetherby would say the same thing, in the same way, as would Mavis Purvis. There was no reply, no justification to bind up those wounds. Not at this far-too-late date.

Once Paul pried the lid off the secrets box, "but you could have told *me*" would make the rounds of lesser friends, spiraling down to bare acquaintances. The latter wouldn't be hurt so much as angry. They prided themselves on knowing everything worth knowing about everybody in town. Their reputations might never recover from an oversight of that magnitude.

Had they only known, affronted townsfolk would say, they'd have seen to it no harm came to Jenna, her boy or her mother—as if six-guns and frontier justice still trod the dusty asphalt streets of Pfister, Missouri.

Next on the wind would be speculation embroidered by plot points from soap operas, *The Sopranos* and outright fabrications. Truth was stranger than fiction, but that didn't mean it couldn't be improved upon.

Jenna knew she wasn't exaggerating. Twenty-three years of deceit and defenses were shabby foundations to build a life on, but it's all she had. She'd be damned if she'd let Paul Haggerty tear it to pieces.

Sam preceded his canine groupies into the kitchen. Jenna tightened the cap on the thermos and put it, the sandwich, two bananas, the leftover muffin she'd brought home to eat for breakfast in the morning and paper napkins in a brown shopping bag stamped with MacArthur Perk's logo.

"You're the best, Mom," he said, and stooped to kiss her cheek. "Love you."

Unable to meet his eyes, she shooed him away.

He nodded at Paul. "Later, pard."

Voice constrained to a whisper, Jenna called out, "I love you, too, Sam."

"Call ya tomorrow." The front door closed behind him.

Hands clasped in front of her, she stood in the middle of the kitchen, listening to the Jeep's retreat from the driveway. Who was she kidding? She had no options. Paul held the ace to her flimsy house of cards. All she could do was try to learn if, when and how he'd play it.

She blew out a sigh. "There's coffee left."

He gently set Festus down on the floor. "Will you drink some with me?"

She shook her head. "I think the occasion calls for something stronger." Gaze still focused on the hallway wall, she went on, "Sometimes I wish I'd acquired Daddy's taste for B-52s. Called 'em boilermakers back then, at the bar he should have owned stock in. Jerzy's Place, if I remember correctly."

Her lips turned up at the corners. "One of those happy coincidences, I guess, that I bought a bottle of St. James Velvet Red this afternoon."

"Jenna…"

She turned. "So, what'll it be? Coffee? Wine? Sorry, but we drank all the beer Friday night—no, actually, it was Saturday morning, wasn't it?"

"Coffee's fine. I'll get it myself."

"No, no. Stay put. Relax, make yourself at home while you fill in all those holes in the truth that kept you an honest man."

He waited until she'd cleaned away the sandwich fixings and seated herself across from him. The hand he reached out for her to take, she ignored. The gesture was step three—seldom lower than five—in various how-to-conduct-a-psychologically-correct-argument manuals. In theory, a physical connection between combatants diluted anger and nurtured a sense of teamwork and intimacy. In practice, it halved the number of fists that could be thrown.

Paul shifted in his chair, frowning, feeling like a swimmer uncertain of a river's depth. "I didn't lie when I said I'm in love with you."

Nor had she. The bastard.

"I didn't lie when I told you I've been looking for you for nearly half my life."

Jenna cocked an eyebrow, remembering the curbside phone conversation. "Clever of you to say that, and that you didn't know my name and didn't know where to start looking. Anyone would assume you were referring to a soul mate.''

"I was." His eyes didn't avert, didn't waver. "I am."

The wrench to her heart, she refused to let show. "It was risky to use your real name, though." She shrugged. "Or not. I suppose you figured time and my poor brain-injured memory were on your side, eh?"

A cheap shot. She didn't care. He didn't respond.

"You said you were from New Orleans."

"No, I told you I *came* from New Orleans. I was there on business before I flew here."

Jenna sipped her wine. The brand name was apt. Its succulent, sweet flavor felt like liquid velvet to her taut, dry throat. "In the scheme of things, it's a minor discrepancy, but no, that isn't what you said. I accused you of having a Brooklyn accent. You told me New Orleans."

He conceded grudgingly. "I did everything in my power not to lie to you, Jenna. Not to anyone if I could avoid it. Careful wording with double meanings? You bet. But I swear, I had every intention of telling you the whole truth when—''

"The time was right?"

The "Yes" he snapped back was adamant and defensive.

She tipped back her head and laughed. "Take it from me, it never would have been. Intentions operate in only two time zones—too soon and too late. The first is justifiable, common sense even. Too late is, well—''

"Why you're terrified of me." Paul's thumb pad circled the rim of the untouched coffee cup. "Sam doesn't know…anything, does he? It follows that no one else, Casper included, does either.''

Jenna started when Herschel crept up and rested his head on her shoulder. Homer was already curled at her feet. Festus, the traitor, was again wearing Paul's lap like a napkin. Dogs weren't more sensitive than cats to human distress signals; they just gave a shit.

Paul said, ''I'm your worst nightmare, even if you believe I love you and that I'd never harm you in any way. You can't trust me. You never will. You can't trust anyone completely. One slip of the tongue, like Aggie's and mine tonight, and your world crashes down around your ears.''

Hearing him say it, his voice a matter-of-fact monotone, was more frightening than thinking it. The glass wobbled in Jenna's hand.

''I don't say this to hurt you, but through no fault of your own, I think you're the loneliest person I've ever known. You can't lay open your heart to anyone, not even Sam. The stakes are too high to let your guard slip. The guilt you're lugging around won't let it fall anyway.''

Jenna leaped to her feet. ''I hate you. God, how I hate you.'' The chair toppled sideward and slammed the linoleum. The hair at Herschel's withers raised. He growled a heads-up at Homer.

''No, you don't hate me. You're afraid of me, and not just because I'm your Ghost of Christmas Past.''

That's precisely what he was, a hobgoblin that didn't belong here, not now, not in this life. If she believed it was possible, a peculiar sort of sense could be made of the sudden recurrence of her flash-backs—a response to recognizing Paul on a subliminal level, but without an alert dispatched to the conscious one. It would account for the holiday her suspicious nature had taken, the connectiveness she'd felt, the strange familiarity.

"Bullshit. You don't look or act anything like the Paul Haggerty I knew. The rookie detective that played poker like a banker. Who tried so hard to be Ace Supercop he didn't have time for second dates, and yes, the guy that followed me around the apartment like a sad-eyed puppy."

Paul grinned. "Ace Supercop is a helluva poker player now."

"Do tell."

"My sorry social life was partly your fault. Rick ribbed me about it every chance he got. He wasn't jealous in the least. Why would he be? You were the funniest, smartest, unconsciously sexy woman either of us had ever met and you were deliriously in love with him."

Yes, she was, but was uncomfortable and a little hurt when Rick bragged on her to his friends, not as if he were proud of her accomplishments, but of himself for having the smarts to take such a capable, multitalented woman for his wife. The distinction was subtle, but as shrill to a woman's ear as an ultrasonic whistle to a dog's.

Jenna paced the floor, arms hugged tight to her chest. Rick's inherent machismo wasn't on trial here. "C'mon, Paul. Tell me something I don't know instead of parlaying what I just told you. You could be anybody. You could be some sick son of a bitch Vildachi hired to find me, and you decided, what the hell, why not get a little first. Mix pleasure with pleasure."

Paul sat back and crossed a leg on his knee. "Bullshit is right. Damn insulting bullshit, too."

Jenna whirled. "What was Rick's nickname for you?"

"Gung-ho Haggerty."

"What did you bring to the hospital when Sa—er, Rob—damn it—when my *son* was born?"

"Oh, man. That's been a while." A thumb and forefinger stroked his mustache—a favorite stalling technique, she'd noticed. A full minute passed before he said, "A pizza—extra cheese, hold the black olives and anchovies. Chocolates, too. Godiva, I think, plus a pair of fuzzy earmuffs and a Jim Croce album I was pretty sure you didn't have."

All she remembered was the pizza and the earmuffs. After a day and a half in the hospital, she was starving for food she couldn't see through. The earmuffs were a joke, intended to force Rick into taking care of the middle-of-the-night feedings. The pizza was phenomenal. Rick's selective deafness foiled the earmuffs, just as his selective sense of smell excused him from diaper duty.

Paul said, "As for the horny hit-man crap, you tell me. How many D.A.'s have there been since Vildachi put out the original contract?"

Probably a dozen. Maybe two. Jenna dismissed the question as rhetorical.

"When the judge declared a mistrial, everyone but Lenny the Bozo knew the charges wouldn't be refiled." Paul waved a hand to belay an argument. "Okay, for a couple of years there was a decent chance of it, especially with the Feds drooling for a conviction so they could turn him.

"Stranger things than out-of-the-blue eyewitnesses

or new evidence happen in cases that hot, but the primary threat Vildachi posed to you was being an idiot. A loose cannon. A wannabe Albert 'Lord High Executioner' Anastasia.''

Jenna knew it was true, but reducing the terror of receiving Polaroids of her baby and her mother with red ink smeared across their faces to what sounded like a sitcom soured her stomach. The pictures were one of many intimidation tactics. Each had the desired result.

"Are you saying I overreacted? That I packed up my family and ran for nothing?''

"No. Absolutely not. Morons have a weird kind of luck. Compensation for being morons, I guess. What else explains Lenny staking out that apartment building on the one night Constantine Manetto's bodyguards snuck off for some female companionship of their own?

"Lenny'd chased his own tail all over Midtown for days. We heard he was getting bored with the vendetta and was about to find a new hobby when the hit—'' Paul pinched the bridge of his nose. "Christ. I'm sorry. Obviously, it takes a moron to know one.''

Jenna stared at the floor. A deluge of what-ifs and if-onlys washed over her, as they had the other afternoon at the shop. Adding Vildachi's disenchantment with the rigors of assassination wasn't particularly upsetting.

But Liz Rivas intruding on Jenna MacArthur's turf was as disorienting as a midnight power outage. It wasn't as if her alter identity had been wrapped in plastic and stored in the attic like Sam's outgrown clothes. In mind and memory, Liz was on par with a friend from college thought of when certain songs played on the radio, or when insomniac channel surfing snagged an *American Graffiti* or *The Big Chill* rerun.

Paul Haggerty had brought Liz Rivas to town with him as surely as if she'd occupied the passenger seat. "Why? Why now? And how did you find me in the first place?"

He set her chair upright and held it. "If you'll stop wearing a trench in the floor, I'll tell you while you finish your wine."

Jenna flopped down and raked her fingers through her hair. She was exhausted, curious, wary. This wasn't a discussion where a recess could be declared. Angst-athons weren't her forte. Paul went to the sink and half emptied his cup, then refilled it with hot coffee from the carafe. A *click* said he'd taken the liberty of turning off the machine. Casually hijacking her kitchen and small appliances wouldn't have rated notice yesterday. Tonight it rankled. She wondered if he now measured their relationship by decades instead of days. If he always had.

Elbows braced on the table, he clasped his fingers and rested his chin in the dovetailed groove. He regarded the newspaper, folded and unread, the day's mail, a crumpled grocery list. "I didn't lie a minute ago, either."

"About what?"

"I won't tell you how I found you."

"Won't?"

"I could've said 'can't,' then you'd have asked why not. 'Won't' cuts to the chase."

Jenna rolled her eyes. For a lyin' son of a bastard, he had a certain charm. She drank to it.

"If you're worried somebody else will find and follow the same trail, don't be. It's a billion to one against."

"Because you're still Ace Supercop?"

"Because I stumbled onto it by accident." He took a sip of coffee. "That case is cleared. Okay?"

"Which leaves why and why now. Assuming you haven't scratched them off the agenda, too."

The umbrage taken to "agenda" was apparent, but he reserved comment. "The why now is like Mount Everest. I wasn't sure I'd go through with it until the shop's bell rang above my head. Even then, I almost said, 'Oops, wrong number' and whipped a one-eighty."

She tilted her head. "Shall I ask why again, or will that be covered in the overall why."

"The overall."

His thought-gathering process commenced. The dour expression returned. An index finger followed the curve in the coffee cup's handle—down, then up again, as though memorizing the shape for posterity. He shifted in the chair as if it were causing his discomfort.

Festus had disappeared, probably to nap in a corner of the living-room sofa. Herschel and Homer had resumed their positions. Hard to tell with the hair flopped over his eyes, but the big guy seemed to have Paul on point. Jenna hooked an arm under his neck and hugged his shaggy block head.

Paul began, "The other night at Casa Juarez, you asked if I had children. My answer wasn't a lie. It wasn't careful wording, either. There's no truthful answer to that question. Not with my heart saying yes but the facts telling me no, and that I'd best get accustomed to it and go on.''

He pulled his wallet from his pocket and removed a photograph. The little girl had chubby, dimpled cheeks, a mop of curly red hair, green eyes and a grin Jenna would now recognize anywhere.

''My daughter.'' Paul's voice caught. He looked away, a corner of the wallet tapping the table. ''Her name is Serena. She'll be eight next month.'' He cleared his throat. The tapping ceased. ''That's an old picture, taken about three years ago.''

Jenna picked the photograph up and studied it, uncertain how to respond. The grief etching his face implied that his daughter was dead, yet he'd spoken of her in present tense.

''She's beautiful.'' Jenna laid the photo on the table. ''She's more than beautiful. There's a sparkle to her, like the world is her playground and she just took a time-out to pose for the picture.''

''That's Serena, all right.'' He returned the picture to its protective sleeve, smiling as if a collage was streaming past his mind's eye. Reluctantly, he shut the wallet and put it aside.

''Serena's mother was—is—fifteen years younger than me. Meredith is a terrific woman—bright, attractive, ambitious. I loved her and I always will, but I was never in love with her. I talked myself into marriage, knowing if I was ever going to settle down and have a family, I'd better get with the program.''

He sucked his teeth. ''She couldn't have asked for a lousier husband. A bigamist, she called me. I married my job, then her, because I liked having someone around on my days off.''

''Ow.'' Jenna winced. ''That's a bit harsh.''

"Maybe, but to say we led separate lives isn't exaggerating. Meredith was a stockbroker, I was Columbo without the trench coat. Her friends from the brokerage house didn't exactly jibe with mine, either. They were martinis to our Budweisers. All of us were snobs, though, in a to-each-his-own way."

Jenna nodded. Birds of a feather, yada-yada. Except cops were more insular than most flocks. Besides common experiences and lingo, cops were avid shop-talkers. Unfortunately, civilians aren't as keen on conversations larded with black-humored descriptions of week-old corpses and drug mules with their stomachs and other anatomical areas chock full of cocaine-filled condoms.

"Meredith thought a baby would cure what ailed our relationship. Hell, I was years past old enough to know better, but I wanted a child, too."

Paul shrugged. "Long story shorter, Serena stole my whole heart the minute she was born. I was a good daddy and a good cop, but Meredith was still short a husband.

"We split when Serena was two. Meredith remarried a few months later—a widower at the brokerage house with a girl a year younger than Serena and a boy two years older."

Jenna pursed her lips. A whirlwind romance? With three tagalong kids? Yeah, right. Decent of Paul, though, to let her do the math.

"Not long after, my car was in the shop, so my partner, Gabe Tolson, volunteered to give me a ride to pick up Serena for the weekend and take us back to my place. We hadn't gone two blocks when a delivery truck blew a red light and creamed us, broadside."

The description of the accident was delivered as concisely as a traffic incident report. Gabe Tolson was declared dead at the scene. Paul wasn't expected to survive transport to the hospital.

The valley of the shadow beckoned a dozen times. Serena colored pictures of lollipop-shaped trees, smiley-face suns and rainbows for her daddy's room and begged her mother to take her to see him.

"Then some kid at preschool told her that I was dead and her mommy just didn't want to tell her because it would make Serena very sad. After all, hospitals have telephones, don't they?"

Paul's injuries and the machinery keeping him alive robbed him of his voice. Meredith's assurances and reassurances failed to refute a four-year-old's logic. Serena was inconsolable. Seeing was believing. Grown-ups fibbed too much to be trusted.

He knew it was a mistake to let Serena visit him, but didn't expect her to take one look at him and run screaming from the room. "Meredith and a counselor tried to prepare her ahead of time, but the monster with the *Phantom of the Opera* face terrified her.

"Her daddy had gone to live with the angels and that was all there was to it. Emotionally, she could handle my being dead—as peaceful and unbattered as Sleeping Beauty. The bogeyman in the hospital bed gave her nightmares. She said Daddy wouldn't scare her like that, not ever."

"Oh, Paul. Dear God, I can't imagine…" Jenna's voice trailed away. Imagine how he'd felt? Or Serena? Who could? Platitudes were emptiest when the inconceivable became reality.

Her situation had been the reverse. It was she who'd begged to see her son. She missed him like a vacuum misses air, and desperately needed to hold and see and touch all she had left of Rick. Her mother refused to bring him to the hospital. She said she feared he'd catch some dread disease, then later admitted she'd told the little boy that Mommy and Daddy had taken a trip and would be home soon.

Another good intention gone awry. Jenna had almost forgotten, but never quite forgiven her mother for it.

Paul scrubbed a hand across his face. A ragged sound, like a stammer tangled in a chuckle, escaped his lips. "It's not funny. God help my baby girl, there's nothing funny about it, but when I think about—" His eyes were watery, bloodshot, red-rimmed. "Serena started having funerals for me. She laid the teddy bear I bought her for Christmas in a doll bed, put a sprig from Meredith's silk arrangements in its paws, then gathered round all her Barbies and stuffed animals for the ceremony.

"It was inspired by that damn *Snow White* video— don't ever let anyone tell you TV has no effect on kids. A child psychologist said it was healthy for Serena to act out her grief. Gradually the 'concept' of my not having died could be introduced."

The strand of hair Jenna twirled around her finger pulled tight. She was a shopkeeper and a mother, not a mental-health expert. Her opinion had not been asked. Her mouth was supposed to stay shut.

Paul continued, "In the tradition of everything hitting the skids at once, complications sent me back to the ICU. Kidney failure, antibiotic resistant infections, a collapsed lung. If I survived, with or without dependence on a ventilator, it would likely be as a paraplegic.

"Meredith couldn't hold off any longer. She told me Chris, her husband, had already transferred to the brokerage's San Francisco office. She was pregnant with their child. Serena was excited about the baby and adored her stepfather, who, much as I wanted to hate him, is a nice guy."

The dogs whined at the back door. Jenna aimed a stern you-can-wait look at them. They wiggled, pranced, pleaded with the same round, frantic eyes of a potty-training toddler. While she let them out, Paul went on, either unmindful or unaware of her leaving the table. "It seemed like the right thing to do. The best thing for Serena. She was so young...so confused. The separation, the divorce, Meredith's remarriage, the car wreck. There were too many changes, too fast, for a little kid to comprehend."

Jenna sat down again, flinching at the ladderback's rheumatic cricks and grumbles. Paul's gaze pierced a focal point right of her shoulder.

"The RNs who witnessed the adoption papers cried. I gave my daughter, my beautiful baby Serena, to her stepfather..." His head lowered, shaking slightly, as if he was bewildered. "Black tears. I'll never forget the nurses crying black tears. They staggered down their faces like wet ashes, not just makeup washing away."

The stark imagery was chilling. A sheaf of white legal paperwork striped by bold typefaced lines. Immaculate winged white caps and uniforms. Cinderblack tears. No matter that nurses now wore bright, color-coded scrubs. Like Bogart movies and newsreel footage, heartbreak's mental replays were almost always monochromatic.

Paul's eyes met Jenna's. "Doing the right thing—

what you believe in your heart and soul is right—should be the easier choice. Easier to live with anyway, by virtue of being right.''

"It would be," she said, "if not for the enormous difference between *believing* and *knowing*. Especially when a decision involves a child. Knowing a right choice from a wrong one is impossible, even in hindsight. That's why living with it is so god-awful hard.''

"No, a wrong one will come to light sooner or later. When it's too late to undo the damage.''

"I don't believe that. I *won't*.'' Jenna lofted the wineglass for emphasis, then sipped from it. "If I did, I'd have to believe Sam was a good kid and grew into a good man because I chose to enter WITSEC.''

Paul deliberated a moment, then gestured capitulation. "A parallel must be in there somewhere but I'm missing it.''

"I do, too, sometimes, but it's the only thing that holds the guilt at bay.'' Jenna propped her forearms on the table and leaned on them. "If Sam had been a juvenile delinquent, became a hard case, a bum or, in general, a blight on society, who and what do you think I'd hindsightedly blame for it?''

Skepticism was the least of Paul's expression, so she answered herself. "I'd blame myself for entering WITSEC. At the time, I didn't believe I had a choice, but right or wrong—and I *won't* ever know for sure—it would be as ridiculous to credit that decision for the man Sam is as it would have been to blame it if he'd become one of the FBI's Ten Most Wanted.''

Paul's mouth curved into a semismile. "Nature versus nurture, eh?''

"I don't know. Probably more of a two-penny lecture on yin and yang." She sat back. "I'm not minimizing the grief you've gone through and still feel. I won't deny thinking, 'Oh, but for the grace of God, go I,' and thanking Him for sparing me.

"But saying 'I'm sorry, I wish it hadn't happened' over and over is as ludicrous as believing any and every bad choice and action Serena makes for the rest of her life is your fault, for allowing the adoption, when death was a cosmic coin toss, dependency on a ventilator was a possibility and paraplegia looked like the best prognosis you could hope for."

"Fools rush in," Paul said. "My sisters haven't spoken to me since, other than to say that our parents were spinning in their graves. If we'd waited and I'd died for real, Meredith's husband could have petitioned the court to adopt Serena."

"What if you and Tolson had left the station house five minutes earlier or later?" Jenna said. "What if I'd ordered dessert that night, or used the rest room, or Rick had made reservations at another restaurant?

"Survivor's guilt comes in all sizes, shapes and colors, Paul. It'll eat you alive from the inside out if you let it."

"What's done is done." It was less a statement than a self-directed sermon. "Right or wrong doesn't matter. Deal with it."

Jenna paused before saying, "Yes, but you might have a little faith in your daughter and your ex-wife. Serena won't forget you. Someday she'll want her daddy in her life. From what you've told me about Meredith, she won't object."

His slow nod indicated hopeful resignation, a frame of mind Jenna had no trouble recognizing.

She'd seen it in the mirror after countless pull-yourself-up-by-the-bootstraps lectures, and on her mother's face every Christmas, on Jimmy's birthday, Mother's Day...every day since she chose exile with her daughter and grandson over waiting alone for a son that might never find his way home.

"Noncompensatory injuries," Paul said. "The first time I heard it, it reminded me of you."

"Noncom what?" Jenna apologized for the attention lapse and sat up straighter in her chair.

"You probably don't remember, or maybe weren't aware of it, but when you were in the hospital, a controversy broke out over your injuries not being sustained in the line of duty. The bean counters decided the department wasn't responsible for the bills. The union rep said there was no such exemption in the benefits package."

"Oh, really." Anger, even the retroactive type, had an enlivening effect. "I had no idea."

"I don't know how it was resolved, but that phrase cropped up a lot after my accident, too."

"After all this time? Gee, I'm shocked."

Paul smiled. "How many bureaucrats does it take to change a lightbulb? Who knows? They're still working on the feasibility study." It was so pathetic and true, Jenna had to laugh.

"I thought about you, wondered how you were, God knows how many times, after you disappeared into the program, but that noncompensatory gibberish was like—" Wincing, Paul massaged the back of his neck. "Waiting for the right time to explain all this was supposed to keep me from sounding like the surgeons who put me back together had neglected to batten down some hatches."

No subterfuge applied to Jenna's look at the Kit Cat clock. Paul noticed, as she'd intended.

"I've dragged this out long enough, huh?" His hands wrapped around the coffee cup. He spoke to it rather than her. "This will sound lame, regardless of how I say it, so here goes. Lying in that hospital bed day after day, I thought about you and Rick and the good times and how nothing ever was the same after he died and you disappeared into the program.

"I got it in my head that if I found you, the clock might restart. Kind of like going to a high-school reunion to see an old girlfriend. Not to take up where things left off, just to recapture a little blast of magic from the past."

He glanced up at her, then lowered his eyes. "I dunno. Maybe a second wind is a better analogy."

Jenna said, "Believe it or not, I understand what you mean. A midlife crisis, sans the little red sports car and half-your-age blonde. Time to take what you have, or have left, fall back, regroup, then move forward from there."

"Well, I could do without the midlife-crisis label, but that's it exactly. You being integral to my regroup phase, when I tried to trace you, I pulled strings, collected on favors—no dice. I'd about given up when, as I told you before, purely by accident, I got a lead."

Jenna felt sick, bereaved, but couldn't, wouldn't, let it show. Jaw rigid, she lofted her chin and said, "And here you are."

"Yeah." Defensiveness rose like an aura. "Easy as one, two, three, if you skip reconstructive surgery, learning how to walk again, building a business from a hospital bed—tiny stumbling blocks in the path of progress.''

''Why didn't you tell me who you were from the beginning?'' She raised a hand. ''The name doesn't count when you knew I didn't recognize it.''

''I wasn't sure how you'd react.''

''After all the hurdles and hassles you went through to track me down, God forbid the door should slam in your new face.''

''You've got it all wrong.''

''Do I?''

''I didn't intend for things to go this far—never expected them to—before I told you who I am and why I came.''

''Well, they did, and you still haven't told me why.''

''I'm not sure I can, Jenna. Not to your satisfaction. Or mine. All I know is, there must be a reason greater than coincidence that I found you. When I did, the chemistry between us was instant and powerful. You can't deny it, so don't even try.''

Paul's voice softened. ''Besides seeing you again, I didn't have a game plan when I came here. Turns out I didn't need one. Mavis instigated our dinner together at the Mexican place. Is she in the habit of setting you up with strangers? I'll bet not. Aggie isn't, either, is she? But she stage-managed our second date.

''I don't believe in coincidence,'' he went on. ''I've never known a cop who did, but bottom line, I don't give a damn about the how and why behind us being together again. I'm in love with you—''

''No, you aren't.''

The phone rang, loud and shrill. Jenna was too

empty to be startled by it. She pushed herself up from the table, as though she were enfeebled. "You're in love with Liz Rivas. I can't compete with her, with all your rosy, good-time memories of her. That hurts more than if you'd lied and you didn't love me at all."

Staring up at her, he parted his lips and slumped in the chair, as if an unseen fist had slammed his belly into his backbone.

She cleared her throat as she brought the phone receiver to her ear.

"Jenna!" Aggie shouted. "Get over here, quick as you can. Casper tripped, fell down the porch steps. He's in horrible pain, talking clear out of his head. Please, help me!"

12

The hospital's waiting room was a windowless cubicle decorated in mauve, pearl gray and a shade of green in the teal-avocado neighborhood but owing allegiance to neither. A ceiling-mounted TV was on. The testimonials of couples who'd made millions in real estate with no money down was blessedly muted.

Aggie and Paul sat in a far corner, speaking in low tones, their knees almost touching. When Aggie telephoned, he'd told Jenna he could drive her to her mother's, or follow her, but he was going there to help regardless.

EMTs were loading Casper into an ambulance when they arrived. The paramedics suspected a fractured hip and a probable concussion from Casper's head hitting a porch step on the way down.

He was in surgery now. He had been for what seemed like a week. There was no clock in the waiting room. Jenna knew a time box was in the television screen's lower corner, but she couldn't see the box, much less the numbers.

"I don't know what in the world I'm going to do," said Casper's daughter, Vinita Potts, for approximately the nine-hundredth time since she'd collapsed in the chair beside Jenna's.

She was in her late fifties, a pale, pinch-faced dish-rag of a woman married to a soybean farmer who likely wouldn't notice if she ran naked through the living room yelling "Fire!"

Vinita had been the pallet factory's bookkeeper for thirty-some years. She cut her own hair, bought her clothes at the Council of Churches' thrift shop and lived in a slightly off-plumb house her husband, Eugene, built from discarded pallet slats. Inside was every limited-edition plate, doll, figurine, chess set and framed collector coin available from the Bradford Exchange on the three- or six-payment installment plan.

"Do you know they dismissed Nedra Dean Johnson's husband two days after he had bypass surgery?" Vinita fanned herself with a tattered issue of *Family Circle*. "Dad will be lucky if he gets breakfast before they show him the door."

"Uh-huh." It had been the essence of Jenna's replies since Vinita slumped down beside her.

"Of course, if they'd let Christie and David Masters bring their baby home sooner, it might not have taken sick and died."

"Uh-huh."

Vinita cast the magazine aside and yanked off her glasses to clean the lenses with the hem of her sweater. The cardigan smelled of mothballs and Febreze. A slipstream of both usually followed her wherever she went. "What do they care if Dad's in no shape to fend for himself and may well be for weeks, months. Why, he could be crippled for life, for all we know."

Jenna made a mental note to call her dentist in the

morning. The fillings in her molars must be ground down to shavings by now.

"*I* certainly can't keep him," Vinita said, as though Casper were a stray dog that showed up at the back door one morning. "Even if I could, I'd have to hire private nurses to take care of him while I'm at work. We *both* know how much *they* charge an hour, and for what? Sitting on their heinies watching TV, that's what. If I had any sense, I'd quit the factory and get a job baby-sitting old folks that don't do much aside from sleeping all the live-long day."

Jenna blinked the glaze from her eyes. That Vinita Potts could converse with a fence post and carry both sides was small comfort. An infinitesimal comfort. Escape was impossible. Twice Jenna had excused herself to use the rest room and twice Vinita had gone along to keep her company, as though peeing in private in a public bathroom invited a crushing type of desolation.

Out of respect to Casper, Jenna had refrained from stuffing the wilted silk philodendron arrangement on the coffee table into his daughter's whiny, lipless mouth. She'd probably swallow it whole and keep on yammering anyway.

Cater-corner across the room, Aggie's hand lay atop Paul's. She was listening to him as though mesmerized. Jenna should be grateful for his distracting her mother from Casper's plight. She should be more forgiving of Paul's sentimental, self-centric journey.

Her heart fluttered, then twisted whenever she looked at him, with every thought of him. Falling in love was emotional parasailing. She'd jumped off the cliff assuming the ground was solid beneath her and now had to build her wings on the way down.

Vinita poked her glasses up her beak until the nosepiece rested in a groove just below the bridge. "Put Dad in a nursing home?" she said as if Jenna had suggested it. "Out of the question. He'd have to sell his house and that ridiculous car to pay for it. It's criminal, *criminal* I say, for a man to work all his life and wind up destitute."

More like, with nothing for his only child and heir to get her bony mitts on, Jenna fumed. How dare Casper waste his accumulated net worth on medical care. Finding an ice floe in Missouri in late October would present a challenge, but crawling onto it and setting himself adrift would be so much more convenient for Vinita.

The wall phone rang, fostering a round-robin glance exchange. Vinita sprang from her chair. "That better be the recovery room. I have to work tomorrow and it's already hours past my bedtime."

Aggie said, "Then why don't you go home? No sense losing out on your beauty sleep."

Vinita unhooked the receiver but covered the mouthpiece with her hand. "I just remembered, Agatha. Dad fell on *your* property, didn't he? Gosh, I do hope your homeowner's insurance is paid up."

Clapping the phone to her ear, she smiled up at the ceiling. "Hel-lo-o, this is the surgical waiting room. Vinita Potts speaking. How may I help you?"

Her eyes shifted to Jenna. "Yes, she is. Whom may I say is calling?" She gasped and jerked away the receiver. "It's your son," she said in the same tone one would use to announce Satan was holding on line one.

Jenna thanked her, then watched as Vinita walked over and sat down beside Aggie, probably to inquire after the amount of Aggie's insurance policy's liability and medical coverage.

"Officer, I'd like to report a homicide almost in progress," Jenna said. "The victim will be Vinita Potts. The perpetrator will be either your grandmother or me."

"Hey, no jury will convict you. Poor ol' Eugene would feel like the governor just pardoned him. Poor guy had no idea that when the preacher said 'Speak now or forever hold your peace,' it was Eugene's last shot at getting a word in edgewise."

"We still haven't heard anything about Cappy," Jenna said. "The nurse told us the surgeon repairing his hip would be in to talk to us as soon as Casper was sent to the recovery room. That was about three days ago."

"If you need me, I can swing by while I'm on patrol."

"That's sweet of you, but there's nothing you can do."

"Is Haggerty still waiting with y'all?"

Jenna looked that way. Her gaze met Paul's and locked. She turned away and shouldered the wall. "Yes. He's still here."

A two-second pause. "Are you all right, Mom?"

Head lowered, she rubbed a spot above an eyebrow with her fingertips. "No, of course not. I'm worried sick about Cappy, which is more than I can say about Vinita."

"I'll bet so."

The dispatcher's voice in the background was an unintelligible drone. Sam said into the microphone, "Charlie 10–32, en route from Fairway and Elm," then into his cell phone, "Got a call, Mom. Page me soon as you hear anything about Cappy." The connection broke with a high-pitched beep.

Jenna felt Paul's presence behind her. So easily, she could succumb to the lure of his arms wrapping around her, giving her someone to lean on, and not just in the physical sense. Sam knew he could count on her. Aggie often called Jenna her rock. Over the years, what once was a warm, fuzzy point of pride had steadily gained weight. At the risk of sounding like Vinita Potts, at times Jenna would love a rock of her very own.

"I'm going to the canteen for a cup of decaf for Aggie," Paul said. "Would you like anything? Coffee? A soda? Candy bar?"

She'd pay ten bucks for a cold can of Dr Pepper. "No, thanks."

Minutes after Paul left, the surgeon entered the room, still wearing green scrubs and paper booties over his shoes. "Mrs. Wetherby?" he asked, walking toward Aggie. "I'm Dr. Moberly."

Vinita stepped between them. "My father is a widower." She introduced herself and accounted for Aggie and Jenna by saying they were acquaintances of her father's. The doctor, who was nobody's fool, sat down beside Aggie, although he spoke primarily to Vinita.

"I was concerned about Mr. Wetherby's head injury in regard to the anesthetic, but he came through surgery fine and is responding as expected.

"Because the fracture was relatively clean, I opted to use a glue substance for the repair instead of pins or screws."

"Glue," Vinita said, adding a syllable and length-

If offer card is missing write to: The Best of the Best, 3010 Walden Ave., P.O. Box 1867, Buffalo NY 14240-1867

NO POSTAGE
NECESSARY
IF MAILED
IN THE
UNITED STATES

BUSINESS REPLY MAIL
FIRST-CLASS MAIL   PERMIT NO. 717-003   BUFFALO, NY

POSTAGE WILL BE PAID BY ADDRESSEE

THE BEST OF THE BEST
3010 WALDEN AVE
PO BOX 1867
BUFFALO NY 14240-9952

MIRA BOOKS,

The Brightest Stars in Fiction, presents

The Best of the Best™

Superb collector's editions of the very best books by some of today's best-known authors!

2 FREE BOOKS and a FREE GIFT!

YES! I have scratched off the gold star to reveal my prize. Please send me the 2 FREE *"The Best of the Best"* books and FREE gift for which I qualify. I understand that I am under no obligation to purchase anything further, as explained on the back of this card.

▲ *Scratch off the gold star to reveal your prize!*

385 MDL DRST   185 MDL DRSP

FIRST NAME   LAST NAME

ADDRESS

APT.#   CITY

STATE/PROV.   ZIP/POSTAL CODE

Visit us online at www.mirabooks.com

® and ™ are trademarks of Harlequin Enterprises Limited. ©2002 MIRA BOOKS

DETACH AND MAIL CARD TODAY!

ening the vowels for maximum crassness. "Do you mean to tell me you stuck my father together like my boys used to do model cars?"

All three of Vinita's sons had enlisted in the navy five minutes after their eighteenth birthdays. That particular branch of service guaranteeing home base would be hundreds of miles from the ocean-challenged Midwest was no coincidence.

"It's a new technique, and the adhesive bond is virtually unbreakable, Mrs. Potts. The procedure is also less invasive, which lowers the risk of infection and speeds recovery."

"Oh. Well. In that case…" Vinita's smile suffered for chronic disuse. "How long, would you say, before he's back on his feet, able to do for himself?"

Dr. Moberly cast sympathetic glances at Aggie and Jenna as he stood. "Mr. Wetherby appears to be in good health for a man his age, but a fall of this nature traumatizes the entire body. Time will tell, Mrs. Potts."

He paused at the door. "Mr. Wetherby is being moved to a patient room. As soon as he's settled, an aide will take you to him."

"Thank you, Doctor," Jenna and Aggie said in unison. Vinita nodded a curt "Yeah, what they said."

He started out, then held the door for Paul, who was juggling three cups of vending-machine coffee. From his jacket pocket, he produced a can of Dr Pepper. "I wasn't sure this was still your brand. If you don't want it, just leave it on the table."

Jenna had been addicted to the soda, once called a Waco for its city of origin, since her first taste of it at Mary Theresa D'Auria's twelfth birthday party.

"Some things never change," she said. The can hissed open, exhausting the sweet scent of black cherries, oranges, a hint of lime and lemon. Brown foam bubbled out of the triangular drink hole.

"Not as much as we may think they do," Paul said. "And not always for the worst."

"This isn't the time or place for one of your carefully worded tête-à-têtes."

In the corner, Vinita made a strangling noise as though a lung was making a break for freedom. "Agatha," she gasped. "That ring. Where did you get it?"

Aggie's eyes averted to Jenna. Paul murmured, "Uh-oh."

"Isn't it gorgeous?" Aggie extended her hand, fingers slanting downward, giving Vinita an unimpeded view. "Your father gave it to me at dinner this evening. We're getting married...December fourteenth. At, uh, at two o'clock. The committee will have the sanctuary decorated for Christmas by then."

"Married!" Vinita sat back in the chair, unmindful of the coffee slopping on her wash-faded corduroy skirt. The mental image of Casper changing the beneficiary to his estate was as plain on her face as the wen on her nose. "You can't do that. I mean, you heard what the doctor said. That's what—six weeks away? No, no, it's simply out of the question. Dad won't be in any shape for a wedding that fast."

"Vinita, dear," Aggie said, her tone as serenely malicious as Jenna had ever heard. "Your father and I will be married in December, whether you like it or not, even if he has to roll down the aisle in a wheelchair to take his vows."

13

Aggie checked her profile in the mirror, then faced it, ignoring the paunch below her nonexistent waist and bulges above and below the black lacy underwire brassiere. The contraption gouged her ribs but did its advertised wonder for her bosom.

Swaying this way and that, she buttoned the scoop-necked, hip-length tunic over matching red slacks. Cleavage aplenty, all right. Nothing scandalous, but Casper would notice, even without his glasses. The naughty old coot would appreciate the peep show a lot more than the flowers and cartoon balloons she'd brought him the past two days.

His daughter would surely notice, too, damn her. Damn me as well, Aggie thought, for telling her the wedding would go on, come what may. The conniption Vinita had thrown about the ring in the surgical waiting room was no excuse.

What I should have done was fib and say I bought the ring for myself, or better yet, given a little gasp and said, "This old thing? Why, I've had it for years."

After all, Vinita has a head for figures, especially those following dollar signs, but not much of anything else. Aggie should have known that telling the truth would be like poking a hornet's nest with a stick.

She leaned over the vanity, her nose a bare inch from the mirror. Her sigh condensed on the glass. A teenager's eyes bagged and smudged after burning the midnight oil before an exam. What hope did a woman in her seventies have of erasing a sleepless night with makeup?

Casper's nighttime sinking spells and daylight rallies concerned his doctor, but not enough, in Aggie's opinion. Yes, Cappy was getting on in years. Yes, he looked smaller and more frail in a hospital bed than he had three days ago when he was helping her get the house ready for Sam's homecoming dinner. But the man hadn't even caught a cold in Lord knew how long.

She just couldn't accept that a side effect of the surgical anesthetic was causing Casper's middle-of-the-night respiratory problems and had said as much to Vinita. Which was another huge error in judgment.

"Being a Pink Lady volunteer doesn't give you the right to question Dad's doctor," Vinita had sneered in response. "Everybody knows old folks and babies always get sicker at night than in the daytime. That's why nurses close the window curtains and leave on a light in the room—so patients won't know if it's one or the other."

Aggie had committed the egregious error of laughing, remembering too late that Vinita couldn't be joking. Casper's pickle-pussed daughter had no sense of humor.

In retaliation, Vinita had exercised her power as Casper's sole next of kin to banish Aggie, Jenna and Sam from his bedside, other than during official visiting hours. To enforce it, Vinita descended on the room like a traffic cop a few minutes before the morning and afternoon allotments ended. Evenings, she sat with Casper until the ten o'clock news was over.

Aggie discovered the first morning that the staff was too busy at shift change to notice or care about a little old lady visitor who jumped the starting gun by an hour or two.

She gathered her purse, keys and a new Donald Westlake novel to read aloud to Casper after *The Today Show* signed off. If he wasn't up to it, she'd pull a chair to the bedside and hold his hand. He liked that. Said if more couples held hands the way they did when they courted, the divorce rate would take a nosedive.

The phone rang just as Aggie went out the door to the garage. It had earlier, when she was in the bathtub. Her stomach took a funny turn. Probably just Blanche Filbert, she decided, pushing the button to engage the garage-door opener. That woman could give Richard Simmons an ulcer.

Vapor purled out her mouth as she scooted around the car to the driver's side. Hoarfrost sugared the grass and shrubbery and the breeze needled her skin. She'd neglected to wear a coat and thought about returning to the house for one, then dismissed the idea. Once inside the hospital, it would be something else to keep track of and carry with her when she left the room.

Last night, when Vinita waltzed in and said her father needed rest not company, and was it any wonder that he had trouble breathing after talking his leg off to entertain Aggie the live-long day, Aggie had stormed out without her purse. Returning for it had earned a snipe about senior moments.

Casper had motioned Aggie to his bedside for a second kiss good-night—no peck on the cheek, but a sweet one, full on the lips—then smiled and said he loved her and would see her in his dreams.

Aggie blinked away tears and gripped the steering wheel tighter. The morning rush hour was gaining momentum. Cars and beefy pickup trucks swapped lanes, as if the clock would fall back a quarter hour if they rode her rear bumper for blocks and jackrabbited from stoplights.

She upshifted to second gear, tut-tutting at their foolishness. What's the sense in laying a patch when you can't go farther than ten feet? It ruins the effect.

The trip to Mercy Hospital took less time than finding a parking space for her '68 Volkswagen Beetle. Jenna had been after Aggie for years to trade it in for a new car with standard features such as the engine under the hood, the trunk in the back and an automatic transmission. For a dealer specializing in pre- and postwar collectibles, her daughter failed to recognize a genuine classic when she saw one.

Jenna was wrong about Paul Haggerty, too. God forbid she should latch on to a man who's smart, good-looking, successful and heterosexual. Not to mention one who'd carried a torch for her for twenty-three years.

The poor man had looked sicker than Casper when he stopped by the hospital for a quick visit yesterday afternoon, knowing that Jenna wouldn't be there. She was still hanging up on him when he called the shop and wouldn't answer the door at home, or the phone, unless she knew who was on the other end. Paul had seen the flowers he'd sent leaned against the trash cans at the curb, waiting for the garbage truck.

Aggie understood why her daughter had reacted the way she did. Paul had charged headlong into a daydream that was Jenna's worst nightmare.

"He should have come to me before going anywhere near my daughter," Aggie muttered, taking a shortcut through the emergency room to an elevator bank. Vinita or that dumbbell husband of hers might be staking out the lobby.

"Things would have been different if Paul had told me who he was and why he was here first," Aggie explained to the control panel button. "It would have taken a while to convince Jenna to meet him and longer to trust him, but she'd have figured out eventually that Paul Haggerty was the one man in the world she needn't keep secrets from."

A phlebotomist exiting the elevator looked from side to side, then at Aggie, amused to catch her in the act of talking to herself.

Her face was still warm from embarrassment when the doors opened on the third floor. Aggie turned left down two corridors, then right through a pair of swinging doors. If not for her once-weekly duties as a volunteer, Mercy's remodeling projects and ratmaze additions would have had her walking in circles, like the majority of visitors.

Her pace slowed, then halted. Jenna was sitting with her forearms on her knees on an upholstered bench fitted into a hallway alcove. Aggie looked toward room 321. The door was closed. The blaze-orange Oxygen In Use sign was gone.

Closing her eyes, she tipped back her head and forced a deep breath into her nostrils. She'd known the moment the phone rang at the house. That's why she hadn't answered it.

Bringing Casper's ring to her lips, she kissed the cool stone. *We'll be together again, sweetheart, by and by. I love you so. I always will.*

"Oh, Mom…" Jenna enveloped her in a tight hug. "He—he's *gone.*" Fresh tears trickled down Aggie's neck. Jenna's whole body quavered with her sobs. "I'm so sorry."

Aggie stroked her daughter's hair, whispering the same consolations she had when Earl died, and then Rick. Jenna needed her to be strong and so would Sam. And if Casper were there, as Aggie felt with all her heart he was, he'd be furious if she broke down smack in the middle of the hallway.

His first wife had been a weeper. He'd stayed with her until Vinita was grown, then, as he put it, swam for shore. The second was a hypochondriac who could watch a PBS special about one disease or another and wish the symptoms on herself. A lightning strike killed her and two other mourners at her doctor's graveside service.

Aggie would never be Casper's wife, but she'd do her grieving in private. She always had.

"Is Vinita here?" she asked.

Jenna shook her head. "When the nurse called her at work, Vinita said if Casper had passed away, there was no reason to come to the hospital. She went to the mortuary to make arrangements instead."

Animosity and sorrow delivered a one-two punch. A soft groan escaped Aggie's lips. Jenna grasped her shoulders and steered her to the bench. Before her throat closed completely, Aggie said, "Do you mean he was alone when…"

"No, Mom. I was with him. It just all happened so fast." Jenna knelt in front of her. "Cappy had a terrible night, the worst yet. If a nurse hadn't checked on him when she did and resuscitated him, we'd have lost him then."

Aggie stared at the carpet's feltlike surface. The suspicion that had been building for days drummed in her mind, growing louder with every beat. It was unthinkable. Abhorrent. Almost unbelievable. Almost, but not quite.

"This morning," Jenna went on, "he seemed to be pulling out of it again. He was asleep when I got here, then after a few minutes he simply stopped breathing." She paused, her thumbs massaging the backs of Aggie's hands. "They think his heart gave out—from the strain."

Through tears she couldn't hold back, Aggie said, "They *think?*"

Jenna's forehead creased. She said yes, as though uncertain whether an answer was necessary.

"Why don't they know? What are they going to put on the death certificate as his cause of death? A big question mark?"

Grief bowed to anger. Aggie welcomed it. She rose to her feet, a little shaky, but the light-headedness had passed.

She didn't recognize the ward clerk or the nurses milling around the station down the hall. Not surprising. Turnover was at an all-time high.

"Mom?" Jenna's voice sounded miles away. "Where are you going?"

Walking toward the station, Aggie took a tissue from her purse and dabbed her eyes. She was the one with a heart condition and high blood pressure, not Casper.

Oh, he had his share of ailments visited on the elderly—arthritis, glaucoma, digestive problems, a fickle prostate and a touch of osteoporosis. But his heart? Casper's doctor teased that the rest of him was on the downhill slide, but he had the heart of a racehorse.

Aggie chose the oldest of the nurses at the desk, though she couldn't be a day over thirty-five. The printing on the photo ID clipped to her scrub top was too tiny to read. Most things were these days.

"Excuse me, miss. My name is Agatha Franks, Casper Wetherby's fiancée."

The nurse's smile wedded sympathy with empathy. "When I saw you visiting him yesterday, I assumed you were his wife."

Just goes to show how carefully you read the charts, Aggie thought.

"I'm so sorry for your loss, Ms. Franks. Mr. Wetherby was such a sweet man."

Two other nurses behind the desk nodded agreement.

"Yes, he…was." Referring to Casper in past tense seemed strangely disloyal, as though the difference between life and death was a small matter of using the appropriate verb.

Aggie gripped the edge of the counter, its laminate surface cool against her palm. "I wanted to thank you all for the care and kindness you gave him, and to—" Her breath and her courage faltered. Summoning both, she finished "—to fill out whatever forms are needed to order an autopsy."

A gasp from behind her told Aggie that Jenna was

as shocked by the request as the nurses exchanging leery glances. A sensation akin to an adrenaline rush squared Aggie's shoulders. "I understand that the official cause of Mr. Wetherby's death will be noted as heart failure, in some form or fashion. At best, that's purely speculation.

"If that was the cause, I believe his daughter and grandsons deserve specifics, for health insurance reasons, if nothing else. In the event a postmortem points to something else, they deserve to know that, as well."

Several seconds passed before the nurse recovered her voice. Her tone was compassionate yet firm. "Ms. Franks, I realize Mr. Wetherby's passing is a terrible shock to you, but at his age—"

"Age, my foot. The man was admitted with a fractured hip and died of heart failure? I want to know how one led to the other." Aggie's eyes narrowed. "Don't *you?* And if not, why not? Good heavens, it might help in treating another patient with the same condition."

Over Aggie's shoulder the nurse telegraphed a visual appeal to Jenna.

"C'mon, Mom. Let's go home."

Aggie jerked away from the hand Jenna laid on her arm. "Stop patronizing me, the both of you. I'm not in shock and I'm not an addled old lady. I want what I want. If I have to, I'll go to the hospital's administrator to get it."

When Aggie pulled into the SeaShell Motor Court's parking lot, Paul Haggerty was shifting luggage around in the trunk of his rented Chevy. He must have recognized the tinny gallop of the Volkswagen's engine, for he straightened, his head turning and body following volte-face. Dark-tinted sunglasses hid his eyes, but the hand thrust in his khakis' pocket said he'd hoped for a clean getaway and would now have to explain himself.

A Beetle doesn't have the tightest turning radius, but wheeling into a smooth wide arc brought it to a T behind the Lumina's rear bumper. Aggie switched off the ignition and cranked down the window a few inches.

"Get in, Paul. We need to talk."

"Aggie, I—"

"Do as you're told, young man. I don't have time to argue."

He squinted at the traffic passing by on Commercial Street, heaved a sigh, then rounded the front of the car, fingers raking his hair like a kid sent to the principal's office.

The Volkswagen tilted sideward when he slid into the passenger seat. The door he left open, one foot planted on the concrete-slab lot. "I'm sorry, Aggie, but there's nothing you can say to change my—"

"Casper passed away this morning." Bluntness somehow dulled the pain of saying it aloud.

The news stunned Paul. The car door closed with a soft thump. Swiveling toward her, he pushed his sunglasses atop his head and lifted her hand from the gearshift knob. "Oh, Aggie, I thought he was… Yesterday afternoon he was *joking* with me…."

He squinted out the windshield, as if expecting Casper to jump out from behind the cabin, laughing at the trick he'd played. "I know he'd had some rough patches, but he seemed to be doing all right, considering."

"That's what I came here to talk to you about," Aggie said. "They're trying to tell me his heart gave out."

Paul's cocked eyebrow relayed the obvious response.

"No, I don't believe it," she said. "The monitor he was wired to was as steady as a rock. I know what those readings mean because I've been hooked up to plenty of them."

By his expression, Paul was framing a reply that wouldn't sound condescending or insulting.

She chuckled without humor. "I guess you'll have to trust me on this, but I'm not plotting a murder mystery to take my mind off losing the love of my life. Bear in mind, Casper and I have been together for over ten years. I know that man, inside and out, the same as he knows me. If they were blaming anything other than his heart, I'd believe it, but that's nothing but a catchall to write on a death certificate."

"Have you talked to Jenna about this?"

"Yes." Aggie looked down to smooth the wrinkles from her slacks. "She thinks I'm having a breakdown. So does Kaiser McMillan, the hospital's administrator." Aggie pinched a speck of lint, pretending it was McMillan's fat head, which bore a striking resemblance to the roll that shared his first name. "McMillan said when hospital deaths occur, only the next of kin can request an autopsy, and that if I had any idea what one entailed, I wouldn't wish a postmortem on my worst enemy."

Her eyes raised to meet Paul's. "Casper didn't die of natural causes. I won't waste my breath asking Vinita to authorize an autopsy, but it's a dishonor to his memory not to try and find out the truth."

Down the way, a cabin's screen door slapped shut. From the street, a note of carbon monoxide drifted into the car, along with snatches of rap music and a screeching fan belt. Aggie's mouth tasted foul. Swallowing didn't help.

Paul had shilly-shallied long enough. She broke the heavy silence with "I can't say I recall much about you from way back when, but you were an NYPD detective and a good one, or my son-in-law wouldn't have taken you under his wing."

Paul smiled. "He had to. Training whiteshields was part of Rick's job. His least favorite, I might add."

"He didn't have to take you home with him. Treat you like family. You weren't just another rookie, Paul. You were Rick's friend. And Jenna's."

He flinched. "That's a damn low blow."

"Not as low as walking into the hospital and being told Casper was dead and that his daughter was making a beeline to the mortuary to pick out his casket."

That got his attention, but not for long. "Vinita is as obnoxious as they come, but from that to harming her father is an awfully big leap."

"Fine. Prove it. I'll pay whatever you ask."

He shook his head.

"If this podunk town had a private-detective agency, I'd be there instead of here," Aggie said. "But it doesn't and I have nowhere else to turn."

"Your grandson's a cop."

"My grandson is my grandson. How much credence do you have with your family? How much do you give your family?" She shrugged. "Jane Doe, he'd listen to. *Vinita,* he'd listen to. But his kooky ol' grandma? Not a chance."

Paul's face was stony, his tone as chill as the draft seeping through the floorboard. "I'd like to help but I can't. You of all people should know why."

"Because of Jenna?" Aggie tossed her head. "This is between you and me. It has nothing to do with her."

"Aw c'mon, Aggie. I've hurt her enough, for God's sake. How do you think she'll react when she finds out you asked me to stay and look into Casper's death?"

"*I don't care.*" Hot tears sprang into Aggie's eyes. "For once I'm putting *myself* first. What *I* care about. What *I* feel is the right thing to do. What I need for my *own* peace of mind."

The shrill, desperate pitch to her voice seemed to redouble, amplified by the car's close confines. An achy pressure beneath her breastbone radiated to her left shoulder. A tab of digitalis would relieve it. So might unleashing the hurts and resentments stacked one atop another like bricks in a fortress wall.

"For twenty-three years, I've done everything in my power to keep my daughter and my grandson safe and happy. It was my choice. I'd make it again if I had to, but in all that time not a day has gone by that I don't wonder if Jimmy ever came home, needing help, needing his mother, his sister, and found strangers living in the house he was raised in.

"Jenna thinks she knows how it felt to choose her and Sam over Jimmy. She doesn't. No one does, or can. I'm not always aware of it, but I look for Jimmy in every man I pass on the street, every face the TV cameras pan at ball games, or crowd scenes, or on the news. Then it hits me that I'm praying to see a lanky, frizzy-haired sixteen-year-old boy, not a fifty-two-year-old man. God forgive me, I'm not sure I'd recognize my own son if I saw him.''

Aggie massaged the inside of her forearm, then surrendered and fumbled in her purse for her medication. Paul took the pill bottle from her hand and opened it for her.

''Angina?'' he asked.

''Um. From hypertrophic cardiomyopathy. That's longhand for a bum ticker.'' Aggie slipped the tiny tablet under her tongue. ''Had it all my life. The doctor warned me not to have any more babies after Jimmy, but, well, in those days, accidents happened.'' She smiled. ''Especially when you didn't do anything to prevent one.''

''My dad had cardiomyopathy, too. The docs implanted a pacemaker.'' Paul's eyes said the procedure was too little too late.

''Then you know what stress did to his blood pressure.''

A wry grin tipped a corner of Paul's mouth. ''They say when it comes to laying on the guilt, every mother is a Jewish mother.''

Aggie batted the air. ''Rank amateurs compared to a lapsed Catholic.''

''Yeah.'' The pill bottle rattled into her open purse. ''All right. Two days. If I don't come up with anything conclusive by then, I'll have a plane to catch.''

Relief felt like champagne bubbles sprinting up a flute. Saying thank-you was a woeful inadequacy. She hadn't simply asked a favor, she'd asked him to spend another forty-eight hours in Jenna's world—one where he was no longer welcome.

As though he could read her mind, he said, ''I

won't help you behind Jenna's back.'' He pulled the door lever. ''Both of you are hurting, and it'll only make everything worse, but you have to tell her.''

''I know.'' Aggie fired up the *rat-a-tat* engine. ''I should probably be ashamed to say this, but I'd rather fight with my daughter than think about never having Casper to bicker with again. Funny, but that's one of the things I'll miss most.'' Tears blurred her vision. ''We were so *good* at it.''

Paul levered himself from the small car, then paused before closing the Beetle's door. ''Are you okay to drive home?''

She nodded. The nitro hadn't kicked in yet, but it would within the hour. There was no magic pill for rattling around in a house that wouldn't ever feel quite as bright or cozy or full again.

14

The parade of casseroles and coffee cakes began an hour before Jenna pulled into her mother's driveway. No point in asking how the sad news had spread so quickly. It always did.

Since then there'd been no time, no privacy, for a mother-daughter talk. Knowing a catfight would ensue if Aggie went to the funeral home, she'd sent Jenna to "help" Vinita with the arrangements. Civility had prevailed, but the ordeal had been exhausting. Jenna wasn't eager to divulge Vinita's plans for Cappy's funeral. She kept reminding herself that the woman had just lost her father, and that everyone grieved differently and shouldn't be criticized for anything they do at a time like this, but it sure seemed as if Vinita couldn't get Casper in the ground fast enough.

Maybe with haste would come closure. Just thinking it reminded Jenna how much she despised that word. Intentional or not, it alluded to some kind of emotional heart surgery. Stitch up the wounds, give the patient a little time to recuperate and, voilà, you're as good as new, so get on with your life.

One look at her son, and Jenna almost wished it were possible. A domestic disturbance had kept him on duty well after the 7:00 a.m. shift change. He'd then raced home to climb into a suit to testify at a drug possession trial.

Sam's weary head had barely creased the pillow when Jenna knocked on the apartment door. When she told him about Casper, he'd sunk onto the arm of a chair, his head shaking and his features contorted.

Feeling more helpless than she had in years, Jenna just stood beside him, kneading the shoulder of the heartbroken boy embodied in a big, tough guy who pulled mangled bodies from wrecked cars and subdued drunks and dopers spoiling for a fight.

Now Sam was sitting with Aggie on the living-room couch, holding her hand, not ashamed to let her and everyone else see the tears in his eyes. "Take it like a man," Earl Bukowski had snarled when Jimmy's best friend died of leukemia. "Cryin' ain't gonna bring him back."

"Big boys don't cry," Rick had chastised when two-year-old Robby fell and split open his lip on the coffee table.

Bullshit. Jenna's disgust held heartache in check for a moment. Whoever came up with that law of masculine behavior probably invented the rule of thumb, too. A real man sheds no tears and never beats his wife with a stick thicker than his thumb.

Too many still adhered to one or both of those idiotic ideas. Thank God Sam MacArthur wasn't one of them.

Casper had been a grandpa to him, taken Sam fishing, taught him to tie his shoes, then a necktie, and was front and center at every school play, choir recital and sporting event. He could whittle Sam down to size, though, if need be, even after the kid shot up a foot in height and outweighed Casper by a hundred pounds.

Jenna grinned at the memory of eavesdropping on the birds-and-bees talk Casper took it upon himself to have with Sam. After a droning lecture on biology with an emphasis on the aquatic abilities of tadpoles, Casper said, "All you really gotta remember, son, is that any girl that'll let you hit a home run has likely had more at-bats than Babe Ruth."

A long silence had ended with a stammered, "S-so, I'm not s'posed to like girls that play baseball?"

Casper had hemmed, then hawed, then blurted, "Just keep your dick in your pants till after the wedding and you won't have a thing to worry about."

Not the worst advice a boy could be given, but Jenna had expanded on the concept later that evening.

The procession of neighbors and friends continued. At times the living room was packed with people who couldn't stay but wanted to tell Aggie how sorry they were about Casper, and about relatives for whom fractured hips had also proven fatal, and to remind her how much worse and prolonged the ordeal would have been had he contracted cancer or had a stroke, and weren't the two of them lucky to have found each other and had so many good years together.

Jenna fled to the kitchen as often as social grace allowed. The outpouring of kindness was truly wonderful, but dear Lord, her overhugged body was as sore as a newborn subjected to too much handling. With each "How are you doin', hon?" it was becoming harder to lie.

Fists planted on either side of the sink, she looked

out the window at her mother's withering flower and vegetable gardens. Bird feeders swung like cradles from boughs stripped to their leafy orange and yellow skivvies. Jenna's nose wrinkled. The cinnamon scent wafting from a bundt cake on the counter could be associated with a hundred things other than hot spiced cider, grizzle-bearded musicians playing "The Tune the Old Cow Died On" in Frisco Park's gazebo and strolling hand in hand in the autumn sunshine with Paul Haggerty.

Damn it. She was supposed to be mourning Cappy, not a love affair that was nearer a ménage à trois. She wasn't Liz Rivas and glad of it. Rebirth in the WITSEC program landfilled a ton of battered, excess baggage.

She sure as hell wasn't twenty-five anymore, either. Didn't want to be, thank you very much. Who'd want to reverse the calendar and make the same stupid mistakes again, which she no doubt would. Human nature was too hopeful, too prone to believe second chances promised different outcomes. If that were true, why did history constantly repeat itself?

"Jenna?" Her mother's voice implied a reluctance to intrude on private thoughts. "How are you doing, sweetheart?"

"I'm fine." Jenna smiled at the conditioned response. Turning from the window, she reached out her hand. "Plenty of room in my hiding place for another refugee, though."

Aggie sighed. "I shouldn't, but that is what I feel like. Everyone is being so sweet, but all of a sudden I just had to get away. Catch my breath a minute."

Those unaware of her heart condition would assume the spots of color at her cheeks was a healthy glow. Jenna knew it had been chemically induced. Aggie's respiration didn't appear to be labored and she was steady on her feet, but brave fronts are heavy to hold up for hours on end.

"Why don't you take a nap, Mom. Let Sam and me do the meeting and greeting for a while."

"Good idea," Sam said as he lumbered into the kitchen, "except I have to catch some z's myself. My head's buzzing so loud it sounds like a 757 coming in for a landing."

He took a plastic tumbler from the cabinet for a drink of water. Leaving the faucet running, he emptied the glass, then set it aside to splash water on his face. "Gotta be back at the cop shop at oh-fifteen-hundred."

Jenna bristled. "Not after a death in the family you don't. Even cops get time off for that."

Sam glanced at Aggie, then slanted a significant look at his mother. "Matt Lorge's, uh, wife is sick. We already traded rosters so he could go to his daughter's dance recital." He swiped his dripping chin with a kitchen towel. "And Matt did cover for me when I was at Quantico."

"But—" Jenna's brain finally received the message. In the police chief's eyes, Casper Wetherby wasn't a family member. "I'm sorry, Sam," she could hear him say when her son spoke to him earlier. "Everybody in town knows how much ol' Casper meant to you. If I wasn't short on manpower, I could finagle the schedule, but you know the bind I'm in."

"It's all right, Sam," Aggie said. "It would be silly for you to miss work. I love you to pieces, but I don't need a baby-sitter."

The comment's aim wasn't exclusive to her grandson. Jenna started to argue, then decided to save it for later. If her mother wouldn't come home with her, Jenna would bunk here the next few nights. Aggie might be perfectly fine by herself, but Jenna wouldn't be able to sleep for worrying about her.

On that thought trailed a fleeting image of her garage's transformation into private, stone's-throw quarters for her mother. Winter was just around the corner and Aggie didn't realize that she and Casper had been as mutually reliant as rain and a rainbow.

No more than Jenna had considered how personally liberating their twosomeness had been. Or how much she'd taken it for granted.

Sam hugged his grandmother to his side and kissed the top of her head. "Promise you'll page me if you need anything."

Aggie nodded.

"I'll come by when I'm out on patrol. Provided it's as quiet as I expect it'll be tonight, I'll get rid of some of this food for you."

"Before you go," Jenna began, thinking *and can easily restrain your grandma when she swears she'll kill Vinita with her bare hands,* "the memorial service is set for eleven o'clock tomorrow morning."

"What!" Aggie said. "Tomorrow?" Sam's hold on Aggie did tighten a bit. "Why didn't you say something before now? I've been telling everyone the funeral would be the day *after* tomorrow at the earliest."

"Calm down, Mom. I stalled because I knew you'd be upset, but there's no sense getting all worked up about it. There's nothing we can do to change it."

"Want to bet?" Aggie pushed off Sam's chest and stomped to the wall-mounted phone above the breakfast bar. "This is Casper's funeral, not Vinita's—though that could be arranged real lickety-damn-split."

Jenna's fingers splayed over the hooked receiver. Her mother hadn't heard the worst of it yet. "Mom, please. The last thing Casper would want is you and his daughter fighting over him like this."

"She's right," Sam said. "Vinita can't disappoint Casper anymore, and she can't hurt you unless you let her."

Aggie looked from one to the other as if they were the enemy.

"How many people do you think have made condolence calls at Vinita's house today?" Jenna asked. "Some, I'm sure, since she *is* his daughter, but his friends and lodge buddies and your friends and neighbors came here. That's what matters. Not Vinita's petty one-upmanship."

Aggie's expression reflected grudging agreement. "Go on. Tell me the rest. I know there's more."

Jenna's hand slid from the phone. "No visitation at Tuft's this evening. Tomorrow will be a memorial service, not a funeral. Vinita's sister-in-law will sing 'What a Friend We Have in Jesus' and 'The Old Rugged Cross.'"

Aggie harrumphed. "That girl couldn't carry a tune in a bucket." Her eyes narrowed. "Sam better be one of the pallbearers or I will snatch Vinita bald-headed."

Jenna glanced at her son, then shook her head. "There won't be any pallbearers. Vinita is having

Casper cremated. She and Eugene and their sons plan to scatter the ashes in Park Lake.''

Sam broke the tense silence with ''I think Casper would like that. We sure pulled a lug of catfish and crappie out of that old sinkhole.''

Aggie's lips pursed and twisted. Other than the mouth movement, she was eerily motionless, staring straight through her daughter to a farm on the north side of town.

''Casper said he'd rather be thrown overboard from a barge trussed up in log chains than be cremated. He never said why, but the very idea gave him goose bumps. Vinita knew that. He told her he didn't care if he was buried in a cardboard box, as long as he went into the ground whole.''

Of course she knew. So did Kenneth, Ken and Kenny Tufts, the lineal morticians whose family had less imagination than the Pfisters. The bottom line was the bottom line for Vinita Potts: crematorium fees were cheaper than caskets and the attending expenses of a traditional funeral service.

''You tried your best, sweetheart,'' Aggie said. ''Vinita wouldn't have honored Casper's wishes for anyone.'' She removed the phone book from a drawer and opened it. ''The question is, why?''

Jenna watched her thumb the flimsy Yellow Pages. ''Because she's spiteful and money-grubbing and had no respect for her father.''

Sam grunted. ''For what it's worth, I don't think it's that personal. This is the first taste of power over anything Vinita's ever had and, oh man, it is sweet. Eugene's henpecked, but make no mistake, he rules the roost.''

''Uh-huh. Well, I think your bachelor's degree in

psychology is showing," Aggie said. "It's personal all right. It doesn't get any more personal than this."

She uncradled the receiver and punched the seven digits in the phone book underlined with a fingernail.

Jenna squinted a square black-bordered advertisement into focus, but not its contents. "Who are you calling?"

"Yes—cabin number four, please," Aggie said into the phone.

What the hell was going on? That was Paul Haggerty's cabin number at the SeaShell Motor Court. Last night, he'd left a message on Jenna's answering machine, saying he was leaving town this morning for his flight back to Baltimore—as though she'd better get with the kiss-and-make-up program or forever hold her peace.

"He isn't? When he gets in, tell him to call Agatha Franks immediately. He has the number. Thank you."

Aggie hung up the phone, then faced her audience, nose atilt and eyebrows arced in a classic, preemptive *Don't you dare give me any crap about this.* "Paul Haggerty has agreed to delve deeper into the cause of Casper's death."

Sam muttered something under his breath.

Aggie's gaze shifted to Jenna. "It was my idea, not Paul's. If he doesn't find anything substantial in forty-eight hours, like he said, he'll have a plane to catch."

Growling through clenched teeth like a large dog on a short leash, Jenna winged her arms over her head lest it explode all over her mother's immaculate kitchen. "So that's what your scene at the hospital was all about. Why you demanded an autopsy. No doubt it was your idea, but Paul jumped at the chance to be your white knight with a spyglass, now, didn't he?''

''No, he most assuredly did not.''

Sam planted his hands on his hips. ''How's about one of you bringing me up to speed.''

''Your grandmother thinks Vinita murdered Cappy.''

''Yeah, right.''

''She does. Ask her.''

Aggie's glare was defiant not defensive. ''Those mother-son smirks are precisely why I went to Paul for help. He doesn't think of me as a brainless old fool.''

''Grandma...''

''There's nothing wrong with wanting to *know* if there could be a reason, other than vindictiveness, for Vinita to restrict visiting hours. Or why Casper's sinking spells were always at night, never in the daytime, even though he was more active then.

''Was it just a coincidence that he fell ill after Vinita's late-night visits? Could be, but why did she visit so late in the first place? When we were in the waiting room after the accident, she whined about it being past her bedtime.

''Then there's the odd fact that no one—not the nurses, or his doctors—expressed any concerns about Casper's heart, and not a single cardiac-related test was ordered.''

The look on Sam's face mirrored Jenna's own. The points Aggie cited were on the thin side, but deserving of answers.

''Finally,'' Aggie said, ''tight-fisted or not, why did Vinita demand that Casper be cremated and rush the services so fast? Her sons can't possibly be here in time. After all, she craves attention. A lot of what she draws is negative, but like a five-year-old child, the wrong kind beats none at all. It makes no sense for her not to play the grief-stricken daughter to the hilt.''

Jenna thought back to pizza-and-beer dinners when Rick and Paul lobbed a case's what-ifs and riddle-me-thises in two-heads-are-better-than-one fashion. The process was fascinating to watch and listen to, and an advanced course in detective-style qualitative analysis. She knew she'd graduated from observer to practitioner when she started applying deductive reasoning to traffic accidents and purse snatchings.

Sam said, ''Why didn't you ask me to check this stuff out instead of running to Haggerty? Great time to find out you've got more confidence in a stranger who isn't even a cop than you do in me.''

''Trust has nothing to do with it. I already told you, I didn't think you or your mother would take me seriously. Plus, there are advantages to Paul being a regular Joe.''

Jenna coughed into her fist to camouflage a laugh. Now there's a good one. And told with a straight face, no less.

Aggie went on, ''You can't question anyone officially, or the chief will have your head on a platter. Unofficially won't fly, either. Everyone knows you're a cop *and* my grandson. Somebody's sure to tattle to Vinita about you snooping around, just for the entertainment value.''

Sam cocked his jaw. His thoughts were as legible as a billboard to Jenna, for hers echoed them. Aggie was on a roll. Her doubts regarding Casper's death were as valid as her take on the official and civilian reaction to the only known cop in the family moonlighting as a P.I.

Pfister hadn't had a scandal with a drop of juice in it for years. One hint of suspicion about Vinita committing patricide and the hills would be alive with the sound of wagging tongues. Amazing how Paul "Ace Supercop" Haggerty had hung around town long enough to become the right man, in the right place, at the right time.

15

The law office was a renovated double storefront in the older section of Pfister. Serious money had been invested to sandblast the grime off the building's block-stone and brick facade to revive its mellow patina.

Snow-bright enamel set off the trimwork. Window boxes planted in some species of dwarf-spreading evergreen exuded a spicy, never-ending Christmas aroma. Painted in arched, Old English gold lettering on the door's opaque frosted glass was Steven W. Abernathy, Barrister.

Paul Haggerty turned the shiny brass knob and stepped inside, not at all surprised to find a continuance of the turn-of-the-century theme. He supposed the pretty brunette seated behind the reception desk had drawn the line at wearing corsets and a green eyeshade.

A request to speak with Barrister Abernathy in regard to Casper Wetherby got Paul ushered into a wood-paneled anteroom adjacent to Abernathy's office. Instead of magazines, there were books ranging from the classics to current thrillers and romances available to shorten the wait. Several copies were marked with strips of cloth from the basket on the coffee table. All of Pat Conroy's novels to date were represented, but there wasn't a Grisham in sight.

Paul grinned. He'd heard that medical professionals didn't fall over themselves to join Robin Cook's fan club, either. Whether from envy or reluctance to engage in a literary busman's holiday, he wasn't sure.

The man who threw open the door to the inner sanctum could have played center for Yale's basketball team. His high, wide forehead and quicksilver eyes said he'd captained the debate team instead.

Paul declined Abernathy's offer of coffee and seated himself in a leather wing chair on the client side of the desk. The lawyer drew himself a refill from a silver-plated urn on the credenza, then settled in a tall-backed swivel chair worn dull at the arms and headrest.

"I was sorry to hear about Casper," he said. "He was a little demanding at times, but a role model for growing old gracefully."

Paul agreed. "When did you last speak with him?"

"On the phone, last week sometime, though he called the office about every other day. In person, not for a month or so. Why?"

"I'm told he had an appointment scheduled with you yesterday."

Abernathy's eyes flicked to the desk calendar. He nodded. "If you're concerned about me sending a bill for failing to cancel, I assure you, there won't be one." A smile subtracted ten years from his face. "I know the old boy called me a shyster and worse, but I'm a tad higher up on the legal food chain than that."

"Are you acquainted with Aggie Franks?"

"Oh, yes. Casper's match and then some." The lawyer sighed. "She must be devastated. I'll never understand why she wouldn't marry him, but I'm sure she's heartbroken."

"Aggie accepted his proposal at dinner the night he fell. The wedding was to be in mid-December."

"God love 'em." Abernathy sat back in the chair, his long, slender fingers curled over the arms. "I don't know who you are, or why you're here, but if it's to take the 'Thank God' out of 'It's Friday,' you're doing a fine job."

"If you'll answer a couple more questions, I'll get to the who and the why."

"Shoot."

"Did Casper have a will?"

"Yes."

"Who's the executor?"

Abernathy hesitated, though the answer was a matter of public record. "I am."

Neither man spoke for several seconds. The attorney was as adept at the silent treatment as Paul was, only he decided the standoff was unnecessary. "Casper wanted Aggie as his personal representative, but I talked him out of it. Her age and health were factors, but I told him that his daughter, Vinita Potts, would raise unholy hell, and it wasn't fair to put Aggie through that when he wasn't here to intervene."

By law, the probate court, an estate's representative and its attorney-of-record received percentages of its valuation, yet Paul was certain Steven Abernathy had acted in his client's best interests, rather than positioning himself to collect two fees instead of one.

"Who did Casper bequeath his property's mineral rights to?"

"Ah-ah-ah… That's three questions."

Paul chuckled, then related a selective résumé of his background, adding that he'd known Aggie for better than twenty years. It wasn't a total fabrication. He'd certainly known *of* her for that long.

"Last week," he continued, "Casper told me all about the lawsuit against the hotel chain—just before he tried to sell me the Bentley."

"You're kidding me." Abernathy unlocked a bottom desk drawer. A sheet of paper bordered in green scrollwork sailed toward Paul like a rectangular Frisbee. "He signed the car's title over to me six months ago, in lieu of payment for services. I've kept the insurance up on it, with him as primary driver, and told him we could settle up after the suit was finalized."

"Well, I'll be damned." Paul returned the title to its rightful owner. "No wonder he didn't take me up on pretty much the same deal."

"Knowing Casper, I'm kind of surprised he didn't. Not that he wasn't as honest as the day is long. Just desperate. I haven't billed him for a lot of the hours I've spent on his case, but I can't afford to work pro bono."

"Yeah, but my second suggestion was to barter the car for the money he owed you," Paul said. "He told me Tuesday night, that's why he made the appointment for Thursday—to see if you'd go along."

"Hmph. I have no idea why he went on lying through his dentures. To save face would be my best guess, but Thursday's appointment was for a meeting with the motel chain's attorneys.''

''To settle the lawsuit?''

Abernathy spread his hands. ''That was their intent. Except Casper wouldn't have accepted the fifty grand they were going to offer. He couldn't. He had to have a hundred, minimum, to pay off the bank loan against his house and buy back his car.''

''I know Casper was holding out for a quarter million, but do you think they'd have ever gone as high as a hundred large?''

The attorney shook his head. ''I can't say for certain, but I think fifty was the limit. Budget Zzz's wants to build on that corner of the interchange. Their bean counters predict a higher traffic volume than on the opposite side, though how those numbers are crunched is beyond me.

''At this point, timing is key. The development must be up and running when the new highway opens in April, but they aren't willing to pay two hundred and fifty thousand for the privilege. Not when they've already shelled out four times that to build an access road and have an option to buy the adjacent parcel for forty.''

Paul whistled backward. ''It would take a helluva lot of sleepy tourists and truck drivers to amortize a million and a quarter, plus construction costs.''

''Yep. A bad winter or a hike in interest rates could eat their lunch in a hurry, too.''

''Which brings me back to question three. Who did Casper bequeath the mineral rights to?''

The attorney's pen tapped a drum solo on the desk blotter. ''I wish I could tell you it was Aggie.''

''Meaning it's Vinita.''

"'Fraid so." He dropped the pen and winged his arms behind his head.

"Does she know she's the beneficiary?"

"Uh-huh. Thanks to another terrific piece of advice Casper ignored. Funny how, despite all evidence to the contrary, parents cling to the notion that with enough incentive, a pain-in-the-ass kid will suddenly metamorphose into a kind, loving human being, instead of continuing as the resentful, spoiled brat he or she has been for his or her entire life."

The phone intervened before Paul could reply. Abernathy signaled *Hold that thought,* then kept up his end of the call with a series of "Uh-huhs" and "Yeahs" before closing with, "Let me get back to you on that, okay?"

He apologized unnecessarily for the interruption, paused to jot down a note on a legal pad, then said, "Casper was big on the rights staying in the family, but from the day he told Vinita the terms of his will, she harped at him to close the deal with Budget Zzz's."

"Did he carry life insurance?"

"Casper called it death insurance."

Paul grinned. "He would."

"He had a small policy years ago, then dropped it when Vinita turned twenty-one. By then, she and Eugene were married and their second child was on the way."

"Eugene's family, Eugene's responsibility."

"Exactly."

"Did Casper leave Aggie anything?"

"The rights to all past and pending patents he'd filed." Abernathy shrugged. "Hey, everybody thought the guy that invented Velcro was loony, too.

How would you like to have been willed those patent rights?

"Aggie also inherits the house, except she cosigned a loan against it—which I had no knowledge of until after the fact. She'll have to sell it to repay back the bank, but better that than Vinita holding the deed and leaving Aggie holding the bag."

"Oh, God." Paul rolled his eyes. "What a convoluted, train wreck of a mess that would've been."

"I get a headache just thinking about it." Abernathy went on, "Other than a few specific bequests, the house's contents go to Vinita, who can sell them to pay off most, if not all, of her father's outstanding credit card debt.

"As for me, I get the Bentley and a percentage of an estate the court will itemize in red ink."

Paul reviewed the day's two conversations with Aggie. The first in the motor court's parking lot and the phone call he'd returned when she told him of Vinita's decision to have Casper cremated.

"Correct me if I'm wrong, Steven, and I sincerely hope I am, but if I follow you, Vinita stands to collect a fast fifty grand from the hotel people for the mineral rights to Casper's property."

"That's about the size of it, yes."

"What about the lawsuit?"

"The plaintiff is deceased."

"So, the transfer of the mineral rights to Vinita—"

"Automatic. She wasn't party to the action filed by her father. If she wants to tie up Budget Zzz's in court, she'll need a brand-new rope. And a brand-new attorney."

Paul's eyebrow crimped. "She won't."

"No way, Jose. I expect the 50K has been accepted, the right's assignment to be formalized the second that probate signs off on the estate and earthmovers to start doing their thing by daybreak Monday."

Paul's finger traced a weathered crease in the armrest. "Aggie called me an hour or so ago. Said Vinita directed the funeral home to have Casper cremated."

"Why, that little—" A hand rose. "That's the last thing Casper wanted and I do mean *last.* Aggie put her foot down, I'll bet. On Vinita's neck, preferably."

"She can't. She isn't his next of kin." Paul let that sink in a moment. "She doesn't think Vinita did it just to save a few bucks on the funeral."

"What other reason would..." The lawyer's mouth flattened. "Wait a sec. Casper passed away in the hospital."

"And other than a couple of nurses and an intern, Vinita Potts was the last person to see him alive."

Paul didn't realize the siren's warning was for him until the Chevy Caprice's grill lamps and light bar filled his rearview mirror and stayed there.

The speedometer read two clicks past forty. He couldn't have been going over forty-three, even if reflex had backed his foot off the accelerator before he checked the dial.

Paul pulled to the curb but left the engine running. Wrists balanced atop the steering wheel, he waited as Sam MacArthur took his sweet time reciting the Lumina's plate number to Dispatch. Gee, wouldn't his daddy be proud?

Well, truth be told, he would. Rick Rivas wasn't

a hotshot ego junkie, but when the occasion arose to throw a little weight around, Rick's lips had always peeled back in a gleeful leer.

"Evenin', Mr. Haggerty."

Back to that, are we? Paul's chin bobbed. "Officer MacArthur."

From Paul's seated perspective, Jenna's son did an exceptional job of looking ten feet tall and bullet-proof. The Kevlar vest expanded Sam's chest measurement an easy six inches, and his midnight-blue uniform, wide Sam Browne belt and holstered Glock 9mm lent a certain je ne sais quoi.

"Mind shutting off the engine, sir?"

As he complied, Paul surmised the request was procedural not grandstanding. Complacency hadn't set in yet. Good. It was every cop's public enemy number one. There was no such thing as a routine traffic stop. Routine anything, for that matter. Thinking of a call as the same old, same old was a common cause of twenty-one-gun salutes.

"I need to see your driver's license, please."

"Okay." Paul hesitated before reaching into his jacket's inner pocket. "Just going for my wallet, Officer."

"No problem, sir."

It would have been had Paul worn a shoulder holster instead of an ankle one. Missouri wasn't a concealed-carry state. Even if it were, cops weren't keen on the idea of John Q. Public having firepower at its fingertips.

Sam read Paul's operator's license and social security number into the mike clipped to his shirt epaulet. The transmission finished with the dispatcher's staticky "Stand by."

Enough was enough. Paul said, "I wasn't speeding."

"I never said you were, Mr. Haggerty."

"Then what was your probable cause for a traffic stop?" Paul's smile was no more friendly than Sam's tone. "You work with law enforcement on every level from municipal to military to federal and you pick up the lingo."

He waved at the rear of Paul's sedan. "I saw your left taillight flickering. There's water sloshing around inside the case. Probably a break in the seal."

Paul had noticed the water that morning when he was packing the trunk. He wouldn't stake his life on it fritzing the taillight, but there was no question about the stop being legitimate.

"The Feds, huh. What branch?"

"All of them, except the Coast Guard and the INS."

Sam's utility belt cricketed as though it were his stomach digesting the information. "I can't imagine a busy guy like you taking the time to nose around this burg just because a sweet old lady asked you to."

The motivation had a quart of selfish mixed in, of which Sam was certainly aware. "I wouldn't for just any sweet old lady. Your grandmother is special."

And so is your mother. More so than you may ever know, kid.

Dispatch relayed the disappointing report that Paul's license was valid and there were no wants or warrants outstanding on him. As if that were news to Officer MacArthur. No doubt he'd already run checks through every law enforcement database, including Interpol.

He handed back Paul's ID. "I'd advise you to have that taillight repaired before you hit the highway for Kansas City."

"I would, if it was my vehicle. I'll contact the rental company, but I don't expect they'll authorize the repair."

"Suit yourself." Sam tipped the brim of his campaign hat. "Just don't be surprised if you get pulled over again, sir. Our department prides itself on bringing safety issues to drivers' attention."

It was a great line. Considerably more subtle than Clint Eastwood's "Feelin' lucky?" Paul leaned his head out the window. "How many officers are there on the payroll?"

"Eighteen. Three are detectives, though." Sam flashed a grin so like Jenna's, it hurt. "Oh, and one's the chief of police."

The lovely, red-haired chief librarian had gone home before lunch, afraid she was coming down with a virus. Paul was sorry she'd taken ill, but it relieved him of hiding his activities from the eagle-eyed bibliophile.

The noncirculated reference books were again the sole providers of the materials he needed. A library aide, who resembled Britney Spears in every way other than wardrobe, granted him carte blanche access to the copying machines and saw no reason why he couldn't use the four-color model copier in Mrs. Haroldson's office, as well—provided he paid a dollar each for the privilege.

Its reproduction of his driver's license photo was slightly blurrier than the original. After he'd meticulously drawn on a pair of eyeglasses, the reproduction of the reproduction was the epitome of a career civil servant.

Next, he duplicated the appropriate pages of the annual Missouri State Directory through the black-and-white machines. Experimenting until the toner heightened the contrast and darkened the text to a bold crispness created a sheaf of dime-a-page rejects he'd later chuck in a fast-food restaurant's trash bin.

Then it was back to Mrs. Haroldson's office to copy the pertinent logo, an incorporation of a caduceus and scale of justice superimposed on a slate-blue, Missouri-shaped graphic.

A blank sheet of photocopy paper, a pair of scissors and a cellophane tape dispenser borrowed from Britney's doppelgänger were laid out on a corner table equipped with a gooseneck halogen lamp.

The cut-and-paste process was tedious. Sliver-thin lines of text that seemed straight as a die tilted a fraction left or right upon closer examination. When Paul finished what anyone other than a phony ID purveyor would call a work of art, the muscles and tendons in the back of his neck were as taut as bungee cords.

A final trip through the color photocopier produced a clear, official-looking photo ID for Wesley G. Felcher, a member of the Missouri Health Facilities Review Committee. The board's function had nothing whatsoever to do with Paul's objective, but the title sounded impressive as hell, and who, other than the committee's nine members, had a clue it existed?

From the library, Paul drove to a pharmacy to laminate his masterpiece, attach a clip-on lanyard and buy a cheap pair of horn-rim reading glasses similar to those he'd inked on the photo.

"Wesley, my man," he said, "you sure don't look much like Paul Haggerty. And if he does say so himself, Paul Haggerty has it all over you, bud."

16

The quilted furniture pad Jenna was using for a blanket smelled as if it had spent its life in the cargo bay of a seldom-vacuumed Ford Explorer.

Fancy that.

But it was warm and she'd already burned half a tank of gas running the engine for the heater, which was doubly stupid because she had no idea why she'd come here and parked under a sad-sack weeping willow to wait in the cold and the dark for a man she wished she'd never met—ever—let alone slept with, and who now wouldn't leave town so she could get on with her advertised fine and peaceful and organized life.

The motor court's sign, shaped like a broad-stroked 7, was corduroyed in yellow, hot pink, red and orange neon tubes. The S's in SeaShell were actually sea horses painted on the metal facade and outlined in marine-blue neon. The tall, angular relic was as bright and hopeful as the decade it represented. Even its constant electric hum was, well, electrifying, though it was beginning to sound as soothing as a lullaby.

About now, she supposed, Aggie was finishing her second bourbon and branch with Joyce Ramsour's mother. Barbara Johnson had arrived at the house armed with an overnight bag, her orthopedic pillow and no-prisoners attitude.

Barbara gave Jenna the up-and-down, scowled, then said, "Go home, feed that humane society you live with, snarf a carton of Dutch chocolate and hit the sack. I don't want to see you, or hear a peep out of you, until an hour before the funeral tomorrow."

"Yes, ma'am."

"Joyce and Barry will pick you up in the morning at ten sharp. Don't wear black. Memorial services should celebrate a life well lived. I can't imagine anything that'd piss off Casper more than everyone who loved him best looking like they'd just stopped by the mortuary on the way to the convent."

Barbara winked. "Leave *that* to Vinita. Five bucks says she'll have on a hat with a moth-eaten veil hanging down to her boobs. Last time I worked at the thrift shop, somebody'd donated three of those suckers."

Jenna blocked the image of Vinita dressed as Vampira, Queen of Darkness, with a mental note to buy the remaining two hats for the shop's vintage-clothing inventory.

MacArthur Perk would be closed all day Saturday in Cappy's honor. She'd have closed it today, if not for Mavis's common-sense argument that customers and other merchants would be calling and coming by to inquire after funeral arrangements, and whether flowers should be sent or donations made in Casper's name to a favorite charity.

"Thank God for Mavis Purvis," Jenna said for the umpteenth time. Without her, the shop would have permanently locked its doors years ago.

Any reasonably intelligent warm body could ring

up sales, answer the phone, keep the coffee urns full and fresh and the tables and flea-market inventory clean. Mavis possessed the rare ability to anticipate needs and meet them, no questions asked, no direction or permission required.

Nike only thought they invented Just Do It. Ha. The slogan was a marker in Mavis's DNA. She'd even managed to sweet-talk, wheedle or, more likely, strong-arm Tammy Zeman at the Feed & Seed into plunking down cash for that Jacobean davenport and club chairs she'd salivated all over for months.

As overcoming seemingly insurmountable obstacles was Mavis's metier, perhaps Jenna should have sicced her on Paul Haggerty. The streaming video of Mavis as John Wayne with a Stetson perched atop her magenta beehive, and long-barreled six-guns prodding Paul toward the city-limits sign, ended when Jenna vaulted bolt upright and conked her head on the Explorer's window molding.

The man leering at her through the passenger-side glass bounced her heart off the truck's roof. Yanking open the console's lid, the .38 was in her hand and swinging toward the window before her muzzy brain connected the face with a name.

"You son of a bitch!" In case he didn't hear her, she clicked on the Explorer's auxiliary power, pressed the electric window toggle and repeated herself.

His imbecilic grin undoubtedly masked raw terror. "My, what a big gun you have, my dear."

Jenna glowered at him, then burst out laughing. She couldn't help it. Couldn't stop. While inwardly cursing herself for being a Guinness record–size fool, she was a one-woman sitcom laugh track, chortling and hee-hawing till breathlessness called a halt.

She stowed the pistol in the console—after a fleeting thought of using it on one of them—then slid from the driver's seat still cocooned in the furniture pad. The adrenaline spike and comic release had leveled off and somehow strengthened the resolve that had brought her here. Now all she had to do was keep it from slipping. Or stand aside and let her inner alpha-chick shore it up if it tried.

Paul wisely kept a yard's distance between them. "I'm sorry. I just knocked on the window to get your attention. I didn't realize you were asleep."

"No problem. The .38 isn't loaded anyway." Paul's bemusement brought a "Hey, I used to be a cop, too. Guaranteed, no bullet in the magazine. I checked and test-fired it."

"Okay, but why carry an unloaded gun?"

"It's a deterrent." Jenna's shoulder hiked. "If you must know, it's about the only memento I have of my former life. I could load it fast enough if I had to, but it'd take a life-or-death scenario to make me use it."

Paul nodded. "Due to fallout in the form of too many questions. Starting with why the serial number traces to an NYPD patrol officer named Elizabeth Rivas."

"Yeah." She sneered. "The only woman you ever loved."

It was a cheap shot, but he took it without a flinch. Motioning at the cabin, he said, "Care to come in out of the cold?"

"No, thanks." It was no sooner said than the hot tea she'd sipped during the wait alerted her to a tactical error. Jenna sighed and gathered up the furniture pad like a Victorian-era skirt. "All right."

The cabin's interior proved that charm and economy of space weren't antonyms. From the double bed's fringed chenille spread to an avocado, single-door Frigidaire and gold-flecked vinyl sofa and chairs, it was the kind of place that you looked around and thought, by God, I could *live* here. Not only could, but *want* to. All I have to do is chuck 99.9 percent of a lifetime's accumulated crap and clutter, toss some clothes, toiletries and maybe a photo or two in the car and, ziggety bang, freedom's just another word for nothing much to dust.

"I'll put on some coffee," Paul said, rinsing the tinware four-cup pot. His gaze shifted to a closed, pine-paneled door. "It's in there."

The bathroom was tiny and showed its age, but was as clean as Ajax and Formula 409 could make it. Paul's razor, shaving cream, toothbrush and paste clung to the rim of the porcelain sink's backsplash. His shaving kit rested on the toilet tank's lid. Other than wicked-looking mustache scissors and a sealed box of condoms, the zippered cowhide pouch had nothing to hide.

Jenna returned to the main room and picked up the furniture pad from the floor. The impulse to wrap herself in it and take what she had to say back outside was as tempting as it was stupid. She folded the pad, laid it on the arm of the sofa and sat down.

Paul settled in one of the club chairs. "That stove is pretty much an Easy-Bake Oven with burners. It'll take a while for the coffee to percolate."

I'll be gone before it does. "You said you'd only stay in town as long as you were wanted. I didn't know that statement extended to include my mother.''

''It didn't, when I said it.'' He scrubbed his palms together. ''And you're the second person tonight to, shall we say, encourage me to hit the road.''

Jenna made a face. ''Sam.''

''In the flesh and in uniform. We parted company after he assured me that water in my taillight would continue to attract patrol units like catnip does cats.''

''Harassment. Pure and simple. Stand by for the saps and rubber hoses.''

No comment.

''Sam was hurt when Mom went running to you instead of him.''

''Understandable. I warned Aggie that he would be. I assume she told him or you or both why she came to me.''

''Yes, she did. I won't say her reasons were inarguable, but she didn't just act on impulse, either.''

''Then why are you—''

''You could have turned her down.''

''I did, Jenna. Several times. In the end, a two-day delay was all I agreed to.''

She scooted forward on the cushion. ''Then I expect you'll be heading out after the memorial service tomorrow.''

''Oh?''

''Vinita didn't kill her father.'' She stood.

Paul's head tipped back to look her in the eye. ''Probably not.''

The qualified agreement put a match to the one-act play Jenna had written, revised and rehearsed while waiting for him in her truck. Out went her regal march to the door, the demand not to ever darken hers again and the poignant valediction that she should have known a relationship that felt so right was destined to go horribly, irreparably wrong.

Except she wouldn't have spoken a word between her leave-starting and the leave-taking. There wouldn't have been a sound but that of the cabin door opening and shutting behind her.

"*Probably* not?" she repeated. "I spoke with the head nurse and the intern on duty. Vinita left hours before the Code Blue was called."

"Yep. So out goes the supposition that Vinita suffocated her father with a pillow. If she'd succeeded, the time lapse would have nullified any need to code him."

Paul's tone was animated, edgy, exactly as Jenna remembered it when he'd brainstormed cases with Rick. Hearing it directed at her pierced her defenses. "Vinita isn't clever or gutsy enough for anything else. If she'd killed her father, it had to have been a spur-of-the-moment crime of opportunity."

"Uh-huh."

Jenna frowned. "A 'but' is coming through loud and clear."

"A small one. Being the genius we all know Vinita to be, what if she *thought* she smothered him but didn't quite get the job done. Or attempted it, then chickened out and ran. In either case, I can't see her checking Casper for a pulse."

Jenna couldn't, either. "Yes, but whether she screwed up or chickened out, he obviously survived the alleged attempt, so what killed him?"

"Even half-assed asphyxiation can do serious damage. Plus, Casper did suffer respiratory distress every night since he was admitted.

"Its cause had the medicos stumped. The guesses—and that's all they were—included a residual reaction to anesthetic, severe sleep apnea and nocturnal panic attacks brought on by feelings of isolation and helplessness."

Aggie would have stayed the nights with him if Vinita hadn't banned visitors from his bedside. Imagining Cappy lying all alone in a strange, darkened room, so disoriented and frightened he hyperventilated, made Jenna want to peel out for Vinita's house and exact a similar torture on her.

"I'm confused," she said. "Are you making a case for heart failure now?"

"I'm the objective one, remember? I'm not making a case for anything." He smacked his lips. "To be honest, I don't like Casper's recurring breathing problems. Emphasis on recurring and exclusively at night. It's a piece that doesn't jibe. Not even with a preexisting but undiagnosed medical condition."

"It could," Jenna said slowly, "if Vinita and Eugene were in cahoots."

"Now *I'm* confused."

"What if on the night prior to Casper's death, Vinita went the suffocation route and failed for whatever reason. The attempt could have compromised his respiration, and it's a fair assumption that she wouldn't have gone home and watched TV with Eugene as though nothing had happened."

"Go on."

"If money was the motive, Eugene had as much reason to want Casper dead as Vinita did. It's another fair assumption that he wouldn't be as squeamish about hastening the inheritance."

Jenna didn't realize she'd sat down again until the

cool vinyl wicked through her jeans to her skin. "Let's say last night's visit was sort of a ruse."

"To continue an established pattern and be certain you and Aggie left and didn't come back."

"Right. Then, hours after Vinita's departure—having no doubt waved a hearty and memorable toodle-loo to the nurses—Eugene snuck in unobserved to do the deed."

Paul looked thoughtful, like a defense attorney pondering how best to discredit a witness. "Spouses can't be compelled to testify against each other."

"But a spouse can waive the exclusion if he or she so desires. That contingent is as useful for mutual protection as it is for blackmail."

"It would be," he allowed, "except for your scenario to work, Eugene had to be as inept at homicide by suffocation as his wife."

"Maybe he was interrupted. He heard someone coming, or a nurse keyed the intercom to check on Casper, and Eugene had to skedaddle."

"Where? Out the window? He'd have been spotted if he went out the door."

Eugene Potts as Spider-Man didn't parse. "Okay, so before Vinita left, she unlocked the bathroom's connecting door. The room next to Casper's *was* empty, you know. Eugene could have hidden in there, then snuck away when the staff converged on Casper's room to answer the Code Blue."

"Well..."

Jenna groaned and crossed her arms at her chest. "Don't waste your breath. Plots don't get much suckier than that one."

"Nothing wrong with the teamwork angle. It's asphyxiation I have trouble with. Even if Casper were heavily sedated, he'd have put up a fight. Lungs don't take kindly to having their air supply cut off.''

"There's a slightly larger glitch than that in the co-conspirator theory," Jenna admitted. "Eugene was up to his elbows delivering a sow's first litter of pigs last night.''

"Says who?"

"Charlene Burretts. Her mother-in-law is a member of Mom's book club. Charlene brought over a veggie tray this afternoon and made a typically well-meant, but foot-in-mouth remark about the sorrow of death yielding to the miracle of new life—meaning the piglets her husband helped Eugene deliver.''

"That's bad," Paul said, laughing. "Matter of fact, that's awful.''

"Damn disappointing if you ask me. I so wanted to nail Vinita and-or Eugene for something worse than treating Cappy like a senile old fool.''

"Hey, they aren't off the hook yet. I dabbled in some computer hacking and invested forty bucks on an online credit report. The Pottses live within their means, but barely. They were a few thousand away from owning their farm outright when they had to take out a second mortgage.''

Jenna nodded. "Vinita hit up Casper for a loan first. Huge corporate operations are holding the soybean market hostage. The little guys are struggling for survival.''

"Could be they got tired of pinching pennies.''

"It does grate on you after a while." Paul's hand-stitched loafers received a significant look. "Guess you'll just have to trust me on that.''

"Something else you said gets me thinking, too.'' She arched her eyebrows and leaned back on the sofa as though she knew precisely which remark had piqued his interest and was eager to discuss it further.

"Anyone who raises livestock is an amateur veterinarian," he said.

Say what? "Um, yes. Yes, that's true."

"And they keep a store of basic pharmaceuticals handy—general antibiotics, wormers, vaccines, etcetera."

Comprehension was swift and horrifying. "Oh, God. Eugene would know which drugs and what dosages are toxic."

"So would Vinita."

"No, she hated being a farmer's wife. When the wind was right, the smell from the pig lot made her hurl. I'm pretty sure the backyard was the closest she ever got to Eugene's secondary cash crop."

"In all the years they've been married?"

A valid argument. Especially now that their sons were grown and gone, there was no one else to help with chores Eugene couldn't do by himself.

She said, "Means and opportunity are there, but without an autopsy—and possibly even with one—how could we prove it?"

"We can't. And the biggest obstacle remains, did either of them have the balls to do it? Wishing somebody dead and cold-blooded, premeditated murder are as diametrically opposed as apathy and anarchy."

Jenna agreed. If they weren't, the global population could be counted on an abacus.

Theoretically, suffocation could befit a crime of passion, unless the perpetrator shopped around for the pillow and brought it along. Choosing and preparing a lethal dosage of a drug, smuggling it to the scene, then injecting it in another human being was not a sane person's method of problem solving.

Paul said, "But they could cheat on their income taxes more profitably and with less risk. Which they haven't, as nearly as I can tell."

"As nearly as you can tell? Vinita does their personal and business bookkeeping. How'd you access their tax records?"

"With the computer, along with pulling in some favors." He glanced toward the kitchenette. "The first rule of homicide investigation still being to follow the money, who else stood to gain from Casper's premature death?"

"Nobody." Jenna slanted a look at him. "You'd better not be implying that my mother had anything to do with it."

"Not in a million years." He rose and turned down the stove burner under the coffeepot. Above its gurgle and the clink of two mugs emigrating from the drainboard, he said, "Aggie, Sam, you and me are about the only ones who aren't on my suspect list."

"Bullshit."

"Uh-uh. I bullshit you not."

She accepted the mug he offered, then set it down to cool on a Get Your Kicks On Route 66 brochure on the lamp table. "I never made the grade to detective, but I'm relatively certain there's no suspect list attached to a death by natural causes."

"Nope."

"And for all intents, we've conceded that Vinita didn't kill him and neither did Eugene."

"Judging by evidence to the contrary, probably not." Paul took a sip of coffee, grimaced and remanded it to a complementary *Guideposts* magazine. "But somebody did."

Jenna stared at him. He was stalling. Had to be. Manufacturing a whodunit to justify staying in town. Trying to lure her into a maze constructed of the proverbial smoke and mirrors and her fallow but unperished cop instincts. Enticing her intellect this time, having already used her heart and her body as substitutes for a ghost that had ceased to exist, except in his memory.

Not once had Paul denied it. Not after Sam's homecoming dinner, when she'd accused him of the cruelest kind of unfaithfulness. Not in one of his telephone messages, or the card sent with his forgive-me flowers. Not even outside a few minutes ago, when she'd said Liz Rivas was the only woman he'd ever loved.

"Is there no limit to what you'll do to manipulate me and my family?" She held up a hand. "Don't bother answering. It was a rhetorical question."

His face flushed, deepening the bottle-green color of his eyes to dull jade. A stab had finally struck home and it *hurt*. Except the triumph she'd anticipated from having drawn metaphorical blood felt a lot more like remorse.

"Stand by for a news flash, Ms. MacArthur. I didn't ask you to come here tonight. Since Casper's accident, I've stayed as far away from you as possible."

"Oh, no, you—"

"Okay, okay, I called a few times. Went to your house *once*. But as easy as it would have been, I never ambushed you at the shop or in the parking lot. I even drove by to make sure your truck was there before I went to the hospital to see Casper.''

Her mouth gaped in disbelief. ''Good God, you're serious, aren't you? I guess that goes to show that the ultimate snow job is one you believe yourself.''

''Careful. Considering the source, that could be taken as a compliment.''

''Why, you—''

''Son of a bitch. If that's the best you can come up with, spare me. I really have been called worse.'' He turned his head and looked at the door then back at her. ''I'm on the clock, okay? I'm not sure how your surprise visit went from civil to a verbal knife fight, but if you believe I'm using Casper's death to sandbag your mother, then you can get the hell out of here and stay out.''

The impulse to do precisely that shot through Jenna. She dug her heels in the shag carpet and splayed her fingers on the armrest. The livid roar in her ears subsided just enough to separate the option from the ultimatum.

''No,'' she said, her stance relaxing but hardly relaxed. ''No, I don't believe you'd be that callous toward my mother.''

By Paul's expression, the allusion that Aggie was the sole valedictorian on his personal honor roll wasn't lost on him. ''So you believe foul play was involved in Cappy's death.''

''Um, well, I'd rather leave it at suspicion of an unnatural cause.''

''You're playing the semantics card again.''

''Not true. It's a homicide investigator's job to be an advocate for the victim. Doesn't matter whether he or she was a crack dealer, a hooker or a senator.''

Noticing the cynical tilt to her chin, he said, "Yes, effort devoted to Jane Megabucks on Park Avenue will be greater than Joe Blow from the projects, but in Jane's case a motive is almost certain to be clearer, means and opportunity more definable, the suspect list shorter and physical evidence more available and less contaminated.

"Odds are, Joe got wasted in an alley in the pouring rain with a stolen gun now at the bottom of the East River for any one of a dozen reasons by any one of fifty people, including a strung-out meth-head Joe didn't know from Adam."

Jenna motioned surrender. "Point well taken— from here to Timbuktu by way of Nova Scotia."

"Actually, the point I intended to make is that jumping to conclusions is a mental form of evidence tampering."

"Gotcha, Ace."

"In addition to out-and-out murder, we can't rule out medical error, malpractice or plain old neglect."

Jenna reached for her coffee, which had cooled along with her temper. "Sure, but again, how would you prove it without an autopsy?"

"I'll be honest. It'll be tough proving anything without an autopsy. Vinita's ordering a cremation still bugs me. According to Ken Tufts, it's a first for her extended family or Eugene's."

Jenna chuffed. "I could have told you that."

"I'm counting on you to tell me a lot of things." He reached over the back of the chair for the legal pad lying on the bed. "In answer to questions I'd rather not bother Aggie with right now."

"Such as?"

"What can you tell me about Steven Abernathy?"

That she'd dated him on and off—mostly off—for a year or so could provoke the green-eyed monster in Paul Haggerty, but another of their implicit truces had been declared.

Thank heavens. He was the toughest, sharpest, most perceptive sparring partner she'd ever met. Whether wounded, enraged or invigorated, their battles freed another type of passion she'd miss like the scent of him after he was gone.

"Steve is a competent, general-practice attorney," she said. "His family is well-to-do. They consider his setting up shop in Pfister akin to a consciousness-raising activity like devoting a couple of years to the public defender's office or legal aid.

"He's been married once. No kids. He's a gourmet cook, a ragtime-piano player, is terrified of dogs and wishes he was a contemporary of Clarence Darrow's."

Paul's fountain pen continued to waltz across the tablet for several seconds. "I guess that explains his office's Early Scopes Trial decor."

"Don't knock it. He's a good customer of mine."

"And why you two are just friends." He looked up. "You know, Festus remains undecided, but Herschel and Homer are crazy about me."

"Uh-huh. And in relation to the Great Scheme of Things, that ranks you somewhere between purple M&Ms and Kato Kaelin."

"Yeowch." That sly, crooked grin of his would also be missed. "You are on your toes tonight, darlin'."

Casual eye contact held…intensified…transformed into visual telepathy. Oh, yes, Paul, I'd definitely rather be on *you,* right now. Straddling you, then under you, face up or belly down, and don't forget spoons and all those other lovemakers in our combined repertoire.

Damn shame you ruined it for both of us, isn't it? For Liz and me, I mean.

He shifted in the chair. This time it wasn't anger reddening his complexion. "Jenna, we've got to talk—"

"Yes, we do. And I'd appreciate it if you picked up the pace. It's getting late and tomorrow is going to be rough."

A long sigh intersected a slow nod. "D. B. Sullivan. What do you know about him?"

She repeated the name. "Never heard of him."

"Sullivan owns the parcel opposite Casper's. The county assessor says neither his land nor Casper's would fetch four hundred an acre, if not for the highway project. A Realtor told me that finding a buyer would be a better trick. The land is too far from Pfister for a housing development and too rocky and irregular for agricultural purposes."

"Good Lord, Paul. You've been one busy man today."

"If you only knew. My tour through the hospital will have to wait until I sort out my notes." He smiled. "It's the 'once a cop' thing. As much as I hate the circumstances, chasing after bad guys again feels good."

Jenna was determined not to get involved beyond being an informant, yet déjà vu strummed chords that reverberated in her bones, too. Dangerous was the only word for it.

"Steve Abernathy and the Sullivan guy—are they suspects?"

"No assumptions, remember? I'm just following the money."

He flipped back a page in the tablet. "My Abernathy notes are from memory, but his explanation of the mineral-rights deal has more holes than Casper's acreage. The hotel people's take-it-or-leave-it offer of fifty thousand is too cheap. Casper's quarter million demand is too high. Something in the neighborhood of a hundred and twenty-five thousand would be just right."

Jenna nodded. A concerted effort had been made to remain ignorant of Casper's litigation. Ignoring the highway project altogether hadn't delayed its construction, but thinking about its effect on Pfister and the business community was ungodly depressing.

"Abernathy told me that Budget Zzz's had a forty-thousand-dollar option on Sullivan's land."

Paul shook his head. "Not."

"Are you sure? I don't recognize the name, but it's been common knowledge for months that the hotel had first dibs on the other parcel as an alternate site."

"An option they have, but not for forty thousand. Try a nice even million."

Jenna studied the yellowed postcard collage on the wall. She was just too tired to do the math, too tired to connect all the zeros.

"I haven't had time to puzzle it out myself," he said, "but I keep coming back to why would the hotel chain draw the line at fifty thousand if Casper's land was the preferable site and second choice would cost them a million?"

"Haven't a clue." Jenna gulped the last of her coffee and set the mug on the table. "But Sullivan had a million reasons *not* to wish Casper dead. If you're thinking that Budget Zzz's knocked off Casper to save a buck, you need sleep worse than I do.''

Jenna clambered to her feet and stretched. Agony and ecstasy. ''Unless they knew something we don't and anticipated snapping up a bargain somehow.''

''Like Casper not being around to negotiate?''

The yawn prying her jaws apart evaporated. ''Sorry, Charlie Chan. That scenario wouldn't pass muster with Mom's book club. Blanche Filbert would call it dumber than dirt on a stick.''

''Not if that opportune bargain circled back to the landowner's daughter.''

Joyce Ramsour had vehicles at her dealership priced in the fifty-thousand range. Would Vinita—or anybody—kill a sweet old man that had never hurt anyone in his life for the price of a new pickup truck?

She blew out a sigh at the memory of arresting a twelve-year old boy for murdering a deliveryman for a pepperoni and extra-cheese pizza.

Life was just too damn full of rhetorical questions.

17

Rather than somber organ music, the gentle ebb and flow of a violin solo drifted from invisible speakers. The Parlor of Rest was painted an ethereal blue with eggshell trim and swagged draperies. Its pastel figured carpet seemed to play havoc with some mourners' bifocals.

At the front, a dais was banked with a multitude of flower arrangements and potted plants. Inchmealing sideward as one would in a receiving line was Casper Wetherby's only child. Vinita was swathed in black from her veiled head to her sensibly shod toes, like a severely depressed beekeeper. Methodically, she snatched each tribute's sender card from its envelope for an arm's-length scrutiny of the sentiment and signature.

Shuffling along behind her was her husband, Eugene. His double-breasted, wool-blend suit was of midlevel bank-executive caliber. His demeanor belonged to a seasonal laborer reporting to the unemployment office for his thirty-sixth and last unemployment check.

Though the memorial service wouldn't begin for another half hour, twenty-some attendants were already scattered or clustered on the crescent-shaped pews on either side of a broad center aisle. Not a one of them looked a day under seventy.

Paul Haggerty stood near the back wall, his hands clasped in front of him. Stationing himself in the funeral home's vestibule had been his first choice, but early arrivals either mistook him for an employee or peered at him like B-movie earthlings examining an alien in a tinfoil spacesuit.

An older man of average height hove into Paul's peripheral vision. The cut of his suit jacket disguised the belly that corresponded to his heavy jowls, slewed gait and the wedding ring embedded on his finger.

"Kenneth Tufts," he said, offering his hand.

Paul took it and supplied his side of the introduction.

"Ah yes, Dolph Haggerty's cousin from back East. I heard you were in town."

Paul weighed the risks attached to correcting the grapevine's misinformation against the rewards of being regarded as a token Pfisterite, much less a relative of the town's favorite son.

No contest. No sweat, either, unless the retired bull rider attended the memorial service.

"I suppose you could say we're in somewhat the same line of work, Mr. Tufts."

"Oh?" The mortician's woolly eyebrows arched. "In what way?"

"I'm a freelance journalist researching an article about SEDS." A two-beat pause implied a solid link between funeral directing and the fourth estate. "I needn't tell you why *Scientific American* is intrigued by the similarities between sudden elderly death syndrome and sudden infant death syndrome."

"*Scientific American,* eh?" Tufts was visibly impressed. "Quite intriguing, yes. I believe someone did a seminar on SEDS at our last convention."

Paul nodded, as though the fatal condition he was making up on the spot had indeed been part of the annual National Funeral Directors' program. "I'm here to pay my last respects to Casper—a grand old gent who will truly be missed—but from what Aggie and Jenna tell me, I can't help but wonder if SEDS may have contributed to his untimely death."

Tufts stroked his chins. "Possibly..."

"You're right, of course. Without an autopsy, it's impossible to be certain." Paul's feigned disappointment switched to feigned confidence. "But, experienced professional that you are, any outward indicators of SEDS must literally jump out at you."

The mortician's gratification at the "experienced professional" reference segued to a mild state of panic.

"Cyanosis, for example," Paul prompted helpfully. "Were Casper's fingers or toes bluish?"

"Oh, *yes.*" Tufts brightened at terminology he recognized. "So was the skin around his mouth." He added, "I'm not a medical examiner, but I'd call the cyanosis pronounced." He glanced down at his own slightly discolored hand. "Comes from a lack of oxygen in the blood. That's why they call a newborn with a bad heart a blue baby."

He crooked a sausage finger to bring Paul nearer. "Now, don't you go telling Aggie this, but if SEDS is akin to SIDS, I don't think Casper had it. He surely didn't just fall asleep and not wake up. Looked to me like he'd fought for his last breath."

Paul urged the mortician on by saying nothing.

"My son Kenny did the prep work when we brought Casper here from Mercy, but it's my custom to have a private word and a prayer with the departed—especially an old friend."

"What do you mean by prep work?" Paul asked. "If the body is scheduled for cremation, no embalming is done, is it?"

"Usually not, but some families still want a traditional visitation the evening before the service. In any event, we examine the departed for a pacemaker's wire leads and scarring from breast implantations, then bathe and gown them before transport to the crematorium."

Anticipating Paul's next questions, Tufts explained, "The hospital is supposed to remove the devices before the remains are released, but we always double-check. Lithium pacemaker batteries create a toxic gas when superheated and silicone implants explode and can damage the retort."

The mortician nodded at several couples moving down the aisle to secure seats. The Parlor of Rest was filling rapidly with people, an amalgam of hot-house flowers, perfumes, colognes and aftershave lotions and the oddly mechanical drone of subdued conversation. Paul had watched the doorway for Jenna and Aggie, but neither had arrived.

Before his source excused himself to attend the mourners, Paul said, "So in your expert opinion, Casper's postmortem condition did not indicate SEDS."

"If I may be frank, Mr. Haggerty, I've never heard of SEDS, so I'm hardly an expert. What was clear to me is that the poor man had vomited something terrible before the end.

"His mouth was split at one corner, most likely from inserting an airway. From the marks on his chest, they must've given him a good jolt or two with a defibrillator, too, but to no avail."

The anguish Paul felt was genuine. A German proverb says death is winter without flowers. For Casper Wetherby, it had been a marathon sprint in a vacuum chamber. Whoever exacted that torture on him would pay and dearly.

"There must be credit given where it's due," Tufts said. "I didn't have to be in Casper's room to be a hundred percent certain the staff at Mercy did everything in their power to save his life."

He turned to the fifty years younger version of himself, who'd sauntered up and was awaiting his grandfather's attention. "Isn't that right, Kenny?"

"Man, I hope to shout." Tufts, the Next Generation, shuddered. "The old guy looked like he'd gone a couple of rounds with Tyson when me and Dad picked him up."

Paul shot back, "What do you mean by that?"

"He was, you know like, kind of lopsided—"

"Go tend to Reverend Sieger, Kenny." An "or else" was implicit in the tribal elder's tone.

"But Dad said—" The young man caught the look in his grandfather's eye. He raised his hands, palms out. "Okay, I'm goin', already."

Watching his grandson slouch to a side door, Tufts waggled his head as if what the world was coming to he knew all too well. "Kenny can be tactless, but he meant no disrespect."

"I'm more interested in what he meant by Casper looking like he'd been beaten."

A pudgy thumb and forefinger kneaded the bridge

of Tufts's nose. "I'm up in years myself, Mr. Haggerty. It's sad to say, but the elderly are as vulnerable as children. If there'd been any sign of abuse, I'd have notified the police."

"I take it you've reported those types of injuries in the past?"

He nodded. "More often every year, it seems. Except that resorting to what doctors call extraordinary means can cause secondary injuries. What Kenny meant by Casper being lopsided was that his right hip was out of place—probably refractured when they were trying to resuscitate him."

"Maybe he fell again."

"No. There'd have been corresponding bruises if he had." Tufts's smile was paternal, not the lip-locked variety peculiar to morticians and defeated politicians. "That TV show, *ER?* They save a lot of patients, but they never show how a stroke victim can end up looking like he was at the bottom of a ten-car pileup the very next day.

"Why, just last week, dear little Wynema Owens came to us with four broken ribs. Us old folks have such fragile bones. Some of them simply can't withstand CPR."

"You're saying this is common?"

"I wouldn't call it *common*, but it isn't unusual, either." Tufts squeezed Paul's upper arm. "If you'll excuse me, there are some things I need to see to before the service."

"Of course. Thank you for your time, Mr. Tufts."

"Oh—and do let me know when your article is published. I'd love to have a copy."

"Sure thing." Paul started away, halted and turned on a heel. "Mr. Tufts?"

"Yes?"

"What was Mrs. Owens's cause of death?"

The mortician scowled, then his features relaxed. "It wasn't SEDS, either, I'm afraid. It was cardiac arrest."

His conversation with Tufts Senior having drawn several curious looks, Paul returned to the vestibule and stationed himself near the guest book. Glancing down, he corrected the duck-footed stance law enforcement officers adopt by osmosis and maintain by habit. It was a tag sure to be spotted by anyone in the profession or wary of it.

The white stretch limousine Vinita and Eugene had arrived in was parked under the funeral home's porte cochere. No such courtesy had been extended to Aggie Franks. Not by the ever-spiteful Vinita, anyway.

Paul smiled a private salute at the pair of showroom shiny Lincoln Town Cars that swung into the lot's half-dozen spaces reserved for family members. Each had a spring-mounted, Ramsour Ford-Lincoln-Mercury dealer plate affixed to its rear bumper.

For all her ditziness, Joyce was a class act. The gesture wasn't one-upmanship directed at Vinita and Eugene, yet how sad and silly the Pottses would look after the memorial, the lone passengers in a limo built for nine.

Joyce had even phoned Paul that morning to ask if he'd like to ride with them to the service. "I don't know what happened between you two, but Jenna needs you. She'd never admit it in a thousand years, to herself or anyone else, but you can take most anything dished out if you've got a good, strong hand to hold. In all the years I've known her, that's the one thing she's never had.''

Paul declined the ride but promised he'd be waiting at the funeral home when the group arrived. ''I need her, too,'' he'd said into the phone after Joyce hung up.

Sam MacArthur opened the driver's door of the first Town Car, then moved to help his grandmother from the back seat. Kathy Baker emerged from the front passenger side and Jenna from the rear.

From the second vehicle, driven by Barry Ramsour, alighted Joyce, Mavis Purvis and a petite, attractive woman in a bright teal dress who Paul surmised was Joyce's mother, Barbara Johnson.

The men wore dark suits, but as Joyce had told Paul, her mother insisted they borrow ties from Casper's collection of hand-painted silk neckwear. Topless hula girls danced across Barry's. Sam's was made to look like a pan-size rainbow trout.

As for the ladies, Joyce was dressed in a bright yellow outfit and Kathy in a russet coatdress. Aggie was in royal purple, Mavis in hot pink, and while Jenna's vintage marine-blue suit was conservative by comparison, the peplum jacket and straight calf-length skirt exuded a Greta Garbo–style sexiness.

Paul noticed the wolfish leer on Kenny Tufts's face as he paused beside the door, ready to open it for the group. The kid wouldn't know Greta Garbo from Marlene Dietrich, but generation gaps don't apply to attractive women.

The greetings ranged from Sam's civil handshake to Aggie's smooch on Paul's cheek. Stepping back, she said, ''Goodness' sakes, I've ruined you,'' then dampened her hankie with her tongue to wipe away the lipstick.

"Let's go on in," Joyce said, having introduced her mother, "so Jenna and Paul can have a minute to talk."

They weren't entirely out of earshot before Paul said, "I'm not sure this is appropriate, but you look wonderful. Wherever Casper is, he's whistling."

Jenna's smile extended to her dark, weary eyes. "Thank you. That's a very sweet thing to say." She regarded the others who'd paused to speak with someone midway down the aisle. "Vinita will be scandalized, but I think Joyce's mom was right. Cappy is—was too colorful for us to wear black for his funeral."

Of that, she'd be certain when she saw Vinita Potts's getup. Paul had a sudden sense that her widow's weeds had less to do with a flair for melodrama than with a willful ignorance of the man who'd fathered her.

"Steven Abernathy came," Paul said. "He's seated on the left, about six rows back."

"Uh-huh. He keeps regular office hours on Saturdays. Decent of him to be here."

"Who are the two men sitting with him?"

She slanted him a look. "God, Cappy would love this."

"What?"

"You scoping out the mourners. Earl Stanley Gardner was fond of perpetrators attending their victim's funerals—except most of his were graveside services. Better atmospherics."

"It wouldn't be a cliché if it seldom happened.

Second in popularity is the suspect-who-should-be-there-but-isn't gambit.''

"Not today it isn't." Jenna's gaze swept the room. The soffit lights had been lowered and the dais and lectern were now spotlighted, albeit gently, by conical ceiling fixtures. "Mom's book club and their bridge groups started a telephone tree, but I never expected this many people to be here."

She nodded toward the far wall. "The heavyset woman in the windbreaker owns the DayLight Donut Shop. Casper bought maple bars and bearclaws from her every week for thirty years.

"Over there is his mechanic, a ward clerk and two nurses, the drafting student that blueprints his inventions, his mailman, four of the Pink Ladies..." Her breath caught. "And Margie Ann Tyler, his favorite checker at the supermarket. She told him when double-coupon days were scheduled and he brought her homemade fudge."

Her lower lip quivered. Her eyes averted to a painting of sunbeams splicing a thunderhead rampart. "Cappy wasn't the greatest cook, but he made the best walnut fudge and divinity I've ever tasted."

Paul's hand bumped hers. Back stiffening, she jerked away, then as if an inner voice had rebuked her, she sighed and slipped her hand into his. Her fingers were ice-cold, the inside-out kind of frigid that betrays the enormous energy expended to hold grief at bay.

"The, uh, the men with Steven," she said. "I'm pretty sure the one wearing glasses is a lawyer for Budget Zzz's. I don't know about the other guy."

By her tone, Jenna thought nothing of a representative of Casper's corporate adversary attending his memorial service. In the company of his personal attorney, no less.

Paul didn't ask why. He couldn't have cared less. Not with her hand in his, her skin gradually warming to his touch.

A lean, silver-haired man responded to Paul's knock. He was dressed in navy slacks and a sweater with Bois D'Arc Hills Country Club and golf tees crossed like sabers embroidered on it.

"Mr. Owens? I'm Wes Felcher." Paul flashed his drugstore ID. "I called earlier about—"

"Yes, yes, and you're right on time, too." The full-view glass storm door opened wider. "Come on in." He urged his guest to take a seat and to call him Bill, then muted the Oklahoma-Nebraska game playing on the living room's big-screen TV.

"Who's ahead?" Paul asked.

"Tied fourteen all. Beginning of the third quarter."

Paul watched Bill's gaze follow what was supposed to be a first down, Cornhusker ground gainer. "The offense will have to make bigger holes than that if they don't want to go to the air."

Bill grunted. "God forbid they pass on a first and ten. You'd think somebody'd keep stats on the number of second and nine-and-a-halfs they rack up in a season."

"It seems like coaches are hinkier about getting picked off on a first down than a second or third. If the other team's going to intercept, what difference does it make which down it is?"

"Amen to that." Bill looked away from one of what would become a slew of commercial breaks.

"Let me get you something to drink. Beer? Soda? Or I could rustle up a pot of coffee."

His grin was sheepish. "I bought a fresh bag of chips for the game at the store yesterday, but damned if I didn't come home without the dip. I wrote out a list, just like Wynema always did. When I got back, there it was, lying bright as daylight right on the kitchen counter."

Joining the after-funeral gathering at Aggie's was expected—by Aggie, anyway—but Paul accepted a soda, rationalizing that keeping the recent widower company for a while was a decent trade for barging into his life under false pretenses.

Strange how the death of a spouse, particularly the wife, left an almost tangible void. The house wasn't suffering for her absence—the furniture was dusted, vacuum tracks spoked the carpet and none of the plants looked dehydrated, or drowned, but Paul sensed the room hadn't always felt quite as spacious or chilly.

Bill returned with Paul's drink and laid an open bag of chips on the coffee table. Starting for his chair, he hesitated, sighed, then tromped back to the kitchen for another coaster, paper napkins and two wooden snack bowls.

Poet Harry Kemp said, "Death conquers all things with his peace, now all your victories are in vain." Paul guessed if the lady of the house were still with them, they'd dig chips straight from the bag, degrease their hands with surreptitious swipes at the sofa cushions, and their drinks would rest on copies of *Reader's Digest* and *TV Guide*.

Bill's sidesaddle position in the swivel rocker divided his attention between the Sooners' offense and

Paul. "You said something on the phone about being sent down from Jefferson City to check up on the hospital?"

Paul had switched entities from investigative journalist to fake-ID-card-carrying Wesley Felcher of the Missouri Health Facilities Review Committee. Where Owens might be reluctant to be interviewed for a magazine article, an opportunity to dump contentions and complaints regarding his wife's care in a civil servant's lap would be irresistible.

Paul recited from memory. "The committee's mission is cost containment through health cost management, assurance of community need and the prevention of unnecessary duplication of health care services."

"Uh-huh." Bill munched a chip thoughtfully. "Sounds like government work, all right."

Paul flipped back the cover of a pocket-size, spiral-topped notebook—the two-for-a-buck variety available at any discount store that law enforcement officers bought in multiples. Its cover was uncreased, and not a page had been used, yet it fit the curve of his palm as though made for it. Or vice versa, he thought. Security consulting was lucrative and challenging, but there was no chase, no puzzle to unravel, no genuine sense of accomplishment.

Bill eyed the notebook dubiously. "You sure you work for the state? I didn't think you people could sneeze without filling out a form."

"We can't." Paul smiled. "I'd just rather concentrate on what you have to say. I can wedge the gist of it into the right boxes later."

The Sooners' fourth-down kick went out of bounds at the Nebraska thirty-seven-yard line. Taking advantage of the break in the action, Paul said, "What was the nature of your wife's illness?"

"Adult-onset asthma. It's fair to say it wasn't Wynema's nature to laze around the house. She's been a go-getter her whole life. A little on the stubborn side, too. Being told she couldn't do this and shouldn't do that had her bent on proving the doctors wrong."

"Was she admitted because of an asthma attack?"

A shoulder hitched as Bill piled chips in his bowl. "Yes, but it was mostly a bad reaction to the medications she was on. Either they didn't work and she couldn't get her breath, or they made her sicker than a dog and so dizzy she couldn't stand up without holding on to something.

"The doctor admitted her for respiratory therapy and to experiment with other meds to see if she tolerated them any better." Bill shook his head. "Don't quote me on this, but I don't think she was taking them like she was supposed to—relying too much on a crisis inhaler when she started wheezing."

Paul recorded the diagnosis and complications. "Did her condition improve after she was hospitalized?"

"I thought so. Her color was better and she was breathing almost normal. In the daytime, anyhow. Along around dawn she'd have a spell. The doctor couldn't figure out why, but unless they got worse, he planned to send her home the day after..." Bill's voice trailed off as his eyes averted to a tire commercial.

Paul couldn't bring himself to ask how Wynema died. If her husband didn't volunteer it, Kenneth

Tufts could supply the information, as mortuaries usually provided certified copies of death certificates.

"They didn't tell me much about the end," Bill said softly. "And I didn't ask. The nurse gave her the pills she was supposed to take around two in the morning. About an hour later, Wynema was choking for air. They called a Code Blue, but her heart couldn't take the strain. Her doctor said even if they'd gotten it going again, the oxygen to her brain had been cut off for too long." He looked at Paul. "It isn't living, just laying abed in a coma, hooked up to machines."

An involuntary shudder tripped up Paul's spine. He'd come so near the same fate. That's why he seldom took the pain medication in his briefcase. Birdsong and the wind in his hair were sweeter reminders of being alive. A man who had almost lost his life develops a peculiar gratitude for every achy bone and inflexible muscle.

"I wouldn't ask if it wasn't important," he said, "but how would you categorize the care your wife received at Mercy Hospital?"

Bill snorted. "No complaints. You can quote me on that. A couple of Wynema's nurses even came to the service."

Paul thought back to Casper's funeral. He wouldn't have recognized the young women who attended as nurses if they hadn't been wearing scrubs under their winter coats. "I've never heard of hospital staff attending a patient's funeral."

"It's a small town. We do things different around here." Bill smiled. "When I was a kid, my mother was a school crossing guard. She passed away three years ago and I think every child she ever walked across Commercial Street showed up for her visitation.''

Paul left a quarter hour later with another name to follow up on, plans for the evening and the Huskers ahead by a field goal.

18

Disembodied voices and laughter clattered out the screened porch's patio door, half opened to ventilate Aggie Franks's small, overcrowded house. The babble and mirth weren't cocktail-party loud or exuberant—with the exception of Casper's lodge buddies passing around a flask to punch up the punch. Such gatherings were a catharsis, a reunion and a reminder of promises exchanged at the last funeral to do a better job of keeping in touch.

The scraggly, toasty-brown marigolds alongside the garden shed looked like victims of arson rather than frostbite. Sunlight angled from its two o'clock axis, but cast more shadows than heat. Shivering made a parody of hand-eye coordination as Jenna tried to light a cigarette off the waning ember of its predecessor.

Joyce Ramsour grunted in disgust. "For cripe's sweet sake. You're pitiful, you know that, MacArthur?"

A thread of smoke staggered up from the end of the Salem. Jenna sucked in a blend of singed, shredded tobacco leaves and a hint of peppermint marinade. The vapor stream she exhaled would have been impressive if it hadn't been nine-tenths condensation.

"I'm pitiful? You're the one that snuck out for a smoke with an empty lighter."

"Almost empty," Joyce corrected. "There were a couple of good flicks left till you got ahold of it."

Jenna shrugged, then sighed, then leaned back against the shed's wall. Still dressed in the suits and high heels they'd worn to the funeral, they sat side by side on napkin-dusted, five gallon–size paint buckets, their knees spraddled in a comfortable but most unladylike fashion. Cigarettes in one hand and swigging from long-necked bottles of Michelob held in the other, they looked like transvestite bouncers taking a break between bar fights.

"Other than freezing my ass off," Joyce said, "this was a great idea."

"Yep."

"Seems like weeks since we've been alone long enough to have a chance to talk."

Jenna's eyes slid in her direction. "Well, it hasn't been, and I didn't come out here to discuss Paul Haggerty."

"Neither did I, but since you brought up the subject—"

Shit. "Things didn't work out between us. Let's leave it at that, okay?"

"Sure." The beer bottle hovered a pucker's length from Joyce's lips. "Fine with me."

A squirrel with a hulled walnut in its mouth crashed through a drift of dried leaves. The neighbor's dachshund yapped at its back door, having learned that persistence, not patience, was its own reward. The lush, sweet scent the earth exuded last spring now smelled dank with a metallic tang, like a rain-washed chain-link fence.

There were no elephants or castles in the clouds. Cirrus are too thin and wispy for caricature, and they didn't bring rain, though they were harbingers of it. Cappy had taught her that.

"It was a nice service, wasn't it?" she said.

The smoke rings Joyce tried to blow resembled lopsided bagels. "Saradene Oxendine must have practiced her hymn singing. She usually sounds like a leaky set of bagpipes, but today she was almost on key."

"She and Eugene don't look very much like brother and sister."

"Saradene was born a month premature," Joyce said, as if that explained the discrepancy.

"What did you think of Vinita's eulogy?"

Joyce chuffed. "She can read Bible verses with the best of 'em. I think she may have mentioned Casper's name in there somewhere, but don't hold me to it."

Silence stretched almost a minute before she added quietly, "Sam brought down the house. He looked so young up there behind the lectern. Everybody's heart just broke, right along with his."

Neither Jenna nor her mother had expected Sam to answer Reverend Sieger's call for personal remembrances. He told of the night Cappy took him out to the rock quarry to discover the wonder of listening to a baseball game on the radio and watching it in your head. Then there were the hilarious ballroom-dance lessons the week before Sam's first prom, helping Cappy build prototype inventions in his workshop and their every Saturday-morning breakfasts with the Liars' Club at the Ritts Café.

Sometime during the tribute, Paul had taken

Jenna's hand again and held on tight, telling her without words that no matter what she felt she'd cheated her son out of by denying him Rick's parents and family, Sam had known and returned the love of a special man who'd *chosen* to be his grandpa.

Paul's gesture was intuitive and compassionate, as well as another reminder of the threat he posed. To blame the romantic triangle he'd lured her into for pushing him away was an easy out. To bastardize Shakespeare, a rose by any other name, address and occupation was still Liz Rivas.

He knew it. She knew it.

Not that his deception hadn't hurt. It had, and mightily, but shimmering behind it was the joy of being remembered, the exhilaration of not having been forgotten. The two were not interchangeable. Memorable was the feel and taste of Paul's lips the first time he kissed her. Unforgettable was the feel and taste of him when they made love. And neither would have happened if he'd been honest with her from the start. The rational side of Jenna understood how he construed knowledge of her past into a sort of sanctuary. It might have been, if she and her mother were actors, but Jenna MacArthur and Aggie Franks weren't stand-ins for Liz Rivas and Ellen Bukowski.

At the beginning, they assumed there'd be an eventual resumption of their former lives, or a tolerable facsimile thereof. Returning to New York City was out of the question, but proximate choices had spieled like a train conductor's station announcements: Syracuse, Amsterdam, Schenectady, Watertown.

Then six or eight months after the relocation to

Pfister, Jenna offhandedly commented on a New York City newspaper strike to the U.S. deputy marshal assigned to them. Eyes narrowing, he'd leaned back in the kitchen chair, his expression wary. "Oh, yeah? What's it to ya?"

The animosity was feigned, but the message was as shrill as the six o'clock whistle atop Pfister's city hall. Never drop your guard. Not to me. Not to your mother. Try to be Jenna MacArthur in public and Liz Rivas in private and, as sure as God made green apples, you'll mess up. You'll blurt the wrong thing, or be overheard at the worst possible time by the least tractable pair of ears.

Like the others laid down by WITSEC, she abided by that rule, except for an occasional pity party with Aggie. Over time, their commiserations and the need for them dwindled as lies and diversions trotted out with little or no conscious thought. Their fictional biographies began to ring true at the same rate the truth took on a mythic quality. All the while, from his southern Missouri twang to his street-ignorant naiveté, Sam MacArthur was growing up a small-town boy. What he knew of New York City started with the Statue of Liberty and ended with the intro to *Saturday Night Live*.

Rather than a refuge, Paul Haggerty represented the menacing side of remembering and never forgetting. He'd spent twenty-three years speculating about, then searching for, Liz Rivas. He could vow to put up his guard and never drop it around Jenna, her mother or anyone, but someday he'd blurt "I remember when Liz..." or refer to Sam by his birth name or his father's again, and it would be at the worst possible time and overheard by the least tractable pair of ears.

If life were fair, Jenna thought, the *too late* mark would have diagonal orange stripes and amber caution lights like a highway barricade. But if such a warning existed, she'd blown by it, just as she had a thousand chances to convert a moment, a mood or a circumstance into a heart-to-heart with her son, a thousand chances to tell Sam who his daddy really was and why his death was her fault.

She remembered more of that night than she'd ever told anyone. The smell of Brut, naphtha and hamburgers wafting from the coat someone slid under her head for a pillow. A towel and the heel of a hand bearing down hard on her opposite temple. Flashlight beams sweeping over shoe tops, sidewalk detritus and a glistening rivulet of blood following a channel in the concrete to the gutter. A voice howling, "Naw-aw-aw. C'mon man, don't *gimme* that. Rivas'll be all right. Help him—ya gotta help him."

Another thanked Jesus that she was alive. A third cursed Him for taking Rick and sparing her. "Ain't she s'posed to be a cop, too? What the fuck was she doing when the shootin' started? Powderin' her goddamn nose?"

"Might as well have been. She wasn't carryin'."

"Why should she? Anything happens, she had big, strong Detective Hubby to cover her back. Geez, who'da thought Rivas might need *her* to cover *his?*"

She had. Not exactly in those terms, but until a few minutes before they left the apartment for dinner, her badge wallet and service weapon were nestled in the oversize shoulder bag she was using for an overnight bag. She and Rick seldom ventured out unarmed, but she wasn't in the habit of lugging around lingerie, perfume, makeup, shampoo, votive candles and a bottle of Kahlúa for the coffee they'd sip after Act One of their second honeymoon.

Ain't she supposed to be a cop, too?

The badge wallet stayed, but she locked the Smith & Wesson in the safe she'd insisted on buying when she was pregnant with Robby. Lightening the load by six or seven pounds wasn't particularly noticeable, but she remembered thinking that at least her lacy silk teddy wouldn't reek of gun oil.

What the fuck was she doing when the shootin' started? Powderin' her goddamn nose?

On average, bullets travel nine hundred feet per second. Rick was hit before he drew his weapon from the shoulder holster. His unit commander and a therapist who specialized in counseling law enforcement officers swore she couldn't have returned fire fast enough to save Rick, even if her weapon had been in her hand.

The majority of their fellow officers demonstrated the compassion and respect due a widow, much less a wounded comrade. Prayers were spoken and candles lighted for her recovery. Squad members treated her bewildered little boy to afternoons at the zoo, Knicks games and the Mets' preseason openers until she realized her son was becoming as confused and withdrawn as a ward of the court shuffling between foster homes.

Anything happens, she had big, strong Detective Hubby to cover her back. Geez, who'da thought Rivas might need her to cover his?

Lenny Vildachi's murder trial was a second chance to do that, a last chance at redemption. Much of the evidence against Lenny was circumstantial, but the D.A. was confident that her testimony would ensure a conviction.

Why did it matter that she couldn't recall what she'd eaten for dinner that night? The precise time they'd left the restaurant? Whether or not the wind was blowing? Whether the alleged assailant's car was black with New York plates, or dark blue with New Jersey tags?

Because a man's life is at stake, thundered Vildachi's lead counsel. He agreed, a selective memory was understandable considering her injuries and the loss she'd sustained, but if her recollection was so flawed and erratic, shouldn't Lenny Vildachi—whose mother swore under oath that she and her son had had dinner, then played Uno until after midnight—be given the benefit of the doubt? Most of the impaneled dozen agreed, but they couldn't convince the holdouts. To this day, Detective Sergeant Rick Rivas had not received the justice he deserved.

By definition, Jenna thought, homicide is the killing of one human being by another. If Sam knew the truth, who would he despise more? Lenny Vildachi for gunning down his father in the street? Or me, for taking Rick's life and burying it under twenty-three years of secrecy and lies?

"Hey, Jen." Joyce Ramsour's face swam into view. "Are you okay?" She pressed the back of her hand to Jenna's cheek, then her forehead. "All of a sudden you looked like you were gonna hurl."

The Salem still forked between Jenna's fingers had burned down to the filter. She stubbed it out on the ground, then flipped it into a cracked plastic flowerpot. "Don't worry, I'm not sick." Not that kind, anyhow. "Just tired."

"Yeah, well, there's a surprise. When's the last time you had a decent night's sleep?"

Since the night before Rick died and everything I believed in died with him, Jenna thought, letting herself slide chin deep in pathos for a moment. Once in a while, when the going gets tough, even the tough say *screw it,* simply because it's easy and feels so damn good.

Joyce said, "My mom is spending the night with yours again tonight. Daddy's deer hunting up in Wyoming at my brother's, but Mom said she'd stay regardless. I know you have plenty on your plate already, but she's worried about Aggie."

"Why?" Jenna's thumbnail vandalized the beer bottle's label the way Paul's had a century ago at the restaurant. "I mean, the way you said it, there's more to Barbara's concern than how Mom is going to handle Casper's death."

Joyce took a long pull from her bottle, then made a retching noise. "How can beer get warm when it's colder'n hell out here?"

"How come everybody says 'colder than hell,' when hell's advertised as a lake of fire with unquenchable flames all over the place?"

"Okay, smart-ass. How can my beer get warm when it's colder than a polar bear's pecker out here?"

"Ask Heloise or the Science Guy. What I want to know is why your mother is so worried about mine."

Joyce's expression turned serious. "She thinks Aggie is obsessing on the idea that Casper was murdered so she doesn't have to come to terms with his death.''

Anger sparked, then flared. ''What if she is? Instead of food, maybe somebody should have brought her a copy of Pfister's *Guidebook for Publicly Acceptable Grieving.* There has to be one, since everybody else seems to know the rules.''

The huffy silence little girls perfect well before they can walk unassisted ended with Joyce's terse ''I didn't mean to make you mad.''

''Ditto.''

''Like I said, I know you have plenty enough on your plate right now.''

''Yep.'' *And about ten tons more you* don't *know about and I wish to God you did.*

''It's just that Mom said that's all Aggie talked about last night. That if Vinita didn't kill Casper so she could stop the lawsuit and sell out to the hotel people, then the hotel people did it for basically the same reason.''

Joyce patted Jenna's arm in a you-poor-thing manner. ''A hit man in Pfister? Can you imagine? It'd be funny if it wasn't so sad.''

''Funny?'' Jenna looked away before the defensive, defiant side of her snapped back, *Oh, yeah? What would you say if I told you a contract was out on me once upon a time?*

''I didn't mean funny ha-ha.'' Joyce's fair complexion flushed crimson. A grass clump received a frothy Michelob baptism. As a final act of contrition, she thunked her cigarette down the empty's craw. ''Vinita could whine somebody to death, but kill 'em for money? Get real.''

"That *is* real. Money is a leading cause of murder."

Joyce snorted. "Vinita won't buy lottery tickets for fear she'll win. Bitching about those pesky annual jackpot checks just wouldn't have the same impact as bitching about shelling out three bucks and change for a package of toilet paper."

"Actually," Jenna allowed, "I'm sort of with her on that one."

"Well, the fact remains, Vinita didn't kill Casper and the hotel people didn't grease Aggie's porch step so he'd fall, then finish him off at the hospital."

Jenna didn't argue. She couldn't. Logic was on Joyce's side. All Jenna had was the persistent itch behind her breastbone that commenced yesterday morning when Casper's eyes fluttered open and met hers an instant before a nurse's aide hustled Jenna from his room.

It wasn't love or delirium or pain she saw. Not the fear of dying or his resignation to it. The look he'd flashed was laced with pure terror.

Gooseflesh rippled up her arms and down her back. Her heels pierced the moist ground when she stood. "You're right. It is colder than a polar bear's pecker out here."

Joyce needed an assist to her feet. "I shouldn't have shot my mouth off, huh?"

"Why not? Your loud mouth is one of your best features." Jenna hugged her around the waist. "If you're really asking if I'm pissed, the answer is no."

"Scout's honor?"

Jenna chuckled. "Next you'll want me to build a

campfire and sing 'Kumbaya.' Which I'd do, if I didn't already have plans for the evening."

Joyce's eyebrows rose like dual crescent moons.

"Plans of my *own*, girlfriend. Nothing whatsoever to do with Paul Haggerty."

19

Miniblinds hanging in the fixed, plate-glass windows sliced the night-dimmed glow within to ghostly slivers. Jenna's reflection followed along a quarter step behind, like a bashful twin.

Mercy Hospital's top-floor offices commanded a panoramic view of Pfister and the surrounding countryside. When the new wing was constructed, the eagle's-roost location was a practical decision not an administrative perquisite. With future expansion in mind, the fourth floor had been prewired and fixtured so all or part could be revamped into patient rooms. Yankees, apparently, didn't have a lock on ingenuity.

In deference to comfort, Jenna had exchanged her pointy-toed heels for a pair of black pumps, but hadn't changed her clothes. After a day's wear, her suit jacket's peplum flapped over her derriere like a wilted lettuce leaf, but an air of class and respectability might come in handy if a security guard caught her rifling through the office's file cabinets.

The video camera that panned the elevator's alcove was identical to the one at MacArthur Perk. It was only a matter of time before one of the two rent-a-cops on night duty decided its blank monitor screen might not be a glitch in the system. He would not be amused to find the lens cap she'd fashioned from a plastic canned dog-food lid covered in black electrical tape.

It was also technically illegal to possess the lockpick set she removed from her shoulder bag, but they were a necessity for anyone who bought and sold antiques. From sea to shining sea, there are millions of dresser drawers with a bowlful of spare keys to everything from a first apartment to the first car ever owned, but somehow, like the second sock to each pair tossed in the dryer, the key to grandma's tiger-oak secretary or great-grandpa's steamer trunk always vanishes without a trace.

To prevent damaging a piece, patience and a delicate touch are needed to open and disable locks stuck fast by time, grime and climatic swelling and shrinkage. By comparison, the bolt securing the administrative offices' door was a cakewalk.

The room was large and lit by a single fluorescent panel and the kaleidoscopic flicker of fish, fireworks and Dilbert screensavers. Other than functional accoutrements, most of the desktops were bare and as tidy as an elementary-school classroom's on Parents' Night. Regardless of season, a cardigan in varied shades of neutral would likely be found in every bottom drawer.

An unexpected whistling-through-a-graveyard sensation rippled from head to toe. Jenna closed the door and relocked it, wondering if real burglars ever got the willies.

Thirty minutes were wasted looking for the records she sought. In hindsight, she supposed she should have guessed that these particular vertical-file cabinets would be sequestered in a windowless anteroom at the far end of a corridor. Convenient access wasn't a priority.

She shut the door to the insurance-department offices across the hall before flipping on the light switch to the closetlike storage room. In the ceiling fixture's bright, artificial glare, the tall, banked rows of steel, hasp-handled drawers bore an eerie resemblance to a morgue.

"Which it is, in a manner of speaking," Jenna said, her voice loud and wonderfully reassuring in the small space.

In its wake came one that trebled her pulse rate. If, in fact, the quiet rattle of a doorknob and the *snick* of retreating tumblers wasn't a guilty conscience joining forces with an overactive imagination.

She killed the lights but stayed in the records room. The monotonous hum of computer hard drives, the ventilation system's respirations, the wind buffeting the exterior walls and a faint rumble beneath her feet subverted any indication that she was no longer alone.

The insurance department across the hall had its own exit, but the office door had squeaked when she closed it. Her sweaty hands balled into fists. Being caught was one thing. Being caught before she'd taken a single peek at Casper Wetherby's medical file was infuriating.

Footsteps. Muffled but unmistakable. Footsteps going *away* from her, toward the billing department's cubicles and administration, public information, secretaries' and human resources offices she'd reconnoitered earlier.

Maybe she could abandon ship before anyone was the wiser. Better yet, hide in the ladies' room until the coast cleared, then scurry back and finish what she'd come for.

Taking a breath and holding it, she peered around the door frame. The status was quo. She edged farther into the corridor. A figure was skulking about the main room. She snapped her head back. Tilted it. Craned her neck for a second look.

In her experience, security guards wore wanna-be law enforcement uniforms, not expensive leather sport coats. Or turtleneck sweaters. Or wore jeans as well as the shapely male butt disappearing into the gloom.

Permission to breathe was granted. She toed off her shoes and padded to the doorway he'd exited into. His scouting mission wouldn't take long. Finding nowhere to hide in the meantime, she flattened herself against the bookcases beside the door.

Beyond the adjacent windowed wall, the beacon atop a municipal water tower strobed like Rudolph's nose. At this altitude, neon signage gave an a-lot-like-Christmas look to the whole town. Jenna could have waxed poetic about the view had she not heard the subtle drum of approaching footfalls.

She gripped the edge of a bookshelf. A knickknack behind her wobbled, then acceded to the power of prayer. Her cheekbone pressed against the upright as though bonding with the prefab wood grain.

Timing was everything. Paul Haggerty was two strides into the main office when Jenna leaned forward and whispered, *"Boo."*

The effect was mesmerizing. He launched like a scalded cat, then levitated a full six inches off the floor. Defying both gravity and physics, he somehow spun around in midair and landed with his arms cocked in battle-ready kung fu position.

Jenna slumped against the bookcases, laughing so hard her knees almost buckled. Chest heaving, Paul's face turned three shades of red, and his eyes, a malevolent chartreuse. He didn't so much as crack a smile.

"Damn you, Jenna. Think it's funny, do ya? Why I ought to— I ought to— Hell with it, I'm *gonna*." Paul's fingers raked back her hair and he pulled her to him. His mouth descended on hers, his kiss at once hungry and tender and exquisitely thorough.

Still reeling from the aftershocks, she stammered, "Is th-that what you do when somebody scares the shit out of you?"

He cupped her face in his hands, his thumbs caressing her cheeks. "Nobody ever has as much as you do, darlin'."

The magical suspension of reality cracked, then shattered. "Same here," Jenna said. "But on a lot more levels."

Without anger pushing her as it had three days ago, stepping back was an act of will, but a precarious one. It might have failed if Paul had resisted instead of dropping his arms to his sides.

They fidgeted a moment, looking everywhere save at each other, both at a loss for what to say or do next. Emotion, need and their ever-strengthening bond mocked Jenna's fears, daring her to give in. To let go. To take what she wanted, damn the torpedoes and the consequences.

If only blissful ignorance of their history had prevailed, but the skeletons and ghosts had refused to stay locked in their legendary closets. She recalled a motivational speaker's remark about the past being a canceled check, the present being cash and the future, a promissory note.

It was a nifty nugget of wisdom. She'd since seen it reproduced on cross-stitched samplers and a bumper sticker. Life just had a nasty habit of not playing by the rules, let alone adhering to banking analogies.

She supposed she should be grateful the haunts and hurts had crashed down around her before she'd fallen totally in like, and probably in love, with Paul Haggerty.

As if she hadn't already.

Paul cleared his throat, then motioned at the room they'd independently broken into and entered. "Great minds and all that, huh." A tentative smile eased the tension in his face. "I've got to say, you're the best-dressed burglar I've ever run across."

She glanced down at her outfit. One stockinged foot roofed the other, as though the gesture made the lack of shoes less obvious. "Yeah, well, I figured if I got caught, the standard basic black outfit would look a skosh premeditated."

"It could arouse suspicion all right," he agreed. "Unlike that spur-of-the-moment, jerry-rigging job you did on the surveillance camera. Which I wish I'd known about before I hiked up four flights of stairs."

"I might have let you in on it," she lied, "if you'd come to Mom's after the funeral. She wondered why you didn't."

"According to Joyce, Sam and Kathy took you home about ten minutes before I got there." Good timing, his tone seemed to inquire. Or bad?

The nonchalant "Oh" she strove for came out

sounding disappointed. She thought, "So what took you so long?" but hadn't intended to blurt it out loud.

"When I spoke with Kenneth Tufts before the service, he mentioned a Wynema Owens who'd passed away as suddenly as Casper did."

Jenna sifted the name through her mental Rolodex. Wasn't that the friend Flogent Lee Pfister had mentioned before the heirloom buy-back ritual?

Paul removed a laminated ID from his jacket pocket. "I called Mr. Owens from the mortuary. He said he'd be glad to answer a few questions regarding his wife's hospitalization."

She scanned the card. "Wesley Felcher?"

"At your service, madam taxpayer, by gubernatorial appointment to the Missouri Health Facilities Review Committee."

The guy had cojones, she'd give him that.

"Mrs. Owens was severely asthmatic," Paul said, "but her cause of death was cardiac arrest."

"Synonymous with heart failure."

He nodded. "She was coded and resuscitated after she was admitted, then her condition appeared to be improving, until her vital signs went haywire in the middle of the night and failed to stabilize."

"Similar to Casper, though I'm not sure I see a connection."

"There may not be any, but I think something in each case gibed in Mr. Tufts's mind without him realizing it."

"In other words, as if we don't have enough tangents to go on, now you're hearing between the lines."

"Could be." Paul scooted a family photo aside

and sat sidesaddle on a desk. "What's the third leading cause of death in the United States?"

Cancer and heart trouble must top the list. Diabetes was on the rise, but stroke must rank pretty high. Jenna guessed the latter.

"Different entities do the math different ways, but stroke usually comes in fourth. Medical malpractice and hospital-borne infections combined win the number three slot by a few thousand victims."

Her mouth sagged open. "Gee, thanks so much for sharing. I'll sleep better knowing if a doctor doesn't kill me, the germs'll take their best shot."

"We still have one of the most advanced health care systems in the world." He grinned. "And a jillion more attorneys per capita."

"How reassuring." She planted a hand on her hip. "Can we change the subject? As in, what does any of this have to do with Casper?" Her eyebrows knit. "Unless you're suggesting malpractice was involved."

"Mmm, not necessarily."

"Did Mr. Owens suggest it to Wesley Felcher?"

"No. He had no complaints about his wife's care and treatment."

The elaboration Jenna expected didn't materialize—or vocalize, as it were. "Obtuse doesn't become you, Haggerty."

"I have my reasons. You'll just have to trust me."

"Uh-huh. What if I don't?"

He slid off the desk. "That's an even better reason for me to tick-a-lock."

She moved not a muscle, batted not an eyelash. "If you recall, I said last night that I'd snooped around the hospital, but hadn't had time to reread my notes or mull them over.''

"Something tells me it was Wesley Felcher who did the actual snooping.''

Paul shrugged away that minor detail. "He didn't net a helluva lot. Mercy Hospital is experiencing an upswing in its mortality rate, but so goes the trend with the general population aging in droves.

"Even in my *official* capacity, the lady who toured me around wouldn't let me get my mitts on any patient files. Privacy issues, don'tcha know. That's partly why I came back tonight.''

"And the other part?''

"Is where trusting me comes in. I have a hunch.'' He raised a hand. "You have great instincts. I'd rather you analyzed whatever info we may find at face value, than with a subconscious bias to prove me right.''

She smirked. "Or wrong.''

"Fine by me. Except the most likely scenario is being up to our necks in inconclusive, circumstantial evidence and the medical community's lousy handwriting.''

Jenna led the way to the paperwork morgue, pausing at the threshold to turn on the lights and slip into her shoes. Odd how an extra couple of inches in height made her feel businesslike.

Paul walked toward the back of the room, taking the ID card from his pocket again. It vanished into the slender cleavage between the wall and a file cabinet.

"Why did you do that?''

"I should have left it in the car. Better to chuck it than have to explain it to anyone.''

She looked at her watch. Almost an hour since she'd blinded the video camera and she'd accomplished exactly zilch. "As if explaining ourselves would be a no-brainer."

"Lest you forget, security is my area of expertise. Breaching the hospital's was as easy as buying a soda at the local convenience store. When I started my company, it was more effective to show prospective clients how lame their systems were before I sales-pitched mine."

"And how many times were you arrested on the way to making your point?"

A thumb and index finger formed a digital zero. "I'm very good at what I do, darlin'."

An understatement, the applications of which she blocked from her mind. "Let's get busy before the law of averages catches up with you."

To their chagrin, the files were arranged alphabetically, not by death date. For the sake of speed and convenience, Paul's chosen time period expanded from the prior six months to the entire year. To narrow the field, he also told Jenna to concentrate on patients sixty-five and over, who hadn't succumbed in IC units, the emergency or operating rooms, or to a terminal illness, catastrophic injuries, or were comatose for a prolonged period of time before they died.

She questioned the department's anal-retentive compulsion to password-protect its computers. She did not question Paul's methodology. Not aloud, anyway. A veteran investigator's gut feelings deserved respect. If more civilians listened to their own, the crimes-against-persons rate would plummet.

The process began at either end of the file cabinets' U-shaped arrangement and worked toward the middle. They didn't talk much, but each kept an ear peeled for footsteps, the *ping* of the elevator's bell and keys jingling on a guard's utility belt.

A couple of facts quickly came to the fore. So far that year, more male than female senior citizens had passed away. And scrutinizing and photocopying medical charts by the ream fit law enforcement's description of itself: ninety-five percent tedium and five-percent adrenaline-spiking terror.

The latter occurred during Jenna's 4:00 a.m. raid on the mini-fridge in the administrator's office. She was so hungry she was shaking, but one look at the available snacks brought tears to her bleary, bloodshot eyes. Bottles of carrot juice stood alongside a carton of soy milk. As for eats, there were rice cakes, dehydrated prunes, pumpkin seeds and sugarless carob brownies.

Grimacing, she opted for the rice cakes. Chased with a jug of Nordic glacier water, they might swell into something akin to real food. She'd just arranged her haul in the crook of one arm when she heard muffled voices—a man's and a woman's—outside in the corridor.

Wood paneling, built-in cabinetry and cushy carpet had virtually soundproofed the CEO's office. Outside the private entrance, a key rattled in the doorknob.

"Get yourself on in there," the man crooned as the door swung open. "It's been three days and I'm so hard I'm 'bout to bust my britches."

Jenna panicked. The leather couch was pushed smack upside the wall. Its easy chairs were too low to hunker behind.

His female companion's throaty laugh sounded forced. "Doesn't your missus *ever* go to bed without a headache?"

Jenna scanned the windows—vertical blinds, not drapes. There was a bonsai tree on a glass brick plantstand. A pencil cactus brambled from a chinoiserie jardiniere.

"It ain't your place to make fun of my wife, Val," the man warned. "I'll thank you to remember that."

"I get headaches, too, you know."

His chuckle had a threatening edge to it. "And I've been known to blab stuff into the wrong ears when I don't get what I want, whenever I want it."

Through the louvers of the slim wardrobe closet she'd squeezed into seconds earlier, Jenna glimpsed the backlit outline of a security guard. He closed the office's door behind a curly-haired woman dressed in scrubs.

The woman whispered something in his ear to which he murmured, "That's more like it."

Jenna gave serious thought to coming out of the closet. Screwing around on the job versus rummaging through deceased patients' files seemed like a stalemate to her. But would it to the couple groping each other a few yards away?

Jenna closed her eyes. She would have clapped her hands over her ears, but couldn't with water bottles and rice cakes hugged to her chest.

How much time had passed since she left the records room? Five minutes? Ten? What if Paul came looking for her? Called out her name?

She buried her head in the administrator's cashmere topcoat and hoped they finished before Paul's curiosity got the better of him.

20

To remove urine stains and odor from carpet, melt a bar of grated castile soap in a double boiler. Stir in one ounce of rosemary oil, one ounce of rubbing alcohol. Pour into an eight-ounce margarine tub and let set before using.

Jenna rubbed the goop into the dried puddles on the living room's area rug. Over the years, she'd cooked pounds of the stuff to clean incoming shop inventory and at home.

"Don't fail me now," she said, her teeth gritted against the ache in her shoulder. "Mom and Paul are supposed to be here in an hour."

Homer and Herschel lay on either side of the Mission oak coffee table. Their snoots were at rest on outstretched paws and their soggy sad eyes pleaded for forgiveness. Well, Homer's did. As usual, a flop of hair concealed Herschel's baby browns, but remorse radiated from every inch of his mountainous, shaggy body.

Festus was reclined on top of the table, the crown prince of feline superiority and personal hygiene. His undulating tail was catspeak for King Richard III's "Chop off his head." Meaning the dogs' heads, as it were.

"It's my fault, not theirs," Jenna said. "You have

a litter box. I should have let them out before I went to the hospital last night.''

And would have, had she known she wouldn't drag her ass home till half-past dawn.

She flipped over the sponge and dipped it in the goop. In all fairness, that made Paul Haggerty partly to blame. And she had more than a sneaking suspicion that the mutts' unusual lack of bladder control was payback for leaving them home alone too much.

''Then why am I the one on my hands and knees scrubbing piddle puddles like freakin' Cinderella?''

She was tired beyond the reaches of an extra few hours' sleep, a snide reminder that she wasn't a kid anymore. Age turned *any* body into a climatic barometer, but when temperatures huddled near the freezing mark, muscles torn by bullets, then surgically sliced, probed and sutured throbbed like abscessed teeth.

Then there was the shop she'd been the mostly absentee owner of since…Tuesday? Try the Friday before last. Closing yesterday in Cappy's honor, and as usual on Sunday, didn't make up for the hours Mavis had put in so that Jenna could be with Paul, make love with Paul, argue with Paul, kiss and make up with Paul, send Paul packing forever, then be the rock Aggie leaned on and the Miss Marple to Paul's Hercule Poirot.

In the manner of misery loving company, Homer waddled over and nuzzled Jenna's elbow. She stroked his droopy, paddle-shaped ears. As dish-raggy and decrepit as she felt, the Slinky on stilts looked the part on a day-in, day-out basis.

''This afternoon's triple header isn't going into overtime,'' she said. ''After I shoo Mom and Paul out the door, you and Herschel can ride along with me to the shop.''

Homer's joy at the prospect was well contained.

''You can watch TV in the back room as easily there as you can here.'' Jenna grunted and groaned into a Cro-Magnon slouch. ''Trust me, homeboy. I'd rather spend the evening curled up on the sofa with you, Herschel and *Antiques Roadshow* than at the store.''

Humming ''Love Will Keep Us Together,'' she gathered the cleaning supplies and gimped to the kitchen. Herschel and Festus saw no reason to interrupt their rest period between naps, but Homer trotted behind her like a kid brother eager to score brownie points while his siblings were otherwise occupied.

A fresh pot of coffee was the first order of business. Hospitality dictated that something chewable also be served, but it was a sure bet that Aggie would bring with her a plate of cookies or a bundt cake. If she was alert to Jenna's psychic signals, she'd deliver a smorgasbord of leftover comfort food, too.

On the table was a banded accordion file containing the photocopies she'd been ordered to read through before the get-together. While Jenna was trapped in the administrator's coat closet, Paul had sorted the rest of the patient files. The pseudo-burglars had then helped themselves to the Human Resources office's time sheets for specific dates and corresponding medical personnel records.

All together the material constituted a ream of homework for anyone, let alone a sleep-deprived, grouchy and not entirely willing accomplice. And a layman at that. Neither of them nor Aggie possessed the knowledge to distinguish protocol from any procedures or lack thereof that could indicate malpractice.

Among the fourteen patient files Paul had culled, males outnumbered females by a ratio of nine to five. No two were admitted for the same cause. A few were housed on the same floor or ward, but Mercy wasn't a sprawling, metropolitan health facility with a menu of specialized units. By the chart notations, each appeared to be recovering, then developed complications and died of some form of cardiac arrest.

"Everybody does," Paul had said. "Whether the mitigating factor is suicide, homicide, terminal illness, injury or natural causes, when the heart stops beating, that's it."

Jenna nodded, saying, "Hence the horrifying decision families must make when a loved one is declared brain dead."

"The will to live is primal. There are patients who've survived in a persistent vegetative state for decades. As long as their hearts hold out, they are medically alive."

Would Casper, Wynema Owens and the other twelve who'd passed away have believed that to be a fate far worse than death? Jenna was certain Cappy would. Being kept alive by machinery was his greatest fear, likely shared by a majority, if not all of the others.

Except the elderly's pragmatic attitude about death wasn't the issue. Paul had remained as tight-lipped as an oyster ruminating a pearl, but seemed bent on proving whether the group fitting his criteria had succumbed to wrong or injurious treatment.

"Or is he?" Jenna inquired of the table at large.

"A paperwork swamp is a fabulous stalling technique. Ask any bureaucrat. Better yet, ask a victim, if you can find any who's still legally sane."

Stepping over Homer, she removed three dessert plates, cups and saucers from a built-in, glass-front cupboard.

"If Paul's malpractice theory is really just an excuse to stay in town a while longer..." Jenna sighed, as people do when a sentence can be completed in various ways, including not at all.

It wasn't an excuse. Paul wouldn't dupe Aggie like that. His promises weren't the verbal equivalent of casual Fridays, either. Leads could be pursued as easily long distance as in person. More easily, perhaps. You don't need a cut-and-paste ID to flimflam sources by phone. An estimable title and the voice of authority are like Pike Passes to the information highway.

In the front room, Herschel began to howl and Homer bayed like the bassett hound branch of his ancestry. Jenna hadn't heard the doorbell, but rarely did when the dogs were in the house.

Aggie bustled inside, her arms loaded with food totes. "Yes, I'm early, but I wasn't about to go back home and futz around for half an hour."

"Okay..." Jenna held out her hands. "Let me take some of—"

"No, no. Just shut that blessed door before all the heat gets out. They hiked natural-gas prices again, you know."

The dogs slunk down the hall to the library. Many house pets are four-legged sadists that derive their jollies from clinging to visitors who aren't animal lovers, are allergic to dander or are opposed to inhaling, eating and wearing hair not of their own creation. Homer and Herschel weren't exceptions, but they had learned early on not to mess with Jenna's mother.

Not that Aggie had ever been mean to them. But during their formative years, she'd gotten her bluff in and perfected a look that seemed to visualize them as wintertime apparel.

As for Festus, Aggie adored the three-legged tabby. He snarfed the canned salmon and the kitty treats she brought, batted at new toys and often snoozed on the mink-lined bed she'd sewn from one of Earl Bukowski's ill-afforded forgive-me gifts. Still, the cat kept his distance, like a call girl who encounters a john at a social function.

"Casper wrote our congressman about the price increases," Aggie went on. "Said the gas companies were gouging us, pure and simple. I told him it was a waste of a good stamp. Politicians couldn't care less about widows and old folks on fixed incomes. The faster we freeze to death, the less they'll spend on social security."

They were in the kitchen now. Jenna watched as her mother hung her coat on the back of a chair, then subdivided her plunder between the counter, the fridge and its freezer compartment.

"Don't mind me," Aggie said. "Go ahead with whatever it was you were doing."

Jenna shrugged. "I wasn't doing much of anything."

The baled lid to a rubberware carrier tormented Aggie's arthritic knuckles. Before Jenna could offer assistance, Aggie employed a butter knife like a pry bar. "I'll listen for the door, while you go finish putting on your makeup."

"I am finished."

Aggie glanced up from the plate where she was arranging cake slices like toppled dominoes. "Well, nobody could tell by looking at you. Go put on some more."

"Makeup isn't supposed to show, Mom. If it's done right, you should look natural, only better."

The carrier's lid snapped shut. "Take it from me, sweetheart. You aren't quite there yet."

Jenna weighed her options. Unconditional surrender. Outrage. Self-deprecating humor. Counterattack. Deductive reasoning. She said, "You're pissed off about something. Want to tell me what, or keep using me for your voodoo doll?"

"I don't appreciate that kind of language, young lady."

"I don't appreciate my mother bossing me around and insulting me in my own house."

"Fine. I'll just go—" The prize-fighter glare Aggie had leveled at everything in her path mellowed to significant irritation. "I should have gone home and cooled off instead of coming here and snapping at you." A hint of a smile appeared. "But you could still use a little more mascara and blusher."

Jenna rolled her eyes. "Want some coffee? Or something stronger."

"Would a cup of tea be too much trouble?"

Yep. To put on the kettle to boil and spoon Aggie's favorite brand of grocery store Earl Grey into a teaball was an enormous undertaking. "Did you sleep okay last night?"

"Better than I expected to. Barbara made hot but-tered rum, then we watched a senate hearing on C-Span.''

''That'd do it for me.''

Aggie sat down in the chair caped by her coat. ''I told her I wanted the house all to myself tonight.''

Jenna was ashamed of herself for feeling relieved. Playing catch-up at the shop didn't sound as much like drudgery if she could come home and veg out with Festus and the boys. ''It's awfully soon, Mom. Are you sure you're ready for that?''

''It's like I told Barb Johnson. Much as I appreciated her company, I missed Casper as much last night as I will tomorrow night, or a week from Wednesday morning, or six months from next Saturday afternoon.''

A lump swelled in Jenna's throat. ''I miss him, too.''

Her mother didn't have to speak to get her thoughts across. *You've never missed anyone like you will Paul Haggerty.*

The kettle was roaring toward a hard boil. Jenna poured the steaming water into a porcelain teapot, then dressed it in a crocheted cozy. ''When you came in, you said you didn't want to futz around at home for a half hour. Did you and Barb go to church and then out to lunch?''

''No…'' Aggie repositioned the cup and saucer in front of her, as though a right angle to the dessert plate prevented the earth's orbit from getting out of whack. ''I was sort of restless after Barbara left this morning, so I decided to put that energy to good use and see if there was something I could do at the hospital.''

Forgive her, Father, for I know she has sinned,

Jenna recited as she set the teapot on a trivet. She wasn't Catholic, but could convert. And would, if prison might be involved in whatever her mother had done.

"Of course, there's no mail delivery on Sunday," Aggie said, "so there weren't any greeting cards to deliver, and all the flower shops are closed, too, but I think the Pink Ladies should be on duty seven days a week. Don't you?"

"I—"

"Yes, we've had trouble finding new recruits, but just because it's Sunday, it doesn't mean there's nothing for us to do. We *are* the hospital's ambassadors. Patients and their visitors expect us to be there. Besides, sick people don't always know what day it is."

"Uh-huh." Absently, Jenna wondered what the symptoms of a bleeding ulcer were.

"Well, to make a long story short, you remember Buddy Rhodes, don't you?"

Jenna most assuredly did. He had the distinction of being her mother's all-time worst fix-up, and not just because Buddy was older than Casper (mature, in Aggie's words), emaciated (a smidgen on the thin side), rude (a straight shooter) and smelled like feet. He was a buzzard-eyed lecher who wanted a mistress, or a wife—it made no nevermind to him as long as she warmed his sheets nice and cozy.

Aggie said, "Buddy hasn't been well the last year or two, but I didn't know the doctor admitted him a week ago, when his liver wasn't acting right (chronic alchoholism).

"I was tracking down the lobby wheelchairs when I ran into Misty, his new wife—child bride is nearer the truth—bawling her eyes out in the elevator. She said Buddy was due to be moved to Extended Care this morning, but then he had a seizure and, *boom,* he was gone.''

''Oh, my God.'' Jenna eased down into the adjacent chair. ''Did anyone tell Misty what happened? What was his cause of death?''

''I asked the same questions.'' Aggie spooned sugar into her cup, poured in the tea, then stirred it. ''Cardiac arrest, they told her. Buddy's had a couple of heart attacks, but Casper saw him at the barbershop back in September sometime and Buddy was as spry as ever.''

Yeah, well, so was Casper until last Tuesday.

''Then I told Misty, if she was smart, she'd have Buddy autopsied and find out whether his heart really did fail. His daughters are three of the nicest women you'd ever want to meet, but that second eldest boy is trouble with a capital T.''

''You said that? To Misty Rhodes? In the elevator?''

Aggie sighed. ''I'm afraid so.''

Jenna's head drooped forward, as though her spine had snapped. Her hands slid over the hump at the back of her skull and joined at the nape of her neck.

''I don't know why you're upset,'' Aggie said defensively. ''I'm the one that got fired.''

''Fired? From what?''

''The Pink Ladies. They made me turn in my smock and everything.''

Disconcerting popping noises accompanied Jenna twisting around to look at her mother. ''How do you get fired from a volunteer organization?''

''The same way you do from a real job. Acciden-

tally mash the wrong toes and you're outta there."
Aggie's pinkie finger curled above her cup as she
raised it to her lips. A tiny experimental sip was fol-
lowed by a healthy gulp. "I felt so sorry for Misty,
I didn't notice who else was in the elevator. Even if
I had, I don't think I'd have recognized Dusty."

"Would that be Buddy Rhodes's second eldest
son?"

"Yes."

"Who's on the Mercy Hospital board of directors?"

"Well, he wouldn't be if his daddy hadn't donated
the money for the new PET-scan machine. I hear
Dusty hasn't shown up for a single meeting, either."

Aggie's expression changed from perturbed to
pensive. She returned the cup to its saucer. "There
was a rumor going around that Misty dated Dusty
first. That's how she and Buddy became acquainted.
You don't suppose they're in cahoots, do you? Dusty
and Misty, I mean. Or what if Dusty was so jealous
he couldn't take it anymore."

This is nuts, Jenna thought. Hit men, matricide,
patricide, serial malpractice—examine any death and
the circumstances surrounding it under a microscope
and something somewhere is bound to look fishy.

"I'm sorry," Aggie said. "I shouldn't have said
anything."

"You're just now figuring that out?"

"I don't mean what I told Misty. She and her bully
of a stepson can go hang for all I care. I shouldn't
have nattered on about who might've done what to
Buddy." Her lips curved into a secret smile as her
thumbs played back and forth along the rim of the
cup. "Casper and I used to read the obituaries and

make murder plots out of them. Bouncing, he called it. Most kind of fizzled out, but once in a while we'd spin a yarn that'd give us both goose bumps.''

Aggie sucked her teeth. ''It's a bad habit to have fallen into, I guess. Ghoulish even, some would say. But you know what? I'm sure going to miss it.''

The doorbell rang again. Homer's and Herschel's barking failed to smother the sound of two overfed mutts *ker-thumping* off the library's couch and love seat they were forbidden to lie on.

''To answer the question rattling between your ears,'' Aggie said, ''no, I didn't bounce up a murder plot when Casper died. Now, are you going to get the door, or wait till Paul is frozen clean through before you let him in?''

It was true that nobody since Bogart had worn a homburg as well as Paul Haggerty, but it was downright gratifying to see him looking as bag-eyed and haggard as she did. The grin he flashed was as ornery as ever, though, and he helped himself to a kiss on her cheek as he stepped inside.

''One of us is in a good mood,'' she said, taking his hat.

''I wasn't until you opened the door, darlin'.''

She could have said, ''Strangely enough, I *was,* until I opened the door,'' but didn't because it was a lie and he'd know it and get a bigger kick out of it than her faking temporary deafness.

Shrugging off his coat released a fog of Icy Hot fumes. In two sniffs, Homer and Herschel were sneezing their empty heads off, backpedaling and banging butts and heads in a scramble to get as far away from Paul as the walls allowed. Festus just wheeled a one-eighty and stalked back into the living room, his sinuses inflamed but his dignity intact.

"Don't take it personally." Jenna laughed. "They learned to detest the smell of liniment when Sam was in football."

"Can't be helped. I was as creaky as the Tin Man when I rolled out of bed." Paul hung his coat on a hall-tree hook, then took a stenographer's pad from the side pocket. "Aggie in the kitchen?"

"Yes, but where is your copy of the copies I made last night?"

"In a Dumpster behind the hospital." He waved the steno book. "I take great notes, though."

"You threw the whole stack away? Why? And why there?"

"Well, let's see. First, since everyone in Pfister seems to be related to everyone else, the SeaShell is about as secure and private a place for them as Betty Bigelow's bed-and-breakfast. The second worst hiding place is the trunk of my car, because I don't particularly care to explain to your favorite municipal taillight inspector how such materials came into my possession."

The sarcastic reference to Sam was justified, Jenna decided. Once.

Paul added, "Which is why I unpossessed myself of them where they'd cause the least curiosity if they were found."

"Makes sense," she allowed, starting for the kitchen. "Other than the lot-of-work-for-nothing aspect of it and our contribution to global deforestation."

"Ah-ah-ah. It wasn't my idea to run a duplicate copy."

"Paul!" Aggie greeted him as though he had just returned from lunar orbit, then her beaming smile lost wattage. "You poor dear, you look *exhausted*. Are you all right? Jenna, get him a cup of coffee and some of that spice cake before he keels clear over."

You poor dear, you look exhausted, Jenna mocked to herself as she fetched the carafe and cake plate. I'm as tired as he is, but I get grief about my makeup and he gets maid service.

He and Aggie chitchatted for several minutes until Paul finally noticed Jenna tapping her wrist where her watch should be. After he suggested they "get down to business," he explained why he'd deleted Vinita and Eugene Potts and a hired killer from his suspect list.

"Virtually anyone is capable of committing a crime of passion. Emotions boil over, rational behavior evaporates and the caveman in all of us takes over.

"But none of that applies to Casper's death, and I just don't believe his daughter and-or son-in-law have the cold-blooded temerity to murder a helpless old man lying in a hospital bed."

Aggie swallowed hard, moisture forming at the outer corners of her eyes.

Paul reached for her hand. "I shouldn't have said—"

"Don't mollycoddle me, young man. I'm sick to death of people chewing their words before they spit them out. Casper's gone and it breaks my heart, but tiptoeing around the facts doesn't change them."

The shoes Jenna would have to try to fill someday stretched three sizes larger. She was as guilty of a one-dimensional view of Aggie as Sam was of her.

Wouldn't it be marvelous if children wised up about their parents twenty or thirty years faster?

Paul continued. "There are two problems with the hired-killer theory. Casper's fall was an accident. Who knew in advance that he'd be hospitalized? It might seem like a bonus, but in reality, it's a huge obstacle. The risk of being seen or caught jumps sky high and that type of elimination is in James Bond's league, not the Knife and Gun Club guys.

"The second—and larger—consideration is Budget Zzz's, Incorporated. The lawsuit was personal to Casper, but just a gnat in the hotel chain's ointment. It's fair to say a mineral rights action was well outside Steven Abernathy's area of expertise, as it would be for most attorneys."

"Do you mean Abernathy was taking advantage of Casper?" Aggie asked. "Doing a song and dance to run up the bill?"

Paul shook his head. "Making sense of, much less a legal precedent from an unclear title originating in the nineteenth century, would be a rat maze for any lawyer. Without a doubt, Budget Zzz's shysters counted on it. What they failed to consider was Casper Wetherby's dog-with-a-bone stubbornness.

"I'm convinced they were sincere about a final offer being final. Let the court decide what the rights were worth, and very possibly stick Casper with the expenses to boot, in keeping with that fine American tradition of the loser paying the tab."

David versus Goliath was a grand Bible story, but in real life the little guy needed more than a slingshot, a rock and good aim.

The tick of the Kit Cat clock's mechanical eyes and tail was the only sound in the room. Aggie's fingertips ironed the place mat's fringe, her chin bobbing in rhythmic contemplation. Her voice was flat and quiet when she said, "Before you got here, I told Jenna I didn't conjure a murder plot from Casper's death. It looks like I did, though, doesn't it? Maybe not on purpose, but a wild-goose chase is still a wild-goose chase."

"Except when it isn't," Paul said.

Aggie started. "I don't understand. Do you think Casper was murdered or not?"

"Not intentionally, but yes, I do. And he isn't the only Mercy Hospital patient who's died under suspicious circumstances."

Paul removed the elastic band from the accordion file and pulled out the stack of photocopied patient and personnel records. Aggie glanced at Jenna, then back at him. "Where did you get those?"

"I refuse to answer on the grounds your grandson is a law enforcement officer."

"Oh, pooh. I'd never tattle to him, I swear. Besides, Sam loves me to pieces, but he thinks my wheels are short a few spokes."

"Where Paul got the records really doesn't matter," Jenna said, neatly excising herself from the commission of a felony without lying to her mother.

Aggie laughed, the first, full-tilt belly laugh Jenna had heard in almost a week. "So *that's* why you two look like you've been yanked through a keyhole backward. I hoped you'd settled your differences and had sex all night to celebrate, but you snuck into the hospital and rifled through the files, didn't you?"

Jenna stuttered random vowels and consonants. Paul pled the Fifth again.

"Time's a-wasting," Aggie warned. "Somebody had better start talking."

Jenna did, beginning with their record sorting process and its extent, then going straight to the summary and conclusion.

"We think Casper and six, or maybe as many as eight, others were victims of medical malpractice."

Aggie gasped and clutched at her sweater. "Oh, my God."

"We do?" Paul's bewilderment appeared genuine. Jenna's most certainly was. "Don't we?"

"Well, you could call it that, but what I suspect is happening isn't malpractice by its common definition."

"But, you said—" No, she realized, other than noting exemplars to tailor the search and bossing her around, he hadn't said much of anything last night.

She leaned back in her chair and folded her hands in her lap. "Okay, Ace. You've got the floor. Go for it."

"Speaking with Kenneth Tufts before the funeral planted the seed of a hunch. My visit with Bill Owens got the germination going." He jerked a thumb at the accordion file. "I wouldn't call the information in there conclusive, but I think Jenna will agree, a few too many patients who seemed on the road to recovery took a sudden, sharp left and ended up at Mr. Tufts's place of business."

Yes, she did agree, but why the effect wasn't caused by some form of malpractice had her stumped—and wildly curious.

"Have either of you seen the movie *The Sixth Sense?*" he asked.

Jenna had, twice at the theater and once on TV,

but the trailers had convinced Aggie that it wasn't her kind of film. For her benefit, Paul synopsized the scene where a videotape is found under a dead child's bed and given to the child's father. The camera had captured the girl's mother spooning poison into her daughter's soup. By various means, the child had been sickened for years to satisfy the mother's craving for attention and sympathy.

"Otherwise known as Munchausen's syndrome by proxy," Jenna said. "A network newsmagazine show did a story on a woman with Munchausen's whose nine children had died over a twenty-year span and were buried in three different states."

It was impossible to comprehend how a mother could abuse one child like that, but nine? With each pregnancy, had she promised herself she wouldn't harm the baby this time? Or fantasized about the compassionate outpouring that would soon be heaped upon the tireless, devoted mother of a chronically sick child.

"A variant of Munchausen's is called factitious disorder by proxy," Paul said. "Instead of a parent—usually the mother—intentionally harming her child, a nurse, a nurse's aide, a doctor or, in rare cases, a dentist, inflicts pain and suffering on a patient. They don't intend to kill them, just make them sicker. They crave the thrill of reviving them, then being hailed as heroes by family members and their co-workers."

"No sane person could do that to someone and think of themselves as a hero," Aggie said. "They're monsters."

"To you and me they are. But factitious disorder by proxy is a recognized psychological condition, and those who have it aren't insane—not legally, anyway. Health care killers know the difference between right and wrong. They just don't let it interfere with personal gratification.''

By Aggie's expression, the faces of every caregiver she'd seen at Casper's bedside were parading through her memory. ''Intentions be damned. Casper is dead. If someone he trusted—we *all* trusted—to help him get well again hurt him, then killed him, trying to earn an extra slap on the back, I want that monster locked up in a cage for the rest of his life.''

''So do I,'' Paul said gently, ''but I have to warn you, catching them won't be easy, and if the perpetrator gets wind of an investigation, he or she will turn tail and run.''

Aggie moaned and rested her head in her hand. ''This is horrible, *horrible.* I have friends scheduled for minor surgeries before the holidays. I'm not arguing the need for secrecy, but what if something happens to one of them? Then who's the monster?''

As Jenna recalled, they'd copied nineteen personnel files—a small army of suspects. ''He *or* she? Jesus, Paul. Can't we narrow it down any more than that?''

''Not yet. Beatrice Crofts Yorker, an expert on medical serial murderers, has developed a profile, but it's sketchy. Health care killers are a new twist on a relatively rare disorder.

''According to Yorker's findings, unlike Munchausen's syndrome by proxy, factitious disorder by proxy affects both genders almost equally. Most are young, in their twenties or thirties. Most were on the night shift. None of them had a criminal record, but their medical histories often showed chronic conditions, or an above-average number of sick days.''

The best lead was the hours they worked. The typical age range should shorten the list of candidates, as well.

Paul agreed that it should, but in the interest of cost containment, hospitals scheduled the least number of employees necessary to care for X number of patients.

"If the X rises unexpectedly," he said, "help is called in. But staff assigned to a ward or wing got wise to that in a hurry. On a scheduled day off, unless they need the overtime, they don't answer the phone.

"I don't know whether Mercy's method of operation differs from other hospitals', but floaters—nurses willing to fill in, either because they need the money or are looking for brownie points from a supervisor—are next on the call list.''

Jenna cocked back her chair and wadded great clumps of hair in her fists. "So the nineteen suspects are either assigned staff or floaters who worked the same nights as the patients we don't believe died of natural causes.''

"Yes."

"Males and females."

"The genders are more lopsided here. Five males, eleven females.''

"All in their twenties and thirties," Jenna said, thinking and thinking aloud at the same time. "Which begs the question, why do so many young people work the grave—er, the night shift?''

As if "night shift" cued a word association to coffee, Paul rose from the table to fetch the carafe from the warmer. "I've always wondered why a lot of cops are married to nurses, but it sort of stands to reason. Because third shift is the least desirable, rookie cops and nurses are stuck with it until they build up some seniority. Whether they get acquainted in the E.R., or at a coffee shop after work, at 7:00 a.m. competition in the romance department is pretty slim."

Jenna laid a hand across the top of her cup to signify no refills for her, thank you. Her stomach was burbling like a lava dome already.

Paul offered Aggie a little coffee with her tea, then topped off his own cup. "Night shift does pay a little more per hour than days, and there are parents who'd rather work while their kids are asleep, see them off to school, hit the sack and stay there till the kids come home again."

Jenna wagged her head. "If I had that much energy in my twenties and thirties, I don't remember it."

"Well, two of our group are pushing forty. I included them because a thirty-six-year-old male nurse at a veterans hospital in Columbia was recently indicted on ten counts of first-degree murder."

Paul glanced at Aggie. "Before you get the idea that Missouri is the factitious disorder by proxy capital of America, health care killers have been charged from Boston, Massachusetts, to Nocona, Texas."

She snorted. "If that's supposed to be reassuring, it isn't. A team of wild horses couldn't drag me to the hospital right now."

"Mom..."

"Don't *Mom* me, damn it. I know all about one rotten apple spoiling the whole barrel. I'm blowing off steam, for pity's sake. It isn't enough to have a homicidal maniac on the loose. Vinita Potts and her stupid, spiteful restriction on visiting hours *played right into the killer's hands.*''

The statement wasn't pure hindsight. Aggie would have stayed the nights with Casper, save Vinita's edict. Not to guard him—they had no reason to suspect he could be in danger—but so he wouldn't be alone. Even without the side effect of medications, a gloomy hospital room—with its unfamiliar odors and sounds—is a frightening, disorienting place, especially for children and the elderly.

Nor could she or Jenna identify any third-shift hospital personnel who'd frequented Casper's room.

"What now, Paul?" Aggie demanded. "We can't sit here twiddling our thumbs."

"We can't rush in without substantial evidence to warrant an official investigation, either."

"It doesn't get any more substantial than catching a murderer in the act!"

Where he'd gotten them, Jenna didn't know, but Paul had smarts enough not to tell an overwrought woman to calm down. He took a paper napkin from the press to blot the coffee he'd spilled on his shirt when Aggie shouted down the roof.

She apologized. He accepted, then explained why laying a trap for the killer was impossible.

"At the moment there are too many suspects, working in too many areas of the hospital. Plus, in prior cases, the murderers have injected an IV line with either a heart stimulant or a paralyzing drug normally used when a patient is intubated."

"I figured as much," Jenna said. "Not the type of

drug, but the MO. Nobody thinks a thing about a nurse injecting something into an IV.''

''And late at night, who's there to witness it? More than likely, the victim is asleep and unaware the IV has been tampered with.''

Like Casper. The thought was unanimous; the sorrowful, round-robin looks they exchanged were identical.

''Questions have arisen that need answers,'' Paul said, ''but I'm closing in. Stats will tell the tale. I just have to interpret them correctly and plug the holes.

''For instance, from the year-to-date patient files Jenna and I skimmed through last night, the first suspect death was in mid-February. Or was it? Were there any, say, last October through December? If not, our killer is almost certainly a new hire, since this year's have occurred at approximately two- to five-week intervals.''

Jenna's mouth opened to speak, then shut again. Paul hadn't misspoken. The deaths began at five-week intervals and were escalating, but he'd reversed the time frame for Aggie's peace of mind.

There would also be a new club formed tomorrow with her mother as founder and president. The Care Bears, maybe. Guardian Angels? No, that hit too close to its actual purpose. Leave it to Aggie to divine something cute, catchy and innocuous.

They couldn't protect every patient at Mercy Hospital, but until the murderer was caught, no family member, friend or neighbor would spend a single night there alone.

21

Mavis Purvis peered down into the shopping bag. "You didn't say a thing about me wearing a wig."

Aggie ran her tongue along her teeth, trying to think of a diplomatic way to tell Mavis that her magenta beehive had as much chance of going unnoticed as Marge Simpson's blue one.

"We can't afford to attract attention, and your hairdo has as much chance of going unnoticed as Marge Simpson's."

Mavis gaped at her, then burst out with the whiskey-hoarse laugh that years of sobriety hadn't mellowed. "You never were one to beat around the bush. It's refreshin' as all get-out, if you ask me."

And a necessity. Aggie didn't have the wherewithal or time to wheedle and curry favor. Her courage was draining away along with her energy.

Jenna and Paul would be furious if they found out she'd confided in Mavis. The retired bartender was as gossipy as the rest of Aggie's friends, but didn't trade secrets she was asked to keep. Besides, two of them prowling the hospital's hallways doubled the odds of catching the murderer. Probably not in the act—Paul was right about that—but the killer's kind of heroism required an audience. Any sign of emergency intervention and she or Mavis would swoop in and take roll.

While driving home from Jenna's, Aggie realized Paul had fibbed about the intervals between the murders. Wynema Owens had passed away ten days before Casper. Fear of discovery might stay the killer's hand a while, but the craving for attention could also be overpowering his or her self-control.

In either event, Aggie couldn't sit home waiting for someone to call and tell her whose funeral she'd be attending next.

Only God knew what Mavis's natural hair color had been, but judging by the clash of coloring between her complexion and the wig, it wasn't platinum blond.

Mavis examined the new do in the mirror above her sideboard. She finger-poked a curl here and a ringlet there, as though minor adjustments would decrease her resemblance to Don Knotts doing a Mae West impersonation.

Of course, Aggie wouldn't win any prizes for her ensemble, either. Like Mavis, beneath her winter coat she was wearing a nightgown and robe rolled up to her waist, secured with strips of duct tape so it wouldn't unroll at an inopportune moment. Having loaned the wig to Mavis, Aggie had wrapped her head in one of the turbans she sewed for chemotherapy patients. It seemed like a form of blasphemy to use it as a disguise, but the floaters Paul mentioned worried her. Not being acquainted with many third-shift employees was faint comfort when it was anyone's guess who might be moonlighting to fatten a paycheck, particularly with Christmas just around the corner.

"Got your house slippers?" she asked.

Mavis patted a coat pocket. "Check."

"Walkie-talkie?"

The other coat pocket was frisked. "Yup."

"Change for the pay phone?" Which Aggie prayed they'd need to call Paul and Jenna and tell them the killer had been caught.

Mavis nodded. "I'm packing a couple of granola bars, too. I don't want to go wobble legged from the sugar shakes in the middle of the action."

Aggie toyed with her car keys. What in the name of heaven were they doing? What was she asking Mavis to do? At their age, they had no earthly business traipsing around town after midnight. They had no business being anywhere but in bed, fast asleep, at this time of night.

"I know what you're thinking," Mavis said, "and it's about ten miles on the far side of positive." She laid a hand on Aggie's shoulder. "Listen here. The worst that can happen is that somebody notices us slinking around and admits us to the psychiatric unit for involuntary forty-eight-hour observation."

Spots danced in front of Aggie's eyes. "Oh, my Lord."

"It ain't that bad—really. Akin to a two-day vacation, if you ask me. The food's good, and you don't have to cook or wash up after. A shrink'll come by and ask a bunch of nosey-ass questions, but other than that, you can watch TV, sleep, play gin rummy or just stare out the window."

Aggie's blood pressure hiked another fifty notches before Mavis laughed and hugged Aggie's shoulder. "Lighten up, will ya? I was only teasing."

Like hell. Aggie wasn't certain how much good it

did to cuss, then pray Jesus watch over them while they trespassed on private property, but issued one, anyway. It couldn't hurt.

Mavis pocketed the extra set of ignition keys to the Volkswagen. By prior agreement, if Security nabbed one of them, a quick "Mayday" into the wal-kie-talkie would warn the other to skedaddle for the car. A half hour was plenty to wait for the other to talk herself out of trouble.

Now it was excitement not apprehension spurring Aggie's pulse. Wouldn't Casper have loved to be along for the ride? A passing streetlight's ambient glow fired the silver-white star in her engagement ring. It wasn't a wish she made on it, but a promise. Whoever had hurt Casper and took him from those who loved him best wouldn't get away with it.

"Where are you going?" Mavis tapped the passenger window. "The hospital's that way."

"I *know* where the hospital is, Mavis. I'm just being cautious."

"About what? Nobody's following us. I'll wager there aren't five cars moving in the whole dang town, and two of them are patrol cars."

Aggie braked for the cruise past Jenna's house. Uh-oh. The lamp was on in the living-room window—a sure sign her daughter wasn't home. She grinned. "Maybe not so uh-oh."

Paul's car was parked outside his pitch-dark cabin at the SeaShell Motor Court. No white Explorer was taking up an adjacent slot. Whoever Jenna was with, it wasn't Paul Haggerty.

The Volkswagen waddled over the slough between the driveway and the street. Aggie shifted into second, wondering if Jenna had been so tired she'd forgotten to turn off the lamp.

As usual, the last possibility should have been the first one tried. MacArthur Perk's plate windows looked all the brighter for being the only ones lit for blocks along Commercial Street.

"What's that girl doing out at this hour all by her lonesome?" Mavis said. "There isn't a thing to be done in that shop that couldn't wait till morning."

"I think she's missed it. At the very least, after so many days away from it, tidying up and getting ready for a new week probably feels like things are getting back to normal."

"Whatever that is." Mavis leaned forward to survey the upcoming intersection. "Doesn't this bucket of bolts go any faster than twenty miles an hour? Or have you got a grade A excuse ready if we happen across Sam or Kathy."

"I'm going the speed limit and we won't be happening across Sam or Kathy. She's on first shift all week with a field-training officer. Sam went off duty at eleven."

"How do you feel about having two cops in the family?"

It was a question Aggie must become accustomed to hearing without the pinch behind her ribs. She answered the same way she had so very long ago. "They're perfect for each other."

Mavis looked sideward, frowning as a music aficionado does when an orchestra's cellist or horn player hits a clinker.

Aggie gripped the steering wheel to force the flashback of Liz and Rick's wedding back into the memory vault where it belonged. "Don't mind me.

I'm a silly old lady that can't feature her grandbaby taking a wife. It seems like only last week I was stitching pipe-cleaner whiskers on his Peter Cottontail costume for Halloween.''

"Time flies, whether you're having any fun or not," Mavis said, chuckling. "I remember that costume. Law, he was cuter than a bug's ear."

"He hated it with a passion, too. He wanted to be a superhero not a 'dumb stupid sissy wabbit.'"

They fell silent as the car chugged up the incline to the emergency room's entrance. A county ambulance hunkered under the portico, its lights off and bay doors shut, but exhaust huffing out the tailpipes.

Parking spaces abounded nearby, yet the cold, metallic-tasting air chafed Aggie's lungs during the short trek to the building. Luck was with them, though. The reception area was empty. The paramedics and medical staff were probably kicked back in the anteroom, drinking vending machine coffee to celebrate the quiet passage of Sunday night into the wee hours of Monday.

Aggie pushed on the side entrance's door, muttered, "Hell's bells," and cocked a hip against the bar handle to hold it in place.

"Whassamatter?"

"Forgot the props." Fumbling under her coat and duct-taped clothing inner tube for the fanny pack she was wearing frontward, Aggie yanked open a flap secured with Velcro. She stowed the car keys, then removed two lighters and two half-empty packs of generic cigarettes.

"What the—" Mavis waved them away. "You know damn well I quit smokin' after the bed caught fire back in '96, and you never started."

"Take 'em." The wad at her waist threatened to unfurl. Aggie wrapped her coat around it and cinched the belt tight. "Anyone asks why you're prowling the halls, say you're going outside for a smoke. They'll give you grief but they won't stop you."

"Agatha Franks, you're a far sight smarter than I ever gave you credit for."

Once inside, they cut right down the broad corridor between the E.R. and Outpatient Surgery. A redwood planter divided the waiting area from a corridor accessing cell-like private consultation rooms where surgeons reported to family members after procedures were finished.

Aggie chose door number three. It was as dark as pitch inside the cubicle, but they didn't need light to untape their nightclothes and exchange their street shoes for slippers.

Mavis said, "Care if I ask you something?"

"Shh. Keep your voice down."

"How come we hitched up our pajammers under our coats if it's okay for patients to go outside and smoke?"

"Because…" Aggie made a face. "We don't have time to stand around gabbing. Hide your shoes under that magazine table and let's get on with it."

By prearrangement, Mavis would take the first floor and Aggie the second. The third floor's east wing was Mavis territory, while Aggie went west, then they'd meet by the elevators and switch routes.

Pediatrics, Obstetrics, the nursery, Intensive Care and, by all means, the psychiatric units were off limits. To Aggie's knowledge, no suspicious deaths had occurred there and the staff was more likely to question an insomniac hall-walker.

As they parted for their appointed rounds, Aggie turned and whispered Mavis's name. "Thank you. For everything."

"Don't mention it." Mavis winked. "To *anybody*."

With her fingers curled around the walkie-talkie in her pocket and her thumb poised to key the talk button, Aggie strode by the information desk, the gift shop, cafeteria entrance and the chapel. Elevator number three got her business. It was beginning to feel lucky and she was beginning to feel like a kindergartner on the first day of school.

The second floor's deserted, shadowy hallway reminded her of a sci-fi movie Casper had dragged her to about a town whose inhabitants had vanished in the midst of their daily routines. In room 202, a patient's respirator clacked and wheezed with the beat of a waltz playing low on his roommate's bedside radio. Farther on, wall-bracketed televisions cast fan-shaped prisms on the acoustical ceiling tiles. Aerosol disinfectants, noxious-smelling in their own right, waged losing battles with sickroom odors, floor wax and the coat of fresh paint drying above the handrails.

Most of the patients she peeked in on were asleep; a few had their mouths wide open, sawing logs with a dull blade. A woman of about Aggie's age and two men several years younger fidgeted and grimaced as if rousing from sedation. She watched each of them for several minutes until satisfied they were uncomfortable but not in distress.

What did she propose to do if she chanced upon a victim, or a twenty- to thirty-year-old caregiver injecting an IV? Call for help? Tell Mavis to come on the double? Throw a hollering, foot-stomping hissy, if need be?

A couple of days' worth of good food, gin rummy and staring out the window was no price to pay at all for being wrong.

Hushed voices and a telephone's ring migrated from the nurses' station around the corner. The sluggish squinch of crepe-soled shoes on linoleum put Aggie on alert. An aide pushing a rubber-tired cart loaded with water pitchers, cups and a basin of crushed ice angled away from the station's pool of light.

Aggie looked around frantically for somewhere to hide. Beside her was a twelve-foot stretch of solid wall. She didn't dare break for the patient room across the hall. No sudden moves, she told herself.

The aide stopped the cart alongside the first doorway on her right. Cups in hand, she entered the room…without a backward glance.

Clammy sweat prickled the nape of Aggie's neck, then soaked the back of her gown and under her arms. Her feet and fingers numbed. She swayed a little, shivering despite the heat suffusing her chest and face.

She damned herself for a ninny, delivered a stern lecture on straightening up, flying right, on having some gumption, for heaven's sake, instead of acting like a dumb stupid sissy wabbit.

The spell began to break, the chill and fever and seasick feeling easing by increments. The bands girding her chest hadn't loosened yet, but would. Mind over matter, Casper always said. Sometimes it even worked. Aggie blew out a breath, like a smoker exhales after several hours' abstinence.

Well, of all the idiotic— Wooden fingertips crackled the cellophane-wrapped prop in her coat pocket. Smarter than Mavis gave her credit for? What a crock. Dumber than Jenna's dogs was nearer the truth. Before the aide startled her, she was fretting over how in the world she'd slip by the nurses' station to the rooms at the other end of the hall.

Lord, let Casper be catching forty winks in heaven right now, not looking down on the weak sister she'd become since he left her.

The aide soldiered on with her trolley. Not a suspect, Aggie decided. The girl hadn't the authority to handle or dispense anything except over-the-counter medications, if those. Charge nurses with access to controlled substances weren't infallible. In an emergency situation, a cabinet could be left unsecured. A harried R.N. with a full house and too few helping hands might allow a trusted, albeit unlicensed, aide to deliver meds to a patient in dire need. But a murderer couldn't rely on anomalies to coincide with his or her heroic urges.

Aggie squared her shoulders and switched the cigarettes and lighter from her right pocket to her left hand. Bold as brass, she checked the remaining rooms, two of which were empty, then sauntered on, her knees jellied but her chin as obstinate as a bulldog's.

The nurse with the phone receiver to her ear was arguing, presumably with a doctor, about a patient's impacted bowels. Another was bent over a pile of charts, her pen dotting i's and crossing t's with machine-gun speed. A second aide of perhaps twelve was slumped on a counter, chewing gum, filing her nails and nodding to the rap beat pulsing from her headphones.

Aggie was two steps, three at most, from an intersecting wall, when a bubble popped loud as a pistol shot. A voice sneered, "'Ey. Where you think you're goin', lady?"

The nurse updating charts looked up. "May I help you?"

"No, no, I'm fine." Aggie waved the cigarette pack. "Rules are rules."

The nurse's gaze lowered to Aggie's wrist. A patient-ID bracelet. If only she'd thought of it, one could have been fashioned from— She couldn't think for the pounding at her temples.

"What's your name and room number, ma'am?"

Aggie tried to smile. "Um, I'm in, uh—316." She pointed at the ceiling. "Just checked in this afternoon. Late. Well, actually this evening. What's the rush, right, when nothing's really wrong. Just tests."

A cleft formed between the nurse's eyebrows. Palms flat against the edge of the desk, she started to push her chair backward. Now the one on the telephone had canted her head to peer at Aggie.

"Oh—oh! Are you coming *with* me?" Aggie clapped a hand to her chest before her heart burst out of it. "That would be wonderful, simply *wonderful.* I have all kinds of questions about those tests I've been *dying* to ask someone, but the nurse on three says she's too busy, though she didn't look all that busy to me."

The chair stopped, as if the castors had fallen off.

"Well, c'mon, dear. Let's shake a leg," Aggie chirped. "After all, I *must* get some rest before tomorrow's ordeal and—"

"Aw, don't sweat it, Kerry. I'll go with her." The aide hopped down from her perch. "I need a break anyhow."

"From what?" The nurse motioned a by-your-leave at Aggie. "I'm sorry, but you'll have to find your own way downstairs. Follow the directories to the E.R. All the other doors were locked at 10:00 p.m."

Aggie almost said, "Are you sure you won't go with me?" but couldn't get her second wind. No sense in gilding the lily. Can't wait to tell Mavis.

The floor took on a life of its own; the linoleum squares rippled and fishtailed. Get to a room. Find a chair. Rest a minute—be fine, then. Her stomach topsy-turvyed as the ivory walls turned a bilious yellow.

The walkie-talkie was as cumbersome as a paving brick. Static sounded like the cheers of a faraway crowd. "Mayday. May—"

It was as if thick, black ink had been dashed in Aggie's eyes. She heard the radio smack the floor....

22

A gust of Estée Lauder perfume stopped Paul at the doorway to the hospital room. Barging into the institutional equivalent of not one, but two, ladies' boudoirs reduced any mature, worldly-wise male to a stammering, toe-digging twelve-year-old kid.

A law of the Murphy persuasion dictated that regardless of the reason for hospitalization, any female patient a guy proposes to visit will be assigned the B-bed parallel to the room's exterior wall. And the A-bed nearest the door is always occupied. And entry to the sanctum will often coincide with patient A engaging in an activity a man could cheerfully live his entire life and likely the next without witnessing.

Aggie motioned from the B-bed for Paul to get a move on. Gaze fixed as frontward as a mounted-police horse, he strode past Aggie's roommate as though she were invisible. The attempt at chivalry earned the snappish *"Well"* that women of a certain age can transform into an obscenity.

Plastic tubing hissed oxygen into Aggie's nostrils. One arm was tethered to an IV; a cardiac monitor blinked and beeped. The sheet and thermal blanket were tucked to her chin, as if she was chilled, but her cheeks were the shiny, rosy shade of pink peculiar to incurable alcoholics and the hypertensive.

"You lied to me, Aggie."

"A tiny little white one." She touched a finger to her lips. "Close the curtain. Please."

The drape's carrier slides whistled on the metal rod. The neighbor took vocal exception to that, as well.

Aggie said, "You didn't call Jenna, did you?"

"Not after promising you I wouldn't when you called me." Paul unbuttoned his leather coat and unclipped the cell phone from his belt. "An error in judgment I'll rectify in about thirty seconds."

Aggie waved her hands. "No, please. Hear me out. What's a few minutes, one way or the other?"

She had him there. Jenna was going to shoot, stab, bludgeon, then hang him from a century tree when she found out he'd come tearing to the hospital at 6:00 a.m. without calling her first.

Aggie smiled and patted the mattress. Paul took the bedside chair, cell phone still in hand.

"I'm not sick," she said.

"Yeah. That's why you're on oxygen."

"It's just a precaution. I'm overtired is all." She crooked a finger. "They think I had a heart attack, but I didn't. I faked one."

"Aggie, so help me…"

"All right, what I did was foolish, but I couldn't just sit home and wait for the next body to drop." She grimaced. "What a horrible thing to say."

"The way it came out isn't what you meant. I do it all the time." He holstered the cell phone. "When I got here, for instance. I hope you know it was worry doing the talking, not anger."

"Don't speak too soon. I haven't finished yet." There was a pillow adjustment made and some blanket plucking before she resumed. "What I set out to do wasn't to prove you wrong about the impossibility of catching the kil—uh, the *person* in the act."

She shook her head, frowning as though telling her thoughts to settle down and behave themselves. "Same difference, I suppose, but I wanted to put a stop to this reign of terror.

"Casper tried. I'm absolutely convinced of it. As convinced as I am that people know when they're going to die. Whether it's the last instant before an accident, or they're sick abed and everyone swears they're going to be fine. They *know* better. You don't live in a body for seventy years and get taken by surprise when it fails you."

Paul nodded. He had firsthand knowledge of that. The body truly is a machine, and it won't quit until it's damn good and ready, no matter how much you beg.

"If he'd known, he wouldn't have come right out and said so," Aggie continued, "but there would have been signs. He was furious with Vinita about the visiting hours, but went along to keep the peace."

"And so did you."

"I chose my battle. Casper had agreed to move in with me when the doctor dismissed him, so I could take care of him."

In other words, Aggie's turf. Aggie's rules.

"The day before he passed away," she continued, "he told me he was working on a new mystery plot—a double-dog of a doozy, he called it. I asked what it was. He wouldn't tell me. That was a first, and I should have realized something was out of kilter."

She took a deep drag of oxygen, then coughed. "My throat's dry as dust from this thing."

Paul poured her a glass of water. It was lukewarm, as cardiac patients aren't allowed to have ice, but she didn't complain.

"Casper didn't tell me the plot because we've been together too long. Soon as I'd had time to think, I'd have guessed his imagination hadn't hatched it. When I did, I'd have raised six kinds of hell."

For all the good it would have done, Paul thought. The chance anyone would have believed them was slim to none. Everyone, including himself and Jenna, would have dismissed it as a figment of a couple of senior citizen wanna-be mystery novelists' imaginations.

Everyone, that is, except the killer. The horrible irony was that if hell had been raised, Casper would be living like a sultan in the blue-over-white house with chateau-style trim at 210 Lyon Street instead of under a grassy knoll in the Sunrise, Sunset section of Pfister Memorial Cemetery.

Aggie said, "I wanted revenge. I wanted to see justice done, have a hand in it. At least, that's what I thought when I snuck in here last night. Somewhere along the way, while I was peeking in rooms, making sure no harm was being done to those innocent, sleeping people, I realized I wasn't out to catch a killer. I was protecting them *from* one."

Her voice was straining and her breathing was increasingly labored. Paul insisted that she rest, said he must let Jenna know her mother was in the hospital—the whys and wheretofores could wait. There was no sense in explaining twice and Jenna wouldn't appreciate hearing it from him.

"I'm not an invalid and won't stand to be treated like one. Now hush up and listen. It's your fault I'm stuck here for observation, anyway."

He pointed at his chest. "*My* fault?"

"Well, I guess Jenna deserves half the blame," Aggie allowed. "I'd have never thought of skulking the halls like a burglar if you two hadn't broken into the business offices Saturday night to search the patient and personnel records."

She took another hit of oxygen. "Wouldn't have done it if you hadn't said a killer nurse was on the loose, either."

"Hey." Paul glanced over his shoulder. "Not so loud, okay?"

Aggie flapped a hand. "That old biddy in the other bed thinks she's a Romanian princess. Deaf as a fence post, too."

Maybe. His grandmother's selective hearing tuned out the boring and inane, but whisper that her housekeeping and cooking weren't what they used to be and she'd shotgun whatever was handy—a tissue box, silverware, the collected poems of Seamus Heaney—like Joe Namath at the top of his game.

Aggie said, "With all that, it's no wonder I had the heebie-jeebies. Then that head nurse on two stopped me and starting asking nosey questions. Didn't believe a word I told her. I just knew she was going to call Security. If they called the police, Sam would find out. So I acted like I was having a heart attack." A wry smile appeared. "Seemed like a good idea at the time."

Acted? The readings on the monitor's LED screens weren't fakes. There was some truth in her story. There'd been some in Nixon's version of the Watergate break-in, too.

"After the E.R. doctor gave me the once-over, I'd hoped they'd let you take me home."

Paul chuffed. "And the whole mess could have stayed our little secret."

She studied a rent in the blanket. Exhaustion and melancholy broke through the brave front she'd struggled to maintain. "Jenna and Sam worry far too much about me as it is. They won't understand the insult in it till they're old and nobody listens to them, either."

"Aggie..."

"Wait'll Mallory comes on duty this evening. She'll tell 'em how the cow ate the cabbage. She knows I was perfectly fine when they hauled me in here last night."

Paul started. "Who's Mallory?"

"Mallory Fergus," she answered, as though he were a simpleton for not recognizing the name. "She saved Sam's life when somebody poisoned his drink with syrup of ipecac at a football game."

"So she's worked at the hospital for several years."

"Oh, yes." Aggie clucked her tongue. "I had no idea what horror that poor girl's been through since I saw her last. Her husband abandoned her after their baby was born with cerebral palsy. I don't know how, but she took care of that sick little boy all by herself till he passed away last Christmas Eve."

Paul flinched with the peculiar kind of guilty gratitude felt by parents of healthy children. There were worse ways to lose a child than by a loving stepfather's adoption.

"You'd think she'd be bitter, but she isn't. She's even transferring to Pediatrics next week."

"That seems like the last place she'd want to work. Then again, who would have more compassion toward the parents of a seriously ill child than someone who's cared for one."

"I told her the same thing last night."

A vague uneasiness had Paul shifting in the chair. He plastered on a grin, hoping it would inflect his voice. "Sounds like the two of you really hit it off. What else did you talk about?"

"Oh, you know, just—" Aggie's lips crooked into a sneer. "Woe to the daughter who has a fool for a mother, eh? Is that what you're implying?"

"No, I wasn't implying anything."

"Don't insult my intelligence then try to wriggle out of it with a lie." She faced the window. "I think it's time for you to call Jenna."

Paul rose to his feet and kissed the top of her head. "I'm sorry, Aggie. I happen to believe that neither Jenna nor her son have fools for mothers."

A nurse with a halo of curly hair was checking the dozing Romanian princess's pulse as Paul left the room. The nurse's back was turned and her concentration focused on her wristwatch's sweeping second hand.

He proceeded into the corridor, then halted outside the door. He could return to Aggie's bedside and wait for a better look at the nurse's face and ID badge. Or bide his time until she exited the room.

His watch read 6:58. Near enough to shift change that the graveyard crew should be gathering up their coats and thermal lunch kits for the drive home. The

usual drill for incoming nurses was to make the
rounds and record top o' the morning vital signs.

Paul hadn't heard the attending "How are we feeling today?" that annoyed the bejesus out of patients
on general principle, but his glimpse of the nurse's
iron-gray hair was reassuring.

Chauvinistic as it sounded, few females in their
twenties and early thirties would let their hair fade
to a premature gray. Today's youth obsession was
propelling a significant number of men down drugstore aisles where hair coloring products were
stocked, as well.

You're stalling, Ace, Paul thought. No time like
the present for Jenna to hand you your head on a
platter and tell you where to shove it.

"Grandma's fine." Jenna's head tipped back to
look her huge, angry son in the eye. "She may have
had a mild heart attack and her blood pressure is
higher than it should be, but she's been under way
too much stress the last week or so."

"Uh-huh." Sam cocked a hip and planted his
hands on his utility belt. "I'm kinda stressed myself
at the moment."

"Well, of course you are. How many hours' overtime have you put in the last few days?"

"That's some of it. Damn sure isn't all of it."

Five seconds. Ten. Neither of them blinked.
Budged. Sam was no piker at visual standoffs, but
Jenna had many more years' practice. And she was
his mother.

"I thought I was hallucinating about 0300 when I
saw Grandma's Beetle eastbound on Walnut Lawn."

A silent "Oh, shit" was followed by a verbal

"You did?" Paul had relayed the details of Aggie's escapade and the inspiration behind it. Jenna hadn't told Sam and had no intention of doing so, but that time and location didn't jibe.

"I pulled her over and was primed to read her the riot act, when who did I find behind the wheel but Mavis Purvis."

"Mavis?" Jenna's voice upticked an octave.

"It gets nothing but better, Mom. The nightgown and robe Mavis had on under her coat didn't throw me for much of a loop, but the blond wig sitting whomperjawed on her head had me scratching mine."

Jenna tottered backward to the nearest chair and sat down hard. She should have known Aggie's caper wasn't done solo. Except, when had Mavis become the go-to gal for harebrained conspiracies? And why had Mavis abandoned Aggie when she passed out? Unless the heart attack scenario was hatched in advance and as bogus as Aggie said it was.

Sam went on, "I didn't have any choice but to buy Mavis's story about borrowing Grandma's car for a hot date with some night-blind old geezer. What was I supposed to do? Call Grandma and check it out?

"I didn't think much more about it." He made a face. "Tried to forget it, truth be known, then what's the nurse tell me when I get here? That Grandma collapsed in the second-floor hallway, already in her nightie, an hour or so before I stopped Mavis."

Jenna crossed her arms atop her head as if her skull might explode. "I should have guessed, but this is the first I've heard about Mavis being in cahoots with your grandmother. Paul didn't know, either. He'd have told me if he had.''

"In cahoots? Why? And what's Haggerty got to do with anything?''

"Grandma called him, instead of me, when she was admitted for observation. She thought if she were released quickly enough, Paul could take her home and none of us would be the wiser.''

After insisting that he sit down, Jenna explained their suspicions that a nurse on staff had murdered several patients, including Casper. Aggie, and apparently Mavis, thought they could catch the killer in the act.

Sam wasn't one to let anger show. But beneath his calm exterior was an explosion waiting to happen. ''A few days ago you and Grandma tried to convince me that Vinita Potts had murdered Cappy.''

"The bottom line is, his death didn't appear natural to any of us. Paul and I are—''

"Who is he, Mom? Where'd he come from? You haven't been out on a date in a year or better, and all of a sudden he hits town and, wham-o, you're joined at the hip. Then you're not and now you are again.''

Jenna shook her head. ''That's not true.''

"Then what is? I go to Quantico for a week, and when I get back, nothing is the same. You spring this Haggerty guy on me, but Grandma and Cappy act like he's a member of the family already. Then they steal mine and Kathy's thunder about our engagement, which would have been okay, if you'd seemed the least bit happy that *we* were getting married—''

"I *was*. I *am*—''

"Next thing I know, Cappy's dead, Haggerty's

still here, everybody thinks you and Grandma have gone off your nut, and now she's maybe had a heart attack from pussyfooting around the hospital with Mavis in the middle of the night.''

Jenna laid her hand on his. ''I understand why you're upset. We've barely said two words to each other since you got home, but this just isn't the time or place.''

He jerked his hand away and gained his feet. ''It never is, is it? Never has been. There's always something more important you have to deal with first.''

''Sweetheart, you're the most important thing—''

''Save it for later, Mom. I'm going to visit with Grandma a minute, then head for the house to get some sleep.''

''The house? You mean, my house?''

''Yeah.'' He snorted. ''Seems like only yesterday, it was ours, but what the hell. Gotta move on—''

''That's *enough*, Sam MacArthur.'' Jenna sprang from the chair. ''You have a right to be angry. I wish we could go off and talk everything—and I do mean *everything*—out, but my mother is hooked up to an oxygen hose and cardiac monitors, and I can't deal with that and you and a shop I have to open somehow in an hour and a manager I don't know whether to fire or strangle with my bare hands all at the same damn time.''

He glared down at her, the resemblance to his father a virtual mirror image, then he rolled his eyes and bear-hugged her shoulders. ''I love you, Mom.''

Her ''I love you, too'' was muffled by his insulated jacket. ''I ought to kick your butt up between your ears for talking to me like that though.''

"Better save that for later, too. I'm so tired, you might get lucky."

Jenna stepped back. "Is Kathy sick? Or are you two on the outs because of me."

He frowned. "She's fine. We're fine. Why?"

"Just curious why you want to crash at our ancestral home."

"We haven't even set a date yet, but the bridal consultant Kathy's mom hired is coming to the apartment at ten."

"Three's a crowd, huh?"

"It is when one of them's trying to sleep. Besides, our fridge is about empty again and yours never is."

Refrigerator. Kitchen. Omigod. "Grandma's got tons more food in hers than I do. And it's quieter— no dogs, or a cat to pester you."

"Yeah, but—"

"Really, hon, you'd be lots more comfortable at Grandma's, and an empty house is an invitation to burglars. Especially so soon after a funeral." Jenna knew she was pushing too hard, but had to dissuade him somehow.

Sam's arm dropped from her shoulder. "You're weirding out on me again. Did you forget you already had a houseguest?" With that, he turned on his heels and stalked from the lounge.

When he disappeared into Aggie's room, Jenna made a mad dash for the elevator. She was panting when she intercepted Paul in the cafeteria line. The cardboard tray he was sliding toward the cashier bulged with pastries, fruit bowls, two large coffees and two orange juices.

"Sam's with Mom. If he asks where I am, tell him I went to the rest room."

"Okay, but where are you going?"

"Home," she answered over her shoulder.

There was no time to explain why. She had to drive home, pitch the files and folders she'd left on the kitchen table in her truck and zip back to the hospital before her son finished his visit with his grandmother.

That he'd see Paul toting a picnic breakfast on a hospital tray, instead of snoring between her sheets, was no consolation.

All those old lies and secrets had been told and kept to protect Sam. In one way or another, the new ones were necessary to shore up the old.

Except now, the person they were designed to protect was herself. And the one they were hurting most was her son.

23

There was no Mallory—Fergus or other surnamed—on the list of full-timers and floaters who'd
worked the graveyard shift since the first of the year.
Confirming that fact was about the only progress
he'd made after hours of telephone calls and Internet
searches.

Paul tossed his pen on the legal pad, then watched
as it rolled off and sank into the shag carpet. Okay,
for one reason or several, including gut instinct, he'd
narrowed the field of suspects by five. It was too
much to ask for the killer's name to have leaped off
the page in a clamor of bells, whistles and exploding
Roman candles.

"It could've, though. Just between me, myself and
the clock on the wall, I was counting on it."

Reaching for the ceiling, he grimaced at the cracks
and pops of joints and vertebrae misaligned from sitting slumped in a SeaShell Motor Court club chair
all afternoon. The aspirin he'd knocked back every
couple of hours might as well have been breath mints
for all the good they'd done. The spirit was willing
but the body felt like an archaeological specimen.

His gaze slid to the telephone he'd moved from
the desk to the floor beside him. The latest report on
Aggie hadn't been good. When the cardiologist had

spoken with Jenna earlier, he'd slalomed between cautious optimism and worst-case possibilities.

He agreed that the onset of arrhythmia and Aggie's failure to respond to treatment might well be attributed to stress, overexertion, disruption of her medication schedule and the onset of depression. Whatever the cause, until her blood pressure was under control, she was at risk of a stroke or a serious heart attack.

As if that wasn't enough for Jenna to deal with, she'd been unable to reach Sam or Kathy. The presumption was that Sam had taken the phone off the hook so he could sleep, and that Kathy had already left the apartment for duty. By now, surely one or the other or both had called Aggie's room to check on her.

Paul switched on a couple of lamps as he made his way to the bathroom to splash cold water on his face. Joyce Ramsour should be arriving at the hospital about now. She'd agreed to sit with Aggie so Paul could drag Jenna to the cafeteria for dinner. She might even go willingly, considering she'd dissected her breakfast rather than eat it, and there was scant doubt that she'd skipped lunch altogether.

"Then what, sport?" he inquired of the mirror. "Between bites of mystery meat, should you casually remind her that today is supposed to be Hit the Road Day and pray to God she asks you to stay? Say nothing and pray to God she doesn't, either? Or tell her she's ten times the woman Liz Rivas ever was and they owe it to themselves to give the future a chance?"

Those questions were still festering in his mind as

he and Jenna finished their salads and started the en-trée course, rumored to be chicken chow mein.

"Not bad," he said.

"Definitely a notch above the usual."

"The canned kind? Or frozen?"

She scooped a generous portion with her fork. "Frozen. My epicurean taste buds tell me this is the canned kind. Please note the overabundance of bam-boo shoots and under-abundance of water chestnuts. They're dead giveaways."

Paul shrugged. "Not bad, though."

"Not bad at all, and thank you for going behind my back and arranging for Joyce to stay with Mom for a while." She laughed. "Don't bother trying to look innocent. You're terrible at it, and I know Joyce didn't just happen by when she did."

"She could have."

"Yeah, and I might have believed it if she'd waited thirty seconds before suggesting we have din-ner together."

They jumped at a toddler's ear-splitting wail, closely followed by the cartoonlike *kaboinks* of a plastic tumbler rebounding on the floor. A few tables away, a sympathizer took up the call, then both chil-dren's cries were absorbed into the generalized din.

At traditional mealtimes, a hospital cafeteria pos-sessed the atmosphere and intimacy of an army mess hall. Paul welcomed the racket and imagined Jenna did, too. Someone once said, "Silence can soothe the soul, or loose upon it the snarling hounds." Bring on the marching bands, he thought, if it would hold the packs snapping at their heels at bay.

"Have you talked to Mavis since this morning?" he asked.

"I don't think that's wise until I'm beyond the death threat stage. The ides of March, maybe. Fourth of July weekend at the outside."

"She didn't instigate last night's caper."

"True, but she could have nipped it in the bud, instead of riding shotgun. Mom wouldn't have had the cojones to go it alone. At least, I don't think so."

Paul sprinkled soy sauce on a gummy dune of rice. "You're not blaming Mavis for Aggie's illness, are you?"

She shook her head. "Hitting the streets in their nightgowns at three o'clock in the morning probably wasn't a real healthy choice for either of them, but Mom hasn't felt that great for a month or two."

As if by mutual consent, they curtailed that conversational path. Having established that Aggie's hospitalization was inevitable, continuing the discussion would circle around to now being the worst possible time for it and Mercy being the last place they'd have chosen for treatment.

Paul was content to survey the other diners, the shuffling line in front of the steam tables, the ruddy-complexioned cooks apportioning their wares. Without them, he'd have no camouflage for watching the woman seated across from him.

The hollows beneath her eyes and cheekbones were shadowed—a sign of fitful sleep and too little of it. She picked at her food as she had this morning, but now she was mining for the choice bits rather than waste a modest appetite on filler. The nails of both hands were bitten ragged, except for the ring finger on one and pinkie on the other—rations, he supposed, for the long night ahead.

It would be a lie to say she'd never looked lovelier, but he'd never wanted her more. He could, he was sure of it, erase the worry lines creasing her forehead, make her laugh, free all the hurt and sorrow locked inside, then hold her, tell her without words that he was there, would always be there, and that there was nothing to be afraid of anymore.

"This is nice," she said.

Paul smiled, adrift in that sweet spot between thought and real time. "What is?"

"Not talking." She batted her hand. "Not feeling like we have to talk, just because couples who don't over dinner must be bored out of their minds, and God forbid we let a roomful of strangers know that the honeymoon is over."

Paul laughed—who wouldn't?—yet he could have done without that "honeymoon is over" line. Though unintentional, a door had opened on the questions he'd asked the mirror but didn't have the courage to ask her.

He thought of another. A compromise. A less confrontational tack with no ultimatums or strings attached.

"You're staying with Aggie tonight," he said as one would a forgone conclusion.

An eyebrow raised. "I would anyway. If they'd let me, I'd feed her cherry Popsicles and a bowl of Mrs. Finkleberm's kosher chicken soup, like Mom did me when I was a kid."

Paul rested his elbows on the table, bracing himself without appearing to be. "How's about we stay with her in shifts? Rotate every three, four hours between the visitor's chair and stretching out on the couch in the lounge."

Now both eyebrows crested. Her mouth tucked at

the corners, in consideration or regret, Paul couldn't say.

Sam MacArthur wasn't easily overlooked, even in a packed house, but Paul didn't see him until he loomed large behind his mother.

"Joyce said you were here. Glad I caught y'all before you left." He bent down to kiss Jenna's temple, then stuck out his hand. "How's it going, Paul?" As their hands clasped, Sam added, "Or should I call you Detective-Sergeant Haggerty?"

Jenna's fork clinked the edge of her plate and fell to the floor. Paul sat stunned, staring up at Sam's hauntingly familiar face.

He appropriated a chair from the neighboring table. "Don't mind if I join you, do you?" He glanced at his mother. "Can't stay but a minute. I'm sort of playing hooky from patrol."

With robotic precision, Jenna plucked kernels of rice from her lap and returned them to the plate. Save the motion, she could have been mistaken for a chalk-white mannequin.

"All I came by to ask is why nobody told me you used to be a cop," Sam said, more confusion and hurt in his voice than anger. "An NYPD Crimes Unit detective, no less."

"It, uh, I guess it just never came up," Paul said. "It isn't as if we've had a whole lot of time to talk."

Sam turned to Jenna. "You knew. Grandma knew. Maybe not at first, but that's why she went to him for help when Cappy died. Seems like it would've been the most natural thing in the world to mention it to me somewhere along the line."

Jenna's sigh was tremulous. "Yes, I suppose it should have been."

Paul marveled at her composure. She didn't explain. Didn't apologize. Her worst nightmare was devouring her from the inside out, but she'd simply looked her son in the eye and given him the only answer she could.

Sam turned back to Paul. "I homed in on you in the kitchen before your butt parted company with Grandma's bar stool. I just didn't know why. My first instinct said you were a con man. It explained why my family was so taken with you so fast. The second told me you were a cop."

He grunted in derision. "The third said dirty cop."

Paul shook his head. Reflex, not denial.

"Yeah, I know. Far from it. Commendations out the ass and the highest clearance rate in the city."

Jenna's eyes were as wide and flat as river rocks. It hadn't been discussed, but they'd both expected Sam to check Paul out—wants, outstanding warrants, even Paul's driving record.

Finding him to be a law-abiding, tax-paying, exemplary citizen wasn't good enough. Not for Officer Sam MacArthur. Dig deep enough and everyone has something to hide. Every freshman criminalistics major knows that.

"Your ears should have been burning around three this afternoon," Sam said. "Me and Dean Cordrey talked for better than an hour. He said you were a shoo-in for captain, if that wreck hadn't put you on permanent disability."

Dean Cordrey was a couple of years younger than Paul and another of Rick Rivas's protégés. *Jesus.* If Cordrey had any idea he was speaking with Rick's son...

"I'm impressed," Paul said. "If your chief had

any sense, he'd promote you to detective. So what do you want for all that effort? An apology? You got it. I should have submitted my entire résumé for your review from the get-go."

Sam cocked back in the chair. His gaze shifted from Paul to his mother. "An explanation is what I want. A reason why I'm the last to know who you are, where you came from and why I had to find out on my own."

Jenna shot Paul a hard look—a demand that he say nothing. He telegraphed a plea for her to tell her son the truth.

Presently, the front legs of Sam's chair touched down again. He stood and returned the chair to its original table. "I'll call the desk later to see how Grandma's feeling."

Jenna's hand brushed his sleeve. "Sam, I—" He stiffened at her touch. She said, "First thing tomorrow morning, I'm having her transferred by ambulance to a hospital in Springfield."

Sam nodded. His rubber-soled oxfords made not a sound as he walked from the room.

Her features waxen, Jenna stared at a place far beyond what the human eye can see. Paul knew she was telling herself what was done was done, but that everything would be fine because she'd make it that way.

Her crumpled napkin fell over what remained of her dinner. She grabbed her shoulder bag by the handle and scooted out of her chair. "I have to go. Have to get back upstairs."

Paul reached out his hand. She hesitated, then took it, her icy fingers entwining his. Neither of them spoke until they reached the lobby concourse. In one direction, a broad corridor led to the elevators accessing the upper floors. To his left was the main entrance.

He guided her beside the windowed wall overlooking the grounds. He started to ask if she was all right, to tell her she'd *be* all right, to assure her that the rift between her and Sam would mend, if not heal, and that Aggie would live to drive her crazy another day.

Jenna looked up at him. She loved him. She always would. It was all he needed to be certain he couldn't stay. He learned when he'd chosen his little girl's happiness and security over his own that sometimes the truest love is the kind that lets go.

Paul smoothed the hair from her face, the strands parting, rippling beneath his fingertips like water. He breathed in her scent, kissed the tears from the corners of her eyes, then her lips, trembling under his.

Maybe at a different time, a different place… No. Don't even think it.

He turned and walked away, praying for a last chance. Listening for her to call out his name, for rushing footsteps, for the touch of her hand on his arm.

Jenna slumped against the window. She stared after Paul, her jaw clenched tight as tears coursed down her cheeks. Don't go. Look back, *please*. Oh, God, once, just once, can't loving me mean staying? Don't leave me like Daddy did, then Jimmy, then Rick.

The hospital's pneumatic doors slid open at their center. *I love you, Paul. Can't you hear me?* He hesitated at the threshold. One second…two, then his shoulders sagged. Without looking back, he strode into the crisp, night air.

Jenna tipped back her head, her eyes squeezed shut, willing herself not to cry anymore. He was right to go. It had to be this way. She loved him too much to make him leave; he loved her too much to stay.

Everything was going to be just fine. She'd stay with Aggie tonight. Keep her safe. All those secrets and lies were safe again now, too. She'd think of something to tell Sam. He wouldn't believe her—not entirely—but he had a life to get on with. With Paul gone from hers, no further explanation was necessary. Just another page to file under things of the past and forget all about.

As insentient as a sleepwalker, she turned and started for the elevators, then ambled into the gift shop. It was just a diversion, a mental recess to collect her wits before returning alone to her mother's room.

Before she was through, the clerk had docked her debit card twenty-eight dollars and change. Weighting the shopping bag was a ceramic basket of potted violets for Aggie, a Toblerone bar Joyce would pretend to strangle her for buying, and a paperback novel for herself, identical to the title stocked two shelves from the top of the bin at MacArthur Perk.

"They're beautiful," Aggie said when presented with the flowers, "but you shouldn't have spent the money."

The nurse replacing a depleted IV bag glanced back at Jenna. Silvery curls contradicted her, at most, thirtysomething face. By her wry smile, her mother left no thank-you unqualified, either.

Jenna craned her neck toward the bathroom. The light was on and the door open. "Where's Joyce?"

"It can't have been more than a minute since she left," Aggie said. "One of the girls called needing her to do something."

Typical. "I hope she remembers to let Homer and Herschel out on her way home."

Aggie looked past her. "Isn't Paul with you?"

"No, Mom. He, uh—he had a plane to catch."

"Oh, Jenna, honey, I'm so sorry."

"Don't be." Her eyes flicked to the nurse, who was apparently preoccupied with timing the IV's drip. "Que sera sera and all that."

The shopping bag and her purse were set beside the high-backed visitor's chair, but Jenna remained standing. If Aggie's condition had improved, it wasn't evident to Jenna, but she asked the obligatory "Are you feeling better?"

"Much better. I knew I would as soon as I got some rest." Aggie wrenched her head around on the pillow. "Didn't I?"

The nurse bent down to check the heplock taped to her patient's forearm. "I wouldn't sign up for any marathons yet, Mrs. Franks."

"Well, a little optimism never hurt anyone." That dictum included her daughter. The next was exclusive to her. "Jenna, are you going to say hello to Mallory?"

Her emotions scraped raw and basted together with filament and library paste, it was all Jenna could do not to pummel the footboard, shrieking like a feral cat. "Yes, I am, the first chance I get without interrupting you."

It was a shitty thing to say and she apologized

immediately. Her mother's assurance of no harm done was supplemented by the nurse's comment that unrelieved stress could cause even the best-natured and levelheaded to snap.

"I honestly don't know how you do what you do," she said. "You don't have just one shop to run, but three, and you work six days a week."

"I hadn't thought of it that way," Aggie said, "but you're right. Even though they're all under one roof, MacArthur Perk is still a flea market, a bookstore *and* a coffee shop."

Four actually, counting the eBay auctions, Jenna corrected silently.

Mallory said, "What a balancing act you've managed all these years. And anyone can guess how worried you must be about the new highway going in. It won't be good for anyone's business, but especially one like yours that caters to the tourist trade."

Don't remind me. The nurse spoke as though she were a long-term customer, except Jenna couldn't recall waiting on her.

"We were just talking on break about how the last thing you needed was a family crisis to contend with," she went on. "Much less…" Her expression and trailing voice implied love gone wrong, a conclusion easily drawn from Aggie's reference to Paul.

Jenna held up her hands as if in surrender. Actually, the last thing she needed was to be grist for the hospital's gossip mill, but saying so would upset Aggie. "I've had better days—weeks, even—but can we change the subject?" Jenna forced a laugh. "You're depressing the hell out of me."

"Watch your language, young lady." Aggie clamped her own mouth shut around an electronic thermometer. When freed, she said, "You look so tired, sweetheart. It's silly for you to sit up in that chair all night when you could go home and sleep in your own bed."

Before Jenna could protest, Mallory said, "And how much rest do you think she'd get, wondering how you were passing the night?"

Aggie sniffed. "I'll pass it fine, thank you."

"So will I." Jenna sat down, took her book from the bag and turned to chapter one.

The nurse started for the door, then turned and rubbed her arm. "It's a little chilly in here, isn't it? I'll bring some of my famous spiced cider, a blanket and a pillow after I finish evening meds."

If anything, Jenna thought the room was a skosh warm. Absently, she said, "I'm pretty comfortable. Don't go to any trouble on my account."

"Oh, it's no trouble, Ms. MacArthur. That's why I'm here. To take care of you and your mother."

Jenna looked up from her book. Eyebrows knitted, her gaze followed the nurse out the door.

"Isn't she the sweetest thing?" Aggie cooed.

24

Paul tossed the briefcase on top of his garment bag and slammed the trunk lid. The earliest flight he could book was at 2:17 tomorrow afternoon. He could almost walk to Kansas City International and make it in time, but he couldn't spend another night staring at the cabin's knotty-pine walls.

He gassed up the Lumina, squeegeed the bug entrails off the windshield, then checked the oil. Prowling the convenience store's aisles netted a soft drink from the cooler, a box of Cheez-Its and an audiobook from the gondola rack.

The crunchy crackers and the story's narrator should silence the voice in his head. It had blatted warnings for the past quarter hour or so. Excuses why he shouldn't leave town was nearer the truth.

Paul keyed the ignition and flicked on his headlights. "Hit the road, Jack," he said, and instantly regretted it. The rest of the song's lyrics wended through his mind and splintered his heart.

He made it a hundred yards past the Y'all Come Back Now, Hear? billboard before he veered onto the graveled shoulder. Fingers drumming on the steering wheel, he alternately cursed himself for a fool and listened to his grandfather lecturing, "It's better to be foolish and wrong than foolish and right."

The Chevy wheeled a respectable bootlegger's turn for a six cylinder. He grabbed his cell phone off the seat and thumb-punched the number for Aggie's room. A busy signal loosened some of the knots in his gut.

About three out of a couple of hundred, he estimated as his foot pressed down on the accelerator.

Hospital security was as hog-tight and goose-proof on a Monday night as it had been on Saturday. Still, he chose the stairs over the elevator, though concrete steps were torture for his reconstructed knees.

As he began the climb, he hit the cell phone's redial button. Never had the monotonal *awp-awp-awp* been so irritating, so mocking.

The door to Aggie's room was closed. Paul pushed it open a crack. Warm, dry air breezed out the aperture. No voices could be heard, other than Robert Vaughn's televised pitch for a Saint Louis law firm.

The bed closer to the door was unoccupied. The Romanian princess had been transported back to the nursing home earlier that afternoon, yet the drape segregated Aggie's side of the room, as if a closed door didn't afford enough privacy.

Paul peered around the curtain, then let out the breath he'd held since he entered the room. Aggie was sound asleep. Her head was lolled to one side and a quicksilver line of drool meandered from a corner of her mouth.

Jenna's coat was hanging on the back of the visitor's chair, but her purse was gone. A rest-room break, Paul supposed, or she'd dashed out for a cup of vending machine coffee.

She will not be happy to find you here when she gets back, he thought. Which would likely be any second.

Careful not to bang into the rolling bedside table as he turned, he hesitated, then looked back at the visitor's chair. On the floor half under Aggie's bed, a paperback thriller was splayed open on the linoleum. Its spine wasn't creased, but a corner of the cover was bent and a section of pages folded inward. A tassled bookmark printed with MacArthur Perk's logo and address lay a few inches away.

Jenna had grinned when she'd tucked one inside the Grisham novel the day he bought it. *Dog-earing books ought to be a felony. And is, as far as I'm concerned.*

Paul ripped aside the drape. On the nightstand, the telephone receiver was off the hook. He snapped on the over-bed light. "Aggie. Aa-ggie." He gently shook her shoulder, fearful of startling her. No response. Her respirations were slow and deep, as though she was sedated. He shook her a bit harder. *"Aggie."*

She stirred, mouthing gibberish. A foam cup she must have cuddled to her chest tumbled off the bed. Paul snatched it up from the floor. The syrupy residue smelled of sugar, cinnamon and apples.

A second cup with similar dregs was in the wastebasket. Paul jammed tissues inside them both and put them in his pocket. Dialing 911 on his cell phone with one hand, he pressed the nurse call button with the other.

The Pfister Police Department dispatcher answered first. "This is Detective-Sergeant Haggerty, NYPD.

Patch me through to Officer Sam MacArthur immediately.''

Pulling rank would speed the connection and Sam would know it was codespeak for Get your ass on the radio.

"Paul?''

"Don't talk, listen. I need you lights and sirens at the hospital. Aggie's okay, but your—uh, another individual isn't in the room and I don't think she walked out on her own.'' In the background, a siren wound up its classic six-note scale. "What's your –20?''

"Other side of town. Gimme five minutes.''

Paul whirled and ran from the room. "Can we stay on this channel?''

"Affirmative. I'm switching to another to alert dispatch. Hang tight.''

"That's a 10-4.'' Paul halted in front of the nurses' station. The aide behind the desk had her back to the blinking light corresponding with Aggie's room number. "Who's the charge nurse for Agatha Franks?''

The aide jumped. "I, uh, I think Valerie Weems.''

Weems. It was on the suspect list. "Where is she?''

"She took Miz Franks to Radiology, then was going on break.''

"No she—'' Paul's hand tented his forehead. Think, *think.* What was that other nurse's name— Sam's savior? Sweet Jesus, it blew right by me when Aggie told me this morning.

"May I help you, sir?'' An R.N. rounded the doorway from an adjacent office.

Paul slapped the counter. "Mallory Fergus. Is she on duty?''

"Mallory? There's no— You must mean Valerie. Fergus was her maiden name."

"Describe her."

"Who are—"

"I'm a cop, damn it. I need a description, *now*."

The nurse spread her hands. "She's average. Five-five, five-six. Medium build. Brown eyes."

"Hair color."

"Blond. Wait, no, I think it's gray again."

"You think?"

"She was very ill a few years ago. Her hair went gray prematurely. Val's forever dying it different colors—blond, red, brown, black. It's hard to keep track."

It would be for a deceased patient's family members, too. "Mrs. Franks isn't in Radiology. She's in her bed, heavily sedated." He sliced the air with his hand. "I know she isn't supposed to be. Just don't give her anything to bring her out of it—*no meds,* got that? Get her up, walk her around. That's it."

"Yes, sir." The nurse started for the corridor.

Paul pushed away from the desk. "Her daughter, Jenna. When did you see her last?"

"Why, I haven't seen her at all."

"Okay. How would you take a patient to Radiology—protocol, I mean."

The nurse gave him a sharp look. "The same way we take one anywhere in the hospital. In a wheelchair."

Breaking into a run, he said into the cell phone, "You there, Sam?"

"Whatcha got?"

"When you get here—shit, stand by." He yanked

down the phone. "Nurse, what kind of car does Weems drive?"

"A Honda? Maybe a Civic?" She flinched. "I'm almost sure it's blue."

Almost sure. Give me a break. "Sam, circle the employees' parking lot. We want a blue Honda, probably a Civic."

Paul jerked open the stairwell door. "Suspect name, Valerie Weems. Gray hair. Average, average. A nurse. Probably wearing scrubs." He paused, then added, "The victim is likely sedated and was abducted from the building in a wheelchair."

"That's a 10-4." Fear laced Sam's voice. "I'm on the scene."

"Meet you outside. Clear." Paul half leaped, half skied down the last flight of stairs, punching up 911 for the second time.

"This is Detective-Sergeant Haggerty again. Alert Mercy Hospital Security of an abduction in progress. This is not a drill. We need a lockdown. All exterior exits, elevator search—passenger, staff and freight. Got that?"

"Officer MacArthur already radioed that alert and suspect ID, sir."

Good man. Fine cop. Paul stiff-armed the door ten seconds ahead of a security guard. "I'm Detective-Sergeant Haggerty, PPD." What the hell. Ol' beer gut won't know the difference. "Nobody comes in or goes out till cleared by myself or Officer Mac-Arthur."

Another "Yes, sir," Paul thought, sprinting for the patrol unit's spotlight sweeping the parking lot's rear quadrant. Lord, how I've missed hearing that.

The spotlight pegged a silver Dodge Neon with a

caved-in passenger side. Sam emerged from the cruiser just as Paul ran up on it. "Tags and registration check to Valerie Weems."

Sucking wind, Paul said, "Always did hate witness reports."

Sam strafed the interior with his Maglite. "Empty. Hood's cold, too."

"I don't get it. Weems killed Casper. Who knows how many more. She's taken Jenna somewhere. I'll stake my life on it."

"You're staking hers, Haggerty."

"Think I don't know that?" Paul squinted at the building. All hospitals were like catacombs. Were Valerie Weems and Jenna still inside? If so, the nurse was trapped—a nothing-to-lose proposition.

The cold stung his sweaty face and neck. Aggie's room had been a sauna. Heat exacerbated drowsiness. Radiology. Coffee break. Jenna's coat was on the back of the chair, but her purse was gone.

Pieces clicked like a revolver's hammer on empty cylinders. "They're in Jenna's Explorer. Weems knows the net's closing in—she heard Aggie and me talking about a nurse-killer. Whatever Weems has planned for Jenna will look like an accident. That's why her car's still here. She's coming back to kill Aggie, finish her shift and clock out. Perfect alibi."

"You sure?"

"Hell no, I'm not sure. You got a better idea, let's hear it."

"Hop in. I know where Mom was parked."

The radio chattered like a battle of the deejays. The fine tuner in Paul's ear had rusted. The cruiser hurtled backward, straight as a laser, then squalled into a hard arc. The light bar flung white, red and blue prisms at the parallel rows of parked vehicles.

"There." Sam pointed left. "It was beside that Ranger pickup when I was here this evening."

A PT Cruiser was in the space now.

"Okay, we've got a vehicle. Beats chasing smoke," Paul said. "If you were Valerie Weems, where would you stage an accident?"

"Park Lake, or the old rock quarry."

"I'll take the lake." Paul scrambled from the cruiser. "Get an A— Uh, get crackin'." Ordering Sam to put out an APB on the Explorer wasn't necessary, either. He wasn't a green-bean rookie.

And I'm not his watch commander. Paul forced his legs into a hobbling jog. The adrenaline spike had peaked, and along with it, the natural invincibility to pain. I'm just a civilian—a crippled-up has-been about two clicks above a wanna-be.

Two more patrol units ramped up the apron into the hospital's lot. They flanked Sam's cruiser a moment, then, like a vehicular ballet, peeled away for the turn around as Sam's car shot into the street.

"Stupid." Valerie Weems glanced at the blanket-wrapped figure in the passenger seat. "Stupid woman. Stupid waste of my time."

She turned onto South Dollison, her gloved hands caressing the Explorer's steering wheel. Abandoning it was the stupidest waste of all. She couldn't keep it and couldn't afford one of her own. Her health was too fragile. She took too many sick days and medical leaves to have a nice car to drive. Or a pretty little house to fix up and live in.

"I'll bet you were never sick a day in your life.

You've never suffered for anything, have you, Jenna? Have it *all*, don't you? I couldn't save my little boy's life, but I saved your son's, didn't I?

"You hear me? I *saved* him and for what? So your stupid mother can call me by the wrong name? At least she remembered. You didn't even recognize me. You never once thanked me—not even after you knew who I was. How's that for gratitude?"

Park Lake was a gigantic sinkhole crater fed by an underground stream. Divers had attempted to measure its depth, but none had succeeded. About twenty yards beneath the surface, the water turned a dark, murky green that absorbed light, be it natural or artificial.

Legend had it that an entire train—locomotive to boxcars to caboose—had once jumped the tracks and plunged into the lake, never to be seen again. It was said the accident happened so fast, the engineer and the rest of the crew had drowned at their posts.

The Lumina crept slowly along the shoreline. Paul scrutinized every inch of ground for tire tracks. If this were New York City, there'd be the homeless to canvass, a dozen junkies and dealers to interrogate, a hooker on the stroll eager to earn twenty bucks without wrinkling her hot pants.

As this was Pfister, Missouri, Frisco Park was as deserted as a beach in a blizzard. There wouldn't have been any witnesses to a white Explorer with its windows rolled down bobbing, then sinking grill first into the frigid, glass-smooth water.

"Haggerty. You there?"

Without taking his eyes off the winter-brown grass, Paul's hand groped the seat for his cell phone.

Loud enough to be heard over Sam's siren, he said, "I got nothing. You?"

"I'm headed back. The quarry's too far out if Weems is on foot."

"What if she isn't? What if she ditches—"

"Shut up." Sam's voice blasted from the dime-size speaker. "Weems is an R.N. She's staging a suicide not an accident. Has to be. Any drug she gave Mom would show up in a tox screen. Weems knows it. She's gotta cover her ass."

Paul's stomach heaved. "You're right. A thousand percent." He cut the wheel away from the lake and floored the accelerator. "Any ideas where she's taking her?"

"Only three places fit the MO—where Mom's vehicle wouldn't be noticed. Nobody's home at Grandma's. That's the best bet. Kathy's en route to the shop. You take Mom's house."

"I'm on the way."

Dirt clods and mud pecked the Chevy's undercarriage. Its rear tires spun and slewed on the hoar-frosted grass. Paul's head snapped back with the car's impact against the block-stone curbing. Its edge skinned off the muffler as slick as a ten-pound mallet.

Hazard lights on flash and manually flicking his headlamps, Paul careered through traffic, sounding the horn at intersections. How much time had elapsed between Weems's spiriting Jenna out of the hospital and his arrival? How much between the first busy signal when he'd called Aggie's room and now?

Enough. Too much. For all he knew, Jenna was already dead when Weems loaded her into the wheelchair.

He made the turn off Fourteenth onto Dollison

Street on two wheels, then fishtailed to a stop at mid-block. No vehicle in the drive. *Shit.*

Grabbing his Smith & Wesson off the seat, he bailed from the car, hit the ground running. No sign of disturbance. The porch light was on. The bunga-low's windows were dark, except for the light cast by the living-room lamp that any self-respecting bur-glar would interpret as a welcome-home sign.

Paul yanked open the screen and wrenched the doorknob. Locked. Then it hit him—the quiet. No barking from the other side. Leg scissored at the knee, he kicked at the door. Again. Three times. On the fifth try, the jamb, not the door, splintered and gave way.

''*Jenna!*'' He ran from one room to the next, flip-ping on lights, yelling her name. He glimpsed Festus diving under Jenna's bed, but no dogs. Not inside, not in the yard.

Halfway up the stairs to the second floor, he spun around and clattered down again. Jenna and Weems were about the same size. There was no way the nurse could carry, drag or push Jenna up a stairway that steep.

No one had been in the house. He was certain of it. But where were the damn dogs? Who'd let them out?

Applying logic to insanity was insanity itself. Maybe Jenna's truck had been at the hospital all along. There were a hundred white SUVs in town. Maybe Sam had mis-IDed his mother's. Maybe he'd gone down the wrong row. Maybe Jenna was… God only knew where Weems could have her by now. At this time of night, there were as many empty rooms in the hospital as there were occupied ones.

Paul ran from the house just as Sam's cruiser swerved into the curb. A second unit pulled in behind. As their sirens switched off, Paul heard a soft drone to his left, slightly louder than the hum of a high-voltage power line. The mercury-vapor light bolted above the garage door was off.

"Sam! Back here."

A few yards from the barnlike building, glass from the shattered fixture crunched under Paul's shoes. Engine exhaust seeped from under the double doors. Heavy-duty steel hasps and padlocks secured them. It would take a bulldozer to force them open.

Paul shielded his eyes and fired at the locks. Tossing the pistol aside, he threw open the doors. A noxious, carbon monoxide cloud billowed out. Staggering backward, choking and blinded by the fumes, he buried his nose and mouth in the crook of his arm and lurched inside.

He felt his way along the side of the Explorer. His fingers closed around a door handle. Locked. Head reeling, his legs rubbery, he cocked back a fist and slammed it into the window.

The glass fractured into a thousand pieces. Ragged chunks flew in all directions. Grabbing the window ledge to hold himself up, he reached in and unlocked the door.

Jenna tumbled out. An arm flailed across her body. Her face was slack, her skin a bright cherry red. Paul caught her, then fell to one knee, keeling sideward.

"I've got her, pard." Sam scooped up his mother's body and ran for the door.

Paul heard, rather than felt, the concrete floor crack his skull.

25

The jackhammer quartet was still at it. There was one at each temple and two doing a trepan maneuver at the top of Jenna's head. Pain reverberated in her jaw, the nape of her neck, and roiled in the pit of her stomach, but if she threw up, if she even thought too much about throwing up, her head would explode.

Helluva way to wake up and find out you're not dead yet.

She peered through her lashes, certain that opening her eyes would trigger a detonation of semilethal magnitude. A greasy cloud hindered her vision, but she'd swear two doctors in lab coats were talking with Sam, Kathy and a midget wearing a white yarmulke.

Her eyelids eased shut again. Pfister had a rather eclectic population, but a Jewish little person was a new one on her.

Sleep's velvety arms reached out again. She pushed them away. Earlier breaks in the fog hadn't been nearly as interesting. It was time to let her son, future daughter-in-law and their short-statured friend know she was all right.

A smile—not much of one, but the needles piercing her forehead said her lips had moved. Not that the caucus at the end of the gurney noticed. A foot wiggle didn't do it, either. She added a finger wave. No dice.

In the nineteeth century, it was common for breathing tubes and bells to be placed in coffins. Embalming was rare, funerals were hasty and people were terrified a loved one might not be entirely deceased and would waken buried alive with no means of communicating the error.

It was an eerie custom, but Jenna would give big money for a coffin bell right now. She swallowed to lubricate her throat.

"Hey," she croaked.

The midget spun around and pointed a white mitten at her. Sam, Kathy and the physicians followed suit.

Jenna's head didn't explode, but her heart almost did. The little person was Paul Haggerty, seated in a wheelchair, his head and hands wrapped in thick gauze bandages.

She was hallucinating. Had to be. The image of him walking away into the night, leaving her and not looking back was as vivid as the dried blood splashed on his shirt and jeans.

Sam started for her, then turned to grasp the wheelchair's handles to push Paul ahead of him. Kathy hastened around the gurney.

"You're in the emergency room," she said, taking Jenna's hand, "and you're going to be fine. Aggie is, too. The cardiologist isn't sure why, but the sedative Valerie Weems gave Aggie stopped the arrythmia and her blood pressure is way down. Paul found you just in the nick of time."

Kathy's voice was calm and soothing, but the

words were gibberish. Who was Valerie Weems? What sedative? Paul found us…where?

"Yeah. Found you, fell down and passed out cold," Paul said. "The hardware in my legs doesn't take kindly to wind sprints. Sam carried you out of the garage, then came back for me. Without him, we'd both be goners."

Jenna's stomach lurched and she closed her eyes. Her mind flashed back to her mother's room. She was slouched in the visitor's chair appearing to read, but not comprehending a word of the novel she held. Aggie was watching a *Golden Girls* rerun on TV.

Mallory Fergus came in with a cup of hot cider for each of them. Jenna's teeth ached at the memory. The cider was gaggingly sweet and mud-brown with cinnamon, but they had to drink it. The nurse had also brought a cup for herself and had perched on the corner of Aggie's bed chatting away until they finished their drinks.

Things didn't jibe. Nothing Kathy said or Jenna remembered made sense. It frightened her, just as it had the night Rick died and she couldn't separate reality from the nightmare because Aggie and the doctors had lied—told Jenna what she wanted to hear instead of the truth.

She pulled her hand from Kathy's. *Go away. All of you. Let me sleep. Or be quiet and let me wake up.*

The gurney jostled. "C'mon, Mom." Sam's wide warm palm caressed her cheek, patting it gently. "Open your eyes. You don't have to talk or anything. The doc said not to let you conk out again."

Screw him.

Kathy whispered from the gurney's far end. "Kiss

her, Paul. It worked for the prince in *Sleeping Beauty*.''

Sam chuckled. ''Worked for the frog, too.''

What the— Jenna's eyes fluttered open. Now Sam was standing on her left, grinning down at her. Paul was still in the wheelchair on her right.

''Damn,'' he said. ''Missed my chance.''

''I reckon you'll make up for it by and by, pard.''

Jenna's eyes slid from her lover to her son. ''Pard?''

''I'll explain that in a minute,'' Sam said. ''Think I'd best bring you up to speed first.''

''But—''

''Hush now and let me do the talking for once. Okay?''

She sighed assent. He'd pay for that when she got vertical again.

''There're a few holes we haven't filled yet, but all those years ago when I had to have my stomach pumped, Grandma misheard the Poison Control nurse's name. She thought it was Mallory and it stuck that way in her mind.''

''Mallory Fergus,'' Jenna said.

''*Valerie* Fergus. Her married name is Weems. Like I said, we don't know the whole story, but it seems she made herself sick for years so folks would feel sorry for her, then may or may not have killed her little boy for the same reason.''

''Oh, dear God.''

''Not intentionally,'' Paul said. ''He was born with cerebral palsy, after all. But from the medical records, his life expectancy should have been early to mid-teens.''

''There's no way to know whether the boy's death

was from natural causes or not,'' Sam went on. ''But when Weems went back to work full-time after he died, she saved a patient—an epileptic—from choking on his tongue during a grand mal seizure. Weems almost got her finger chewed off in the process. The patient's doctor and other nurses dang-near built a statue of her for the lobby.

''Great while it lasted, but when those 'atta girls' wore off, Weems got the idea of injecting patients' IVs with succinylcholine. It's packaged full strength in liquid form, but also comes as a powder that is mixed with sterile water before being injected.''

Paul said, ''The powdered kind is stocked on the hospital's crash carts. It's a controlled substance, but Weems could have helped herself to a few grains now and then with no one the wiser.''

''Is that what was in the cider Weems gave me?'' Jenna asked.

''No, she slipped you and Aggie some type of a sedative. Gave some to Herschel and Homer, too, to shut them up, before she locked you in the garage with the motor running.''

Jenna gasped.

''The dogs are all right, darlin'. Groggy, but no worse for their little nap, I swear.''

''To God?''

''Yep. To Him and anybody else you want me to.''

After a moment's pause, he went on. ''As for succinylcholine, it halts the natural gag reflex so that a breathing tube can be inserted. That's why it's stocked on crash carts.''

Sam said, ''It's injected before surgery, too, but

not until the patient is anesthetized because...well, pardon the French, but it's scary shit.

"Like Paul said, it does stop the gag reflex you'd have awake or under anesthetic, but it actually paralyzes your entire body in less than ninety seconds. You can't breathe and your heart stops anywhere from seven to fifteen minutes later."

An E.R. nurse chose that moment to check Jenna's vital signs and the IV inserted in her arm. When the nurse leaned over, a laminated ID badge swung from a lanyard around her neck. The photo was as complimentary as one issued by the Department of Motor Vehicles, but Louella Gayle Piven, R.N., was printed in large, bold type.

"Doesn't that badge get in the way?" Jenna asked.

"Constantly. We all hate 'em, but let a supervisor see you without it, or tucked in your pocket, and they dock your paycheck twenty-five bucks."

Jenna was certain Mallory-Valerie hadn't been wearing one. If she had, Aggie would have introduced her by the correct name and Jenna might have recognized it from Paul's original suspect list.

Nurse Piven produced a syringe from her pocket and snapped off the safety seal.

Jenna caught her wrist. "What is that?"

"Don't worry, it isn't a shot, hon. It's an injection for your IV to help your headache."

"Oh, no, you don't." Jenna shuddered. "Just bring me a couple of extra-strength aspirin and a cup of coffee." Jenna winced. "No, just water. Plain ol' tap water. Please."

The nurse looked to Sam for intervention.

"Thanks, ma'am, but if Mom wants aspirin and water, I suspect that's what she ought to have."

"All right, but if it upsets her stomach..." The nurse left the consequences to their imaginations.

Kathy volunteered to fetch Jenna a cup of coffee from the cafeteria. Her future mother-in-law smiled gratefully and blew her a kiss.

"Okay, so I'm paranoid," Jenna admitted after Kathy exited the room.

"We'll all be for a while, Mom. Paul wouldn't let the doc give him a local to have his cuts stitched up, either."

"Cuts?" Jenna eyed Paul's bandaged head and hands, as if noticing them for the first time—which, technically, she was with a now-functional brain. "From what?"

"Putting a fist through your truck's driver's-side window." His tone suggested he did so on a daily basis. "Weems locked the doors when she left it running in the garage and—"

Sam cleared his throat. "How about we wait and cross that bridge when we get there."

Paul's raised mitten signaled agreement.

Sam sat down on the edge of the bed. "Paul didn't tell you, but between Kenneth Tufts saying Casper's hip was refractured and a newspaper article he found on the Internet about that VA hospital's killer nurse, he suspected succinylcholine was the drug being used here. In some people, it can make muscles spasm so tight they can rebreak bones."

Sam's controlled cop voice belied his sick-at-heart expression. "We haven't told Grandma any of this. All she knows is that the nurse who murdered Casper is in custody."

"Except Weems can't be charged with it," Paul said.

"Why not? Sam just got through saying that she gave him that drug."

"Suspecting she did and proving it are two different things, darlin'. Vinita had Casper cremated— Weems's idea, or so Vinita says. We don't have any remains for postmortem toxicology.

"Even if we did and found succinylchorine, we couldn't prove Weems administered a lethal dose. From Casper's symptoms, she must have kept giving him just enough to cause respiratory distress so she could rescue him."

Jenna made a fist. "Intentional or not, that's homicide, damn it."

Paul shook his head, obviously wishing he could let the subject drop. "The last time, whether Weems overdosed him or Casper reacted more severely to it, the Code Blue team also injected him with the succinylchorine on the crash cart. They had to in order to intubate him and put him on a respirator."

Jenna clamped her hands over her face. Revulsion shuddered through her and she tasted bile. How could anyone be so vicious, so *evil*. Valerie Weems didn't just play God with Casper's life. She stood back and watched the people fighting to save him unwittingly kill him with a second injection of the drug.

"The security guard Weems was screwing let her in when she snuck back to go after Grandma," Sam said, "but another one caught her in the hall before she could do anything. Weems has been charged with two counts of attempted homicide—yours and Grandma's. The prosecutor won't have any problem convincing the judge to deny bail, pending further investigation.''

He gently took Jenna's hands from her face and clasped them in his. ''It'll take weeks of paperwork and disinterments to charge her with first-degree homicide, probably a half-dozen or more times over, but I promise you, Mom, Valerie Weems is never going to hurt anybody again.''

Jenna nodded her understanding. There'd be justice for Cappy, just not by name. Others would be left off the roll of victims, as well. Weems would stand trial only for cases the prosecution could prove without a shadow of a doubt.

But she *would* stand trial. Weems couldn't cop a plea. Factitious disorder by proxy didn't meet the legal standards of insanity.

Paul murmured, ''We should have waited, Sam. She's been through enough. She didn't need to hear this right now.''

''Nobody does, regardless of when they're told,'' Sam said, ''but the straight-out truth hurts less in the long run.'' He looked to his left. ''Doesn't it, Paul?''

There was a clattering and soft grunts of pain, then the mattress buckled beside Jenna's pillow. Paul whispered in her ear, ''Sam knows, darlin'. He always has. Not everything, but you can't keep secrets from a kid. Once they're on to one, they'll sneak and peek and listen at keyholes till they root it out.''

Jenna nodded as tears began to straggle down her face. A part of her had sensed he'd done exactly that. That he knew more than he let on or she was willing to admit. Sleeping dogs lie. And lie and lie and lie— by omission, if not outright.

''All Sam's ever wanted is for you to tell him,''

Paul continued. "The whole truth and nothing but. That's what the dustup in the cafeteria was all about. He thought if he confronted you about me, the truth was bound to come out right there and then."

The other side of the mattress keeled heavily to port as Sam positioned himself near her left ear. "Remember how you always said, no matter what I did, you'd never, ever stop loving me? Why didn't you believe the same went for me?"

"I did, sweetheart. It just never seemed like the right…" Jenna's voice trailed away. She looked into her son's dark eyes, so much like his father's, then into Paul's bottle-green ones. "Last I knew, you had a plane you had to catch."

"Not anymore. That is, not unless you want me to." He eased himself down onto the wheelchair. "Even if you do, it just so happens that I've gotten pretty fond of this one-horse burg. And a cop friend of mine says the department's been beating the bushes for a crippled up, has-been, big city detective to put on the payroll. Lord knows, there's a wet-behind-the-ears patrol officer that needs somebody twice as smart and half as cocky to take him under his wing and teach him the ropes."

Paul wheeled backward from the gurney. "For now, though, I think I'll see what's taking Kathy so long with that cup of coffee."

"Wait up a sec," Sam said. "I'll go with you and let Mom get some rest."

Jenna tightened her hands around his before they slipped from her grasp. She'd never been more certain of anything in her life. Certain of her son's love and trust. Certain of a future with Paul—one without a single cloud or shadow to hide behind or haunt them.

The well-intentioned but vicious circle that had begun twenty-three years ago in a hospital's emergency room was destined to end in one.

The time couldn't possibly be more right.

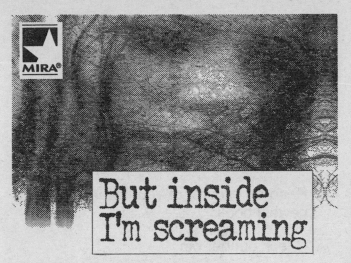

But inside I'm screaming

A remarkable debut novel from

ELIZABETH FLOCK

While breaking the hottest news story of the year, broadcast journalist Isabel Murphy unravels on live television in front of an audience of millions. She lands at Three Breezes, a four-star psychiatric hospital nicknamed the "nut hut," where she begins the painful process of recovering the life everyone thought she had.

But accepting her place among her fellow patients proves more difficult as Isabel struggles to reconcile the fact that she is, indeed, one of them. In order to mend her painfully fractured life, Isabel must rely solely on herself to figure out what went so very wrong, and to begin to accept an imperfect life in a world that demands perfection.

"…an insightful, touching and, yes, even funny account of what it's like to lose control as the world watches…"
—*New York Times* bestselling author Mary Jane Clark

Available the first week of September 2003, wherever books are sold!

SUZANN LEDBETTER

66925	WEST OF BLISS	___ $6.50 U.S. ___ $7.99 CAN.
66848	NORTH OF CLEVER	___ $5.99 U.S. ___ $6.99 CAN.
66797	SOUTH OF SANITY	___ $5.99 U.S. ___ $6.99 CAN.
66597	EAST OF PECULIAR	___ $5.99 U.S. ___ $6.99 CAN.

(limited quantities available)

TOTAL AMOUNT	$_____
POSTAGE & HANDLING	$_____
($1.00 for one book; 50¢ for each additional)	
APPLICABLE TAXES*	$_____
TOTAL PAYABLE	$_____

(check or money order—please do not send cash)

To order, complete this form and send it, along with a check or money order for the total above, payable to MIRA Books®, to: **In the U.S.:** 3010 Walden Avenue, P.O. Box 9077, Buffalo, NY 14269-9077; **In Canada:** P.O. Box 636, Fort Erie, Ontario L2A 5X3.

Name:_____

Address:_____ City:_____

State/Prov.:_____ Zip/Postal Code:_____

Account Number (if applicable):_____

075 CSAS

  *New York residents remit applicable sales taxes.
   Canadian residents remit applicable GST and provincial taxes.

MIRA®